RISE OF THE SMYRNIANS

The Apocalypse : Episode One

DAVID O. BULLOCK

Black Rose Writing | Texas

ISBN: 978-1-68433-375-2
PUBLISHED BY BLACK ROSE WRITING
www.blackrosewriting.com

Printed in the United States of America
Suggested Retail Price (SRP) $19.95

Rise of the Smyrnians is printed in Calluna

*As a planet-friendly publisher, Black Rose Writing does its best to eliminate unnecessary waste to reduce paper usage and energy costs, while never compromising the reading experience. As a result, the final word count vs. page count may not meet common expectations.

To the memory of my mother, Katherine Bullock
She loved her family and Jesus
and looked forward to His return
I miss you every day momma

ACKNOWLEDGMENTS

Jesus, my Savior for showing me pure love and giving me real life. You have done for me what I describe you doing for the characters in this book. I am eternally grateful.

My high school sweetheart and beautiful wife, Glenda, for standing by me as I pursue my dreams. I love you more with each passing day. You will always have my heart.

My dad who taught me what it means to be a true man of God. You loved me, taught me, inspired me and helped make me the man I am today. I aspire to be like you.

Lena Godby, Lisa Brown and Rodney Whitis. In battling cancer, you showed us what true faith is. Now we live in faith, knowing you are in the presence of Jesus forever.

The people of Eagle Heights Church for more than 22 wonderful years. I will never forget the miraculous times we shared. We made an eternal difference together.

Black Rose Writing and Reagan Rothe for giving me the opportunity to put my first fictional novel in print. I am grateful to you for believing in me and this book.

SPECIAL THANKS

To Dawnetta Smiley, for my author photo and for all of her help and hours of hard work.

To Jeanne Lose, for reading the book and using her expert editing skills to make it better.

In the darkness of a late summer night, a solitary figure on a white horse ominously descends upon planet earth. In his hand, he holds a bow. On his head is a conqueror's crown. His target is the earth...the entire earth...every person on the earth. Below an unsuspecting populace goes about their lives, having no clue what is about to hit them. All the while, slowly, ever so slowly, the rider descends.

The year is 2029. The day is September 11. It is a normal late summer day, but it is no normal day. On this day 28 years earlier, terrorists from the Islamic extremist group Al Qaeda hijacked four planes and carried out suicide missions against targets in America killing over 3,000 people. It is also the Feast of Trumpets, Rosh Hashanah, the Jewish New Year. Each is a day like no other, as this day also promises to be.

Around the world, people are sleeping, eating, working, enjoying recreational activities and other things human beings do on any average day. Then in an instant, everything changes...a deafening sound unlike any sound that has ever been heard. It is too loud for thunder. It could be an explosion but no explosion would be heard worldwide. A sonic boom, maybe? No one knows for sure, but almost no one misses it. People pour out of homes, restaurants, work places, sporting venues and places of entertainment in shock and fear. It is a day they will never forget.

It happened so fast most did not see what happened, but some witnessed it, though there was little to see. A brilliant flash lit up the sky and turned the entire earth into a brief moment of blinding light. It appeared to be a streaking bolt of lightning as it shot across the sky from east to west, clearly visible on every continent, rapidly disappearing as quickly as it had come. Then an eerie silence engulfed the planet. Something was not right and everyone knew it. A spine-tingling chill caused a worldwide shudder so real you could feel it. Something was wrong. Something was terribly wrong. People stood for what seemed like hours, many failing to notice they were standing alone or that others were conspicuously absent. Most stood dazed, as if in a trance. Soon enough the stunned silence would be interrupted by the sound of blaring sirens. Phones would begin to ding with news alerts. All TV programming would be interrupted with breaking news. But in these eerie moments, there was nothing but silence, complete silence. Within minutes all of that would begin to change.

The real news was about to hit like a ton of bricks. Millions of people from around the globe have vanished, gone in an instant, without explanation. Conservative estimates put the number of missing at 500-600 million. Others say it could be as high as 2 billion, possibly as many as one fourth of the world's population gone, having disappeared without a trace. There are no terrorist groups claiming responsibility, no plague or major disease that could possibly have caused this inexplicable tragedy. Are there no answers? The world is about to find out.

RISE OF THE SMYRNIANS

CHAPTER 1

Reporter Blake Thompson is fast asleep in his New York City high rise luxury apartment when he is suddenly jarred awake by the loud blaring of an old car horn. It is his phone. He chose the ringtone to ensure that he would never miss a call. And at 3:00 a.m. on this Tuesday morning in the city that never sleeps, he does not miss this one. Blake takes his job very seriously. After all the hard work he has put in to get this far, he is not about to do anything or have any lapse in his responsibilities which would jeopardize that. After graduating from college with a degree in journalism, he struggled to get his foot in the door with a credible news agency. Following a couple of years writing for a small town newspaper, he had finally landed a job as a beat reporter covering crime for a small market television station. His big break came when he broke a story about an expansive drug ring that, as it turned out, had international ties. It was investigative journalism at its best. As a result, a powerful drug lord was captured, convicted and sent to prison. A huge pipeline for drugs into the states was stopped. Blake's work caught the eye of a major network. They had flown him to New York for an appearance on their morning show. That was followed by what amounted to a courtship period, and ultimately led to his hiring as a field reporter. His willingness to work long hours, weekends and holidays, even his birthday, endeared him to his employer. Those things were natural to Blake because he was not married and his work was his life. That and his rugged good looks and on camera charm made him one of the most eligible bachelors in America. His ability to gather information and investigate leads also gave him a leg up on other reporters. He was able to speak from memory and had a magnetic screen presence. No story was too big or too tough. He was typically the first to break major stories. Due to those attributes, his rise to fame in the TV news industry came quickly. He became the headliner for the network, their "go to guy." There was even talk that he might someday move into the position of anchor. Yes, he had put a lot into his career and gotten a few breaks along the way, and on this life-altering day he was ready.

"Blake, have you heard what happened?" asked his producer, his voice uncharacteristically cracking with emotion and what sounded like fear. Blake had never heard him like that before. The man was normally in complete control: calm, cool and collected. If he was ever anxious or concerned, no one would know. But this time was different. Blake knew immediately that this was no normal call and no normal story. Thoughts raced rapidly through his mind, even as a reply was preparing to come from his mouth. Devastating tsunami? Massive earthquake? The assassination of a world leader? Another major terrorist attack? What could be so catastrophic that it would elicit such emotion from Benjamin Abramson? The man prided himself on his Jewish heritage and was a tough and savvy businessman who fit the prototype of a hardnosed producer for a major news network. He never missed a story. News had been his life. Ben, as those closest to him knew him, lived to get the news out to the public and thrived on seeing that happen. His Jewish faith was important to him, having been passed down from generation to generation. He was a regular attender in the synagogue with his family. He observed the Jewish festivals. Those were the only times during the year you might not find him on the job. The Sabbath, which began at 6:00 p.m. Friday and ended at 6:00 p.m. Saturday, was holy to him and he kept it religiously. He obeyed the Law of Moses as found in the Torah, the first five books of biblical Old Testament to the very best of his ability. Eating kosher food, that which adhered to the dietary laws of Judaism, was often a challenge during the parties and meetings he attended as required by his executive position. But he would never fail to eat by those standards, regardless of what foods he had to bypass. He prayed three times a day: morning, noon and night. A mezuzah was attached to the door frame at the entry to his house, as also required by the Torah. Mezuzah means "doorpost." It contains a small piece of parchment inside with the words of Deuteronomy 6:4-9 and 11:13-21 written on it. Those verses comprise the two parts of the *Shema* (so named for the Hebrew word translated *hear*) which is one of only two prayers commanded in the *Torah*. It has been repeated every morning and night since the time of Moses. The first part is the most basic expression of Jewish faith.

⁴ Hear, O Israel: The LORD our God, the LORD is one. ⁵ Love the LORD your God with all your heart and with all your soul and with all your

strength. ⁶ These commandments that I give you today are to be on your hearts. ⁷ Impress them on your children. Talk about them when you sit at home and when you walk along the road, when you lie down and when you get up. ⁸ Tie them as symbols on your hands and bind them on your foreheads. ⁹ Write them on the doorframes of your houses and on your gates.
Deuteronomy 6:4-9 NIV

Ben was reminded of those words every time he left and entered his house. And he diligently taught them to his family. During his morning prayers, he wore without fail, a phylactery which was held tight to his forehead by a leather strap around his head. It contained the aforementioned verses, with the words of Exodus 13:1-16 added. His faith was not just a *part* of his life; it *was* his life. His children and grandchildren were faithfully following his example. But while he considered himself a man of strong faith, nothing could have prepared him for the events of this day.

"Wh...what?" Blake finally managed to get out, his composure surprisingly shaken too in light of the sound of the voice on the other end. His mind was in a spin by now. The answer came quickly, driven home like the strike of a hammer slamming into his brain.

"Something terrible happened at midnight tonight. Millions, possibly billions of people worldwide suddenly disappeared. All over the world: everywhere, every country, every continent. This is the worst catastrophe in history. I need you out there Blake...now! No one knows what, or who caused this. There are no answers. But if anyone can find answers, it's you."

Blake sat again in momentary stunned silence, his mind trying to process what he had just heard. That was not possible, was it? He grasped for words to formulate an answer that would not betray his emotions at that moment. Finally, regaining a measure of composure, his reply came out sounding like the professional he was. "I'm on it Ben," he shot back as he was already pulling on the pants he had laid out before lying down for the night. He was always prepared in advance, ready to go at a moment's notice. He finished dressing in a matter of minutes, taking only time to make sure his always perfect hair was just that...perfect, even when the dress code was casual. Blake was not used to being the last one to hear big news. But he was used to being the first to discover and report the facts before most others had even started their investigations. He ran out the door, no more than 30 minutes after his conversation with Ben, back in reporter mode now and calling his cameraman as he ran. "Meet me in Times Square."

"On my way," said Anders Norstrom. His parents were Norwegian immigrants. They had come to America when he was less than a year old, hoping to provide their young son the best opportunity possible to succeed in life. Thankful for their choice, Anders was living his dream. He loved the news game and being in the thick of the action. And he especially loved working with Blake Thompson. The man had a thirst for adventure and a drive for perfection that matched perfectly with his own. He was Blake's right hand man and knew his next moves, often he thought, before Blake knew them himself. Anders had a wife and three children at home who were fully supportive of his career and his passion for it. They knew he loved them and how important they were to him. When he was home, he spent every moment with them he possibly could. His kids were his pride and joy. He tried hard to make it to every one of their activities. His twin sons were crazy about soccer and his daughter was in band. His job prevented him from being there for every one of their activities, but when he could not be there, he always called to let them know they were on his mind and to wish them well. There was only one thing they missed from him. Even before they were born, his wife began attending a church near their home. She had been invited by friends. Church had never been Anders' thing. So, when she became a Christian, he supported her decision but told her to never push her beliefs on him. She had honored that as best she could. The occasional mention and invitation to attend church with her was the only time she felt rejection and coldness from him. His kids were also active in the church and had committed to Christianity. It changed nothing as to how he felt about them, and he never mocked them or tried to prevent them from going to church or attending church sponsored events. Like his partner, his job was his life and he had no time for things like church. To him, it was a waste of time and something that interfered with the profession to which he had given his life. His love for his job was what had caused him to sprint from his house this morning as quietly as he could, trying not to wake his family. But even now, he could hardly believe they had slept through the explosive roar that had split the air. He had jumped from bed and run outside to see what caused it. But surprisingly, almost unbelievably, the night was eerily still with no evidence of anything that could have caused such a sound. He had not returned to bed. That explained why he was loaded up and ready to go well before Blake's call ever came. And he knew it would come.

CHAPTER 2

Blake was wasting no time. It was only a 5-minute walk from his posh apartment in the Theater District to Times Square. As he walked, he speed-dialed one of his sources. The man was in D.C. and was almost always in the know on big events that affected the country or world. In this case, world leaders have already been scrambling to find an answer. And they have arrived at the conclusion that there is only one thing which could possibly explain such an immense and instantaneous disappearance of millions of people. The source answers his call with two words.

"Alien invasion."

"What???"

"Alien invasion, man. UFOs. Little green men. Earth is under attack by forces from outer space. It's invasion of the body snatchers, for real!"

"Are you sure?"

"I'm telling you man, it's true. World leaders have already collaborated and spoken with scientists and experts in space exploration and found clear evidence that this is the work of aliens. They are in complete agreement. There is no doubt about it, man. It has finally happened. Even NASA has confirmed it, and you know they have always denied the existence of aliens. A worldwide announcement will be made within the hour, with the leader of every country holding a press conference. You don't have a lot of time, but you can still be ahead of the game, if you hurry. As far as I know, no one else knows about this. You can be the first to break the story!"

Blake never knew how his source always seemed to know things before anyone else. The man was amazing. Whoever his sources were, they had to really be on the inside to know every single scoop.

"Man, you had better be right. If you're not, and I do this, it will destroy my career. This is the most devastating day in history. I can't afford to get this wrong. But let's face it, if you're right, we are all in trouble."

Blake's mind was even more in a spin now. Secretly, he had always believed in UFOs. After all, he reasoned, anyone who has any intelligence, has known for years that alien life forces exist and have entered earth's atmosphere many times. And since the events of Roswell, New Mexico in 1947, that had become a common belief for a lot of people. Many buy into reports of an elaborate government cover-up denying the reality of an alien spacecraft crashing in a field near there. Blake had certainly bought into them. He had read multiple books on the incident. He had even traveled to Roswell to investigate for himself. It was hard for him to see how anyone could doubt the facts in the case. In early July, 1947 a rancher had discovered several large pieces of metal debris scattered across a field. A trench of several hundred feet had been caused by the crash of an unidentified flying object. There was plenty of evidence for the identity of the object. As an investigative reporter, Blake had made note of each piece. There had been several UFO sightings in the U.S. that summer. Research said the military had been tracking an object that had crashed at the same time outside Roswell. The debris being examined was shown to be made of indestructible material and definitely not from any man-made flying object. The army had issued a press release stating they had found a flying disk. Eyewitnesses had also reported seeing the dead bodies of alien life forms. And that was only a brief summary of the evidence he had found. Ultimately, the army issued another press release stating the debris was simply the remains of a weather balloon that had crashed. But Blake, like many others, had always believed that was simply a way of concealing the truth. Furthermore, several early astronauts and high flying pilots had told multiple stories of UFO sightings. Astronaut Gordon Cooper had so many close encounters that he was certain of the existence of life on other planets because he had seen their spaceships for himself. He had sent a letter to the United Nations saying he believed extra-terrestrial vehicles and their crews were visiting earth from other planets. More recently, a decade ago, astronomers had used the Hubble Telescope to search for atmospheres around planets the size of earth beyond our solar system. Clues had pointed to the potential for habitability. In the two decades prior to that, other telescopes had discovered several worlds like earth which could potentially sustain life. The truth is, he thought, there has long been evidence pointing to the likelihood of life in outer space. So, it was easy for Blake to believe this worldwide tragedy was in fact an attack of alien life forces invading the earth. What was not easy for him was reporting that information to a world full of people who were not only in shock and grieving but also in imminent danger themselves of another attack occurring at any time. All nations had better begin uniting in preparation to defend the earth and its inhabitants.

Blake and Anders were now set up and ready to go in Times Square. 3, 2, 1 and "Go," as Anders pointed at him. "This is Blake Thompson reporting live from Times Square. At midnight Eastern Time tonight a worldwide tragedy occurred which simultaneously caused the disappearance of millions, or possibly billions of people. From what we know, every nation has been affected. None has been left out. Some have been devastated; others have experienced minimal loss, by comparison. But make no mistake, all have been touched by this. Millions of families on every continent are grieving today. The world is searching for answers. It has come to my knowledge that world leaders, working with scientists and experts in the field of space exploration, have discovered the cause of this shocking and catastrophic event. Simultaneous press conferences will be held soon in nearly every country to announce it. I feel obligated to tell you now because it may mean all of us are in grave danger. It is possible that what happened earlier today could happen again at any moment and more of us could be gone. I do not want to cause a worldwide panic, but what has been feared for years has happened. In the blink of an eye tonight, at least tonight for those of us living in America, the world was attacked by alien life forms from another planet. The spaceships did not land at any point, but simply hovered in the atmosphere and snatched people away in an instant. The deafening sound you likely heard and the blinding flash of light that some of you saw were caused by the UFOs leaving at warp speed, after stealthily getting into position and perpetrating their heinous act. For years, there has been speculation by some that this day would come. At the same time, there has been denial by the very government agencies who should be protecting us. Well, today is that day. Folks, I fear that we could be near the end of Planet Earth if the nations of the world do not band together and come up with a military plan to prevent this from happening again. I also suggest that each one of us should be on guard as well and ready to protect ourselves and our families as much as possible. Keep an eye toward the eastern sky because that is the direction from which this attack appears to have originated. Okay, I am hearing that the presidential news conference is about to begin. So, we will switch to the White House for the President's statement now. I will be back with you right here in Times Square as soon as it ends."

From the Oval Office of the White House, the President of the United States sits behind his desk preparing to speak to Americans. His press secretary appears on camera and introduces him. "Ladies and gentlemen, the President of the United States of America."

"My fellow Americans. Instead of my normal press conferences in the James S. Brady Briefing Room, I am addressing you from the Oval Office today with no reporters present. This is no time for questions because answers are limited, at best. It is my sad duty to inform you that our nation is under attack. An atrocious act of war has been carried out against us. I know many of you are grieving the loss of friends and family members as I speak. There are no words to express the heartfelt grief I share with you. I too have lost family members and colleagues. Several members of the House of Representatives and Senate are missing. Some were considered political rivals, but I cared for them, as they cared for each other in spite of disagreements on important issues that challenge our nation. Every state in the union has been hit hard. Some have lost as much as half of their population. The grief that our nation is experiencing now is unparalleled in its history. But Americans are not the only ones who are mourning. The entire world is grieving. Every nation on the planet has suffered significant loss of life. Granted some have lost far more than others, but all have been affected to some degree.

The enemy who perpetrated this horrific aggression is no normal foe. In fact, it is not an earthly foe at all. World leaders in space exploration, including NASA have determined that this is the work of extraterrestrial beings. For years, there has been much speculation as to whether life actually exists outside of our own planet. Today, what has previously been portrayed only in movies has become reality. At midnight Eastern Daylight Time this night, a clandestine invasion was carried out against the entire world. This was accompanied only by a blinding flash of light and deafening sound. Few saw, but many heard. It is my duty to tell you that we are preparing for war and any future attack. However, there is no guarantee that we can stop such an enemy because it is difficult to fight an enemy you cannot see. We have placed our entire military on alert and are preparing with everything that is at our disposal to defend our country. I only ask that each of you do everything you can to protect your family and stay as safe as you possibly can. Please be on the lookout for anything suspicious in the skies and report any such activity to law enforcement or military personnel as quickly as possible. Peace be with all of you. And may God bless America, and the world."

CHAPTER 3

Blake stood in the middle of Times Square trying to process his own thoughts. Sure, he had always believed deep down that extraterrestrial beings existed, but now that there was not only proof, but an actual attack from outer space, it changed everything. All he knew was he had work to do, and there was going to be hardly any rest in the weeks, and likely months to come. But little did he know as that thought entered his mind just how true it was. He was jarred to his senses by the hustle and bustle of New Yorkers and tourists. The early risers were beginning their day, seemingly unaware of what had taken place. But that awareness was about to hit them like a tidal wave. News crews scrambled for position, looking to find anyone who may have seen the flash of light or hoping to even find someone who may have seen a spaceship or anything else that would confirm the alien invasion. No one could be found who fit the latter category. And among this group at this hour of the morning, they have yet to find people in the other category either.

As Blake looked around, he saw the one person he was looking for most: Beth Jennings. Of course, she was on the job as quickly as he was. He would have expected nothing less. It was always hard to get a leg up on Beth. She was his chief competitor, the top reporter for another major network. They were the two aces when it came to the news in America. But he admired her. No, more than admired her, he was intrigued by her. Oh, who was he kidding. If there was a woman anywhere with whom he could see himself in a relationship, it was Beth. Every time he got close to her, he could feel his heart rate increase. Her long blonde hair and sky blue eyes seemed to draw him in. His feelings for her were more than admiration and intrigue; they bordered on infatuation. In many ways, Beth was like the female version of Blake.

She had also come up through the ranks of the news industry and finally arrived at the top. She had never married either, and like him, her job was also her life. She had little time for a social life and had never seriously dated anyone. Born in a small town, she was the only child of lower middle class parents who worked hard to provide everything she needed. She was a high school cheerleader, homecoming queen and editor of the school paper. She was also voted most likely to succeed by her peers and had determined that she would live up to that title, whatever it took. That, and her parents' example, had driven her to work harder than most of her colleagues. Most of them would call her a workaholic. She had excelled in college, a journalism major like Blake, graduating Summa Cum Laude. After graduation, she was given the opportunity to work overseas for a year, learning the ropes in London. She had learned from the best, working as an understudy to the renowned English correspondent, Oliver Barton. While she had not made any of his trips to the Middle East with him during her tenure, she had still gleaned from his immense knowledge of foreign correspondence. His knowledge of that area, his work in Israel and Jerusalem, along with most of the surrounding countries, his assignments in war zones and his understanding of how that volatile part of the world functions were priceless to a young reporter trying to learn all she could.

Upon returning to the states, Beth went to work for a television station in a large market and excelled. Her rise to the pinnacle of her career was a bit faster than Blake's but she had her bumps along the way. She had been widely criticized for an expose she did uncovering the disreputable business dealings of a beloved senator. It ultimately resulted in the woman stepping down and escaping prison time in exchange for a guilty plea and an agreement to repay five million dollars to the people she had defrauded. Beth had never been one to shy away from the tough stories. More than once she had reported controversial news. That endeared her to the networks and accelerated her rise up the ladder of success. Now she found herself a superstar among TV reporters. She had certainly made her parents' investment in her life and future pay off. They were very proud of her. And Beth had taken every opportunity she could to pay them back. She had bought them a nice house in the suburbs and sent them on several trips. They deserved it. No one ever had a better mom and dad. She loved them dearly. She tried to call them every day, if at all possible.

However, today Beth was worried. Her concern had caused her to try and contact her parents many times in the wee hours of this morning. But all of her calls had gone unanswered. She had been unable to get an answer from any of their neighbors and close friends who may know their whereabouts. She could not help but fear they had been taken by one of the UFOs. No! She would not allow herself to even consider that possibility. They were probably fine and still asleep, maybe not even aware of the fact that the world had changed overnight. The same was almost certainly true of the others she had tried to call as well. Most of their neighbors were retirees, like them. She would hear from them, or get in touch with them before the day was over. She was sure of that. But for now, she had work to do and after all, reporting the news, especially on this day, was more important than anything else, even them.

As Blake stood near Beth, he could tell she was not her usual self. The normal professionalism and perfect appearance were there but her face displayed a look of concern he had never seen before. He wanted to approach her and ask what was wrong, but like her, he had work to do and it was urgent that he not allow anything to interfere with that today. His thoughts were interrupted from the studio as he heard "Now we go back out to Blake Thompson live in Times Square for more on this developing story that deeply affects every one of us. Blake?" Anders was set up and ready. He gave Blake the signal, and right on cue he began.

"You just heard the president confirm our worst fears. As I reported prior to his address, an alien invasion has occurred which has devastated the world. I have been informed that the armies of the world have been mobilized. Every nation has its military on high alert. I am of the mindset that all the nations of the world *must* come together and join forces on this. The future of the world is at stake. If we do not fight together, we will almost certainly fall together to a formidable foe."

From the studio: "Blake, I want to interrupt you for a moment. We have just received some astounding images that were captured by the James S. Webb Space Telescope. They show the exact moment of the departure of the alien spaceships. I'm going to put them on the screen. I must warn our viewing audience to be careful as you look at your televisions. The term 'blinding flash of light' hasn't been used without reason." As the images hit the screen, even Blake was taken aback. The telescope revealed the earth completely engulfed in brilliant light. The entire 25,000-mile circumference of the globe appeared to be ablaze. Within a matter of less than five seconds, the images went from a normal view of earth to the blinding explosion of light and back to the normal view again, as if nothing had happened. But something had happened. Within those few seconds, millions of people had disappeared. It was the most awe-inspiring thing Blake had ever witnessed.

There were no words to describe it, except maybe, *otherworldly.* Whatever it was, it was not of this world. The intriguing thing was the absence of UFOs among the images. There is no possible explanation for how the telescope had missed them. One thing everyone knew was, the earth was dealing with forces beyond the scope of human comprehension. Which made this war seem less and less likely one that human beings had any chance of winning.

Blake quickly gathered his thoughts and began to speak again. "I have never seen anything like that, and my guess is, neither have any of you. What caused that flash of light is inexplicable, but how millions, or billions of people could just disappear within those few seconds is even more impossible to explain. I suspect we may be in for more than any of us can possibly imagine right now. I would be lying if I did not tell you that I myself am frightened. I promise to search everywhere I can for answers and report to you any information I find as soon as I discover it."

Before Blake could even say "back to you" to those in the studio, it seemed as though the scene changed instantaneously. In spite of all that had gone on in what already felt like an eternity, he realized it had only been six hours since the attack occurred and three hours since he was awakened by the call from Ben. He had been on the scene and reporting before 4:00 a.m. The president had spoken at 5:00 a.m. Many people who had heard the earth-shaking noise were awake and tuned in. Now things were moving fast as the news began to spread like wildfire. There were no scenes like the horrific images in New York City that shocked the world on September 11, 2001 but people were still once again stopped in their tracks and glued to any television station they could find. Many were sitting with their eyes glued to smartphones and tablets. And the same was true worldwide. In that moment, it could literally be said that the world stood still.

CHAPTER 4

The air was suddenly filled with the sounds of sirens as calls came pouring in from multitudes of people who were just realizing that their loved ones were missing. NYPD was overwhelmed with the number of calls, having no chance of responding to all of them. People were pouring into the streets begging for help. The most chilling screams came from parents whose children were gone. It was becoming apparent that babies had been the most targeted of all. In fact, in the days to come it would become clear that not a single baby or young child was left remaining on the earth. For those who knew the story it felt eerily similar to the biblical account of the first-century slaughter of the infants in Bethlehem. Whatever the country, the reports were the same: the children had been taken. Blake was confronted by a young mother who pleaded for his help.

"Mr. Thompson, I watch you on the news every day. Please tell people my children are missing. I have two: a 2-month old baby girl and a 3-year old son. They're gone. Here are their pictures. Please help me find them… Please. I want my babies." She began to sob uncontrollably.

Blake knew he was powerless to do anything to help. All of these children had been taken by the aliens. Who knew their plans for them? Young minds would be easy to shape and control. But why were so many adults taken? From the young to the elderly, so many were missing. It made no sense, but it was what it was. Then something occurred to him.

"Anders, have you called your wife? I know it's early and I don't want to frighten you, but I think you should call just to make sure she and the kids are okay."

"It is early. I hate to wake them. I'm sure they are fine." But he could tell by the look on his partner's face he was not going to be satisfied until he confirmed their safety. And by now, Anders was becoming concerned himself. Yes, he should at least call. He pulled up the favorites on his phone and touched his wife's number. The phone rang several times then went to voicemail.

"Hi, you've reached Angie. I'm sorry I can't take your call right now, but if you'll leave a message and your number, I will call you back as soon as I can. Just remember, Jesus loves you!"

It was that cheerful voice he loved so much. He left a message: "Good morning baby. Hope I didn't wake you. But if I did, you may as well call me back. I just want to make sure you and the kids are okay. I don't want to scare you, but if you haven't heard, an alien invasion has taken people from all over the world. I am in Times Square with Blake reporting live. Please just let me know..." A ding signaled that the time had expired for him to finish his message. She would call him back as soon as she got up. He would get back to work and wait to hear from her. If that did not happen soon, he would try again.

"Did you get her?" Blake's voice showed genuine concern.

"No, it went to voicemail. I left her a message and told her to call me as soon as she wakes up."

"We need to go check on them Anders. Your family is more important right now than the news." Blake could not believe he had said that. The news was his life. But something about this day told him nearly everything needed to be temporarily put on hold.

Anders' job was important to him too. It provided a good living for his family. Along with his wife's income, they lived well. "Let's wait for now. I'll try to call her again in a few minutes. If she doesn't answer then, we will go."

Blake admired Anders' commitment to getting the news out. He was a true professional in every sense of the word. He longed to see the man recognized for his work. He tried to show him every way he could how much he appreciated him. He often reminded him that he could not do what he did without him. As Blake turned around, he saw Beth. This time she was not reporting. She was seated on the curb crying. His spine tingled and his flesh crawled with fear. He could not stop himself. He went to her quickly. He had interviewed thousands of people in his career. But it was hard for him to get out her name. He finally reached down and touched her shoulder as she sat with her head buried in her hands.

"Beth, what's wrong. I'm here for you. No reporting for now. The camera is off. I promise. Please tell me what I can do to help."

"My parents are gone Blake. They're gone," she sobbed.

"How...how do you know that?" he stammered.

"After trying to reach them several times, I finally called the local police and asked them to go and check on them. They were flooded with calls, but because it was me, they went. Within 15 minutes, they called me back and told me there was no answer at the door. I told them to use forced entry and I would take responsibility if they found them. I stayed on the line as I heard them go into the house and search every room. When they got to the bedroom, their bed linens were crumpled where they had been sleeping. The bed hadn't been made and no lights were on. And I don't understand this. Dad's pajamas and mom's nightgown were lying there as if they had just evaporated from them. They're gone. My parents were my world, and just like that, they're gone. What am I going to do Blake? My life is shattered. I know a lot of other lives are shattered too, but this is me. This is *my* mom and dad. Is that how aliens take prisoners, or worse yet kill them? All I know is, I have to get to Missouri. I can report as I go, and I can report from there, if I must. But I have to go."

Blake knew nothing else to do but sit down beside her and put his arm around her. He held her as she wept. All he could say was "I'm sorry Beth. I'm so sorry."

She rose, hugged him and thanked him. The consummate professional, she began to share her story on the air. Her tears were genuine and her words slower than normal. "There are times when those of us who report the news to you, our listening audience, are affected by the same tragedies that have caused you unimaginable pain. At this moment, I empathize with all of you who have lost friends and family members in this horrible attack on our planet today. I have just learned that my parents who lived in our home state of Missouri have also disappeared. I am preparing to leave immediately and travel there. What I would like to do is take you on this journey with me. You will share my pain as I share yours. Right now, we are going to take you to several other places around the world and hear from our correspondents in those areas. I will rejoin you from Ozark shortly after I arrive. May all of us find peace in this turbulent time."

Beth knew this would be the most poignant story she had ever reported. It would be her own. It would be personal. She knew it would test her as no story ever had. But she would report it like the professional she was. It would help those who heard it, and maybe, just maybe it would be therapeutic for her too. With that, she headed home to quickly pack a few items. Then it would be off to LaGuardia as fast as she could to fly home.

As Blake looked back at Anders, the man had his phone to his ear again. As he got closer he could hear his pleas. "Please call me, baby. I need to know that you and kids are okay." This time he had tears rolling down his cheeks. We have to go Blake. I have to know they are safe. Blake hugged his cameraman and said, "Let's go."

Quickly Blake shared with his viewers and the studio what was happening and where he had to go. Like Beth, he promised to continue reporting as they went. Anders was committed to filming if he could manage to hold the camera still. He was shaking now, his fear taking over. They headed for the subway, which was still running in spite of the day. It had lost some operators, so it was running on a limited schedule, but it was running. In a sprint, they made their way to the Times Square Station and boarded the Downtown A for Brooklyn. Anders knew the ride would seem like hours. Typically, he could be home in 20 minutes or less, but today would surely feel a lot longer.

As they rode, Anders filled his time recording Blake as he recapped the events of the morning and interviewed the few other passengers who were on board as they went. Most had not experienced any loss. But they were fully aware of the alien invasion and were preoccupied with the things that had happened. Blake barely recalled a day much like this, twenty-eight years earlier. Having been raised in New York City, it was very personal to him for multiple reasons. He was the only child of upper class parents who had each earned six-figure salaries. They were determined to give their son anything he wanted. He had been enrolled in an exclusive private school and had just begun first grade. He was only six years old, but he could still remember the look on his teacher's face when the principal came and whispered to her, telling her about the terrorist attack on the Twin Towers of the World Trade Center. Blake was too young to grasp the severity of what had happened and how it would affect his life in the years to come. School had been dismissed for the day, but there was no one to pick him up. He recalled sitting with a few others waiting for parents who never came. They were cared for by teachers and later taken to a place where other caring people would watch over them. Blake would later learn that both his mom and his dad were among those who died in the towers. His grandparents lived on the West Coast in California and Oregon. His mom's parents were world travelers. They were making the most of retirement as jetsetters who were rarely home. Whether it was seeing the Aurora Borealis in Norway or a safari in the Australian Outback, they were fulfilling their thirst for adventure. Sadly, for Blake, they had little time for a young boy in their lives. It did not mean they didn't love their only grandson. They often sent him lavish gifts from their travels and came to visit a couple of times a year. But bringing him to live with them was a different story. It was not a good situation for raising a young boy.

His dad's parents were completely the opposite. They lived modestly in Oregon, constantly struggling to get by. His grandfather had battled alcoholism, although Blake had not known it at the time. It was always hush-hush in their home. The alcohol had torn away at his health and he was now battling cirrhosis of the liver. His grandmother was a paralytic who had been wheelchair bound for years. Maybe that had contributed to his drinking, Blake would later think. Nonetheless, there was no way they could care for a little boy. He only had one aunt and uncle on his dad's side and they had been estranged from the family for many years. No one even knew where they were. All four grandparents felt his chances were better in New York. Time would prove they were right.

Blake lived in some wonderful foster homes but was never adopted. With private school now out of the question, he had gone to public schools. Moving from one set of foster parents to the next, due to varying circumstances, he often changed schools more than once a year. It was not an easy life, but instead of destroying him, it made him stronger and determined to succeed in life. That determination had caused him to go out on his own when he turned sixteen. As he finished high school, he also worked and made his own way. He shared an apartment with a few of his high school buddies during his junior and senior years, then went off to college. His last employer had taken a liking to him. He was a very wealthy philanthropist. He believed so strongly in this hard-working young man with a drive to succeed that he chose to fund his entire college education. Be it fate or luck, Blake never forgot it and maintained a close relationship with the man until his death. The man had been very proud of him and followed his career with very personal interest.

Through the years Blake had seen the images of planes crashing into the Twin Towers again and again. He could still see the pictures of people jumping from windows dozens of stories up and many others running, covered in ash, from the towers as they collapsed sending a wall of the stuff billowing down the streets of Lower Manhattan. He could see the towers falling and first responders working to save everyone they could. He could hear the reports of the increasing numbers of people who had perished. And he had to live with the fact that his parents were two of them. That had been a life-changing day for him and many others.

Yes, that was a day the world would never forget. People remember where they were when they first heard the news. It was a horrendous day for

America. But as horrible as it was, this day was far worse. Instead of thousands, millions and most likely billions of people had perished. Instead of only New York and America, this time it was the entire world. And instead of terrorists, this attack came at the hands of an enemy no one could see. There were no faces to show and no images to fill the mind; only the disappearances, accompanied by a deafening sound and a flash of blinding light that rocked the whole earth. Nothing more, simply that and a world forever changed.

Anders had been five years old on 9/11, as it was still known to this day. His parents had arrived in the USA just over four years earlier. He vaguely recalled the events of that day. They were somewhat hazy in his mind, as you might imagine for a five-year old. He could remember his dad being distraught at having moved his family to this new country in hopes of a good life, and now being gripped with terror after witnessing such a horrific disaster. A few images remained in the back of his brain, but honestly he could not tell whether they had been there from childhood or had come from years of seeing them over and over again on television. But *this* day he would always remember. There would be no forgetting it. Fear clawed at his mind as he maintained a faint hope that he would not remember it for the worst of reasons: losing his wife and children in the massive invasion of aliens against the people of earth. No, when he got home they would be there, happy to see him as always. Fear...hope...anticipation...agony... This was definitely the most gut-wrenching trip he had ever taken.

CHAPTER 5

Beth had made a reservation online for her flight home. She threw her bags into her shiny BMW and made her way to Central Park West headed toward 97th Street on her way to LaGuardia. The drive would take about 30 minutes. She had made this trip many times. Her flight went into Springfield-Branson National Airport. Then she made the 30-minute drive to Ozark. But those were good times when she was flying home to visit her mom and dad. Already, memories of those trips began to flood her mind. Tears welled up in her eyes as they did. She had to get control of her emotions. It is never good to drive in New York with either your vision or judgment clouded.

Because of the *Invasion* Beth was unsure whether flights would even be taking place. She had discovered that while flight crews, air traffic controllers and airport personnel were limited, most major airlines were still operating. Also, understanding that one plane crash is one too many, crashes had been very few in number. In only a couple of cases were both the pilot and co-pilot taken by the invaders. In most instances, one was left to fly the plane when the other disappeared. What was really strange was that many flight attendants and passengers simply vanished in mid-air while the aircrafts were in flight. There was literally no rhyme or reason to the aliens' intent and actions. One thing was for sure. The fear of people in the air was equally as great as people on the earth, if not greater. The sad thing is that many of them had family members taken who had been seated right beside them. Every flight was filled with frightened and weeping passengers. Flight attendants who remained did their best to keep everyone as calm as possible. And when planes landed, as passengers disembarked, they were met by sobbing family and friends who ran to them and hugged them, grateful to see them alive. Because of those things, one would think all flights would be cancelled. But the refrain of the airlines was the same.

"We cannot allow the aliens to win. As we did on 9/11 twenty-eight years ago, travel must go on. People still have places to go. If the world shuts down, we show them we are controlled by fear and have given in to them. We will do everything possible to ensure the safety of our passengers."

Beth had to admit that she would have a bit of trepidation when it came to boarding the plane and would be very anxious when it actually took off. But her determination to get to her parents' house outweighed her fear. The same question filled her mind that filled everyone else's mind. Was another attack imminent? Were the aliens finished with the invasion? Or were they waiting for another opportunity to attack again? Everyone knew it could happen anytime, but life had to somehow continue. There would be funerals with no bodies, empty homes to go back to and companies missing tens, hundreds or even thousands of employees. But tomorrow would come. Yes, grieving would happen and adjustments would have to be made. But somehow, some way, the world would have to function. It would not be easy, but it must happen.

Beth was fully aware that she was speeding. But she hoped New York's finest were too consumed with their duties on this day to worry about speeders. Finally, she exited Grand Central Parkway and began the drive toward her terminal. She entered long-term parking, not knowing how long she would be gone. She grabbed the two bags she had quickly packed and ran toward the terminal. There was no time to wait for a shuttle from the parking lot. She had to get there! She was a workout enthusiast and in good shape, so she could make it faster by herself. Beth knew exactly where she was going. Once inside, she jumped aboard the tram that went to her terminal and got off as soon as it stopped. LaGuardia was not its normal self. Passengers were few and the counters were available to walk up and get checked in. She printed her ticket, checked one bag and began sprinting toward her Gate. One thing that was even tougher than normal was security. She could tell that this was not going to be a simple process. Her carry-on bag was searched, in spite of having been screened. Every item was removed and inspected. She was patted down even though she had gone through the x-ray scanner. Such scrutiny may be important in light of a terrorist attack, but she was obviously not an alien! She allowed herself a light smile at the thought. Security completed, she quickly made it to her Gate. A check of the screen showed that her flight was on time and would be landing any moment. She had been fortunate to find a direct flight from LaGuardia to Springfield-Branson that gave her just enough time to catch it. That *never* happened. But somehow today, it *did* happen. She stood waiting in the Gate.

There was no way she could sit. Come on plane...land!

Blake and Anders exited the subway station in Brooklyn, hailed a cab and headed for Ander's house. They could walk, but not today. The cab would get them there fast. Anders gave the driver the address and said, "Step on it." The driver understood and sped off. He knew what the situation must be, by the look on Ander's face. Nothing else needed to be said. The streets were not nearly as busy as normal. Besides, the cabbie knew how to make his way to a destination. After all, he was a *New York City* cabbie. After what seemed like an eternal twenty-minute ride on the subway and less than ten minutes in a cab, Ander's house came into view. As it did, his skin began to crawl. He could feel the hair standing up on the back of his neck. He began to shake, his hands visibly trembling. As they grew closer, the house seemed quiet. But why wouldn't it be? The kids would be at school, and Angie may be sleeping in. It was her day off. But what if... "Stop," Anders told himself. "Everything is going to be okay." The cab stopped in front and he jumped out. Throwing a $20 bill in the seat, he started toward the front door. It was a nice three-bedroom house in a good part of Brooklyn. Anders considered himself to be very fortunate. Fate had been good to him. As he went, Blake became both cameraman and reporter. With the camera on his shoulder, he talked as he followed Anders. He would not go in the house with him, though. This was for him to do alone. Blake was hoping for the best, but his mind feared the worst. This was his friend, his companion and partner. He was like the brother Blake never had. If the worst had happened, what would Blake say to him? How could he be there for a man who had lost his entire family in one fell swoop? He watched as Anders stopped at the door as if taking a deep breath and steeling himself for what he may or may not find.

Anders walked inside. It seemed as though time stood still as he stood there gathering his courage to go farther. Then coming to his senses, he realized he heard a sound. It was continuous. Angie's alarm! Why would it still be sounding? She would not leave it on. His knees became weak and shaky. He walked to their bedroom and quietly opened the door. The blinds were pulled. She always liked the room dark when she slept. "Angie," he whispered. No response. "Angie, are you okay?" He felt sick to his stomach as he reached for the light switch. He flipped it on. Nothing. Their bed was empty, except for...was that the top of her nightgown sticking out from under the sheet? It was! It was lying there sideways facing his side of the bed. One arm was lying straight out in the place where he had been sleeping. Angie always slept on her side, under the sheet, with one arm around him. The sheet had not been disturbed. Neither had her gown. It looked like she had just floated up out of it. Wait, the kids! He leapt up and sprinted up the steps to their rooms. No reason to be quiet this time. He burst through the boys' door and again flipped the light switch. The scene was the same. Their twin beds were crumpled and the covers were on the floor. They were both wild sleepers. Their pajamas looked the same as Angie's, as if they had just floated away from them. From there to his daughter's room. The same. Wait! They would be at school! Grabbing his cell phone, he dialed the school. The voice on the answering machine said, "We are closed today due to the tragedy that struck the world last night. We hope and pray that you and your children are safe. We will be closed for the remainder of the week." Anders slumped to the floor, his head in his hands, sobbing. He sat for a moment, then got up and made his way back downstairs to the master bedroom. He gently pulled the sheet back and lay down beside Angie's nightgown. He could smell her. She always took her bath at night. The bed smelled like her soap. He placed his arm on top of her gown and sobbed, "Angie, Angie. Please come back. Please, I need you." Nothing but silence. He reached over, turned off the alarm and lay there weeping and calling her name and the names of their kids. Anders had never believed in God and now he believed even less, if that was possible. There were no better people in the world than his Angie and their kids. They went to church and worshiped *God.* If there was a God, he would never have allowed this to happen to three people he loved so much. His grief momentarily turned to anger, then quickly back to grief. Blake. He was outside. Anders started back toward the front door.

When Blake saw him, he knew. His faced was streaked from tears. His eyes looked hollow. He appeared to be a shell of a man who was completely empty on the inside. Blake had always been able to keep his emotions in check. He was much more a thinker than a feeler. That is one thing that made him a good newsman. But this time was more than even he could bear. He went to his partner, grabbed him, held him tight and wept with him. It was minutes before either uttered a word. Finally, Anders pulled back and said, "They are gone Blake. They are all gone." Then he buried his head on Blake's shoulder and began crying again. Blake could feel the warmth of his tears as they soaked his shirt. How could this have happened? How could the world have changed so much in one night? Not just in one night, but in a few seconds in one night. Anders took him by the hand and began to lead him inside the house. He was not sure he could do it. But he must for this man who meant so much to him. Blake could not fully understand. He had never married and had no children. He could not empathize with Beth either. He could not really remember what it felt like to lose someone who was so dear to you. But he had to walk through this with Anders. The man did not have many friends. His work truly was his life.

Once inside the house, Anders led him to the room where he and Angie slept, then to the kids' rooms. Blake had heard stories, but seeing it shook him like he had never been shaken before. The world had not even known a blip of what aliens from outer space could do. It had always been assumed that they were beings of superior intelligence to our own, but how did they pull this off? Bodies disappearing right out of their clothes? No evidence. No signs of struggle. Nothing. Then Anders shocked him. "We report the news Blake. People need to know. They need to hear. They need to see." Blake understood what he meant. He wanted to report the news, even if it meant showing his situation and sharing his grief with the world. He went outside to get the camera. The microphone on the camera should be sufficient to record his voice. They briefly discussed how they would do this. Anders would do the filming as he always did. Blake would report. Hopefully the mic would pick up his voice. He was sure it would. Anders would not speak. He could not. Blake would share his story from an eyewitness perspective. Apart from that, the video footage would do the rest, maybe even better than he could. Anders focused the camera on him. "3-2-1...Go."

"This is Blake Thompson with you again from Brooklyn. I am with my cameraman, Anders Norstrom at his house. We arrived about forty-five minutes ago to a horrifying discovery: his wife, daughter and twin sons are missing. They were taken in the *Invasion*. When Anders entered his house, he heard the sound of his wife's alarm still beeping. It was set for 6:30 but was still going off at 10:00. A call to his kids' school yielded only a recorded message stating that it was closed until at least the end of the week due to the critical nature of this time. Many of you have heard stories describing houses where this happened. But most of you haven't been able to see that for yourselves. Even as he grieves, Anders wanted to share with you what it is like; how people have disappeared leaving behind clothing looking as if they had simply floated out of it. He is unable to speak about this because it is so fresh for him right now. But being the consummate professional when it comes to the news, he wanted to give you this firsthand look. You cannot imagine how difficult it will be for him, but he will film as we walk through his house and visit each of the three bedrooms where his wife and children were sleeping when the invasion occurred. Come with me and take a tour that will give you a chill and break your heart at the same time, as it did for Anders, and me. I warn you; some of the images may be disturbing.

As you can see, everything else in the house is normal. There is no sign of struggle or forced entry. Nothing has been stolen. But Angie and the kids are gone. We are entering the master bedroom now. I want to show you the bed because there is nothing else to show. Notice that her nightgown is lying on its side, the way she always slept. The sheet was still covering it when Anders came in. It is as though she just evaporated out of it. Both it and the sheet were completely undisturbed. Other stories that are coming in are just like this one. It is incomprehensible that something like this could take place. There is no human explanation for what these beings of superior intelligence have been able to do. You know, I think that is enough for now. With Anders' permission, we won't go any farther. I can't bear to see him go through anymore of this. We are going to go back to the studio and hear more of what is happening around the world."

CHAPTER 6

After a wait that seemed much longer than it was, Beth boarded her plane right on schedule. As always, she was flying first class and among the first to board. The flight attendant who greeted her attempted to smile but the look of concern on her face was evident. The pilot standing nearby did not appear very confident either. Not exactly what you want to see minutes before your flight, but none of it mattered to Beth. At least, that is what she tried to tell herself. Deep inside, her nerves were jumping. Her arms and legs were trembling as she put forth her best face, trying not to let it show. She assumed her efforts were not much better than those of the pilot and flight attendant. What is more, every passenger on board exhibited the same concerns. No one really wanted to be on the plane, but each of them had somewhere they needed to be. Otherwise, none of them would be flying on this day. Many of them were taking trips for the same reason as Beth. Their faces also gave away the pain that was tearing at their hearts. Beth settled into her seat and fastened her seatbelt as tight as she could. "This is crazy," she thought. "If the aliens want to take me, this belt is not going to stop them. Not after all the reports I have heard." She had seen Blake's report from Anders' house just before getting on the plane. If a person could disappear from under a sheet and out of her nightgown, this seatbelt would be powerless to keep her from being taken. And if other pilots had been taken, the same could happen to hers. She certainly did not need to be thinking about that as they flew! The flight would take a couple of hours, but it was very doubtful that she could sleep. She would have to find a way to keep her mind occupied. She kept checking the news until she finally had to turn off her phone as the plane prepared for takeoff. As it taxied toward the runway, she pulled out a book she had half-finished and began to read. As they sped down the runway, her anxiety spiked to a new high. But when the plane had lifted off the ground, her mind settled down somewhat. At this point, she was committed. There was no going back now.

The flight was fairly smooth, although every period of turbulence was met with a heightened sense of awareness. It was a beautiful day outside, so the view was amazing. How could the world have endured such a tragedy just hours ago? Things looked so peaceful from up here. You would never know, if you had not heard, that billions of people had been abducted from the earth. But Beth did know. And she knew that her parents were two of them. Her grief returned like a flood bringing her back to the horrible reality of the day. Her parents were gone. How was she going to be able to handle that? How could she stand to walk in their house and see things like Blake and his cameraman had seen? And this would not be someone else's family. This would be *her* family. She was overwhelmed with a sense of dread. The pilot was beginning his descent. Soon they would be on the ground. Beth was about to face the toughest moments of her life.

She left the plane and headed to grab her luggage. From there, it was to the rental car counter. She was quickly in her car and pulling onto the road toward Ozark. The thirty-minute drive only took twenty-five minutes. Speeding would surely be forgiven by Missouri's finest too. Turning onto her parents' street, Beth saw some neighbors walking around. It was obvious that her mom and dad had not been the only ones taken. From what she was seeing, it appeared that number from this neighborhood could be significant. When she pulled into their driveway, she was met by some who were aware of the disappearance and were concerned for her. After some hugs and tears, Beth walked toward the back door, where she always went in, and asked for privacy. She wanted to be alone. She put the key in the lock and turned it. The door opened and she stepped inside. She was not ready for this! The house felt dark without any lights on. It was spotless. Her mom was a clean freak. The same could not be said of Beth. Her mom had taught her well, but she was too busy to clean like her, she reasoned. The coffee in the pot was cold. It had been set to automatically come on, but its contents had not been touched. Beth had gotten them a single cup coffee maker but they preferred their standard coffee maker. "I like my own coffee better than what comes in those little cups," her dad had said. So she had gotten them the little reusable cups to put their own coffee in. But her dad had said they were too much trouble. She saw his television remote laying on the table near his chair. His slippers sat on the floor below. He was a college football freak and the previous week had brought the opening of the season. Mom would sit and read as he watched and pretend to be interested. He knew she was not. The bathroom looked untouched. Mom took her baths in there every morning, but it was apparent that no bath had been taken today. Beth was stalling and she knew it. The bedroom door loomed before her. She knew she had to go in but would have to force herself to do so. She reached out her hand, took hold of the knob and slowly turned it.

The room felt strange, she thought. There was an eerie feeling, or was it just her? She flipped on the light. Again it seemed clear that there had been no activity in this room today. The pants dad had planned to wear were laid out on the chest at the foot of the bed with his shirt on top. He always got them ready the night before. His shoes were there too. He had been ready for the day and most likely had plans already made for what they would do. Beth made her way to the bed. She had tried to focus her attention away from it and had succeeded to this point. But now it was time to face the inevitable. She saw it for herself. Her dad's pajamas and her mom's gown both lying there unoccupied. She had never seen anything like it before. They were flat and empty, but by the way they were lying you would swear there was someone inside them. Her dad slept on his side with one arm under his pillow supporting his head. His PJs were lying in that exact position, as if he was still in them. The legs were straight down with one on top of the other. Her mom liked to sleep on her side turned away from dad and hugging a pillow. Sure enough, there was her nightgown, one arm over the pillow she had been hugging and the other under the pillow on which she was sleeping. No one would believe this if they did not see it. But the sad thing was, many people had come home or awoken to see the same thing. The scene was peaceful. She could almost hear the sound of their breathing as they slept. It was surreal. Strangely, the eerie feeling was gone now. There was a sense of peace in the room like Beth had never felt before. She should be weeping again, but she was not. She could not. It was as if they were telling her they were okay. Where was that coming from? She did not understand it at all. But it was a welcome thing to her after all the grief she had felt. Whether it was only a momentary thing or a part of the grief experience, she was not sure. But she *was* sure that she would bask in the calmness for these few minutes in her mom and dad's bedroom.

Then she remembered: she had promised to take her listeners on this journey with her. She had told them she would rejoin them from Ozark. And she had said she would allow them to share her pain as she shared theirs. But for some reason her pain was now peace. Her grief had been turned into gratitude for the feeling that flooded her mind. This could give hope to a hurting world! Beth headed quickly to the car to retrieve her camera from the back seat. It was a smaller camera, one from which she could record the story and get it back to the studio within minutes to show on the air. She suddenly felt blessed to have this opportunity to offer triumph in the midst of tragedy. She would have to be a one-woman show, something she had not been used to doing in a long time. But she was ready. She was also keenly aware that this could be the biggest story of this day and of her life. "This will top Blake Thompson's report," she thought, then erased that thought from her mind. There she went being the newswoman again. Today, she wanted to be known more for reaching out to people who were hurting than for reporting the news. She could do that by sharing her personal story and letting people enter her mom and dad's bedroom with her. She smiled briefly at the thought of taking millions of television viewers on a tour of their room. But for some reason she felt they wanted her to. Camera in hand, she stopped outside the back door and put the camera on a tripod.

"This is Beth Jennings coming to you from Ozark, Missouri where my parents lived. I say *lived* because they were taken in the *Invasion* last night. I have shared the grief that many of you have been feeling for the last several hours. But at this stage of the day, my feelings are different. I can't explain why, but it is true. I am about to take you into their bedroom in hopes that you can somehow feel it too. We are people, human beings. We are Americans. We have never let anything stop us. For some reason, I believe it is my role to tell you there is hope. Right now, I feel hope. Hope in what, I do not know. Come with me and see if you can feel it too."

Beth turned off the camera, picked it up off the tripod and placed it on her shoulder. She would film and record at the same time. She turned it on and began to walk and talk. "As we walk through the house, you will see that everything is normal. This is the coffee maker which was automatically set to brew at 8:00 a.m. It is full and has not been touched. This is my dad's chair where he was almost certainly watching football last night. The house is spotless, as my mom always kept it. It is obvious that nothing traumatic happened in this house. There was no burglary and no break-in. It is obvious that no person took their lives. Now, we are walking into their bedroom. It is just as I saw it when I came in earlier. Let me turn on the light. You can see my dad's clothes laid out and ready for him to get dressed for the day. But he never got to put them on. Now, let me show you the bed. Again, I am certain that many of you were met with a scene like this one when you awoke this morning. For those of you who were not, you need to see for yourselves. It will give you a look at how the aliens invaded our planet and snatched so many people away in the blink of an eye. How they did this cannot be understood by any human wisdom. We have no technology that can come close to understanding what we know has happened. Look at mom and dad's bed. I have not touched it or disturbed it in any way. Dad slept on his side with his arm under his pillow. His pajamas reveal that was exactly how he was sleeping when he was taken. You can see them in that position, but flat as if he just evaporated without moving. The same is true for my mom. Notice how her nightgown is lying. She slept on her side hugging a pillow. You will see that her sleeve is lying across the pillow as if she is still hugging it. The other sleeve lies under the edge of the pillow she was sleeping on. The bed is not rumpled. It has not been bothered. It is clear they were sleeping soundly when suddenly they just disappeared. That is not possible! Or, is it? The truth that remains says it is. How the aliens did this, we do not know. We just know they did.

But I must tell you, when I walked into this room less than an hour ago, everything changed for me. I can't explain it any more than I can explain the abductions. But as they are real, what I felt and still feel is also real. After a few minutes in this room, when I came near mom and dad's bed and saw the things you just saw, an overwhelming feeling of peace settled over me. It was as though they were here telling me they are okay. It is one of the strangest feelings I have ever experienced. Like you, I do not understand what happened, but I do know I am supposed to let you know there is hope. But even with that, I also feel that there are harder days ahead than we can know right now. The world may get more difficult before it gets better. But we can all have hope of a better day when the sun will shine brightly again. How do I know? I'm not sure. But I stand here today in the most difficult time of my life to tell you it is true. My hope is for you to feel what I feel at this very moment. This is Beth Jennings reporting from Ozark, Missouri."

CHAPTER 7

In Chicago, Evan Ryles sat in his college dorm room, alone, and yes, scared. He had never been one to be scared. He considered himself to be bold and brash, almost cocky. But he was not feeling cocky today. His entire family had been taken. They were all gone, except him. He had been glued to the news and seen more reports about the *Invasion* than he cared to see. He had watched Blake Thompson and heard all about the alien abductions. He had seen the video inside Anders Norstrom's house and how his wife and kids had just disappeared right out of their nightclothes. He had heard so many identical stories that he was not sure he could watch anymore. Whichever network he watched, the news was the same. It was like watching re-runs every time he turned the channel. He finally turned the TV off and sat alone in the dark. The thing that haunted Evan was, he knew they were wrong. He knew it was not aliens. Even worse, he knew what it really was. And the thought of what that meant for him and billions of others sent a cold chill down his spine.

Evan was not one to believe in such things. He was a biology major, a practical thinker and a lover of the sciences. He loved studying the origins of life and how the universe works. Obviously, he had thought, the theory of evolution was more than a theory; it was fact. He was especially interested in astronomy. During his studies he had come to believe that there is unquestionably life on other planets. So when he heard the initial reports of the *Invasion*, he believed them. He had expected something like this to happen for years. But now that it had, he was amazed. When he heard the potential numbers of the missing, he was stunned. But when he saw descriptions on the news, the truth hit him like a ton of bricks. He had immediately called home and gotten no answer. He had called his parents' cell phones and tried to get his brother and sister too, but only heard their voices when their phones went to voicemail. He did not have to go and check on them or call anyone to do that for him. He knew. They had told him it was coming. They made sure he heard, even though he did not want to. He had heard all about it a few months ago but had laughed it off at the time. He called them fools for believing something so ridiculous could happen. His was a learned mind. He was the youngest of his siblings and the first to go to college. Such nonsense was beyond him. Evan had to talk to someone, but who would believe him? Ally. He needed to call Ally. She had to know. She would believe him. If she did not, she would at least hear him out. He would tell her, gauge whether she really believed him, then take it from there.

Ally Fromm was a German student who had come to study in the states. She was also a biology major and had several classes with Evan. They had become close friends; not like boyfriend and girlfriend, more like brother and sister. Ally was bilingual and spoke fluent German and English, although with an accent that often caught the attention of guys who were listening. She had been awakened by the sound at 11:00 p.m. Chicago time and witnessed the accompanying flash of light. It frightened her so badly that instead of running outside to see what had happened, she had cowered in fear in her bed. After all, Chicago had become a dangerous place to live. She loved living there, and she loved school, but she also understood the safety concerns. After hearing what she thought may have been the loudest explosion she had ever heard and seeing her room illuminated with light that would likely have blinded her if she had not closed her eyes, she had pulled the covers up over her head and curled up in a ball clutching her knees against her chest. After several minutes of lying in that position, she called her roommate's name five or six times but got no answer. She finally summoned the courage to crawl out of bed and go check on her. Surely she had not slept through that! When she turned on the light, she noticed something. She was gone! Maybe she had just gotten up to go to the bathroom or get something from the kitchen. She called her name as loudly as she dared. Still no answer. Then Ally noticed her bed. What she saw sent chills throughout her body. She was not aware that there had been an *Invasion* yet, but the strong feeling she had that something was wrong was confirmed by the sight that greeted her eyes. The covers were still pulled up to her roommate's neck, but she was not under them. There was no mistaking it: she was *gone.* She tried to convince herself otherwise but the scene in the bed left no doubt. There lay the cotton pajamas she always slept in, unmoved and lying straight out as if someone had placed them there. It was as though she had just left them. But how was that possible? No one could disappear like that with nothing being disturbed, could they? Maybe she had sneaked out and wanted Ally to believe she was there. No, she would never do that. Not her. She was straight-laced and as good a person as Ally had ever known. She was a Christian, something Ally could not understand, and lived the kind of life that she said "pleased Jesus," who had changed her life. She had talked to Ally about that many times, but honestly she had no time for such things. When she turned on the news later, she heard that aliens had invaded earth and taken millions, if not billions of people. Why would they take someone so good, so wholesome as her roommate? Why hadn't they taken her? How could one person be taken right out of her bed and another left in hers? These were questions without answers, not just for her, but for the entire world.

When Ally finally came to her senses after hearing what had transpired, she had called her family and discovered that they had experienced the same thing but were okay. They were fully aware of the *Invasion* and had heard the ear-splitting sound and witnessed the brilliant flash of light as they were preparing to get out of bed at their home in Germany at 6:00 in the morning. As they did, the boom from the heavens rattled the windows and shook their house. Their thoughts went from *earthquake!* to *what the???* almost simultaneously. They could hardly separate the two, or distinguish between them. The sound was accompanied, or followed quickly by blinding light that lasted only seconds. With daylight coming soon, they thought the sun may have exploded as it prepared to rise. They had jumped up and run outside only to see nothing that indicated anything out of the ordinary had happened. But, they told her, there were two things: a chill that caused them to shudder deep on the inside and a very real feeling that things were not the same, and even more, would never be the same again. Even though there was no evidence of any cataclysmic event, they knew in their hearts something was wrong; something was terribly wrong. It was impossible to tell where those feelings came from but they were unmistakably real. They experienced fear and anxiety none of them had ever felt. Her parents and teenage brothers all felt it and had been afraid to leave the house for the rest of the day after that. They had watched the news and were very much aware of what had happened. They confirmed with a few calls that some of their relatives had been taken, but most were safe. However, they were experiencing the same feelings of fear and dread. Then seeing news reports that the event had occurred worldwide, their first order of priority had been to make sure their daughter in Chicago was okay. But her call came first.

When they heard each other's voices the relief for both brought tears of joy. They learned that all of them had witnessed the same things at exactly the same time even though they were in Germany and she was in Chicago, seven hours apart. Each told their story about the moment of the *Invasion* and found them to be, not just similar, but identical. The one difference was Ally's discovery that her roommate was missing and the description of her bed and pajamas. It was also identical to the stories they had seen on TV. They could hardly bear the thought of their daughter being so far away with the possibility of another invasion coming. But they knew she would not come home and accepted that fact. She felt the same about them but could not leave college so early in the semester. So they ended their conversation by pleading with each other to take every possible precaution to protect themselves, knowing full well if another invasion occurred, that was not possible.

Ally sat alone throughout the day in shock because of what had happened during the night. She sat on the sofa trying to put it all together in her mind. What would the world do? How would it function tomorrow with so many people whose jobs were to keep it running suddenly gone? What would be the impact on her life? In a nutshell, what did the future hold for the planet? As she sat in deep contemplation, her phone rang nearly causing her to jump off the couch. With her heart racing and hands shaking she picked it up and saw that it was Evan. She grabbed the phone and answered quickly and excitedly.

"Evan, it is so good to hear your voice! Have you heard what happened? Of course, you heard. Are you okay?"

Evan's trembling voice replied: "I'm safe, if that's what you mean. But I'm not okay. My whole family is missing. I'm the only one left."

"Oh no! Not your family. I am so sorry Evan. Give me time to get ready and I'll be over there. You don't need to be alone at a time like this."

"How about your family, Ally. Are they okay? I'm just glad to know you're safe and sound."

"My family is okay. I called and talked to them. But Allie is gone. She vanished right out of her bed and pajamas. She was such a good girl, Evan. Why? Why her?"

"That's terrible, Ally. I can't believe it. You are right. Allie was one of the best. It is hard to believe she is gone, just like that. I know how close the two of you were."

"I am coming over to be with you, but honestly, I'm afraid to be by myself. I miss Allie. I don't like being alone. Evan, the *Invasion* occurred at the exact same moment in Germany as here. The news is right. It was worldwide. The entire planet has been hit. Where do we go from here?"

"Just get here as soon as you can. I know the answer. I know what really happened and what's coming. I don't know if anyone else on the earth knows what I know. I have to share it with you. I don't know if you will believe me or not, but I have proof. Please just come. I need to tell you!"

Ally's mind was a blur now. What did Evan know? Was it true or something he had imagined in his mind? Did he really have the answer? All she knew was, she trusted her close friend. He had never lied to her or let her down before, and she could not make herself believe he would do that now. She was a mess. She had not showered or cleaned up at all. She grabbed some clothes and almost ran to the bathroom. She had to shower, but she also had to hurry!

Evan was pacing the floor by now. He had retrieved an important document containing what he considered to be potentially confidential information. He had also scanned through a website and found a video which spelled out the information more fully. He was ready to tell Ally everything. Where was she? It was only a 5-minute walk from her dorm to his. Hurry, Ally. Hurry!

CHAPTER 8

September 11 had possibly been the longest day of Blake Thompson's life. Anders had returned home with him at his insistence. He could not bear to leave the man home alone with his entire family missing. Anders did not want to be there either. They arrived at Blake's apartment at 9:00 that night exhausted from a draining and incomprehensible day. They needed to be back on the job before daylight. Blake had been researching any information he could find about the *Invasion*. He had gone over Roswell, New Mexico and 9/11 again and again in his mind. It had finally happened. What he had known for years had been proven true, but in a way he would never have dreamed possible. As he researched, he did his best to console an inconsolable Anders. How do you comfort a man who has just lost his wife and kids in a single instant? There were no bodies to identify and no evidence to be examined. They were just gone. Taken. Disappeared. Vanished. Everything about that defied human logic. Anders needed some time off to deal with his grief. Blake knew he would not take it. He was too devoted to his work, and even more work would help occupy his mind. Sleep. They had to have sleep. At this point, only 4-5 hours were possible before they had to be up and at it again. After much time talking and crying together, both men went to bed hoping to somehow get at least a couple hours of sleep.

Anders lay in the guest bedroom. He had left on the light in the closet so he would not be in the dark. Why did he do that? He had always needed the room completely dark before he could get to sleep. But right now he could not stand the thought of being alone...in the dark. Thoughts of Angie and the kids flooded his mind. He could smell her in the bed beside him. The wonderful aroma of her bubble bath seemed to fill his nostrils. He rolled over on his side, placed his arm around her and hugged her close. She was there in his arms, wasn't she? Then the cold reality hit again and he began to weep. Now he was on the sidelines at his sons' soccer match, yelling and encouraging them as they ran up and down the field. Was that the band playing at halftime? He could see Jenny playing the trumpet. She was so good. She had a bright future as a musician. Wait. The band would not be playing at the boys' soccer match. There it was again: the pain and heartbreak of knowing he would never see them play or watch her marching in the band again. He sobbed and could feel his pillow being soaked with the tears. But somehow his exhausted body and mind fell asleep. He was restless. He dreamed of them over and over. But he slept.

Blake fell asleep almost as soon as his head hit the pillow. The utter fatigue of the day overcame him and he slept deeply. For him, there were no dreams and no restlessness. There was only sleep. Then well before it was time for his alarm to sound, he was abruptly awakened by a voice. Anders stood in his bedroom doorway.

"Blake, are you awake?"

"I am now. What's wrong?"

"Where do you think they are, Blake? They were taken, alive. Their bodies were taken...by aliens. Where did they take them? What are they doing with them? Did they take them to be their slaves? To do experimental testing with them? To train them to be like them? To populate another planet? I need to know, Blake. This is driving me crazy. I need answers. All I can think about is where they are and what is happening to them. You're the best investigative reporter in the world. Please help me find answers. We will find them together, whatever it takes."

Blake was still trying to wake up. He was half asleep, but Anders' questions were like a cup of cold water thrown in his face. How was he supposed to respond to them? As a reporter, his rule of thumb had always been: telling the truth is always the right thing to do.

"There are no answers, Anders. I wish I had them or knew where to begin to find them. But we're dealing with the unanswerable here. I'm sorry; I really am. But I don't even have a clue where to begin. These are beings from outer space, another planet. We don't know anything about them or how they operate. Their technology and intelligence are obviously far greater than ours. There is no way to investigate. I'm sorry. I know you're hurting, and I'm hurting for you. But I don't know what to do. We just have to believe that answers are going to come from somewhere." Blake had no idea how right he was about that last statement and how soon it would come to pass.

"I just don't know what to do. I know you're right. I know they are gone.

And I know there are no answers. But my world is shattered. I don't know if I can go on. I know I said I would keep working and be with you as you cover this *Invasion*. But I don't know if I can. Please help me, Blake. I know you don't have a wife or kids, so I don't expect you to understand. I'm sorry. I didn't mean for that to sound like it came out. I know you will be here for me. Please, help me."

Blake knew sleep was over for the night. "Let's go to the kitchen, get a cup of coffee and talk. We will talk about all your questions and rack our minds for answers."

Anders followed him into the kitchen where they fired up the coffee maker and made two cups of *Red Eye*, coffee with double shots of espresso. This was no time for wimpy coffee. They sat and talked as they drank their coffee. At least Anders was talking, and Blake was listening.

Evan was standing by the door waiting for Ally's knock. It came at last. He threw the door open, grabbed her and wrapped her in a tight embrace. She hugged him just as tightly. Neither wanted to let go. Evan finally broke the silence, and the hug.

"Come in and sit down, Ally. I have to explain something to you. I hope you understand what I'm saying. I can prove to you that it's true. I need you to believe me. If I'm right, and I know I am, we have a long and scary road ahead of us."

"What are you talking about Evan? You know I trust you and always seem to end up believing you, even when it doesn't make sense. But what do you mean, you know what happened? We all know what happened. Aliens invaded earth and took millions, maybe billions of people. I'm so sorry your family was among them. They were nice people. I'm glad I met them when they came to visit you. I can't believe they are gone."

"Ally, you have to listen to me. It wasn't aliens. It was something far different."

"How do you know that? The news, world leaders, even NASA and other space programs around the world have confirmed the *Invasion*. How could you know something they don't? I want to believe you, but this had better be good!"

"It *is* good for those who were taken, including my family. But it is bad, really bad, for us who were not taken. The world is about to go crazy, and we have to live in it. They don't."

"What do you mean *about* to go crazy? It already *has* gone crazy, if you ask me. Nothing like this has ever happened before. If they're right about this, another attack could come any day. We're all in imminent danger. But

I'm listening. Tell me what you know, or what you *think* you know."

"Four years ago my parents begged me to go to church with them..."

Ally interrupted him quickly. "Come on now, you're not going to tell me this has something to do with religion, are you. You know I don't get into that stuff. It's just a crutch for weak people. God didn't create people. People created God in their own minds. Only weak people believe there is a God, and I am not one of them. So, if you are going to try and convince me that some religious teaching had the answer to this, it may be the first time I haven't believed you. But go ahead and take your best shot. I'll listen as best I can. But I can't promise you I will listen with an open mind. It's pretty closed when it comes to that stuff."

"Ally, you know me. I have never believed in the Bible either. I have always considered it to be filled with man-made stories, with some history mixed in. And my studies as a biology major have convinced me even more that is true. If what I heard hadn't matched perfectly with the things that just happened, I still wouldn't believe it. But the preacher that day predicted this whole *Invasion* thing and described in detail everything that would happen. And it did happen, just as he said it would, but even more, *how* and *when* he said it would."

"Okay, I'm all ears. Tell me what he said and don't leave anything out."

Evan took a deep breath: "Okay, here goes..."

Blake sat and listened to Anders for over an hour. He had never considered himself to be a counselor but at least he knew what counselors do; they listen. He was not usually a good listener. Most good reporters like to talk. That is what allows them to be good at what they do. But this time he listened. It was gut-wrenching. He knew Angie and the kids. They were like his own family. And Anders was like a brother. It was tough, but Blake allowed him to bare his soul. Sometimes he would stop for a minute as if in deep thought. His questions and statements came slowly at times. At other times they came so fast that he could not keep up with them.

"Angie was so beautiful, inside and out. I got lucky when she agreed to go out with me. I never thought I would get so lucky that I would have her as my wife. I didn't deserve her Blake. She was such a good person; far better than I deserved. She treated me like I was her knight in shining armor. She always said I was her Prince Charming. But she was the princess. I was just the guy who was lucky enough to marry her. I had the best wife any man ever had."

Blake certainly agreed with that. He nodded in agreement and let Anders go on.

"And my kids. I will never get to see the boys play soccer again. Everybody said they were really going to be good. Their coach was really high on them. He had me already thinking college scholarship. I loved getting out and kicking the ball around with them, but they always ran circles around me. I remember the time A.J. (short for Anders Jacob, named after his father) hit me in the nose with a line drive kick. It bloodied my nose, and I hit the ground. They came running over and jumped on me laughing like crazy."

The look on his face said it all at that point. It was a faraway gaze, as if he was in another place. Staring past Blake as if he wasn't even there, he went on. "And Jenny. I won't ever get to hear her play the trumpet again. She loved it, and she was good too. I was so proud of her. It was her instrument. She said an angel was going to blow a trumpet when Jesus comes, so that's why she loved it. You know I've never been into the Christianity thing. But if I could have them back, I would go to church with them. Anything to be with them. Whatever they wanted me to do."

This time Anders buried his head in his hands and sobbed loudly. All of his emotions and memories spilled out as the tears rolled down his face. His whole body was shaking uncontrollably. Blake's eyes moistened. Tears began to pour from them too. His heart was breaking for his friend. They sat and wept together for a long time. It was the kind of moment that defined this terrible time for Planet Earth and its inhabitants.

CHAPTER 9

Ally sat and looked intently at Evan anxious to hear what he had to say. He was so sure of what he had heard. Could he be right? Of course not. This was an invasion of aliens. The whole world knew that. But what if he was right? What did he mean by things being really bad for those who *hadn't* been taken, like him and her? Things were bad now. How could they get worse? Unless another *Invasion* was coming. She looked at him with a face that said, "I am ready to hear." It was obvious that he was serious as he looked her straight in the eye and began to speak.

"This is the handout they gave us at church that day. I had no plans to listen. I didn't even want to be there and resented my parents for pushing me so hard to go. When the pastor started talking, my attitude wasn't very good. I decided to take notes so I could show them to my buddies at school and give them a good laugh. But something about the way he said it captured my attention. It went against everything I believe, but I listened. It kind of made sense that day, but I shrugged it off. But right after the so-called *Invasion*, it not only made sense, I knew it was true. Ally, will you listen to me with an open mind? I know you will see what I see. I am going to go straight through this outline from the handout for you and try to explain it as best I can.

You and I have studied the origins of the universe and of life. We have been taught that the earth is about 4.5 billion years old. But he said the earth is only six thousand years old."

Ally smirked at that, but tried to go easy because she knew the trauma he was going through. "Come on Evan, you and I both know that's a lie. There is no way the earth can only be six thousand years old. Carbon dating and fossil records, for two things, prove that is wrong. Scientific studies of the universe leave no doubt. I trust you but there's no way I'm buying that."

"You promised you would listen. You have to hear this Ally. It is too important. I know what the pastor said is true. I don't care what we have learned about carbon dating and fossil records and studies about the origins of the universe. It is all a lie, Ally. It is a lie! Those things prove nothing. But what the pastor said and what just happened prove the truth."

"You're right, I said I would listen. I can see how passionate you are about this. There has to be something to it that made you, of all people, change what you believe."

"There is Ally. I promise. Listen to this. He said the universe is six thousand years old and God created all of it in six 24-hour days. Now, before you start shaking your head and rolling your eyes, hear me out. The biblical account of creation explains that. Even some people who are Christians have tried to combine science and theology by explaining that each *day* of creation according to the first chapter of the Bible, Genesis 1, was actually millions or billions of years long and God was creating throughout that period of time.

But that is false. First of all, the Hebrew word that is translated *day* in Genesis 1 is *yom*. That is the word for a day with 24 hours, not a day that lasted millions or billions of years. And there's more. After each day of creation, the Bible says there was evening and morning, Day One, Day Two, and so on. Evening and morning equals a 24-hour day. Why does it say evening and morning? Doesn't the day begin with morning and end with evening? Not the Hebrew day. They saw the day as beginning at 6:00 in the evening. So, evening was first, then morning. The Bible clearly says each day of creation was a 24-hour day. Are you with me so far?"

"I'm with you, and I get what you're saying. But all of that presupposes a belief in the Bible. I'd rather put my stock in what science says. I prefer scientific proof over the words of a book that is thousands of years old. I'm with you so far, but it's going to take a lot more than that for me to be convinced. So, go on, I'm still listening."

"Okay. The pastor explained how the Bible clearly states that each day of creation represents a thousand years of the history of the earth and humanity. It says a day is like a thousand years with the Lord. Then on the seventh day, God rested. So, the pastor said history will last for six thousand years and after that, there will be a thousand-year rest on the earth for the people who believe in Jesus. He read that from Revelation chapter twenty. Then after that God will create a new heavens and a new earth where those people will live with him forever. At that point, I was just like you. I thought 'yeah, right.' I laughed at him, trying not to let others see the smirk on my face. In fact, I was still laughing about what he said until yesterday. Now, I'm not laughing anymore. His words proved true! I knew that as soon as I heard about the '*Invasion*.' (He moved his index and middle fingers on both hands like quotation marks to show he knew that word was only a term that disguised the real truth.) Have I lost you yet?"

"You haven't lost me, but I'm still not buying what you're saying."

"Well, get this. I didn't know anything about the Bible characters. I had heard their names, but I didn't have a clue about their place on the timeline of history. Turns out, that is very important. It was two thousand years from Creation, or from Adam and Eve to Abraham, one of the main characters in God's plan. It was another two thousand years from Abraham to Jesus Christ. And it has been two thousand years from the time of Jesus until today. You're pretty sharp, Ally. What is two thousand plus two thousand plus two thousand?"

Ally was shaking her head, but she answered to appease him: "Six thousand."

"That's right: six thousand. Now, if the six days of creation really do equate to six thousand years of history before the earth comes to an end, where are we on the timeline of the earth?"

"We're at six thousand years, Evan. I know that. But first of all, I still don't believe it. And second, it doesn't prove anything to me."

"Maybe not, but that's only part of the equation. Just suppose with me for a moment that we are at that point in history and six thousand years signals the end. Next the pastor talked about the Feasts or Festivals of Israel in the Old Testament. There are seven of them and God commanded the Israelites to observe them every year."

"What do feasts have to do with what just happened? You're making less sense as you go."

"They're not feasts as we think of feasts. They were festivals they observed to celebrate, and to remind them about God. The Hebrew word is *moedim*. It means appointed times. Yes, they were times appointed by God, and they were commanded to keep the appointments. But the pastor said there is much more to them than that. He said everything in the Old Testament points to Jesus in the New Testament. So the feasts point to times God had appointed during Jesus' first and second comings, and each feast pointed to significant times related to both."

"Evan, you know I don't believe that stuff about Jesus. He is just a figment of the imagination for people who call themselves Christians. I don't think he really existed, but if he did, I can't buy into him dying for my *sins* and rising from the grave. And I sure don't believe he is *coming again* to judge the world. And all that stuff about heaven and hell is ridiculous. No one who thinks for themselves accepts that as true. You have to give me more than that."

"Okay, I will. Remember, there were seven feasts: Passover, the Feast of Unleavened Bread, the Feast of Firstfruits, Pentecost, the Feast of Trumpets, the Day of Atonement and the Feast of Tabernacles."

"Wow, those make a lot of sense. Sounds like something out of a fifties movie."

"Wait till you hear how they match up with Jesus. The first feast was Passover. It was initiated on the day God set the Israelites free from slavery in Egypt. They had been in bondage for over four hundred years. God sent ten plagues on the Egyptians. It took the last one for the Pharaoh, the king of Egypt, to let God's people go: the death of every firstborn in the entire country. God told the Israelites that each family must kill a lamb and put some of its blood on each side of the doorframe of their house. When the angel who came to kill the firstborn saw that blood, he would pass over their houses and their firstborn would not die. Only the blood of a perfect lamb would protect them and allow them to live. They did that and God spared them!"

"Evan...that may be the craziest thing you have said yet. What has happened to you? And there goes that thing about God brutally murdering a lot of people, many of them innocent children. How do you expect me to believe in a God like that?"

"I understand Ally. That always tripped me up too. But when you see the big picture none of that stuff matters anymore. At the end of the day, it's all about Jesus. And the feasts are one of God's ways of showing us his exact plan for history. The pastor said something interesting that day that stuck with me when he was talking about Jesus. I thought it was just a catchy slogan at first. But now it totally makes sense. He said, all of *history* is *his story*. In other words, it's all about Jesus.

You see, the first three feasts match perfectly with Jesus first coming. I thought the pastor was crazy at this point too. And I continued to think that until yesterday. I suddenly realized that he had nailed everything right on the head! What day do you think Jesus was crucified on?"

"I have no idea, Evan. And I have heard just about enough of this nonsense. I know you are hurting because you lost your whole family. I'm not trying to be mean, but I think you are trying to find something you can hang onto that will help you deal with their loss. Can we stop now?"

"Not yet. You promised to hear me out, right?"

Ally sighed and said, "Okay. Go on." Without hesitation, he did.

"Jesus was crucified on Passover...the exact day. John the Baptist, who came to introduce Jesus, called him the *Lamb of God* and said he takes away the sin of the world. Somewhere else, I don't remember where, the Bible calls him our Passover Lamb who has been sacrificed for us. You see, Ally, Jesus died on the cross as God's real Passover lamb. He died for us, so we can live. All we have to do is apply his blood to our lives! I have to tell you something, Ally. Last night I did that. I prayed. I had never done that before, so I didn't really know how. I just talked to Jesus and told him I believe what the Bible says about him wanted to apply his blood to my life. I wanted him to forgive me and be my Savior. That's how the pastor put it that day, so I just did what he said. And I can't even begin to describe how I felt. Something happened inside me, Ally. Something good."

"Evan! Are you telling me you became a Christian? I can't believe what I'm hearing!"

"I did, Ally. Let me tell you more." He held up a hand to stop her as she was about to speak again. "Jesus wasn't only the Passover Lamb; he was the *perfect* lamb. The Feast of Unleavened Bread began the day after Passover. Unleavened bread is bread made without yeast. It is *pure*. Jesus was pure, perfect. His body was laid in the tomb and was in the grave when that Feast began.

And then there was the Feast of Firstfruits. It was the day after the Sabbath, the Sunday following Passover. This was the day the Israelites brought the first fruits of the grain harvest and presented them to the Lord. It was an offering of thanksgiving for the blessing of the crop which would come after that. Jesus rose from the grave on Firstfruits! The Bible says he was the first fruit of everyone else who would be raised because they believe in him. That means he fulfilled the first three Feasts perfectly and right on the dates!"

Evan continued so quickly that Ally did not have a chance to interject, though it was clear she wanted to. "Pentecost is the fourth and middle Feast. It was held fifty days after Passover. The Book of Acts says that is the day Jesus' church began. The Holy Spirit came and filled the believers and they spread the word about him in the language of everyone who was present in Jerusalem for the Feast. Something I remember the pastor saying was, God never does anything by accident. He said Pentecost was also the day the Law was given to Moses. That's when he came down from the mountain and found them worshiping a golden calf idol. Moses was so angry that he told a group called Levites to go through the camp and kill people. They did and three thousand people were killed. On the Day of Pentecost when the church began, three thousand people put their faith in Jesus and became part of his church. When I heard that, I wondered for just a moment if what he was saying could be true. Then I dismissed it as nonsense and put it out of my mind. Then he got to the fifth Feast. It was the first of the three Fall Feasts called the Feast of Trumpets."

"Look Evan, I still don't see what any of this has to do with the *Invasion*."

"Call it that if you want Ally, but I'm telling you that's *not* what happened."

"Say what you will, but you haven't proven anything different to me yet."

"Well, here is the clincher. I will try to make it quick. I know I have been rambling, but I took so many notes that Sunday, not knowing how important they would be now. The Feast of Trumpets is what we know as Rosh Hashanah, the Jewish New Year. It was commemorated with trumpet blasts. Jesus said the time when he gathered his people home would be accompanied by a loud blast of a trumpet and be like lightning that flashes from the east to the west. Do those two things sound familiar to you?"

"I know what you're getting at, the blinding light and deafening sound, as they put it on the news."

"That's right. Jesus said he would send his angels at that time to gather his people from all over the earth at once. And it would happen in the blink of an eye, so fast that people wouldn't even know what hit them. And he said at that time, one would be taken and the other left. The pastor said Jesus gave us a clue when that would occur when he said no one knows the day or the hour when it would happen."

"I don't see how that can give us a clue to when, if he said no one knows when it will happen."

"Well, the pastor said the Feast of Trumpets was known at that time as the Feast of no one knows the day or the hour because the priests waited for the sliver of the new moon to show. As soon as they saw it, they blew the trumpets signaling the beginning of the new year. The new moon could be obscured by clouds and not be seen until the next day. So they waited and watched for it. Jesus told us to wait and watch for his coming to take his people home. It was all Feast of Trumpets language. The pastor said it would be like asking someone 'what is that holiday when guys give their sweethearts chocolates and flowers?' Their answer will immediately be 'Valentine's Day' because they understand what you're talking about. So, he said Jesus told us he would send his angels to bring his people home on a

Feast of Trumpets at some time in the future. Ally, do you know what day Tuesday was?"

"Are you telling me it was the Feast of Trumpets?"

"That's exactly what I am telling you. Do you want to hear something else?"

Ally was stunned. Evan could hear it in her voice when she said, "Yes..."

"The pastor said two other things that seal the deal for me now, even though I rejected them then. First, he went back to the 6,000-year history of the earth. He said *if* he was right, we had to be near the *Rapture* of the church. That was a term I had never heard before. He explained it as the time when Jesus will call his people home, like I just explained."

"But if he's right, we're already past that time, right? You said it would be two thousand years after Jesus came."

"No, if he's right we're actually right at the time. He said it would happen two thousand years after the most significant event in the life of Jesus: his resurrection. So it would happen two thousand years later on the Feast of Trumpets that year."

"Well Evan, that happened in 33 C.E. I have seen enough to know that."

"Wrong, Ally. First of all, it isn't C.E. or the Common Era. It is A.D. or *Anno Domini*, the year of our Lord. We have been trained to believe Jesus either wasn't a real historical figure or didn't matter to history by changing A.D. to C.E. and B.C., before Christ, to B.C.E., before the common era. As you know, I bought into that completely. Not anymore! Here's the deal: Jesus wasn't born in 0 and crucified and resurrected in 33 A.D. The monk who set the calendar, I can't remember his name, was off by at least four years because Herod the Great was still alive when Jesus was born. Herod died in 4 B.C. If Jesus was born in 4 B.C., he was crucified and raised in A.D. 29. What is two thousand years from that year?"

"2029..." Ally breathed out softly.

"The *Invasion*, I'll call it what they did, occurred on September 11, 2029, two thousand years after the year of Jesus' death and resurrection on the Feast of Trumpets. And it occurred exactly as Jesus himself described it. The pastor threw in one more thing just for good measure. He said right after Jesus talked about the trumpet blast and his angels gathering his people home from all over the earth, he talked about the fig tree."

"What does the fig tree have to do with this?"

"I'm glad you asked, Ally, because I was about to tell you. Jesus said when we see the fig tree begin to put out leaves again, we will know the *Rapture* is near. The fig tree is often used in the Old Testament to refer to the nation of Israel. He was saying when Israel became a nation again, it was almost time for Jesus to call his people home. He said it would be right at the door. In other words, it was in the imminent future. And he said that generation would not pass away until they saw that happen."

"But the generation that heard him say that passed away a long time ago, Evan."

"Not *that* generation Ally; the generation that saw Israel become a nation again. That happened in 1948. Some people say a biblical generation is forty years. But Psalm 90:10 says it is seventy years and possibly eighty. Let me test your math again. What is eighty years from 1948?"

"2028. But you said 2029."

"2029 for the Rapture, yes. But Jesus said when Israel became a nation again, we could know it was getting very close. It would be like it was standing at the door, getting ready to happen. That would indicate that it wouldn't occur in 2028 but in the very near future. 2029 would fit the bill, don't you agree?"

Ally nodded her head slowly again, her face turning almost ashen white.

"They call it the *Invasion* and say it was without question an attack of aliens against the people of earth. And millions, or billions, of people were taken. They were taken alright, but not by aliens. I guarantee you, if you could check, you would find that every person who is missing was a follower of Jesus Christ. But I think there's another reason for people believing it was an alien invasion. Do you know what year the supposed alien spacecraft crash in Roswell, New Mexico happened? 1947. The year before 1948 when Israel was re-established as a nation. That all ties together. I know what happened yesterday, Ally. That's why I'm not grieving anymore for my mom, dad, brother and sister. I know they were *taken*, but they were taken to be with Jesus. I'm excited for them! But what you and I are about to face causes my skin to crawl. All I know is I have work to do, and I hope you will join me."

"Evan, you're scaring me. Now I see what you mean by the pastor making sense. Does the Bible really say all of that? I believe it, Evan. I know it is the truth. My family didn't believe in Jesus. I didn't believe in Jesus either. And you didn't believe in Jesus. All of us are still here...left behind. Your family did believe, and they are gone. Allie believed and she is gone. Evan, I believe, and I want Jesus to be my, what did you call it, Savior?"

"That's right Ally. Then all you have to do is tell him that...ask him to forgive you and come into your life."

Ally did that, right there on the spot. Evan couldn't control his excitement. The smile on her face and tears of joy running down her face said it all. Evan grabbed her and held her close. This awful time for the world had just become the happiest day of his life. As they embraced, Ally had another question for him. He did not look forward to answering it, but knew he must because the time was short and she had to know.

"What did you mean by what you and I are about to face?"

CHAPTER 10

Beth returned to New York after taking three days to deal with issues related to her mom and dad's estate. In ways it had been emotionally draining, but she still could not understand the feeling of peace she continued to have on the inside. It had started in her mom and dad's bedroom as she stood looking at their vacated nightclothes. They looked so peaceful that it gave her the feeling they were okay. How they could be, she could not explain. If they had been abducted by aliens, how could she have peace? She should be filled with terror at what they may be going through. But she could not be. She felt like she had somehow been given the task of helping others who had lost friends and family feel what she was feeling. But she had no idea how she was to do that.

Blake and Anders knew they had to get back to work following a memorial service for Anders' family the evening before. Several people had come by to express their condolences. The truth was, so many people had loved ones taken there was no way people could get around to visit with all of them. Anders forced himself to return home after it was over. Sleeping in his bed without Angie was the hardest thing he had ever done, but he made himself do it. He did not touch the kids' rooms. He left them just as they were. He went in that night to kiss them and tell them goodnight. He was determined to keep their memory alive. Blake called him too, just to make sure he was okay. The good news was, they had to fly out the next morning for an assignment in Chicago to report on the *Invasion* results there. Like New York, the city was struggling to function after losing so many people. Fortunately, their flight did not leave until around noon, so they could sleep in a bit and get some much needed rest. There was no reason to be at the airport the standard two hours early since fear still kept many people from flying, and many were still dealing with the loss of family members. An 11:00

arrival time would be fine. Both were looking forward to getting away from New York City after all that had happened and experiencing a change of pace in another city. They knew the atmosphere would be the same, but for them it would hopefully bring some relief from what they had been through.

As Evan looked at Ally, this was the part he had dreaded to tell her. The other was easy because it was good news. But this was bad news in its worst form; as bad as it could get. He was so excited about her decision to follow Jesus, though, that he was ready to tell her the rest. Once again he looked her in the eye and began.

"This is the part the pastor explained that would have scared me half to death if I had believed everything else he was saying. But now that I know it's true, I am scared, but not as scared as I would have been if I didn't know the first part of the story."

"Just tell me Evan. Now that I know Jesus, I feel like I can handle anything!"

"Okay, here goes...again. There is a period of seven years that follows the Rapture of God's people. In seven years, Jesus is coming back to take the rest of us who have now put our faith in him home to be with him, *and* with our friends and family who were taken home the other day. These seven years are called the *Tribulation*. And they aren't called that for nothing.

A world leader will arise soon who will speak a message of peace but will really be a messenger of doom. People will believe him and follow him. The pastor called him the *antichrist*. He will be the antithesis of everything Jesus is. After he rises to a position of leadership, he will turn into a brutal dictator who will be empowered by Satan and kill all those who do not worship him. That puts you and me in grave danger. But what I know is that since we know the truth, it is our job to tell that truth to everyone we can and try to bring them to faith in Jesus too. I'm not sure how we will do that, but somehow I believe God will raise up an army of Jesus' followers who will join us in that task. Well, it will really be *war*. We just have to figure out where to start. One more thing the pastor said that is not in my notes was about one of the seven churches which were written about in Revelation chapters two and three. It was the church at Smyrna. I remember him reading verse ten of chapter two as both a warning and a word of encouragement for those who would be left behind because they hadn't committed their lives to Jesus. I wish I would have heeded his warning. But now that I'm here, I take it as a word of encouragement as we enter these seven years before Jesus comes to take us home."

"What does the verse say Evan?"

"I dug out this Bible my mom and dad gave me when I was fourteen. They hoped I would read it and see the truth. But I was a rebellious teenager who was falling for every lie Satan threw at me. That got worse when I got to college. I looked up Revelation 2:10. Here is what it says."

"Do not be afraid of what you are about to suffer. I tell you, the devil will put some of you in prison to test you, and you will suffer persecution for ten days. Be faithful, even to the point of death, and I will give you the crown of life."

"That's talking about us, isn't it? We are the ones who are about to suffer because we believe in Jesus. The devil will use the antichrist to persecute us and maybe even throw us into prison. Many of Jesus followers will be killed for their faith. But we have to be faithful no matter what happens knowing he is going to give us the crown of life when he comes and takes us home! Is that right?"

"That's absolutely right! I am amazed at how easily you got that from that verse!"

"I don't know. I can see what the Bible means so clearly. I'm not sure why I didn't see it before."

"I have been reading some. I read in the book of John that when the Holy Spirit comes, he will teach us all things. He came on the Day of Pentecost after Jesus had gone back to heaven. He comes into us and fills us when we place our faith in Jesus. That's why, Ally. That is how you can understand the Bible so clearly. The Holy Spirit is teaching you!"

"I have so much to learn, Evan. I guess that will come as we move forward. I will read the Bible as much as I can. And I will tell people the good news about Jesus and the truth about these seven years and the end of time. So, where do we go from here?"

Blake and Anders arrived in Chicago and checked into their hotel. The city was not nearly as busy as normal. They would not waste the remaining daylight hours. They would get out and begin interviewing people to get stories of how the *Invasion* had touched their lives. Blake had already scheduled an interview with the mayor and a leading senator. That would come tomorrow, but for tonight he would be reporting live from outside the 108-story Sears Tower. Then he would ascend to the Skydeck on the 103rd floor where he would stand on the ledge that extends over four feet out into the air overlooking the city. Such a feat was not for the faint of heart! But Blake would go to any length to report a story. And this was the place to be in Chicago.

Beth was back at work in New York. She decided to focus on the churches for a few days, as she continued to interview survivors and spend some time in the studio. Everyone who had been alive on 9/11 remembered how churches were filled, not just in the city, but across the nation as people sought refuge and answers. That had even been true in her home state of Missouri. She still had images of that burned into her memory. But something was different about this time. Churches were, for the most part, empty. It was becoming increasingly evident that nearly all, if not all of the people who were missing were Christians who had been faithfully connected in their churches. But when she visited mosques, synagogues and temples, she found them open and going about their normal times of worship. She was granted interviews with Imams, Rabbis and Brahmans. They were gracious but expressed their confidence in the fact that Christians were taken because of the false beliefs they held about God. This must surely be God's punishment against them for failing to recognize and worship him. For the Imams the failure to worship Allah and Muhammad, his prophet, labeled the Christians as infidels. The Rabbis saw them as worshiping three separate gods since they believed in a Father, Son and Holy Spirit. They were monotheists who held to belief that there is only one true G-d, the G-d of the Torah who demanded to be worshiped. They believed his name was so holy they would not spell it out when they wrote it but put a dash between the first and last letters, leaving out the middle letter. They were serious about their worship. The Brahmans believed in many gods, so they saw the Christians as narrow-minded and missing out on true wisdom and the hope of reincarnation. Beth was getting more confused by the minute. It was time to interview some pastors, if she could find any.

She started attempting to contact pastors so she could talk to them to get their opinions about what had happened. But as she began making calls to churches, she increasingly found that nearly all pastors were among the *taken*. The few she was able to get in contact with refused an interview. Not one of them was willing to talk about the *Invasion*. Most had lost a vast percentage of their congregations and parishes. They were basically left jobless, if you can call the pastorate a job. "There must have been something about pastors that made the aliens want to take so many," she reasoned. What was it? Was it that they were good people from whom they could benefit? Did the aliens seek spirituality of their own? Pastors and children were the two groups most among the taken. *Every* young child had been taken. That made sense in a way. The aliens could shape and control their young minds to do whatever they wanted to do with them. That was the one thing that had crippled the world. But pastors? There had to be a purpose behind that, but Beth could not come up with an answer, no matter how hard she tried. That Saturday evening and Sunday morning she went to multiple churches but found the majority of them empty. Some doors were locked with signs posted that services were cancelled until further notice. A few were open, but attendees were sparse. She attempted to interview a few with very little success. Some who were willing to speak had no idea what had caused so many of their fellow worshipers to be taken. Many of them were people who had rarely attended, other than maybe Christmas and Easter. But others used a word that was unfamiliar to her, at least in the context they were using it: *Rapture*. They talked about the coming of Jesus and his people being *taken* home to be with him. She knew what the word meant: joy, delight, ecstasy. But how could they refer to this event in those terms? The other way they described it, she would have to research. Did it have to do with the reason so many pastors and church people had been taken? Was it the reason so many children were missing? Could it be...could it be why *her* mom and dad were gone? They were committed Christians. Beth immediately set out to investigate this term, not just rapture but *The* Rapture.

Blake had finished his report from outside the Sears Tower in Chicago. He had talked about how quiet the city was, much like New York. And about how the same seemed to be true for cities throughout America and many parts of the world. Grief-stricken people were struggling to return to their normal daily lives. Many businesses were closed, with others operating on a limited basis. Wrigley Field and U.S. Cellular Fields were closed with all sporting events temporarily cancelled. Baseball season had been in full swing and coming down the home stretch toward the playoffs when the *Invasion* happened. Many teams had lost as many as half of their players. The opening weekend of the NFL season had also been postponed. Yes, Chicago was a shell of its former self from only a few days earlier. Blake and Anders got on the elevator and began their ascent to the 103rd floor of the Tower and the Skydeck where Anders would film Blake as he stood on the glass enclosed ledge 1,353 feet above the city. Blake always got a thrill from standing on the ledge and looking through the glass bottom at the city below. It was an amazing view! Yet, each time he had to take a deep breath and gather his courage before stepping out on it. The elevator stopped, and they got off and walked toward the deck. Blake went through his normal procedure, then slowly took a big step into the middle of the ledge. He had the urge to grab hold of something to keep himself from falling to his death below or to turn and run back into the safety of the deck. But he knew he had to report, and Anders was ready. 3-2-1, he pointed at him, and he began to speak.

"This is Blake Thompson coming to you again live from the ledge of the Skydeck on the 103rd floor of the Sears Tower, high above the city of Chicago. As you can see, there is nothing below me but a layer of glass, and air." Anders pointed the camera down through the bottom of the ledge. "From this vantage point, the city appears serene, calm, as if nothing had happened in the last few days. But all of us know something has happened. An *Invasion* of our planet by aliens has taken many good people from all over the globe. Down below people are grieving and trying to find a way to get on with their lives. You and I are grieving and trying to do the same. There is not a one of us who has not been touched in some way by this awful tragedy. It is my hope that we will somehow find the strength to rise above it and rediscover the tranquility that I feel standing here. It seems the world is at peace. It is a beautiful day that could cause us to feel that the world is returning to normal..."

Suddenly the camera began to sway, then landed on the floor of the deck, leaving viewers to wonder what had happened. From its place on the floor, it showed Blake leaning to the outside glass wall of the ledge as it shook violently. He was desperately trying to right himself and run back to what he hoped was the safety of the deck floor. The tremor lasted only a few seconds, but it was enough to shake even the strongest people. Blake scrambled onto the deck from the ledge on his hands and knees breathing hard and thankful to be alive. Anders lay nearby with a look of fear on his face that revealed the question, "what else can go wrong?" It was a question that would be answered soon, but would be asked again and again during the next seven years. Anders had recovered the camera and Blake had stood to his feet again, ready to continue reporting a terrifying story in which he had personally been involved.

"Folks, it appears that we have just experienced an earthquake, or at least a tremor. It lasted only seconds, but I can tell you that I thought I was going to die as the ledge shook and felt as if it would disengage from the Tower and send me falling over 1,300 feet to the streets below. And I can tell you that I am still shaken and we need to get out of the Tower. Alarms are sounding, as you can hear, and people are being ordered to vacate the building. At this point, elevators are working so my cameraman and I are headed that way. I will hopefully come to you again shortly, from outside where we are safe. If you live in Chicago or other places affected by the quake, please be safe."

In New York, Beth was just preparing to exit the last church she had visited when she felt it. The floor under her feet began to shake. She felt unsteady then fell to the floor. A chandelier crashed to the floor, just missing her. The few people in the building were screaming and trying to get out. As Beth tried to stand, the shaking stopped as quickly as it had begun, nearly causing her to fall again. She stood, shaken but alert enough to get out of the church and report what had happened. Her cameraman, who had traveled with her to film interviews, was obviously shaken too but had already set up the camera, ready to film. She quickly called the studio, hoping they were still on the air, knowing they had experienced the same thing. They were. Audiences had witnessed the coverage and had seen the commotion live on television. Quickly they stopped in the middle of their coverage and said, "We are just getting word that Beth Jennings is live from outside the Brooklyn Tabernacle. Beth, are you there?"

"I'm here," Beth reported, still visibly shaken. "I was inside the church to interview the few people who were present. There were no pastors and the famed Brooklyn Tabernacle Choir chairs sat empty. It was a strange sight to behold. I was getting ready to leave when the quake hit. I was thrown to the floor and nearly struck by a falling chandelier. I fear we are in grave danger of a major quake striking very soon. We all need to get out of buildings, especially high rise structures, and as far away from them as possible. As soon as my cameraman and I get to a safe place, I will be back with you. This is Beth Jennings live from the Brooklyn Tabernacle. Back to you."

"Wait a minute, Beth. We are getting reports from all over the world that the same thing has happened simultaneously, everywhere on this planet. This is unprecedented. Never has an earthquake struck the entire globe. It seems that it has traveled throughout every fault line on earth. Seismologists are already reporting that it was a mild tremor, but is likely a portent of a major quake to come."

"That is unbelievable!" Beth immediately chastised herself for sounding so unprofessional. "This following so closely on the heels of the *Invasion* will cause concern that the end of the world is near. Doomsday prophets will be preaching that message. I encourage all of us to stay positive. The world has endured things like this many times before and survived. None has ever been worldwide, but whatever comes next, I say to you with all confidence in technology and the strength of humanity, we will survive." Beth knew she was beginning to share her positive message. What she did not realize was that it would take a far different turn in the near future.

Blake and Anders were thankful for the secure footing underneath them as they stood outside the Sears Tower. Blake reported to the studio that he was ready. They in turn informed him of the worldwide nature of the tremor. He was shaken again, this time on the inside. How could that be? No quake or tremor could be felt over the entire world...or could it? None of this made sense. He feared for the future of the earth. With all of that going through his mind, the feed went live again.

"This is Blake Thompson again safe on solid ground outside the Sears Tower. I can tell you that the relief I feel is like nothing I have ever felt before. I know many of you are feeling it at the same time with me. I can only hope that your friends and family are okay and there has been no more loss of life following the devastation of the *Invasion*. I have just been informed of something of which you may already be aware. This tremor occurred at the exact time across the entire world...everywhere. If we didn't know that to be true, I wouldn't believe it. But if so, as we did with the *Invasion*, we are forced to accept that fact. I don't understand it, just as you don't understand it. There is no record of anything like that in history. I am hearing that seismologists are saying it was a mild tremor, but they also feel certain that it could be an indication of a massive quake coming soon. There is no reason to believe it will not affect the entire world as well. Be safe folks. This is Blake Thompson reporting. Back to you."

CHAPTER 11

Evan and Ally were frightened by the tremor that had shaken Chicago. They had run outside Evan's dorm room and into the spacious quad that formed the beautiful, grassy center of the campus. They were safe there, as long as the earth did not open up and swallow them. Once they felt safe to do so, they went back inside, although this time alert to the possibility that danger could strike any minute. They turned on the news to see what they could find out about the quake. They learned it was a mild tremor that sure did not feel very mild! They saw Beth Jennings report from outside the Brooklyn Tabernacle in New York, then flipped the channel just as Blake Thompson was reporting from the Sears Tower about his terrifying experience on the ledge of the famed Skydeck during the tremor. The combined fear and relief in his voice came through loud and clear.

He was in Chicago! Neither of them was surprised to hear that the tremor had occurred worldwide. This may be the beginning of sorrows Jesus had talked about. It was certainly an eye-opening kickoff to the time of tribulation that had not been seen since the beginning of the world to now, and would not be seen again. That was another thing Jesus said. As both reporters said, the world had never seen a worldwide tremor. They looked at each other as if to say, "It has begun..."

"Ally, I think I know what we have to do next!" Evan exclaimed excitedly.

"Tell me," she said. "We don't have time to waste a single minute!"

"Did you see where Blake Thompson was reporting from? The Sears Tower! He is right here in Chicago!"

"What does that have to do with our next move?" she asked.

"He is the best investigative reporter in the world. He is always on the lookout for any lead he can get. We have to get to him. We have to tell him what we know!"

"How are we going to do that? We don't even know where he is going next. Besides, what makes you think he will want to talk to us. He has bigger fish to fry." (That was an amusing American phrase she had picked up. Her brothers had taken it back home with them.) "Does one of us stay glued to the news while the other is out trying to find him?"

"Email, Ally. We can get his email from the network website."

"That's right! What are you waiting for? Look it up and let's send that email!"

Blake was in full investigation mode now. His first appointment was with a professor he knew who would be fully in the know about the tremor and potential upcoming quake. He sat in the professor's office engaged in serious discussion. This was not a social visit between friends.

John Baldwin was professor of Seismology, Geology and Tectonophysics. He was renowned for his work in the field. He had published several articles on the subject of major earthquakes, documenting destructive quakes in history and pointing to the possibility of such quakes in the near future. He had suggested the potential of a quake that could affect large portions of the United States and of similar quakes in other countries. However, even he had never suggested that something like this could happen. As Blake sat talking to him, his questions were focused.

"John, do you really think this quake was worldwide, or did that only come from initial reports? Is a simultaneous worldwide quake even possible?"

"As you know Blake, I have spent my entire career studying earthquakes and how to predict them so as many people can be aware and kept as safe as possible. It has been my goal to be able to predict them early enough to allow people to escape areas where a quake will hit. I have seen the possibility of massive quakes striking large areas of different countries along major fault lines. But I have never seen any indication that anything like this was possible. I am being honest with you when I say I have no clue as to how this could even happen. If we are indeed in store for a massive earthquake that strikes the entire globe, the result will be the greatest disaster the world has ever seen. The devastation will be greater than anyone can imagine.

Now, that said, I am looking into the possibility that this could have been caused by the *Invasion*. I'll be honest, I don't see how that is possible from an earthly standpoint, but who knows how flying objects from outer space coming so near the earth and using technology beyond our comprehension to 'beam people up' could affect the geological makeup of the globe."

"John, were you a Trekkie back in the day?" Blake tried to interject a little humor into the conversation, but it clearly didn't work. Humor did not work at a time like this.

"That is the only way they could have taken people directly from what they were doing, leaving behind the appearance that they had simply evaporated into thin air. Essentially, they had to have beamed them up into their ships and exited as quickly as they came. I believe an invasion like that could have an impact on the earth geologically, as well as it does atmospherically. The explosive power of the arrival, and especially takeoff, of such powerful vehicles could send off shockwaves that would trigger a seismic tremor along fault lines, ultimately resulting in major quakes. Now understand, that is only a hypothesis, but it is one I am preparing to examine closely, beginning immediately. If such an event is coming, the world needs to know!"

"That is exactly what I'm determined to find, John. Do you mind if I stay in touch with you as you conduct experimentation? I would love to interview you sometime soon, but I know you won't agree to that until you have more factual information rather than simply a hypothesis."

"You know me all too well, Blake. I hope I will be ready for that interview soon with information that can save a lot of lives. I assure you that you will be the first person I call. And when that happens, my interview with you will be the first time the world will hear that news. Trust me, I will already have things set in motion to protect us from a major worldwide quake, if that is possible. But through you, I will let the world know the truth."

As Blake left John's office, he took a moment to check his email. There were many, but one in particular caught his eye. It was from a young man named Evan who just happened to be a student at the same university where he had just met with a professor who specialized in the very field Blake was investigating. He began reading the email, as he would any other lead he might receive. He deleted many of them quickly. But this one intrigued him enough to keep him reading.

"Mr. Thompson. I have been keeping close watch on your reports about the *Invasion*. I can only hope you will believe me when I say, I know what happened. It is not what is being reported. In fact, it is far more significant than that. I know this may sound ridiculous to you, but I am very sincere. I *do* know what happened. Please let me share it with you. You are the one person I know who can get the word out so people will know. I would love to meet with you while you are in Chicago. This is of the utmost importance. I would call it urgent. Please let me know if we can get together and talk. I hope you will reply ASAP. Or if you can call, here is my number. Please get in touch with me before you leave town. Sincerely, Evan Ryles."

Blake did not know if this should be taken seriously or not, but he never turned down a lead. When he got into his car, he dialed Evan's number. He answered on the first ring.

"Mr. Thompson?"

"Yes, this is Blake Thompson. Is this Evan Ryles?"

"Yes, it is. Will you meet with me? It is urgent to me that you do."

What Blake discovered next stunned him. In the news world, there are those occasions when you happen to be in the right place at the right time. This was one of those times. Whether this would yield any information that might assist his investigation, he did not know. What he did know was he was not about to miss this meeting.

"I just finished meeting with a dear friend of mine, Professor John Baldwin. I am here on campus. If you will give me your address, I will be right there."

"That is amazing! Thank you so much. Mr. Thompson, I believe it is a miracle that you happen to be in Chicago right now. But there is no way you being right here on campus at the very time you received my email can be a coincidence. I will be waiting for you to arrive."

Blake wasted no time. Evan's room was close by and he was there in a few minutes. He knocked on the door and was greeted by a young man who looked intelligent enough, but he was not necessarily the professor type. However, he did look somewhat like a journalist to him!

"Evan?"

"Come in, Mr. Thompson. I cannot believe I am actually talking to you right now. It seems a bit surreal. But I have this information which I must share with you. By the way, this is Ally Fromm. She is my friend and fellow student. I beg you to hear us out."

Ally interrupted. "Mr. Thompson, before Evan shares with you what he knows, I have to tell you, I didn't believe him at first either. But by the time he finished, I knew it was true. And what he showed me has already changed my life, and I assure you, my future. All I can say is, the future of the entire world is at stake. It is urgent that you hear this, and hopefully believe it."

"I detect a noticeable, and somewhat catchy accent Miss Fromm. Do you care to tell me where you are from?" He could not help throwing in those catchy lines. It was all a part of being a good journalist. And from the look on Ally's face, he was pretty sure she caught it.

She could not help but smile and blush at that. "I am from Germany," she replied.

"Before I hear from Evan, do you mind telling me what impact this has had on your family there? What did they see and hear? How does it compare to what happened here in the United States?"

"It was identical. They heard the deafening sound. It was so powerful that it shook their house. Even though it was daylight in the early morning there, the flash of light still lit up the house and was so bright they thought the sun may have exploded. Fortunately, they were all safe. I wish the same were true for Evan's family."

"Your family was taken, Evan? I am so sorry."

"My mom, dad, brother and sister were all taken. I will be honest with you. I don't think I could have handled that if I had not discovered what I am about to share with you. It has changed my entire outlook and given me a mission for the future…for the next seven years to be exact."

"Okay, tell me what you know."

"I would rather let you hear it from the original source than go through the long explanation I went through with Ally. I searched the archives of messages from the church my mom and dad attended and found the one I want you to hear. What I would like to do is play it for you and let you watch it. It is just over an hour long, but it is the most important thing you will ever hear. I heard it in person and didn't accept it at all at the time. In fact, I didn't believe it until now when I discovered that what the pastor predicted that day all came true, right down to the very day and year. I think you will find it compelling, and I think when you hear it, you will believe it too."

"So, this 'news' has to do with some preacher's sermon? I'm not sure how that can have any bearing on what just happened, and on the future. I'm not much of a church guy myself. I have never had time for that sort of thing. My work is too important. The world is depending on me."

"Trust me, I was the farthest thing from being a church guy too, even though my family was."

"Me either," Ally cut in again. "Neither is my family. So for me to see the truth from this and believe it cannot be taken lightly. All I ask is that you will take the time to watch the video Mr. Thompson. And I ask that you put your phone away. You do not need to be disturbed during the next hour. I know you are an investigative journalist, so I hope you will take copious notes."

"Okay, I'll watch it. I have a couple of hours before my next appointment anyway. No use wasting that time. I admit, I'm not very convinced based on what you said. But I will give it a listen and see what he has to say. You wouldn't happen to have a good strong cup of coffee, would you. I never could stay awake trying to listen to a preacher." He gave a wry smile. Evan and Ally nodded in agreement.

"I am a *red eye* guy myself," said Evan. "If you have never had it, I guarantee you it will keep you awake through just about anything!"

"Now, you are speaking my language! I am a *red eye* man too."

Soon the cup of strong coffee with a double shot of espresso was sitting in front of him and Evan had his laptop connected to the TV, so he could watch the video on the big screen. Evan had pulled a soft living room chair up in front of everything else and directly in front of the television. He did not want Blake to miss a single thing. The video popped up on the screen, ready for action.

"Are you ready?" asked Evan.

"As ready as I will ever be," said Blake. "This is like having a front row seat at a movie, minus the popcorn, of course."

"I'm sorry we don't have popcorn. I wouldn't mind having some myself. But once you get started watching, eating will be the farthest thing from your mind. I promise! Okay, here we go. Ally and I will be sitting back here so we don't disturb you. But we are here if you need anything at all."

Evan pushed the *Play* arrow and the video began. After a brief clip about the church and introducing the message for that day, they saw the pastor come to the stage and welcome everyone who was there. He said this was the most important message any of them would ever hear and stated that it detailed some urgent things the Lord had revealed to him. That brought the day flooding back into Evan's memory again. He only wished he had believed what he heard that day and put his faith in Jesus. If he had, he would not be worrying about any of this now.

As they watched, the pastor went into detail about everything Evan had shared with Ally. She was amazed at how detailed he had been. Both of them were praying silently for Blake to receive the truth. They watched him as intently as they watched the video to try and gauge his reactions. For the first 30 minutes or so, it was the same as Evan's had been that day at church and equally as identical as Ally's had been to the things she heard. Blake was taking notes, but at times he would stop for a while after shaking his head or moving his hands in obvious disdain for what he was hearing. Both Evan and Ally knew exactly what he was thinking. They continued praying for him.

"Can I take a potty break?" Blake asked. "This *red eye* has got to come out." He quickly apologized to Ally saying, "Sorry, I forgot there was a lady in the house. Please forgive me. And Evan, you may as well make me another cup. This preacher has just about put me to sleep."

Ally assured him she was used to hearing things like that as she hung around Evan and some of the other guys on campus. He smiled at that. Evan showed him to the bathroom and went ahead and made him another cup of coffee to ensure that he stayed awake. He considered an extra shot of espresso just to make sure. Blake returned and settled back in his chair, taking a couple sips of coffee as he prepared to watch the last half of the pastor's message. Both Evan and Ally knew he was getting to the good part, as they would put it. It was go time. He would either believe or not believe. They could hardly wait to find out.

Blake watched more intently now. Things were heating up. Their hopes went up when he turned to Evan and asked, "Can you replay that part for me? I want to make sure I have those facts straight." It was the pastor's second time of going through the six thousand years as he led up to giving the date of 2029 for the year the Rapture would take place. Evan gladly hit *Back*, then *Play* again to make sure Blake did not miss a single thing.

They watched his reactions from behind, wishing they could see his face. But they did not want to disturb him. However, it was clear to both of them that his reactions had drastically changed. There was no more shaking his head or moving his hands. And he was writing as fast as he could. Then he turned to them and asked if they could please stop the video again.

"Did he say 2029?!"

"That is exactly what he said!" Evan and Ally replied at the same time, smiling at each other as they did.

"Okay, let's go again."

Evan hit play. Now, the pastor was getting into the part about the Feast of Trumpets being the day Jesus would come and take his people home. The pastor had explained that Jesus had intentionally given us the day by saying things the Jews of the day would understand referred to that particular feast. As that seemed to hit home, he turned to them again and asked, "Do you know what day the Feast of Trumpets is on this year?"

"I sure do," answered Evan. "It was September 11..."

This time Blake's face turned the same ashen white color as Ally's had when she heard that. They were thanking God and praying even harder under their breath. Evan took Ally's hand in his as they prayed, both asking God to reveal the truth to this man whose reporting could do more for the world during the Tribulation than either of them could possibly do.

Now the pastor was explaining about Israel and the fig tree. Blake looked a bit bewildered as he talked about Israel being re-established as a nation in

1948. But when he gave the biblical length of a generation as 80 years and said the generation that would not pass away until they saw the Rapture would be people who had witnessed the rebirth of Israel, Blake dropped his pen, then immediately reached to pick it up. When he included the events of Roswell, New Mexico that happened in 1947, Blake knew the truth. Evan and Ally knew too. They knew the truth was hitting home. More than that, they knew this meeting was orchestrated by none other than God himself!

As the pastor was finishing, he spoke softly to his hearers:

"I am telling you that I believe God has shown me based on what Jesus said, the Rapture will occur on the Feast of Trumpets in the year 2029. That date will be September 11. Now, I'm not saying I am right. Time will tell if I am. But I am telling you to do what Jesus said, 'watch and wait' for His coming, because I believe it is very near, as Jesus would say, 'right at the door.' Remember how Jesus said it would happen. If you see that, you will know for sure. Two things will signal that event: the *loud* sound of a trumpet, that I imagine will be the loudest sound the world has ever heard, and a brilliant flash of lightning from east to west that I suppose will also be the brightest light the world has ever seen. It will happen in the blink of an eye; within seconds. People from all over the world will be taken to be with Jesus. They will simply disappear. World leaders will try to explain it in ways that people will believe. This is only speculation, but I suspect their explanation will have something to do with the supposed alien spacecraft crash in Roswell, New Mexico in 1947, because that event is tied so closely to the rebirth of Israel in 1948. What better way for the world to explain such a significant disappearance of people than an alien invasion? That doesn't come from scripture, so I could be way off base. But it makes sense to me."

Evan had forgotten all of that! He must have zoned out at that part. The pastor had not only predicted the day and year and described the how, but he had also said the explanation of world leaders would be directly tied to the alien encounter of 1947. Wow! No one could miss that, not even Blake Thompson. The bloodhound had caught the scent and was on the trail! In his closing remarks, the pastor was speaking directly to the three of them in that room, and to everyone to whom his words applied.

"If you happen to be watching this after the Rapture has occurred, listen to me. You still have time to put your faith in Jesus and receive him as your Savior. If you are listening, please stop this video and do that right now. Tell Jesus you believe in him and ask him to come into your life. He said 'I stand at the door and knock.' That door is the door to your heart and life. If *you* open the door, *he* will come in! Make the decision to follow him for the rest of your life, no matter what!"

Blake turned to Evan and Ally. "Stop the video," he whispered. "The pastor is right. There could be no other explanation. I believe. I know the answer now. And I want to give my life to Jesus."

Ecstasy may not have been a strong enough word to describe what Evan and Ally were feeling! They listened as Blake asked Jesus to be his Savior. They saw the same look and the same tears of joy falling down his face as had fallen down theirs. The three of them embraced in a hug only true followers of Jesus could understand during this time in history.

"There is one more thing," Evan said. "It is the tough part."

"Let me hear it," said Blake. "I feel like I am ready for anything."

Evan hit play. The pastor was almost finished.

"Listen closely to me for another two minutes. No more, I promise. If you just said yes to Jesus, this is very important. There are seven years of time remaining before Jesus returns to conquer evil and set up his earthly kingdom. Those years will be called the *Tribulation*. It will be the most horrible time the world has ever known. The entire earth will be shaken. Evil will prevail. You will be hunted, chased down and possibly imprisoned for your faith. Some of you will be murdered by the antichrist and his evil forces. Whatever you do, keep the faith! Do not turn back. Do not receive the mark of the beast. You will understand that when the time comes, if you survive that long. Be God's witnesses to the truth during those seven years. Tell everyone you can about Jesus. And to you I say, 'Welcome to the family of God! I will see you in seven years...or less.'"

CHAPTER 12

Evan, Ally and Blake sat together in Evan's dorm room. They formed an unlikely trio but were determined to make the most of the seven years they had remaining to live on the earth, if they could survive them. A self-proclaimed wild child and black sheep of his family; a girl from Germany who came to America serious about getting an education and a college degree; and the most well-known newsman in America. Their first task was to create a list of people they wanted to bring to the team, and by nature of that fact, to faith in Jesus. For Evan, that was not so easy. He would not call himself a loner, but he had a very small circle of friends. Among that circle, a couple had been taken in the Rapture. He could only wonder why they had not really talked to him about Jesus. He knew they went to church, but they had never asked him to go. Most in his circle had been as adverse to faith and church as he had been. He knew they had not been taken. He was determined to talk to them. It was time for him to come out of his shell. As he saw it, Jesus had come into his life and cracked open his shell, so he was ready to go and be a nut for Him! He could not help but smile at that thought. It made complete sense to him now.

Ally's first priority was her family. She could not bear the thought of them falling for the devil's lies during the Tribulation and missing out on being with her forever. They were a very close-knit family, and although they had not been Christians, they were good, moral people. They had never cheated, lied to or mistreated others. In fact, just the opposite was true. They had always helped anyone they could. Ally had been taught from childhood that every person has value. Now she understood that better than ever, just in an entirely different light. She got it. People were valuable to Jesus; so valuable that he had died on the cross for every single one of them. And now people were important to her. She would do her best to tell as many as she could about him, but she would start with her family. She had a call to make.

For Blake, making a list was easy. They would come in this order: Anders, Beth, Ben Abramson, John Baldwin (well, maybe he would just get him before he left campus) and others. He did not really have family members to tell. Maybe some of his foster parents or people who had helped him along the way. But he knew by virtue of his position in society and the news world, he would have an opportunity to do what many others could not. His contribution could make the difference. That is why he needed Beth Jennings, Anders Norstrom and Ben Abramson on the team.

"Let's talk about a few things before we part ways," said Evan. "We need a game plan. And from what I have read, the things that are coming are laid out for us in the Book of Revelation. As long as we follow it, we will never be caught by surprise. It is a good thing to know what is coming before it happens! We will be one step ahead of the enemy on that. Blake, there is a verse I read to Ally that really cuts to the chase in telling us what it's going to be like for us and what we have to do. It is Revelation 2:10. It says, *'Do not be afraid of what you are about to suffer. I tell you, the devil will put some of you in prison to test you, and you will suffer persecution for ten days. Be faithful, even to the point of death, and I will give you the crown of life.'* It was originally written to the church at Smyrna. What does it mean to you?"

"Well, it is pretty obvious, isn't it? It speaks to everyone who follows Jesus during the Tribulation. We will suffer and be persecuted. That is a given. It is going to happen. We will face possible imprisonment and even death. But we have to remain faithful to Jesus, no matter what. I can't wait to receive that crown of life! How about you? But we have a lot to do before we get it." Evan and Ally nodded in agreement.

"We are going to be Jesus' army for the next seven years," said Ally. "And I hope we will gain a lot of new recruits and grow this into a major movement. I was thinking, we need a name. Something that defines who we are and what we do. Does either of you have a suggestion?"

"Well," Blake offered, "we could go with something simple like God's Army or Jesus' Warriors. Or something that sounds strong and mighty. Soldiers of the Cross? The Blood Bought? The Cross Crew? How about the Fighting Followers? Heaven Bound? No, those are weak. I just threw them out because I've heard all of them before. I didn't like them then, and they don't ring a bell now. I don't know. I'm new at this thing. But then all of us are."

Evan spoke up. "I have an idea."

"Well, let's hear it!" Blake said excitedly.

"We have been talking about the verse that tells us what the road ahead will be like."

"Revelation 2:10," Ally confirmed.

"That's right, Ally. Revelation 2:10."

"I'm not sure I see a name in there," said Blake. "It talks about suffering and imprisonment and even death. It does talk about being faithful. So maybe the Faithful Few? That makes sense because we will sure be outnumbered! And it talks about the Crown of Life, so maybe Crown Crew instead of Cross Crew? I'm just not sure any of those fit."

"What are you getting at, Evan?" Ally was intrigued. She knew he could think outside the box at times. She liked that. He must have something turning his wheels.

"I'm not talking about the verse itself. I'm thinking, who was the verse written to? Do you remember?"

"I think it was the church in Smyrna, right?" asked Blake.

"That's right, the church in Smyrna. They were the prototype for what we, and every Christian, will be experiencing during the Tribulation. You're probably going to think I'm crazy, but I just ask that you consider it, that's all."

"Come on Evan. Tell us what it is!" Ally was getting impatient.

"Okay. It is a name that will fly under the radar. No one will apply it to the followers of Jesus, at least until we become Public Enemy Number One. I say we call ourselves the *Smyrnians*."

"I like it!" Evan was almost surprised to hear that from Blake. "*Rise of the Smyrnians*! Let the war begin!"

Ally agreed. She liked it too! It was different, unusual, but on point with who they were. "Yes!" she exclaimed. "*Let the Smyrnians arise!* Let's start building this army today!"

"I think we should pray before we go out and begin the recruiting process."

"You're right Blake," said Ally. Then she added, "But I'm not very good at that yet. I'm not sure either of us is."

"The best I can tell," said Evan, "we just have to talk to Jesus like we did when we asked him to be our Savior. That's kind of what the pastor said. And that's how I remember him praying when he finished his message that Sunday. He talked to Jesus like he was carrying on a conversation with his best friend. If you want me to, I will pray for us this first time. I may stumble a bit, but we have to start somewhere. Let's hold hands as a sign of our unity."

They stood in a circle and held hands as Evan prayed.

"Jesus, thank you for allowing us to see the truth. Each one of us believes in you and has placed our faith in you. We know the years ahead are going to be tough. But we're ready to do whatever you want us to do to help other people see the truth. Help Ally as she tries to get through to her family. Help Blake as he talks to his friends: Anders, Beth and Ben. And please help Professor Baldwin to see the truth too. Jesus, I hope you are pleased with the name we chose. Please bless the Smyrnians! Help us rise up and lead your army all the way to the end! Amen."

Anders was waiting back at the hotel, his family still on his mind. "This will never end," he thought. He was trying hard, but how does a man go on after losing everyone he held dear. He absolutely treasured his family. They had been everything to him. He loved his job, but it was always secondary to them. Many men never get to experience what he had: a beautiful and loving wife, a true life companion if ever there was one, and three of the best kids any father ever had. He honestly did consider himself the luckiest man in the world, even the luckiest man who ever lived. He thought about Blake. He had never known any of that. He was too busy with his job to have a family that held him down. He had often told Anders that having a wife and kids would have prevented him from rising to the top as the most well-known news personality in America. But Anders knew better. He had seen the look on Blake's face when he was around him and his family. He knew there was something missing in his life and knew what it was: a wife and kids. He had always hoped Blake would find that, but then if he had he might be feeling the emptiness he himself was feeling now. He would not wish that on anyone, especially his best friend. But he would wish for him to know the happiness he had known as a husband and father

That took Anders thoughts back to his family again. Where were they? What planet had they been taken to? Were they even alive? Were they being held as slaves, brainwashed or worse, used as experiments by the aliens to learn more about *earthlings?* The sad part is, he would never know. Unless...what if they planned to try and learn some things from them then return them?! He imagined walking into his bedroom and finding Angie sleeping peacefully. He could see himself lying down beside her, putting his arm around her and feeling her snuggle up against him. He allowed his mind to drift into his kids' bedrooms and finding them sound asleep before he left for work. Maybe this was all a bad dream. Maybe he was going to wake up and find them there again. Maybe the *Invasion* had not really happened after all! Then he slowly returned to reality and the pain and heartache came flooding in again. Where was Blake? He had been gone a lot longer than he said he would. What if something had happened to him? What if there had been another invasion, and he had been so deep in thought that he missed it? He had to call him, just to satisfy his mind and to know what their next steps were. They were not supposed to be in Chicago long.

Blake had just left Evan's dorm room. The elation he felt was so real! He almost felt guilty for feeling so happy while others were grieving so deeply. If only they knew what had really happened to their families and friends. They were not on some faraway planet held hostage by space creatures. They were with Jesus and experiencing more joy and happiness than anyone could comprehend! If they would only reason it out in their minds. They surely knew their loved ones were Christians. Why hadn't he thought of that? Anders wife and kids were Christians. Beth's mom and dad were Christians. There was a common denominator here that no one could miss if they just thought about it for a few minutes. But wait, most of those left behind did not know about the Rapture or the things Jesus said that described perfectly what had happened. Someone had to tell them! That would be the purpose of the Smyrnians. They would surely have a fight to the death on their hands. But they must fight to stay alive so they could tell the good news to as many people as possible. He began to think about what his role in that might be. Yes, that was it! It would be dangerous, but he had spent most of his adult life preparing for it. The thought of it invigorated him and caused his mind to race in a thousand different directions. He was jarred back to the present by that familiar sound, his phone ringing.

"Hello, Anders. Look, before you say anything, I know how late I am. And I still have one more important stop to make. Why don't you take a swim or grab a bite to eat. I'm not sure how long this is going to take."

"I am just glad to hear that you're okay. You should have called me! I was beginning to worry. I even thought that there may have been another *Invasion* and you had been taken! I'm not up for a swim, and I'm not really hungry. I'll just hang out and wait for you. Maybe I'll take a nap or watch some TV. Try to get back as soon as you can. I hate to admit it, but I just don't want to be alone. It gives me time to think, and that hurts too much. I wish I had gone with you."

Blake wished the same thing. If only Anders had been with him to see the video of the pastor's message. He would have seen the truth, just as he had. But he had a copy saved to a flash drive. Anders would see it. If he would believe, it would change his thinking and his life! Besides, the Smyrnians needed the things he could contribute to the team. In fact, they were essential!

"I'll get back as soon as I can. This next appointment will take at least an hour, and hopefully longer. But I'll do my best." The appointment he had mentioned to Evan and Ally would have to wait. It was not even important now anyway. Meeting with John was essential.

With that, their call ended. He felt bad for Anders. He knew he wanted him there. But he had to see Professor John Baldwin again while he was on campus. He hoped he was still in his office. If he only knew; the tremor was just the beginning! If he could see that and trust in Jesus too, he would also be valuable to the team. That is it! Each of the people on his list would bring invaluable knowledge and potential to the Smyrnians. He knew that was not the most important thing for them, but he could not help but feel that God had planned this all along. He called John's cell phone.

"This is John Baldwin. May I help you?"

"John, this is Blake Thompson again. I know I just left your office a couple of hours ago, but I have discovered some new information that I know you will want to hear. Are you still there? If you are, can you give me some time? This is very important, so it may take a while. But if you can take the time, what I have to share with you will make all the difference in your research."

"You know I work long hours, especially when I am trying to find answers for something like this worldwide tremor. Come on over. If your information is that important, I want to hear it!"

Beth had left Brooklyn and was on her way back to Lower Manhattan. Her mind was abuzz with all kinds of thoughts. On the one hand, she considered how easily she could have been killed. If the chandelier had hit her on the head... How crazy would it have been to miss being taken in the *Invasion* only to die, inside a church of all places, as she was out investigating? It had taken this to get her inside a church, and even then she did not feel all that comfortable. For that to happen to her in there may prove she was not meant to be in a church after all.

But mostly, her thoughts were consumed with the worldwide tremor. How was that even possible? Scientifically, there was no answer. Historically, it had never happened. She was an investigative journalist, a reporter who was always able to find an answer for the viewing public. She was up to the challenge, or at least she hoped so. It must have had something to do with the *Invasion*. The two had to somehow go hand-in-hand. Could the aliens have caused it? Was it meant to frighten the people of earth to, what had she heard it called, get their bluff on us? Their intelligence was so much greater than ours. They could probably do just about anything they wanted to do, and humanity was powerless to stop them. It really could be the end of Planet Earth. She knew Blake Thompson already had a head start, so she did not have any time to waste. She had better get rolling!

Blake walked into John's office. He was greeted with a cup of coffee. He sat down and took a sip. It was not *red eye*, and for once he was thankful. He was already about as wired as a man could be after the last couple of hours. He did not need any more help with that!

"Okay, what is it that is so important it couldn't wait? All of my computer research and the musings of my scientific mind aren't yielding any results. At this point, I can't find any reasonable explanation for the cause of a tremor that would cover the entire globe at the same time. It is not possible Blake; it's just not possible. And yet it happened."

"What if I told you I know the answer, John?"

"*You* know the answer? I know you're a good journalist, Blake, the bloodhound of the news industry, as some call you, but I don't see how you could have found an answer so quickly."

"Oh, I found it John. The source was a surprising one, but it is there as clear as a bell."

"Don't tell me you're into Nostradamus."

"Nope, never been a fan. Never been a fan of this source either...until today. I need you to watch this video with me," he said, holding up the flash drive.

"How did you find answers on a video? I have researched online all day."

"I was turned on to this by a source who contacted me. I chase down a lot of leads. But sometimes you get lucky, or should I say blessed?"

"Who recorded this video? Is it anyone I know? A seismologist? Geologist? Another professor?"

"None of the above. Someone I promise you have never heard of. But if you'll watch all the way to the end, you'll understand. It is like reading a good book. You can't stop in the middle. You have to read all the way to the end. The answer is there. But you have to make me a promise before we begin. You have to promise you'll watch the entire video, all the way through."

"Why not? I need answers. I know you, Blake. If you didn't think this gives answers, you wouldn't have brought it to me. Another cup of coffee before we start?"

"No, I'm fine. If you are ready, I'll fire it up."

CHAPTER 13

Back in her room, Ally saw things in a new light. She dug through a couple of drawers and her closet and found some items she could use. A cabinet yielded a cake mix she and her roommate loved. And of course, there was ice cream in the fridge. There was *always* ice cream in their fridge! Some would think the *Invasion* had caused her to lose her mind. But an hour later, the bedroom was decorated with streamers and confetti. Every light in the room was on. And on the bedside table sat their favorite cake, yellow with chocolate icing. On it were nineteen candles, one for each year of Allie's life on earth. Yes, their names were the same, just spelled differently. They jokingly called themselves twins, though they looked nothing alike. They had often dreamed of how they would one day change the world. Beside the cake sat a small gift-wrapped box containing her special gift for Allie. With everything in place, Ally lit the candles and sang to her missing roommate:

"Happy first day to you; Happy first day to you. Happy first day in heaven. Happy first day to you."

She knew it was not the first day by now, but it was the party she now knew Allie deserved. She had not been *taken* by aliens. She had been *raptured* by Jesus! Ally blew out the candles and cut two big pieces of cake, one for her and one for Allie. She placed two big scoops of butter pecan ice cream beside the cake on their plates. It was their favorite. Once or twice they had eaten a whole half gallon before bed. It was time to eat! Ally downed her cake and ice cream, then proceeded to eat Allie's too. It was the right thing to do. Finally, it was time to open her gift. She gently untied the bow and unwrapped it, being careful not to tear the paper. She opened the small box and removed a folded piece of paper. "This is for you Allie," she said, then began to read.

"Dear Allie. We did so many things together. People said when they saw one of us, they knew the other had to be nearby. You were my bestie, and I miss you so much. But today, I'm celebrating because I know where you are. You are with Jesus! I'm sorry I wasn't ready to go with you. The only place I didn't go with you was church. I'm truly sorry for that. But, I have awesome news. I gave my life to Jesus today! I knew you would want to know. That means I will see you again in seven years, or maybe less depending on what happens. Thank you for being such a great friend, for always listening to me and supporting me. I am so happy for you. Enjoy heaven! I will see you there. Your BFF and roommate...Ally. P.S., I ate your cake and ice cream for you! Lol"

That was fun! But with that item now crossed off her agenda, it was time to get serious about the work she and the other Smyrnians had to do.

Blake started the video and the pre-recorded message came on giving the name of the church and introducing the pastor's message for that day.

"Blake! Is this a joke? You came here to play some preacher's sermon for me? I don't have time for junk like this. I have scientific research to do. You can turn that thing off before it gets started."

"Not happening, John. You promised you would listen. My reaction was the same as yours. I promise you that you will find the answer you are looking for before the message ends."

"Grrr..." John growled. "Okay, play the thing so we can get this over with." Blake complied.

John was obviously not a happy camper as the pastor was speaking. He turned to Blake multiple times with that "if looks could kill" kind of stare. The stare made him feel as if his friend, the professor, was burning a hole right through him. Blake knew what was coming at a certain point in the video. He had already prepared himself for it.

"Six thousand years?! I am a scientist, a geologist. That is an outright lie! That's one reason I hate this religious garbage. They deny the scientific evidence for the age of the universe. We have proof that the universe has existed for four and a half billion years! I do not have to listen to this!"

"Yes, you do John. You gave your word. If I have known you to be anything, it is a man of your word. And my promise hasn't changed. If you will watch the entire thing, you will find the answers you are looking for. And remember the date of this message. It is from four years ago! So, the more you sit and listen, the sooner you finish. Want *me* to get *you* a cup of coffee?"

"No! Just keep this thing playing."

John showed his displeasure but stayed true to his word. As had happened with Blake, his demeanor changed when the pastor began to explain his reasoning for the day and year of the Rapture. He sat very still with his eyes glued to the screen as he described the deafening sound and brilliant light that would accompany Jesus' people being taken home. When the pastor tied in 1948 and the rebirth of the nation of Israel, combined with the 1947 alien scare, his interest was clearly piqued. As he mentioned his suspicion that it may have something to do with how the event would be explained, the professor had the look of a student on his first day of class.

When the pastor offered the opportunity to stop the video and trust Jesus as Savior, John was silent. Blake took the chance and paused it himself.

"John?"

"How did he know all of that Blake? He may get lucky and predict one thing correctly, but there is no way he could hit the nail on the head with all of them."

"The Bible, John. It is all in the Bible. I had never read it. I didn't have a clue about the things he was talking about. But after hearing it, I believe. I believe, John. I am telling you that after watching this video, I became a Christian, a follower of Jesus Christ. I am praying for an army of followers to help us take on the enemy for the next seven years before Jesus returns. I hope you will join us."

"That is a lot to absorb all at one time, Blake. I need some time to think about what I heard."

"Let me play this last part for you. It is brief. It is specifically for those of us who made the decision to follow Jesus, but it also contains the answer you are searching for about the tremor." He pushed play and the pastor's words came again.

"Listen closely to me for another two minutes. No more, I promise. If you just said yes to Jesus, this is very important. There are seven years of time remaining before Jesus returns to conquer evil and set up his earthly kingdom. Those years will be called the *Tribulation*. It will be the most horrible time the world has ever known. *The entire earth will be shaken.* Evil will prevail. You will be hunted, chased down and possibly imprisoned for your faith. Some of you will be murdered by the antichrist and his evil forces. Whatever you do, keep the faith! Do not turn back. Do not receive the mark of the beast. You will understand that when the time comes, if you survive that long. Be God's witnesses to the truth of Jesus during those seven years. Tell everyone you can about him. And to you I say, "Welcome to the family of God! I will see you in seven years."

"Did you hear what he said John? *The entire earth will be shaken.* That has happened. It is scientifically unexplainable. But the pastor said it would happen. Now seismologists, including yourself, say it may be the precursor to a major earthquake that affects the entire planet. May I read you a few other verses from the Bible?"

"I suppose I will let you. After all, this is research. What does it say?"

"I noticed these on the screen as the video was ending. I took a quick look at them as I was on my way back over here. I think God may have shown them to me to give to you. These are apparently the things that occur immediately after the Rapture. This is what they say."

I watched as he opened the sixth seal. There was a great earthquake. The sun turned black like sackcloth made of goat hair, the whole moon turned blood red, and the stars in the sky fell to the earth, as figs drop from a fig tree when shaken by a strong wind. The heavens receded like a scroll being rolled up, and every mountain and island was removed from its place. Then the kings of the earth, the princes, the generals, the rich, the mighty, and everyone else, both slave and free, hid in caves and among the rocks of the mountains. They called to the mountains and the rocks, "Fall on us and hide us from the face of him who sits on the throne and from the wrath of the Lamb! For the great day of their wrath has come, and who can withstand it?" (Revelation 6:12-17 NIV)

"That sounds like an earthquake that will affect the whole earth, doesn't it John? As a geologist and seismologist, you can understand some of that, can't you? Many of those things are an exact description of the effects of a great earthquake. I want to run three things by you from those verses for you to think about. First, it says there will be a *great earthquake*. Second, it says that *every* mountain and island will be removed from its place. That sounds like a worldwide quake because it moves *every* mountain and island out of place. And third, the people run to the *caves* and *rocks of the mountains* to hide. Sound like a strange place to hide in an earthquake? Well, it would be if they were actually *hiding*. But what they do is beg the rocks and mountains to *fall* on them. Does that sound like something that may be the result of an earthquake?"

"You have made your point, Blake. The evidence is compelling. Yes, that sounds like an earthquake. It describes one perfectly. And the wording sounds like one that will shake the entire earth. And yes, I have no doubt that the tremor that just shook us all is a warning of a massive quake to come. I guess I just need more time. We scientific types need time to process things before we accept hypothesis as fact."

"But John, this is more than a hypothetical situation. Sure, if all we had is what the Bible says, it could be said to be pure conjecture. But with the pastor's message from four years ago being fulfilled to the most minute detail, that's pretty hard core evidence for it being factual. I think even you would have to agree with that. And since he gleaned every part of his prediction, or maybe prophecy, directly from scripture, that would be surefire proof of the Bible's reliability. Then the tremor, and the verses I just read to you? I know how difficult it is for men of science to be men of faith, but this seems to combine the two: fact and faith. The fact is what has happened. The faith part is trusting Jesus and the Bible to be true about everything else he says will happen in the future and following him. I was as cynical as you, John. It is almost as hard for an investigative journalist to accept things by faith as it is for a professor of science. Don't you see, John? This is the answer to your questions. It was spoken 2,000 years ago by Jesus, then written down by his followers then spoken as fact four years ago by a man of faith. And it all happened exactly as he said it would. You can wait, or dismiss what you heard if you want, but you'll see the major worldwide earthquake occur within the next year or two. Or you can accept the facts, yes that's what they are, and trust Jesus for yourself. Then you can join the movement of truth. *And* you can be ready to go with Jesus in seven years or less. That sure beats the alternative. But I can get into that with you later. The decision is up to you. Examine your heart and mind. Then make your choice based on what you feel and know. And you *do* know it because you have lived it with the rest of us for the last few days. I have said enough. I will leave the rest to you. I will be in New York if you need me."

Blake turned off the TV and removed the flash drive. He shook John's hand and turned to walk out the door with one final word: "Goodbye John. I will pray for your decision." The door was already open and he had stepped into the long hallway when John spoke.

"Wait, Blake. You're right. Four years ago, the pastor's message was purely hypothetical. Now, it has become fact. As a scientist, I would be remiss if I refused to believe fact. And in this case, it is impossible to deny the truth. I guess I don't want to be one of the ones hiding. I have never believed in God or the Bible, but if the *Invasion* wasn't an alien invasion after all, and if it really was Jesus taking his people home, and if the remaining seven years of history really are the time of Tribulation before Jesus comes back, I do need to make a decision, don't I? I have to either believe that is true, or not believe. You have convinced me Blake. Tell me what I have to do."

"Just do what the pastor said on the video, John. Just talk to Jesus and tell him you believe in him. You are feeling his knock on the door of your heart right now. I felt it too! And I opened the door and asked Jesus to forgive me for not believing for so long and to come into my life. You will feel something like you have never felt before! I promise!"

"You haven't lied to me yet. And obviously neither has God. I hate that it took this to cause me to see the truth. I want to be in your army Blake, on your team. I may not be good at this, but if you will excuse me, I have to have a talk with the Jesus I never believed in before."

John's prayer was sincere. Blake thought what an incredible moment that a man of science would place his faith in Jesus and what the Bible teaches, to the exclusion of scientific knowledge. When John finished his prayer, his face was radiant! Blake almost thought he may have become an angel. It was an amazing transformation. He could not wait to see the same happen for Anders and Beth!

"Well Blake, tell me about this army, this team. What do we do next? It sounds like it's going to be dangerous and many of us may not survive for the full seven years. But if we don't, we go to be with Jesus, right? Just like those he took home a few days ago. But if we are going to do this thing, I intend to stay alive and fight for the entire seven years! How about you?"

"Absolutely, John! We're in the recruiting stage now, and we'll always be doing that, even as we fight. We want as many people to trust Jesus as possible. But for now, while we recruit, we also have to study and put a plan together. You enjoy research. You're going to eat this up and help us put the battle plan together! If we're right, the Book of Revelation tells us everything that's coming, in the exact order! So, we'll have a leg up on the enemy. We'll know his every move before it happens! I believe, just like the pastor's message, we'll see each piece come to pass like we did four days ago. Hey, we have a name for the army. Do you want to hear it?"

"Sure. It had better be good!"

"We are the Smyrnians."

"The *what?* What in the world does that mean?"

"Read Revelation 2:10. I think you'll get it. That is the last book of the Bible, by the sway. The one I read from earlier. It is our playbook, our military manual, if you will. Welcome to the team John. I could not imagine doing this without you! We will all meet together very soon."

"Blake? Thanks for not leaving me out. I will be a good team member, I promise."

"I have no doubt you will, John, absolutely no doubt."

Blake could hardly wait to call Evan when he left John's office. "I am one for one!" he exclaimed as their conversation started. "You are two for two. Now, I'm going after Anders. This truth will change everything for him, if he will only believe it."

Evan did a little dance when he got off the phone with Blake. But he really did not have time to celebrate for long. There was too much work to do. He was poring over The Revelation like crazy, digesting every verse and putting together a battle plan for the next seven years. He did not understand it all, but he knew the Holy Spirit would help him. And the entire team would assist with the process too. Part of what he read got him excited. But other parts caused him to shudder to think of what was coming. He knew they would need each other and prayed for many more recruits for the Smyrnians. The more he thought about that name, the more he liked it. *Rise of the Smyrnians*. They were getting ready to rise indeed!

Beth had begun her research. She was on the computer looking at websites. Nothing she could find suggested any possibility of a worldwide tremor. Basically, it was not possible. But it had just happened! She had written a list of scientists she could call and would start on that first thing in the morning. Some were world renowned. She only hoped they would speak with her. She was more than willing to go anywhere she needed to go. But talking by phone was the only way she could realistically do the interviews. Of course, they would talk to her. After all, she was Beth Jennings. They knew they could trust her to not misrepresent anything they said. Knowing she was behind time after seeing a few reports and interviews already, she would work continuously. There was no time for taking a break at a time like this. But she also knew deep inside there was very little, if any chance of finding any real answers because deep inside she knew there were not any.

The strange thing for Beth was how she continued to feel. She still felt at peace with everything that had happened. That was not normal for a news reporter after an alien invasion with millions or billions of people suddenly missing, *including* her mom and dad. She should be horrified! But she was not. She felt what could almost be described as a sense of call, as if she was being called to a special task which would reach to the ends of the earth. What it was she did not know. The one thing she did know is that she was ready and up to the task. "Bring it on," she thought.

Ally was on the phone for one of the most important calls of her life. She admitted she was nervous and that it was even a tough call to make. Even now as she talked to her family, she was trying to find the courage to talk to them about what had happened to her. One thing was for sure, that did not need to happen over the phone or by just sending them a flash drive. With all of them on speaker phone, she finally addressed the subject in a subtle kind of way.

"Hey, I was wondering if you guys could come and visit me? I haven't seen you since Christmas. I really wish you would come. The new semester just started here, so there's no way I can come home. We lost several students and a few professors in the... (she couldn't bring herself to say *Invasion* and they wouldn't understand the term *Rapture*) ...in what happened Tuesday. Did I tell you that Allie was taken?" (She could use that term because she *was* taken, by Jesus!)

"Yes honey, you told us," said her mom. "We are so sorry. I know you have Evan and your other friends, but you miss her a lot. Your room must feel awfully empty."

"It does, mommy. That is one reason I need you guys to come. Something else happened to me that I can't get into over the phone. It really changed my life in a lot of ways. I just need to see you guys. I know it is asking a lot but it would mean so much to me if you would come."

"Why can't you tell us," her dad sounded gruff. But then he always did. He was the typical German male in many ways. Well, that is how many people would see it. She knew most guys were not like that. She had seen many American men who were equally as gruff. He was who he was, and she loved him just the way he was. She just wanted so badly for him to know Jesus.

"I can't daddy. It has to be in person, face-to-face. Please tell me you'll come."

"We'll see what we can arrange, honey. Your dad and I both have some vacation time remaining that we need to use. And if you could see your brothers' faces. They would love to come back to Chicago. They love it there, especially that Chicago pizza! They would have to miss some school too. Well, wait a minute. They were to start back the day of the *Invasion* but school has been cancelled till the end of September. They will make up the time by skipping their Fall holiday. If we're going to come, this is the time to do it. And we would love to see you, especially after all this. After we got off the phone with you the other day, all we could think about was wishing you were here with us. But the other option was us being there with you. We had talked about it. I don't know that we can, but we will see. Don't pay attention to your father. If you need us that badly, we will do our best to try and find a way."

"That would mean so much to me. I really do need to see you and hug you and talk to you. It is very important that I do. Please, please try to come."

"We will let you know as soon as we can. We love you honey."

"*Love you Ally!*" chimed in her brothers, but in a silly kind of way.

When the call ended, she quickly called Evan and told him to pray that her family would come so she could explain to them everything the pastor had said. She would have to do that verbally because she feared their limited English vocabulary might cause something to get lost in translation if they were listening to the video. After all, it worked when Evan explained it to her!

CHAPTER 14

Blake was headed back to the hotel. If Anders was asleep, he would not wake him. The man had been through so much. He needed all the rest he could get, and with their hectic schedule he would need to sleep when he could, to be able to have the energy and stamina to keep up the pace. Blake's mind was running a million miles a minute. (Possibly as fast as an alien spaceship, he thought with a smile) He was anxious to dig into *The Revelation* too, even though he knew Evan was doing the same. It was something each of them would have to do. He also wanted to be alert to upcoming events in the world that would need to be reported. He had a lot of freedom with the network and would volunteer to be on assignment for the major ones. He could be undercover for as long as possible and get inside information that would give them insight to the enemy's way of thinking and next moves. He understood the danger in that but knew he was the only one who might have the capability to do it. His thoughts turned to Beth. If she would believe, they could be teammates, both doing that in different areas. That would double the impact of their investigation. He could not help but think again that he would love for her to be more than a teammate. He had always been attracted to her. They shared so much in common. What if...? He only had seven years at the most to experience the wonder of marriage. He knew if that was going to happen, he would not want it to be with anyone else. "Okay Blake, stop it! You should not even be thinking about that. There are far more important things you need to be focused on." Or were there? He forced himself to think about something else. But then Beth was not married either...

Anders. He had to be his primary target for now. No, research, examining the Bible. Wow, he had a lot to do. They all did. The fight would begin soon enough. The leaders would have to gather in a room and determine what their initial moves would be, as they also planned tactical maneuvers for further down the road. Those could be adapted, if necessary. But it helped to have a game plan.

Blake's cab pulled up in front of the Ritz Carlton. The perks of his job allowed him and Anders to fly first class, stay in posh hotels and have an expense account that made it possible for them to do nearly anything they wanted to do, when they had the time. Unfortunately, they were so committed to their work, the last part seldom mattered. But it was what set Blake apart from most other reporters. Except for Beth. She was just like him. Why couldn't he keep his mind off her? He would get to talk to her soon enough. He paid the cab fare and walked through the beautiful front doors into the stunning lobby of the Ritz Carlton.

"Good evening Mr. Thompson," he was greeted by the concierge. "I hope you've had a good day."

"Better than you can imagine!"

"That's wonderful sir. May I get you anything before you retire for the evening?"

"No, thank you. I will just head on up to my room. Good night."

"Good night, sir. I hope you have a wonderful night."

Blake took the elevator to the 37th floor and walked to his room. He quietly opened the door, not wanting to wake Anders. Sure enough, he was sound asleep in his separate bedroom. After a quick shower, Blake sat at the desk and began to pull up websites that resulted from a search of the word *Rapture*. Talk about research! There were millions of them. He quickly discovered that there were three lines of thinking among Christians when it came to the event. One was rejected by nearly all current theologians. He could understand why. A *Post-Tribulation* Rapture was definitely out of the question at this point. It had now been proven false. So had a *Mid-Tribulation* Rapture because it was obvious that no portion of the Tribulation had happened yet. It was evident that the *Pre-Tribulation* was not only the correct view, but it had actually happened! The pastor had been right on target with that one. He sure was glad God did not allow his people to go through any part of this awful seven-year period at the end of the world.

Since that one had happened and was abundantly clear, he closed that search and typed in the words "*The Tribulation*." Millions of hits again. He began to read a few and suddenly had a tremor of his own inside his body at the prospects of what awaited those who became believers after the Rapture. This was going to be worse than he had even considered. Better get the

Smyrnians ready.

John was still in his office doing late night research. That was not unusual for him. When he was surfing the information overload known as the World Wide Web, he found it hard to stop. Every website he read from, every message he listened to confirmed what he now knew. Jesus had taken his church home in the exact same manner and at the exact time he had said he would. There was no denying the evidence. The more he read, the more intrigued he became. This would be the culmination of his years of work in the field of science. He felt a sense of satisfaction knowing the contribution he would make to the work of Jesus and the far-reaching consequences it would have. There was so much to be done that he hardly knew where to start.

Blake decided to turn in for the night. He and Anders had some final reporting to do in Chicago the next morning. Their flight to New York departed at 2:30 in the afternoon. He had to find the opportunity to talk to Anders before they left! He could not take the chance of something happening to him before he did. He would either have to awaken him early or take the time between their work and flight time. That decision was made for him when they were both up and ready by 7:00. He decided to go out and report, then return to the hotel to spend the remaining time with Anders before they left for the airport. They were granted extended time until 1:00 before they needed to be out of the room. They ate a quick breakfast and were on Michigan Avenue, set up and ready to go by 8:00. Blake pointed out how much slower than normal things were. Traffic was at a minimum and pedestrians were few and far between. Chicago was almost like a ghost town, compared to a week ago. There were no traffic jams, honking horns or throngs of people attempting to cross busy streets before lights turned green again. Street vendors were limited, and many shops were closed. Most mainline businesses and corporations were open but numbers of both clients and employees were low. As he made clear, that was not at all surprising considering the two recent events and projections for the near future. The *Invasion* had taken so many people, and now the tremor brought the threat of a massive worldwide earthquake at any time. Chicago was not the only city affected. Every city, every town, every rural and remote area had experienced the same thing. Blake reported briefly on attempts to discover information that led to a cause of the tremor being worldwide and the futility of such attempts. It was seismologically impossible. He knew the only ones who could possibly know the answer were those who had seen or heard and believed the truth of the Bible concerning the last days of Planet Earth. He so badly wanted to say that on the air but knew he could not yet do that. The time would come, maybe, but until then he would have to be undercover.

Beth was on the streets of New York City interviewing people from all walks of life who had different experiences related to the *Invasion*. Some interviews were heartbreaking. Speaking with young couples who had lost young children was especially hard. It took everything she had to hold herself together during those and time to recover before she could talk to someone else. There were people who had lost no one, but were hurting for those who had. Many compared it to the events of 9/11 and the emotions that had gripped the city then. However, most expressed their knowledge of how much more far-reaching this had been. Several talked about the fear, terror may be a better word, they had considering the possibility of a massive earthquake or another *Invasion*. The uncertainty had crippled most peoples' normal daily routines.

Beth knew she was only going through the motions. She had a purpose. She just did not know what it was. She was waiting for someone. But she did not know who. With each interview, she looked for an indication that this may be that person. But time and again she was met with the reality that he or she was not the one. Leaning on every word, she sought a clue as to what her purpose might be, but it never came. She was so certain, that she would not give up the search. Whatever it was, she knew she was meant to be a major player in the world during this time and in the future.

Blake and Anders were back in the room before 10:00. Blake had plenty of time for what he needed to do, but he also knew he did not have time to waste.

"Anders, I need to talk to you about something very important, something that happened to me yesterday while I was away. I need to do this before we leave for the airport. We're both packed, so I need you to sit with me and hear what I have to say."

"You didn't get fired, did you? Of course not. We were just out reporting. Did you get robbed? Are you okay? What happened that is so important you have to tell me now?"

"None of those things. Those are all bad. This is very good. It is very, very good. I did my interview with John Baldwin. When I left, I noticed an email from a student at the university. His name is Evan Ryles. What he said intrigued me, and since I was doing research anyway and was already on campus, I called the number he left and went right over to his dorm room. There I met Evan and a young German student by the name of Ally Fromm."

"Ah, is there something special about this Ally Fromm?!"

"Come on, Anders. You know better than that. She is a bit young for me. But now that you mention it, there is something very special about her. It's just not what you think. The same is true for Evan. He showed me a video that answered my questions about the *Invasion*, the tremor, and everything else that has happened in the last few days; and everything that is going to happen after this."

"Blake, you are starting to sound a little weird. What kind of video did they show you? A psychic, or something like that?"

"No, nothing like that. I just need to show you the video. It is going to answer some questions for you that will rock your world and change your thinking."

"It is going to have to be awfully good to do that, Blake. All I can think about is Angie and the kids. I don't think anything can change that."

"I don't think it will change that. But I do think it will change the way you think about them. Time is getting away from us. I need to pop the flash drive in and let you watch the video. I must warn you, it freaked me out when I saw it. I almost got up and walked away. It freaked John Baldwin out when he started watching it. Oh yeah, I forgot to tell you that I showed it to him. Believe me, it changed his life in a big way! You're probably not going to like the source any more than he and I did at first. But you have to watch all the way to the end. I couldn't force John to do that, but I did get a promise from him that he would. You are my best friend, but I am also your boss. So I am ordering you to watch it and pay close attention. There are things I want you to know and remember after it is over. It contains things about Angie and the kids that you need to know." He knew that would get Anders' attention.

"Blake, that's no joking matter. I don't see how..."

"It does. Trust me. Have I ever intentionally lied to you about anything?"

"No, but..."

"No buts about it. Sit here and watch. I'll be here if you need to ask me anything. The video is a sermon by a preacher from four years ago. I'm telling you up front so you won't be like John and I were. From the Bible he foretold everything that has happened in the last few days right down to the most minute detail. If you listen closely, you'll discover what happened to your family. It will be the most wonderful news you have gotten since that night. You already know it, if you just understood. Well, you are about to understand. Ready?"

"I have never been into preachers or church. You know that. But I have been thinking if I had known this was going to happen, I would've gone to church with them. I would've sat there beside them. So, maybe this is something I should have heard a long time ago. I'm ready."

Blake already had the flash drive in and the picture up on the screen. He put the cursor on the arrow and touched Play. Anders was up on the edge of his chair, listening closely to every word.

Ally was back in Evan's room. She had news she could not wait to tell him. Her family was coming from Germany! She had talked to them and begged them to come, telling them she had to tell them something she could not say over the phone. Besides, she had said, she really needed to see them. Her mom had called a little while ago and said they had made arrangements at their jobs, booked a flight and would be departing for Chicago the next day. They would be staying a whole week! She was so excited she could hardly stand herself. Their flight was scheduled to arrive at O'Hare at 4:00 in the afternoon. She would be there to greet them and wondered if Evan wanted to tag along.

"Absolutely! I'd love to," he said. "It will be awesome to see your mom and dad and brothers again. But even more, I know what is in store for them if they will believe. We need their boots on the ground in Germany!"

Anders was already misty-eyed when the video started. He listened patiently as the pastor walked through the 6,000-year teaching. You could tell that it was already beginning to hit home with him, much more quickly than it had with the others, including Blake himself. He had looked at Blake and whispered, "We are at that 6,000-year mark right now!" He knew how significant that was. Then as he listened to the pastor explain the day and year of Jesus taking Christians home, tears began to roll down his face.

"They *were* taken Blake!"

Blake nodded with a smile on his face. He watched his friend closely. He saw despair being replaced with hope, grief with joy, pain with peace. Sharing this news with Anders had to rank at the top of the list of everything he had ever done. What a privilege it was to let him know the truth!

Anders let the video play all the way to the end, as if he did not want to miss a single word. When the pastor gave the opportunity to open the door to Jesus, Blake saw him bow his head, tears streaming down his face, and heard him talking to Jesus, giving his life to him. The tears rolled down Blake's face too.

"How did I miss it for all these years, Blake? Why couldn't I see it? Their lives shined with the glory of God, but I was too blind to recognize it. They tried so hard to get me to go to church with them. I know it hurt them for me to say no and reject their faith. But now I have no doubt where they are. They were *taken* by Jesus! At the exact moment I heard that ear-splitting sound, they went to be with him. Right then! In that exact moment! I can't help but wonder if I would have seen it happen if I had been in the bed with Angie. I know I wouldn't have, but a lot of other people did see their loved ones disappear right before their eyes. We have to spread that word. They have to know what I know now. I just let Jesus in, Blake. I just gave my life to him. Now I will see them again! Seven years is a long time to wait, but we have so much to do during that time that I doubt it will feel like seven years. A part of me wants to go on right now and be with them. But the other part of me knows Jesus needs me, he needs all of us here on the earth during the Tribulation. Thank you so much for showing me Blake. I knew it was something good when it started. Now I belong to Jesus just like they did. What do I need to do now?"

"As you heard the pastor say at the end of the video, we're going to be at war with evil for the next seven years. We're forming the army right now and getting battle plans ready. So far, our army consists of Evan and Ally, John, you and me. I know there will be many more, and there are probably others out there all around the world who have trusted in Jesus too in the last few days. I'm pretty sure we aren't the only ones who know the truth! I think the Lord will find a way to connect us all together or use each of us in our respective locations, then let us meet in heaven. I'm not sure how it will all work. I just know I'm ready to fight! By the way, our army has a name. Want to hear it?"

"Tell me!"

"The *Smyrnians.*"

"I have no idea what that means, but I am proud to be a Smyrnian!"

"Revelation 2:10 is written to a church called Smyrna. It describes exactly what we'll be going through as followers of Jesus during the Tribulation. Listen to what it says:

Do not be afraid of what you are about to suffer. I tell you, the devil will put some of you in prison to test you, and you will suffer persecution for ten days. Be faithful, even to the point of death, and I will give you the crown of life.

Sounds appealing, huh?"

"Anything sounds appealing now that I know Angie and the kids are safe and happy, and that I'll see them again...*and* be with them forever! I'm ready Blake! Let's get this party started!"

"Right now we had better get to the airport so we can get the flight started and get back to New York. We have a lot to do. But there is one more person I need to tell about the pastor's message."

"Beth Jennings."

"Yes. How did you know?"

"I know you two are competitors, but do you think I haven't noticed how you look at her? You get all goofy when she is around. I used to think she made you nervous. But I realized over time you weren't nervous. You were, what was that word in the old *Bambi* movie you gave my kids for Christmas that year? *Twitterpated?* Yes, that's it. When you're around Beth, you're twitterpated."

"Anders, you can be a real clown, you know it? Stop with the twitterpated nonsense. Beth just needs to know the truth. She needs Jesus like the rest of us did. And we need her on the team."

"Whatever you say." Anders raised his eyebrows. "But you're right. She does need Jesus. And we desperately need her. But admit it or not, you *are* twitterpated!"

"It is good to see you have gotten your sense of humor back."

"This is the happiest day of my life, Blake. My wedding day and the days my kids were born fit that bill before. But now, this day tops them all!"

With that, they grabbed their bags, went downstairs and loaded up in the shuttle to O'Hare. They were headed home. And Blake was headed directly to Beth Jennings when he got there. *Twitterpated...*that Anders. Thousands of comedians out of work and here he was trying to be one. Funny guy. But on the inside, Blake knew he was right. Yes, he was twitterpated. And the object of his twitterpation was Beth Jennings. There, he admitted it, at least to himself. For now, his goal had to be helping her discover faith in Jesus. Everything else could wait. But he did hope there could be something else. Yes, he really did.

CHAPTER 15

Professor John Baldwin sat in his office again, deep in thought. He had spent his life and career believing and teaching science. He had convinced many students of the truth of evolution and the falsehood of belief in creation. "No rationally thinking person," he had said, "could possibly believe in something he cannot see. You can't show me God, but I can show you the universe and how it has evolved through billions of years." He had asked every class, "Which came first, the chicken or the egg?" And his answer was always, "The egg, because without the egg, the chicken isn't possible. That is how the universe works. Everything that exists, including human beings, evolved from things that already existed." Sounding very un-professor like, he asked out loud, "How could I have been so stupid?" He saw it clearly now because he was seeing through the right lens. He had always looked through the lens of science, when the truth could only be seen through the lens of scripture. "Duh," he said as he hit his forehead with the palm of his hand. He had seen many of his students do that when they suddenly got what he was teaching them. Now it was he who was seeing the truth. If everything came from something that was, that something had to be God. How else could any other something have existed if not created by him. So the answer to his career long question was obviously the chicken, not the egg. God created all living things, and the reproduction process from which other living things would come. So obviously, God created the chicken, and the chicken laid the egg, which produced another chicken. That sounded so simplistic and unscientific, but it was the truth. He felt really dumb. But he could not change any of that, and it would be useless to beat himself up. What he could do was spend the rest of his life telling people the truth and fighting for that truth in the face of pure evil.

Ally had been online checking flight schedules. Her family's flight was delayed by an hour. *Of course it was.* But Ally would not be deterred. Nothing was going to interfere with the courage she had built up to talk to her parents and brothers about Jesus and the pastor's message. She sent Evan a quick text to let him know they would wait thirty more minutes to leave for the airport. She also asked him to come over early and help keep her entertained while she waited. That was one of his specialties. When the time finally came, they drove to O'Hare and rushed to the gate to wait for the plane to arrive. It was a tear-filled reunion after everything that had gone on in the last week. There was an underlying realization that this moment could not have happened. But that realization only affected her parents. Ally knew better by now. She understood that all of them were left behind because they had not believed in Jesus. But her family, especially her mom and dad, were grateful that their daughter had not been *taken*. They just did not understand what *taken* meant.

The family was hungry, so they headed, where else? To Ally's favorite pizza joint for Chicago style pizza. Her brothers put away a large pizza all by themselves. Everyone else shared another large. Then it was off to their hotel near campus to get a good night's sleep. They would all meet up tomorrow and spend the day together. Ally was free all day. Evan was free in the morning, but happened to have a "prior engagement" in the evening so she would be able to talk to her family alone. She was eager to talk to them, and she would be ready when the time came.

Blake and Anders were back home. It was now easier for Anders to go to his house. It was still tough to be there without his family, but knowing where they were was a real game changer for him. He cleaned house and threw out any of his stuff that he deemed to be unchristian. He placed an open Bible on the living room table and a cross he had picked up on the wall. He was new at this but he tried to remember the things his wife and kids had done. Unfortunately, Christian radio and TV stations had closed their doors. There was no one left to operate them. With Christian broadcasting non-existent and most churches closed, he and the other Smrynians were pretty much on their own. He determined two activities would be priorities for him: reading the Bible and praying. His wife had made those two things absolute priorities in her life. As he had once told Blake, "You can mess with just about anything else, but whatever you do, don't mess with her *Jesus time.*" He had never understood that. He just knew he had to either leave her alone during that time, or pay the price! And it was the only thing that could cause her to use that *tone* with him. Now, he knew he needed to have his own *Jesus time*. She had taught him that. He was going to make it a priority, even when the Smyrnians were in the thick of battle. He had already fallen in love with Jesus in the last twenty-four hours. He knew now that far more than telling him about being a Christian, she had shown him how to be a Christian. He whispered, "Thank you Angie. Sorry it took me so long." His kids had done the same. He wished he had joined them earlier but also knew that now was better than never. He was going to make the most of the next seven years. He would be a good soldier, a good team player, a good Smyrnian for Jesus.

Blake had gotten unpacked and settled back into his apartment. He had just stepped into the kitchen to grab a bottle of mineral water out of the fridge when he heard the familiar sound and felt his phone buzzing in his hand. Without even a glance, he answered.

"Blake?"

"Yes, this is Blake Thompson. Who's calling?"

"Blake, this is Beth Jennings."

He was stunned. He had not had the privilege of hearing that voice on the phone before. He did not have to call her; she called him! He could not waste the opportunity to set up a time to meet with her and let her see the video. And...there was that twitterpated feeling again. Anders had really messed him up by using that word.

"Blake, are you still there?"

"Uh, yes, I'm here Beth. I'm sorry. I just got home and put things away. It's good to be back in New York!"

"I don't want to bother you. If this is a bad time, I can call later."

"No, no, no, this is a good time. I'm really glad you called. What's up?"

Get a grip Blake. Stay focused.

"I need to talk to you. I know we have never spent time together. After all, we have been rivals, right? First, I want to say thank you for being there for me the morning of the *Invasion* when I learned that my mom and dad were missing. I sensed something special in you, a true caring heart. Your hug and your words of concern helped me so much in that moment. I wanted you to know that."

"You're welcome Beth. I knew you needed someone, and I was honored to be that someone."

Did that sound silly? He knew he was grasping for words. He had wanted to talk to her for a long time but had not been able to muster the courage to do it. Now here she was calling him, and he sounded like a schoolboy with a crush on the head cheerleader. Calm down Blake. Calm down.

"That made me feel like I can talk to you about anything. Would you be willing to meet me somewhere? I really need to talk to you."

"Name the place, Beth, and I'll be there. Right now, if you want."

"Can you do that? You just got back home. I don't want to impose on you. I'm sure you are worn out."

"I'm never too tired for you Beth. No, we haven't spent a lot of time together, but maybe it's time we break that barrier and get to know each other. After all, we do have a lot in common."

Was that too forward? He could not believe he had said that. He hoped it hadn't scared her off.

"I appreciate that, Blake. I agree. Where do you want to meet? It will mean the world to me."

"I could use a good cup of coffee. How about you?"

"That would be great. How about that little coffee shop on East Broadway?"

"Perfect. See you there in 20 minutes?"

"Yes. Thank you so much."

Blake was excited, nervous and thankful all at the same time. He whispered a prayer of thanksgiving to God and started to head out the door. Wait a minute! He could not meet Beth looking like this. He had thrown on an old pair of comfortable shorts and a tee shirt. He ran to the bedroom and grabbed a pair of jeans and button down shirt. That was better! Now he was ready to go. He hustled out the door. This was one time he could not afford to be late!

Ally had a good day with her family. They laughed, had fun, and some serious moments as well. She was a decent cook and had told the family she wanted to make dinner for them. It was going to be interesting feeding all of them in her tiny place. But she knew Allie would not mind them sitting on her bed. She would be more than happy for them to use it since they were going to hear about Jesus! And her brothers would get a kick out of being allowed to eat on the bed. She had made her specialty, pot roast with potatoes and carrots, corn on the cob, green beans on the side and biscuits. Good American food for her German family. She knew they liked it. They should be coming back any minute. She was ready. Nervous, but ready.

Blake arrived at the quaint little coffee shop, one of his favorite places, just before Beth came in. This was the right place for a late evening chat. But this was much more than a chat to him. He had just sat down at a table when she walked in. How did she always seem to look so perfect? He could not help but feel this was a meeting that was set up by God.

"What can I get you?" he asked.

"I think I'm the one who invited you, right?"

"It doesn't matter who invited who. This gentleman is going to buy for the lady."

"Okay, if you insist, sir." She bowed her head down and to the side with a smile. "I will have a white chocolate latte with plenty of whipped cream."

"Perfect," he said. "Would the lady like anything else to go with that?"

"The lady appreciates the offer, but no, she would not. My favorite latte is enough."

Blake ordered her latte and his usual *red eye* and brought them back to the table.

Beth opened the conversation. "Do you wonder what people will think if they see us here having coffee together? They may accuse us both of fraternizing with the enemy."

"They can call it whatever they want. It is the gentleman buying the lady a drink and being there for her. What's going on, Beth? In spite of being a reporter, I am a good listener." ("Forgive me, Lord, if that was a little white lie," he whispered in his mind. He could be a good listener when he needed to. And tonight he needed to. Then he needed to talk to her; he really needed to talk to her.)

"I have had this strange feeling since standing in my mom and dad's bedroom after the *Invasion*. The feeling came over me that everything was okay, and it has not left me since. It feels strange to be complaining about a feeling of peace. I'm not complaining. I just cannot understand why I feel that way after losing my mom and dad. And I feel like I'm supposed to share this positive message with the world. I don't know what it is unless it is to tell them everything will be okay.

Then there is this feeling that I am to play a major role in the world in the future. Even after the tremor and nearly getting clobbered by a falling chandelier, I still can't shake that feeling. I have no idea what that role is supposed to be. I just know I am going to meet someone who will tell me. I have interviewed a lot of people, and each time I ask myself if this could be the one I am supposed to meet. But I know that I have not met that person yet.

Does all of that sound strange to you? I really don't think I am crazy. But the feeling is so strong that I know it is real. I just don't know who it is that I am supposed to meet or what it is that I am supposed to do. I'm ready. I just need direction."

"Beth, this is your day. Our meeting is not by accident. There is something I have to tell you. If you had not called me, I was going to call you. We need to talk."

"You, Blake! You are the person I'm supposed to meet. I didn't realize that when I called you. But now I know. I'm not fraternizing with the enemy. I'm finding the answers I have been looking for!"

"Beth, if only you knew. And you will know this evening. This is more important than you can imagine until you hear it. I could hardly wait to get back to New York to meet with you. Please don't misinterpret my motives, but can we go back to my place after this so I can talk to you? There is also something I need to show you. I hope you know the lady can trust the gentleman."

"Talk about fraternizing with the enemy! I do trust you, Blake. And I believe this meeting was meant to happen. I feel that now. I know you're the one. Yes, let's go to your place and talk."

"You know, as important as this is, I think it can wait until we finish our coffee. How about you?"

"Yes, I do. But let's not take too long. I have waited several days for this meeting."

"Beth, you've been waiting longer than that. You've been waiting your entire life."

Anders was all alone at his house, but that is where he wanted to be. He felt like he was there spending time with Angie and the kids again. He could feel them, and it seemed like he could even hear them, all over the house. The twins were fighting with their sister. She was perturbed and yelling for her mom and dad to do something. There was no frustration, only a smile. He almost called out to them to tell them how much he loved them and remind them how they should love each other. He basked in their very presence. He knew they were not there, but knowing where they were now made all the difference. He wondered, could they see him? Did they know he had put his faith in Jesus? Had they been told he would come and be with them in no longer than seven years, and maybe sooner? News reports had told of a large number of suicides all over the world since the Rapture, or the *Invasion*, as they called it. He admitted, the thought had crossed his mind. But now it was the farthest thing from his mind. He wanted to be with them, but he knew he needed to make up for lost time. He wanted to live for Jesus and be one of his warriors for the next seven years. He would still be working with Blake, which made it all the better. He was up for the task and ready to get it on. It was time to pull the army together and start making plans. He was also thinking of people with whom he needed to share Jesus so they could become a part of the team.

CHAPTER 16

Ally's family arrived a few minutes early. That was fine with her. She had dinner prepared and was ready for them. And it would give her even more time for that important conversation after they finished. The boys were like, "we're starving!" So they jumped in front and grabbed plates. You could feel the air getting sucked right out of the room when Ally said, "Wait. Before we eat, we have to thank God for the food." Her brothers stared at her.

"What are you talking about thank God for the food?" one of them asked. "We're hungry!"

Her mom and dad looked at each other with that "what has happened to our daughter?" look.

Ally said, "I won't take long. You can bow your heads if you want, but you don't have to. Dear God, thank you for this food. Let us enjoy it and have a good time together. In Jesus name. Amen."

They all appeared to be in shock but filled their plates and dug in. It didn't take long for her brothers to return to normal. They were laughing and bouncing up and down on the mattress as their mother chastised them and ordered them again and again not to spill food on the bed. Everyone did enjoy the meal and had a great time. Mom helped Ally do the dishes, then they all crammed in her tiny room to sit and talk. Ally did not waste any time. She did not want to let her courage weaken.

"You know I wanted you guys to come so I could tell you something. I'm sorry I couldn't get into it over the phone, but telling you in person was important to me."

She had to get it out. No use beating around the bush. She would tell them first and get into the pastor's message, Rapture, and Tribulation later.

"After we got off the phone last Tuesday, I was still in shock but just glad you guys were okay. Allie was gone, and I was still here. I was all alone. Then

Evan called. I have never been so glad to hear someone's voice in my life! He is my best friend, well along with Allie. He told me his entire family was gone, but because of something he heard with them four years ago, he knew the truth and wanted to tell me immediately. I told him I would be right over."

"Ally, of course Evan knew the truth," her mom said quietly. "We all did. It was all over the news."

"No mommy, you don't understand. They were all wrong. It was *not* an alien invasion."

"Come on, Ally. Do you think Evan is smarter than scientists? Than NASA and all the other space agencies? We know what happened, and there's no use trying to deny it or explain it away. You need to grow up and accept the truth. You're not a kid any longer, and this is not made up. So stop this nonsense about knowing the real truth." Her dad almost sounded angry this time.

"Stop it, Bruno." (an appropriate name for her dad, Ally had always thought) "Let her talk."

His angry stare betrayed his feelings, but he decided to keep his mouth shut and listen. His wife was the only one who could keep him under control, and sometimes even she could not do it.

"Go on honey. What did Evan say. We will listen to you. Boys! Stop mocking your sister. You will sit still and listen to her too. Do you hear me?!"

They knew that tone. Their mom was one of the sweetest ladies ever. But when she spoke like that, she meant what she said. They sat still on the bed and tried to listen to their sister.

"If you will hear me out, I think you will see the truth too. Evan went to church with his family four years ago, even though he didn't want to. You know how much he despised church and religion. But that day he went as a favor to his parents. The pastor was bringing a very important message that he said everyone needed to hear. Evan went and took good notes. Not because he bought into what the pastor was saying but so he could show it to his friends at school and have a good laugh. He dug those notes out after the so-called *Invasion* and read back through everything the pastor had said. He made some bold predictions based on what the Bible says and the words of Jesus. Let me just tell you up front: he described what happened in detail."

"Ally, is this like that *Bible Code* thing that came out a few years ago. Anybody can take words and phrases from any book and make it say whatever they want it to." Another look from her mom made him stop abruptly. "Okay, okay, I'm sorry. Go on. You were saying?" There was a clear hint of disdain in his voice, but at least he said nothing more.

"Daddy, I really want you to hear this. I love all of you so much that I cannot bear the thought of what will happen to you if you don't believe it."

This was it. The moment of truth. She had to get this right. Maybe she should just show them the video. No, then she would have to translate some of it for them to make sure they understood. She made a decision. She would tell them a shorter version of Evan's explanation then show the video if she still needed to.

"There are three or four parts to this. Please listen to all of it before you say anything. It comes straight out of the Bible. Okay, here goes.

The Bible says God created the universe in six 24-hour days. Genesis chapter one uses the Hebrew word *yom* which means a literal 24-hour day. Now, I have never, ever believed that. I'm a biology major. We have been taught that evolution is true and that the earth is four and a half billion years old. I have *always* believed that. I know you have too. You were excited when I decided to study biology. I don't want to disappoint you, but now I have to choose the Bible over biology. If you will hear me out, I believe you will too.

The pastor said the Bible also says that one day is like a thousand years with God and a thousand years is like a day. So, he said, since God created the universe in six days, that means it will last 6,000 years, and then it will end. On the seventh day, the Bible says God rested. That means He will rest for a thousand years after that, and it says those who have believed in him will rest with him. With the arrival of the year 2000, the earth hit that 6,000-year mark. That means it is time for it to end.

The second thing: The Bible gives seven Feasts or Festivals God gave the Hebrews to celebrate, and to continually remind them of him. The first three Feasts were fulfilled on the exact days in the first coming of Jesus. I will abbreviate this part, but it is very important. You see, everything in the Old Testament, the first half of the Bible, points to Jesus in the New Testament, the second part of the Bible. Evan said he heard someone say all of *history*, that is 6,000 years, is *his story*, that is the story of Jesus. It's all about Jesus! He died on Passover as the Lamb that would forgive our sins and help us have a relationship with God if we will believe in him. He was in the grave on the Feast of Unleavened Bread, which was bread without yeast, meaning he was perfect. He never sinned. He rose from the grave on the Feast of Firstfruits, and the Bible later said that meant he was the first fruit of everyone else who would do that too.

The fourth Feast was Pentecost. It was fulfilled on the day when the Holy Spirit came and Jesus' church began. So, that Feast represents the church age. It lasts for 2,000 years, and then Jesus comes to take his people home to heaven. This is where it gets interesting.

The fifth Feast is the Feast of Trumpets. It is Rosh Hashanah, the Jewish New Year. Jesus gave us clues that is the day he will send his angels to get his people. He said no one will know the day or the hour. That was the nickname of that Feast. He said his people should watch and wait for that day to come. That is what the priests did back then. They waited and watched for that sliver of the new moon to show up. When it did, they blew the trumpets and called the people of Israel to come to the temple to worship God. Jesus also said when his people were *taken* home, there would be a deafening blast of a trumpet and a blinding flash of lightning, and it would happen in the blink of an eye. Then some people would be taken and others left behind. Sound familiar?

The pastor said that would happen 2,000 years after the year Jesus rose from the grave. He was not born in 0, but in 4 B.C. We know that because King Herod did not die till that year and he was still alive when Jesus was born. That means Jesus was crucified, died, buried and came back to life in 29 A.D. So, the pastor said if he was right, and the Bible proves it to be true, the *Rapture*, that is the word for the day Jesus would call his people home, would occur in 2029. Mom, dad, what year is this? It is 2029. And the pastor said, Jesus told us he would come and take his people home on the Feast of Trumpets that year. Do you know what day that is? It is September 11, 2029. What happened the other day was not an alien attack. It was Jesus taking his people home, exactly *how* and *when* he said he would.

Think about it. The exact day and year he said. The deafening sound, an angel's blast of a trumpet, and the blinding light, a flash of lightning from east to west, which is the direction the telescopes in outer space showed it to go. Then people just disappeared, right out of their clothes. Another thing: everyone who was *taken* was a Christian, somebody who believed in Jesus, church people and pastors. Everybody else, like you guys and me and Evan and our biology professors were left here. All the other people who are gone believed in Jesus and lived their lives for him."

Ally took a deep breath. She hoped she had not messed that all up. It was too important.

"There is one other thing. The pastor said the Bible talks about a 7-year period that comes after the *Rapture*. Some people will see the truth and accept Jesus after the Rapture happens. A world leader will arise who will be controlled by Satan. He will hunt down Christians and persecute them. He will kill many of them. After that seven years, which the Bible says started on September 12, the day after the Rapture happened, Jesus will come back and defeat evil and reign on the earth with all of his people who believed in him. I believe that. It doesn't just make sense. It has to be the truth. It happened just like the Bible said it would. I put my faith in Jesus. I am going to live for him for the next seven years, no matter what happens. If I get killed, I go to be with him just like the people did the when the Rapture happened. I want you to believe in Jesus too.

You have seen the reporter, Blake Thompson, on the news. He happened to be on campus here interviewing Professor Baldwin after the tremor hit. By the way, the Bible said that would happen too, all over the world, and that a massive worldwide earthquake is coming soon. Evan emailed Mr. Thompson and asked if we could talk to him. Since he was here and doing an investigation, he came to Evan's room and met with us. Evan showed him a video of the pastor's message with all the things I just told you. He believed and asked Jesus to be his Savior. He went back and showed it to Professor Baldwin and he did that too! Do you know what a big deal that is? A long-time biology professor and scientist saw the truth and turned from his belief in science to put his faith in Jesus. All of us are talking to our family and friends hoping they will do that too. That's why I wanted you to come so bad. Now, I want to show you the last part of the pastor's message. I have it set to play. Please watch it and listen to what he says."

She remembered, she had left out the last two Feasts and the part about the rebirth of Israel in 1948 and the alien scare of 1947! It was not that important. She had gotten the important stuff in...the Biblical truth. They sat silent as she started the video. She was just praying they understood what she had said and got what the pastor said. The pastor came on the screen. His words felt as powerful to her as they did before.

"If you happen to be watching this after the Rapture has occurred, listen to me. You still have time to put your faith in Jesus and receive him as your Savior. If you are listening, please stop this video and do that right now. Just tell Jesus you believe in him and ask him to come into your life. He said 'I stand at the door and knock.' That door is the door to your heart and life. If *you* will open the door, *he* will come in! Make the decision to follow him for the rest of your life, no matter what!"

Ally stopped the video and looked at her parents without saying a word. A full two minutes went by before her mom broke the silence.

"Bruno, it has to be true. I know we have never even read the Bible. It was just an ancient book to us with old stories that didn't matter in today's world. But how can we deny it? That is too accurate. It predicted the exact day and year. And described exactly how it happened. Everything. Even the tremor. And now the experts are saying it is a sign that a big quake is coming. The Bible said that too. I want to know Jesus, Bruno. I want our whole family to believe in him. We can all be together forever, or we cannot. You want to be with Ally, don't you?"

"I don't know Mila." He was never one to admit he was wrong. "Does it have to be true? I mean, look at what scientists said happened? People have been predicting an alien invasion for a long time too. There have been a lot of books written about it and a bunch of movies made about it. Maybe I would rather believe them than something from a book that was written thousands of years ago. Today's technology can prove things. All they could do 2,000 years ago was use astrology to try and predict things. To me, science is a lot better."

"But daddy, God made the universe. I think he knows more about how the world works, and when it will end than science does. They're really just guessing too." Ally spoke softly. She respected and loved her dad very much. She just wanted him to believe so badly.

"Bruno, I believe. I am going to do what the pastor said. I know Jesus is knocking on my door. I believe in him, so I am going to ask him to come in. I know it may be hard to believe your daughter has found the truth in America, especially when she attends a liberal arts college and majors in biology, but she has. Can't you accept that and believe like she does?"

"I'm just not ready, Mila. I have to think about this. You do what you have to do. I'm not going to stop you. But I'm not going to do that yet. You and the boys do what you think is best."

"Please, daddy," Ally pleaded. "It is true. I know it is. And when I believed in Jesus and asked him to come into my life, I cannot tell you how good it felt. He changed my life, daddy. You can feel that too, if you'll just do this. I love you, daddy. Please do it, for me."

"I'm not ready for that, Ally. Can I watch the whole video? I trust you, but I want to hear everything the pastor said, for myself."

"Yes, daddy. I'll play it for you. But right now, if mommy's ready, I want to let her ask Jesus to be her Savior."

"I am ready, honey. Can you play that last part for me again so I will know what to do?"

Ally complied. When it ended, Mila bowed her head and with everybody listening said, "Jesus, I believe in you with all my heart. I believe what I just heard. I know you took your people home the other day. It was not an alien invasion. It was you coming just like you said you would. Jesus, please come into my life and be my Savior. I receive you right now. I pray in your name. Amen."

The look on her face left no doubt what had happened. Her smile was electric! It went from ear to ear. It looked as if a halo sat on top of her head. She grabbed Ally and hugged her. Both were weeping with tears of joy that cannot come from anywhere else. They looked at the boys.

"Boys, what do you think? I can tell you it is the truth. Jesus just came into me. I want you to know what that feels like. Will you ask him to come into your lives too?"

They had been confronted with the truth just as Evan had in church that day when he was just about their age.

"Yes, mommy" said one. "I know it is the truth. I want to do that now. I don't want to wait!"

His brother agreed. Both of them prayed together and asked Jesus to do the same for them. All Ally had to do was look at them, and she knew it was genuine too. That only left one.

"Daddy?" she asked.

"I told you I'm not ready, Ally. Let me watch the video. You all go shopping or to the lake or something. Take your time. Get some pizza. Just leave me here so I can watch the video. I need to think about everything he said. I can understand it after listening to you. You go on and leave me here."

Ally put the video in and paused it at the beginning. All her father had to do was hit play. He told them to take their time because he would stop it a lot to think about what the pastor had just said. He would probably rewind it several times too. It was like scientific research for him.

Then they left him there and went out to celebrate. Who knew what they would do? They were all ecstatic and wanted to celebrate what had happened to them. None of them had ever felt joy and peace like this before. Only one thing was certain. Their celebration would include pizza!

CHAPTER 17

Evan was walking the floor, praying and talking. "What is going on, Ally?" he asked out loud. He had never minded talking to himself. He had joked with her many times that is what he did when he wanted to have an intelligent conversation. She would always punch him in the shoulder or roll her eyes when he said that. Now he realized just how opposite of *intelligent* he had been. He understood it is faith that brings intelligence. All of the scientific theories he had believed were nothing more than hypotheses. The Bible was *fact*! But it took *faith* to see it. He remembered a Bible verse his mom had quoted to him once that said something like, "Faith is being certain of what we do not see." He could not see it, but he was certain the Christians had been taken to be with Jesus. And he was certain of what the next seven years would hold for him and others who put their faith in Jesus. He could not see him either, but he knew he would! He had to admit, he loved living by faith! Finally, in the midst of his musings, his phone rang. Ally! It was about time. He had been going crazy to know how things had gone with her family.

"Ally, talk to me. What's going on? I have been going crazy!"

"Great news Evan! My mom and brothers put their faith in Jesus! We are on our way to celebrate right now."

"That's awesome! I'm so excited! Wait, you said your mom and brothers. What about your dad?"

"You know daddy, Evan. He is a stubborn, hardheaded man. Faith is not easy for him."

"So, he didn't believe? No, Ally. Please tell me that is not true!"

"I think he wants to, but it is hard for him to give in. Even after seeing my mom and brothers do that, he said he still wasn't sure. He did ask us to leave him there alone, though, to watch the entire video by himself. I only showed them the last part where the pastor told us how to receive Jesus into our lives. He wanted us to give him plenty of time to process it all and run it through his practical, unbelieving mind. He told us to stay gone awhile so he could pause at certain points and look things up to make sure they are accurate. I know him well enough to know he will do a lot of going back and watching things again too. So, it could take some time. Mommy and my brothers are so excited that it's easy for us to celebrate. But daddy is on our minds as we do. Pray for him Evan. Pray that Jesus will knock on his door so loudly he can't deny it."

"I will," answered Evan. "You can count on that. Tell the guys to eat some pizza for me."

Blake and Beth had just arrived at his apartment and walked inside. "Wow, this is nice!" she told him. "You sure know how to live the high life."

"I thought I did, Beth. But I had no idea what the high life was until now!"

"What are you talking about? First, you tell me you are the one I was supposed to talk to. Now, you start talking about living the real high life. Go ahead, the lady wants to hear what the gentleman has to say."

"Open door!" thought Blake. And he silently prayed, "Help me, Jesus. Beth is important to you. And you know she is important to me."

"Well, I would love to pound my chest, give my best Tarzan yell and say, 'I am da man!' But I can't. I brought you here to introduce you to the man, who will introduce you to the man."

"What are you talking about? Is this the man who is going to tell me why I have been feeling such peace and tell me what I am supposed to do?"

"Yes ma'am, he is. Do you mind walking into the next room? Remember, you trust the gentleman, right?"

"Yes, I trust the gentleman. So, what is in the next room?"

"Come and see."

They walked into the spacious living room with a large balcony overlooking Manhattan.

"Blake, this is beautiful! I have a nice view too, but it is nothing like this!"

"It is a big reason why I chose this place. I never get tired of seeing that. I spend time out there sometimes just thinking. But for now you have something far better to see and hear. Come and sit. I would rather show you who you are supposed to hear from than tell you about him."

He led her to the sofa, sitting just the right distance away from his 70-inch TV to allow for ideal viewing. "Please sit down and relax. May I get you anything before the video begins?"

"No, I'm ready. Blake, what is it that you are going to show me? How long is it? I don't need to be real late getting home. Tomorrow is a big day."

"I'm just going to show you the video. All you have to do is watch and listen. You'll understand very quickly why you were meant to watch it tonight. I can tell you, it changed my life. And it is also going to change yours. If you have any questions for me at any time, let me know. Otherwise, just watch. I'll be sitting right over here if you need me."

Blake started the video. As he had seen every time, it began with words scrolling on the screen introducing the sermon for the day. Beth shot him a questioning look as if to say, "sermon?" then settled in to watch. Blake knew he would never grow tired of showing the video to people. The pastor may have been taken to be with Jesus, but he was still delivering the message every time someone watched. It was almost unbelievable how God brought Beth right to him. He didn't have to do a thing. One thing he knew: they were going to make a great team!

Anders had tried to call Blake a couple of times and knew he must be busy. "I wonder what he could be doing that would cause him to turn off his phone," Anders thought. Oh well, they had just gotten back home from an emotional and life-altering trip. Maybe he went to bed early and was sleeping so soundly that he did not even hear his phone. No, it went straight to voicemail, so it had to be turned off. Beth! He was with Beth! He had to be. He could not wait to find out tomorrow. But as for Blake and him, they had plans to make, things to figure out and a team to pull together. Blake said he and Anders would work undercover as long as they could. It would allow them to be in places where they could be privy to insider information that would help the Smyrnians know the enemy's every move. Espionage for Jesus! It caused his heart to pound. Dangerous, yes, but he was ready. And Beth would surely be a part of that too.

As soon as the pastor began to speak, Beth turned to him and put up her hand as if to say "Stop!" Blake thought, "No! She's not even going to watch it. I knew she wasn't into church, but…"

"Blake, I know that man! Well, I don't really know him but I have met him. He spoke at my mom and dad's church one time when I was home. I tried to go with them whenever I was home on the weekend just so I could spend time with them. They never missed. They loved their church. We took the pastor out for lunch after the service. He was a wonderful man and powerful speaker."

"Two more people who loved Jesus and were taken in the Rapture," thought Blake as he smiled to himself. He loved hearing those stories.

"This pastor was the visiting speaker that Sunday. They were excited about hearing him and wanted me to hear him too. They knew I didn't go to church, and the only reason I went when I was there was to be with them. They told me that day I needed to hear this message. It was going to be about the Rapture of the church when Jesus came to take his people home to be with him. Honestly, I didn't know what that meant and wasn't sure I really cared. But I still listened closely. Blake, the title they just showed is the same title of his message that day. I'm getting chills. I believe I was meant to hear this again and was shown that the moment I walked into mom and dad's bedroom. That's where the feeling that they were okay started. And it grew into the feeling that I had a purpose, a role to play in the future of the world. If this is the same message, I remember the gist of what he said. I hadn't even thought about it since the *Invasion*. But now I'm realizing it was not an *Invasion* at all!"

Blake fought the urge to run over and hug her. She knew! She just needed to be reminded of what she had heard. "Do you want to continue?"

"Please!" she said. He started the video again.

Beth sat and listened carefully. He could see her nodding with an "I remember that!" kind of look. She asked him to stop it again after the pastor finished talking about the 6,000 years and Feast of Trumpets and before he gave the year and day of Jesus' coming.

"Let me guess," she smiled. "September 11, 2029."

"You are right on the money!" Blake proclaimed.

"I knew it! He said it that day when I heard him speak, but I thought he was just another one of the crazy men who was predicting a date for Jesus' return. I thought, 'Oh no, mom and dad are going to sell everything and move into some compound with this guy and a bunch of other gullible people.' I had heard a lot of people talk about Jesus coming back, but it never happened. I was sure it never would because I didn't even believe in Jesus. But as I continued to listen to him, he planted a seed in my mind that never left. That is why I've been feeling all those things. I should have known when I saw their nightclothes lying there on the bed. Why didn't I realize that? Okay, let's finish watching. I remember some things about Israel becoming a nation again in 1948 and the alien scare from Roswell, New Mexico in 1947. I'm trying to recall how that ties in."

"You *do* remember well! Okay, here goes with the rest."

"Hey, I am a journalist, aren't I?"

She watched it all and connected all the dots as the pastor continued to speak. It was like every piece of a beautiful jigsaw puzzle had fallen into place for her. When he ended by asking his listeners to tell Jesus they believe in him and ask him to come into their lives, she spoke calmly.

"You can stop the video, Blake. I know what I have to do. I'm sure you and others who have watched this said the same thing, but I will say it too: I can't believe I missed it. How did that happen? I had two Christian parents who loved Jesus and went to church faithfully. I went to church with them several times. I tried to avoid visiting on weekends, so I wouldn't have to go, but I still went enough to hear about Jesus. And that Sunday, I heard all of this. I knew what was coming. I just tried to deny it and put it out of my mind. Now I am ready to say 'yes' to Jesus."

"Just go ahead and talk to him right now Beth. That's what I did. It was the greatest day and best feeling of my life! I've been so anxious to share this with you and see you have that too!"

"No, not here."

What? She was going to wait until she got home? Or maybe go to a church and accept Jesus? He had so badly wanted to be with her when she did.

"Out here." She walked toward the balcony. "I can't think of a better place to put my faith in Jesus. Will you join the lady as she makes the biggest and best decision of her life?" She held out her hand and Blake took it in his.

"The gentleman will be honored," he said.

As amazing as all the other times had been, this one was extra special. He stood holding Beth's hand as she looked over Manhattan and prayed to Jesus.

"Jesus, I am so sorry for missing the truth. But I am just as thankful that you allowed me to have another chance. I believe in you with all of my heart. I hear your knock clearly. I open the door to you right here in this beautiful place. Please come into my life and be my Savior. I give all that I am and all that I have to you." When she finished, she turned to Blake and looked into his eyes.

"The gentleman is elated," he smiled.

"The lady is overjoyed." She began to weep. "Oh, Blake, I will see mom and dad again. They really are okay. I am going to be with Jesus forever." He held her and wept with her, just as he had done that day in Times Square. It felt like an embrace that should not end. When it did, she had one more question. "When does Jesus take those of us home who put our faith in him after the Rapture?"

"That is the final part of the video. Finish watching and you'll get that answer too."

She went in and sat back down. The look on her face showed obvious concern as she realized the full truth of what it meant to miss the first time Jesus took his people home. When the pastor finished and the video ended, she got up and walked over to Blake.

"What is our next step? I'm ready. We'll have a fight on our hands, but this lady is not afraid of going to war!"

"We have a name for our army. Do you want to hear it?"

"Sure."

"We are the Smyrnians."

She smiled. "Only you would come up with a name like that. You know what? I like it! It is different, but I like it. Where did you get it?"

"It comes from Revelation chapter two, verse 10. Jesus was talking to the church at a place called Smyrna. I don't have it with me right now, but he told them they would suffer but not to be afraid. The devil would put some of them in prison, and some of them would be killed. But they must be faithful, even to the point of death and he would give them the crown of life. I think I'm about to learn that verse! That's what it is going to be like, Beth. But we'll all go through it together. And by the way, the name didn't come from me. It came from a young man named Evan Ryles. He's the one who showed me the video and helped me put my faith in Jesus, after he had done that himself. You'll meet him soon. The Smyrnians are coming together! How much time do you have? I would love to talk to you more about the next seven years and your role in them. Or we can meet again tomorrow, or another day. I just don't want to wait long."

"I have all night. Let's talk."

Ally and her mom and brothers returned home after three hours of having fun, celebrating and eating far too much Chicago pizza. When they came in, they saw her dad still sitting in his chair with the TV turned on and nothing on the screen. He was sitting and staring at it.

"Daddy?" Ally called his name. "Daddy, are you okay?" She was worried about him.

"I'm okay, little girl." That was what he had called her since she was born. She was still his little girl, as far as he was concerned. She may be in college, but that would never change.

"Well, did you...I mean, did you ask Jesus to be your Savior." Her voice gave away her pleading wish in that question.

"Not yet, little girl. Not yet. I can't deny any of the things the pastor says, except maybe the part about the next seven years. How am I supposed to know he is right about that? For that matter, I still am not 100% sure I believe everything else he said, even though he was right about it all."

"Oh, daddy, please. Please put your faith in Jesus. Please, daddy. I can't bear the thought of what will happen if you don't."

"A part of me wants to Ally. It really does. But I have so much on my mind. If I *receive* Jesus, I have to *give up* so many things that I'm not sure I'm ready to give up."

"None of those things matter, daddy. Only Jesus matters. From what the pastor says, we are all choosing sides for the last seven years of this earth. We are either choosing to be on God's side or the devil's side. Daddy, you have to choose God's side. Mommy and the boys and I have done that. We don't want to be on different sides. And we sure want you to be in heaven with us. Won't you just do it, please? Do it for me."

"Well now, if I did it for you little girl, it wouldn't really count, would it? It is something each of us has to do for ourselves. I don't know if I can right now. I'm not sure I believe like I should. Maybe I need a little more time."

"Bruno, you are so stubborn" said Mila. "You know the truth. You just won't admit it! You can be stubborn with the rest of us, but don't be stubborn with Jesus. All you have to do is look at the last week and you know what the pastor said is absolute truth."

"Don't be giving me a hard time, woman." (He already knew he should not have called her that!) "I make my decisions when I'm ready, not when everyone is ready to make them for me."

"You're right, daddy. We can't make this decision for you. We can pray for you, but it's still your decision. We all love you, but we won't let you stand in the way of our living for Jesus and fighting for him the next seven years. I just hope you'll come to your senses before it's too late."

He was taken aback. His little girl had never talked to him like that. She was serious about her decision to follow Jesus. She left no doubt about that.

"I need to take a walk." That is what he always did when he felt himself reaching the boiling point. But he had a different reason this time, although he didn't want them to know what it was. His mind was not as made up as he let on. But he had not decided to follow Jesus either. He was swaying in the balance. He wanted to talk to Professor What's His Name about this. He wanted to know what made him turn back on everything he had lived and worked for all those years. He wanted to hear what he had to say. He didn't believe, and now he does. What changed his mind?

"Bruno, it is late. We need to get back to the hotel. You can take your walk there if you need to." Mila stopped him as he was walking out the door. You could hear the Grrr...under his breath, but he turned and came back in.

"Whatever you say, Mila. Boys, get in the car. Your mother is ready to go."

"I love you, daddy," said Ally as he started out the door again. She ran to him and hugged him. "I love you no matter what you decide. Nothing will ever change that."

She was the one who always melted his heart. He always had trouble saying, "I love you."

"I know that little girl. You probably shouldn't, but you always have."

With that, they were out the door, in the car and on the road, leaving Ally alone with her thoughts.

CHAPTER 18

"So what are we going to do, Blake?" asked Beth. "It is going to be dangerous, but I have always lived for adventure, as I know you have. We are like two peas in a pod. We are both willing to go to just about any lengths to get a story."

"You are so right, Beth. Here's what I'm thinking. You and I can work undercover for as long as possible. No one will have to know that we are followers of Jesus. We can travel wherever we need to go to cover stories. When we do that, we can get insider information that will benefit the Smyrnians in our fight against the enemy. We will lay low when we meet with them because they will almost certainly become public enemy number one. So will you and I when we're found out, probably even more than the others. But how about this? When that happens, maybe we can create our own station from where we can report the truth to people and tell them about Jesus. Talk about an adventure! I bet we're both up for that."

"Wow, that gets me excited! Count me in! We have enough contacts between the two of us to get into just about anywhere. What is that thing I heard about an antichrist? I remember that from the pastor's message that day at mom and dad's church too."

"That's where the danger will come from. He will be indwelt by Satan himself. He will be revealed soon. Priority number one for us is to study what the Bible says about him and his role in the next seven years. *He* is the one who will be public enemy number one. The problem is, most of the world won't recognize that. He will be the exact opposite of Jesus Christ. That I do know."

"Where do we start?"

"We do a lot of research. You and I can both do that. And we have a meeting of all the Smyrnians very soon. In fact, I'll try to make calls tomorrow and see if we can schedule that. The tough part for all of us is, we are still going to have to work as we do that. I'm guessing most of it will have to happen by text or email at first. But we will *have* to make sure our phones and computers are secure. We can't take any chances. We need to survive! And I know we can."

"Who else do you know that we need on the team, or in the army, as the case may be. Someone comes to my mind immediately. I worked with him during my year in England before I came back to the states to get started. You know him well. At least you know his name: Oliver Barton."

"You worked with Oliver Barton? I don't think I knew that."

"I worked closely with him for a year. I never went to the Middle East with him, but he knows that area like the back of his hand. If I recall from other things I heard at mom and dad's church, that is where a lot of the action is going to take place. We can definitely use Ollie. I'll call him as soon as possible. But how do I explain the pastor's message to him?"

"You can send him the link to the video from that church website and let him watch it for himself. Then ask him to call you when it's over. If he doesn't, you call him!

That reminds me of someone too, but he will be hard to convince. Ben Abramson, my producer. He's a dedicated Jew, and I've heard him say there is only one God, not three as the Christians worship. He doesn't believe in Jesus. Neither did we, but it's different with him. His family taught him from childhood that Jesus is not real. He's going to be a hard sell. But you mentioned a lot of the action taking place in Israel and the Middle East. Ben travels back there every year. If he's on our side, he'll be invaluable too! If he and Oliver could work together...wow, what a team!"

"I don't know about you, but I'm ready to get to work. This is going to require careful planning and strategizing. Between the two of us, I think we know how to get that done! Maybe I should go and get some sleep. I don't want to because my mind is running a million miles a minute with this stuff. Is there anything else we need to cover tonight?"

Blake was feeling a bit nervous, but courageous at the same time. Why not now? What better time for something like this than the present?

"Just one more thing, Beth. Would you be willing to go out with me, on a date?" Then anxiety took over briefly, and he finished with, "But if you don't want to, I will understand. I probably shouldn't have asked that. I'm sorry if I just ruined a great evening."

"The lady would love to go on a date with the gentleman. When and where would you like to go, sir? It will be my privilege and joy. If you don't think this too forward, I can hardly wait. Shall we make it soon? I would like that."

Blake hoped he was not misreading the look he was sure he saw on her face. "How about tomorrow night? I will treat the lady to the best because she deserves nothing but the best."

"Tomorrow night it is. Pick me up at six?"

"You bet. I will be there with bells on! Well, not bells, but you know what I mean."

"I certainly do. I will have my bells on too." She smiled.

Blake was ecstatic on two levels. Beth had received Jesus as her Savior and joined the movement! And she said yes to going on a date with him. The lady said yes! Wow, what a night! He doubted that he would get a wink of sleep. But if he did, he would probably dream of Beth.

Bruno Fromm did not sleep very well that night. He dreamed over and over. The same dream. It did not change. Each time he woke up just before it ended. The family was back at home in Germany. Ally was a young girl again and the boys were two and four years old. He loved his little girl very much. He also relished having boys to carry on his name. He sat on the front porch of their house and watched them playing together. Mila was hanging laundry on the wire that stretched from the bedroom window to a wooden post in the yard. Suddenly a loud boom rocked the entire house and he was blinded by a bright flash of light. As it cleared and he could see again, they were all gone. The kids clothing lay in the yard where they had been. Mila's dress lay under the line with some clothing still hanging and some left in the basket. He screamed "No!" and bolted from the porch swing. He awakened at that point every time, perspiring heavily and shaking all over. After the second dream, he got up and went to a chair in the corner of the room so he would not wake Mila or the boys. He sat in the chair and fell asleep. The dream came again. He awakened at the same point. The same perspiring and trembling. Morning could not come soon enough.

John Baldwin was back in his office early, as were many other professors. They were focused on their classes which would begin again in a few days after what they termed a disaster break to deal with the tragedy of the *Invasion*. They knew some students and a few of their colleagues were missing, but they would go on with their studies. It would not be easy, but the educational process and the shaping of young minds was important. But Professor Baldwin was neither thinking about his classes nor preparing for them. He was doing research, not to teach students but to learn all he could about the Bible's teaching concerning the next seven years. He was so into what he was doing that he barely heard the knock on his door. It came once, then turned into loud rapping as if someone was getting impatient for the door to open. He opened it and looked into the face of a somewhat large and gruff looking man who appeared to be European. John stumbled backwards, nearly falling.

Evan was up early and hanging out with Ally as she waited for her family to come. They had both prayed for her dad throughout the night. She did not want to see him go back home without saying yes to Jesus. But she had made up her mind that she would be undeterred in her mission if he did. She knew they would have the continental breakfast at the hotel, so she and Evan had a bowl of fruit loops and sat and waited.

Blake was still reeling from the events of last night. How could all of that have happened with Beth and him in one evening? He had only one answer: Jesus. He had surely arranged all of it in advance. Oh no! He realized he had forgotten to turn his phone back on before he went to bed. He had not wanted anything to interfere with the time he and Beth had together, especially as she was watching the video and making the most important decision of her life. But he could not kid himself. He did not want their private time to be interrupted either. And it worked on both counts! She had apparently kept her phone off too. He was glad she did. (There he went again) In spite of all that, not having his phone on was almost unforgiveable for a television reporter, and the top dog at that. He always kept his phone right beside his bed so he would not miss any call that was important to his job. Fortunately, there were only two missed calls, both from Anders. He needed to eat something for breakfast and get himself ready to do some work. It sure was going to be hard balancing his new life with his old job. He would be reporting the news and spying for the Smyrnians at the same time. No easy chore, but he had no doubt that he, and Beth, could handle it. They would be working together, very closely together, he hoped. He sent Anders a quick text before throwing a couple of frozen waffles in the microwave.

"Sorry I missed ur calls. Had phone off. Forgot 2 turn back on. Was with Beth. Come over and I'll tell u all about it!"

"Ur a bit late, buddy. Already on my way!"

"Ok. c u soon."

Blake was not surprised. Anders never missed a beat. He would have to be in "work call mode" to be ready by the time he got there. He downed the waffles, then showered and shaved in ten minutes. Not an all-time record for him, but not far from it. He took enough time to get his hair just right and was dressed and sitting in his recliner seconds before the doorbell played its familiar chimes.

The moment he opened the door Anders greeted him with, "Tell me all about it, in detail!"

"A bit anxious, aren't you?"

"You're stalling. Spill the beans."

"She called me."

"No, seriously. What happened? Did you call her? Or did you wimp out?"

"I told you. She called me. I had gotten unpacked and ready to sit down for a little while when my phone rang. It was her. She said she needed to talk to me."

"Really?" Anders interrupted him.

"Yes, really. I asked her if she wanted to meet for a cup of coffee and she said yes." Those words flashed through his mind again: the lady said yes! It was still hard for him to believe.

"So, you really went for coffee? At that time of the evening?"

"Yes, we did. You know that little shop on East Broadway? It's open late."

"Yep, I know the one. I've been there. Great place to sit and talk."

"It is, and it was. She had a white chocolate latte with lots of whipped topping. I had a *red eye*."

"Twitterpated, I knew it! Every detail. You remember every detail. Tell me more!"

"Would you stop it. We had a great talk...*about* what she was feeling and all of her questions. She has had a good feeling about things since she stood in her mom and dad's bedroom that day. She couldn't shake the feeling that they were okay."

"She was right about that one, even if she didn't know just how okay they were!"

"She has also felt that she has a purpose. She is supposed to do something that will affect the whole world in a positive way."

"Well, she is two for two so far, *if* she believed in Jesus and accepted him as her Savior, that is."

"I knew I couldn't let the opportunity pass to tell her the good news. So, I invited her to come back here with me."

"That may have been a little forward..."

"She said yes, again. We came back and I showed her the video."

"Please tell me she said yes to Jesus."

"When she started watching, and the pastor's face came on the screen, she put up her hand for me to stop it."

"No! She rejected it right up front? Before it even got started?"

"Will you let me tell the story?"

"Okay, tell your story. Don't blame me for being a little anxious to hear it."

"She knew the preacher. She usually went to church with her mom and dad when she was there visiting them on the weekends. That's why she avoided weekends, if at all possible. But that day this pastor was a special guest speaker. And he preached the same sermon as the one we saw!"

"That's crazy! What are the odds of that happening?"

"Are you going to let me tell my story, or not?" Anders motioned with his hand as if to say, "go ahead, tell your story. But hurry. I can't take much more!" "She remembered most of what he said: the 6,000 years; the Feast of Trumpets; the rebirth of the nation of Israel in 1948 and how it tied in with Roswell in 1947. The date of the Rapture was easy for her to believe. It all was. She was ready to say yes to Jesus! But something cool: she loved my balcony when she first walked in here. She was ready to receive Jesus, but she didn't want to do it in here. She wanted to ask him to come into her life out there overlooking the city. She took my hand in hers and prayed right there. It was a magical moment! She's one of us now!"

"Yes! It sounds to me like there was a little twitterpation going on too..."

"Well, you may be right, even though I hate to admit it." He gave him a wry smile. "I brought her back in to show her the last part about the final seven years. She is so in and cannot wait to get started. She is excited and energized about going undercover with us. She knows she's going to see her mom and dad again so she's ready to lay everything on the line for Jesus. And do you want to hear something else? She worked with Oliver Barton when she was an intern!"

"*The* Oliver Barton? The Middle Eastern correspondent from England?"

"One and the same. He can be valuable to us. It seems that a lot of the action during the Tribulation will take place in Israel and other parts of the Middle East. We could use him! Beth is going to contact him soon. She wants to send him the pastor's video, but being so far away, she's not sure whether he should watch it by himself. She's praying about what to do. And I'm going to work on Ben. As you know, he is Jewish and travels back to Israel at least once a year. Imagine pairing him and Oliver Barton helping us over there. That could be amazing!"

"Wow, all of that is amazing! This story just keeps getting better. I hope it really gets better!" He gave Blake a wink and another smile.

"*And*, want to know something else...?" Now it was Blake's turn to wink at his partner.

"I knew it! Tell me Romeo."

"She loves the name Smyrnians!"

"That's all? She loves the name? That's all? You know I was hoping for much more."

"Well, I thought all of that was really good. You're disappointed? How could you be disappointed about Beth saying yes to Jesus and all of those other things falling into place? I would say overall, it was a pretty good night, wouldn't you?"

"It was! I'm not disappointed. I was just hoping for one more thing. Maybe it will come later."

"Oh, one more thing…" Anders head popped back up. "I asked her out on a date. And she said yes! She said she would love to go on a date with me. And she hoped we wouldn't wait long. So, I said, how about tomorrow night? She said yes. I am picking her up tonight at 6:00."

"I knew it! I knew it! Way to go partner! I love watching twitterpation at work. One bit of advice: don't mess things up tonight." One more smile came out of the corner of his mouth.

John Baldwin looked over the large man standing at his office door before he finally asked "May I help you?"

The man, speaking with a distinct European accent (German maybe? John was not sure), asked "May I come in?"

"I'm kind of busy right now. May I ask what this concerns?"

"You know a television reporter named Blake Thompson. He met with my daughter and her friend here on campus, then came and talked to you."

John was not sure if he should prepare to defend himself. It was too late to call security. Had someone told on him for believing in Jesus? Was this the persecution of the Tribulation already beginning? It occurred to him that he could die right here before it even started!

"Yes, I know Mr. Thompson, and yes I spoke with him. What does that have to do with you?"

"My daughter is Ally Fromm. I'm her father, Bruno." (An appropriate name, John thought to himself) "Ally is a student here at the university. She is a good girl. She talked to me about the same thing Blake Thompson talked to you about. I need to know what made you believe that and change your mind about the things you had always believed before. You spent your life teaching and shaping young minds like Ally's to think for themselves and follow the truths of science, and now you leave all that for this. What would cause you to do that? I need to know."

"Come in Bruno. I would love to explain that to you."

Ally's phone rang. She saw it was her mother calling.

"Good morning, mommy. I was wondering what happened to you guys."

"Honey, when we got up your daddy was gone. None of us heard him leave or have any idea where he went. We have tried calling him but he's not answering his phone. You know your father. Sometimes he needs his space, and you have to give it to him. But we're stuck here with no way to go anywhere. Can you come and get us?"

"Of course, I can. Is it okay if Evan comes with me? I don't know if he can, but I'll ask."

"You know it's always okay for you to bring Evan. He's like another son to us. And he's so good to you. We love him."

"I'll check with him and be there as soon as I can. You might want to leave daddy a message and let him know where you are."

"So, Mr. Fromm, I assume you saw the video."

"I did. Ally explained it to our whole family first. My wife and kids bought right into it and prayed to Jesus. But I wasn't sure I was ready for that. I asked them to leave and let me watch the video by myself. I do not deny that it makes sense describing everything that happened in the *Invasion*."

John knew it was the wrong word, but allowed him to go on. Hopefully he would accept the truth soon. Bruno set about expressing his doubts.

"I'm thinking it may be like that *Bible Code* thing that came out several years ago. They said you can find letters in some kind of order on pages of the Bible and they were supposed to predict things about the future. All of that died out, and a lot of it proved false. It sounds to me like the pastor on the video may have been doing sort of the same thing."

"There is a big difference here: these things *did* come true, not only in *how* the Bible said they would, but exactly *when* it said they would. And with that being said, I can no longer deny the clear Bible teaching that God created the universe in six literal 24-hour days, as proven by the use of the Hebrew word *yom*, which means exactly that, a 24-hour day. Then the verse that says a thousand years equals a day with the Lord and a day equals a thousand years seems to say the earth would last 6,000 years, matching the six days of creation, then end just like God's creative work did. I admit, that may have been a little suspect had it not just happened. As a scientist and biology professor, I had always believed in the evolutionary process rather than creation. You are right, I spent my life teaching that to many students, like your daughter. That teaching has always been based on scientific *proof*. But that proof was always hypothetical at best. What happened last week, which was described perfectly in the Bible and predicted by the pastor four years prior to it happening, is real *proof.* It is not hypothesis. It is proven fact. When I was confronted with the facts, I had no choice but to accept them. Does that make sense?"

"I suppose it does. It's just that I have always believed more in natural selection instead of intelligent design by some higher power that we can't see."

"Me as well, Mr. Fromm. But if I put something under a microscope and see the facts for myself, with my own eyes, I can't help but believe what my eyes and mind have experienced. Does that make sense too?"

"It does. That is how I think. It's why I have a love for science. We can't really put the Bible under a microscope and prove anything."

"We just did, Mr. Fromm. The events of September 11, 2029 did exactly that. I would never have known that if a theologian, I think it is okay to call the pastor that, had not put the Bible under the microscope and proven beyond the shadow of a doubt that what it said would happen, *did* happen. And ultimately, the one who foretold the *how* was Jesus. Everything from the deafening blast of the trumpet, to the blinding flash of lightning, to some people being taken and others left, was said by him. And don't forget, he is also the one who foretold the day, the Feast of Trumpets, or Rosh Hashanah, which happened to fall on September 11 this year; which also just happens to be 2,000 years after his resurrection. I can't deny that Mr. Fromm. I would urge you not to deny it either. Faith is difficult for us scientific types. But this is certainly faith accompanied by fact."

"I do see what you mean. I hadn't thought about it like that."

"Mr. Fromm, I encourage you to do what the pastor asked us all to do at the end of his sermon. Put your faith in Jesus, open the door of your life and invite him to come in. I did that, and I can assure you it was the most life-changing reality I have ever encountered!"

"I really needed to talk to you. Can you help me do that? I want to. My wife and children already have. I have never seen them as happy as they were at that moment."

"The same can be true for you, Bruno. Then you can be assured of living with them forever in the presence of Jesus in the very near future. The pastor said we only have seven years of history remaining. Then Jesus will return to take all of his people home. Those seven years will be a living hell on earth, from what I understand. But those of us who have already put our faith in Jesus, including your family, would love to have you on our side in the fight. You appear to be the kind of guy who could fight well, if you get my drift."

Bruno Fromm managed a smile at that, then said, "Okay, you have convinced me." Then he prayed without any further encouragement or another word. "Jesus, I do believe in you. I believe what the Bible says. I'm sorry for not believing before. Will you please forgive me for that and come into my life like you said you would. I receive you as my Savior."

Boom! It felt louder and brighter than the *Invasion* (oops, he meant Rapture) had to Bruno. It was as if his entire body was illuminated with a light so bright that it dispelled all the darkness that had consumed him before. The big hulk of a man fell to his knees and wept. John went over and placed a hand on his shoulder.

"I know just how you feel, Mr. Fromm. I do indeed. Welcome to the family of believers."

CHAPTER 19

Blake had no idea how he was going to approach Benjamin Abramson with the truth about Jesus and recent events. Ben was not only set in his ways but had also been indoctrinated by his family from birth to the present. He had to give him credit. He was a good Jew. Blake was not so sure Ben would not fire him if he knew he had made the choice to become a Christian. They had always had an understanding of each other's beliefs, or in Blake's case, the lack thereof. But this could be the proverbial straw that broke the camel's back for Ben, especially considering everything that had just taken place. "Lord, please help me find a way to do that," he prayed. He did not know if he would be successful, but he was determined to try. He needed to report in.

"Ben, this is Blake. I thought I had better check in. Anders and I just returned from Chicago yesterday evening. It was a fruitful trip!"

"Blake! I thought the two of you got lost. It really wouldn't hurt to check in while you are away. At least let me know how things are going. But you know I trust you. You are the man when it comes to the news. I'm just thankful you are on our team! I saw you reporting from the Tower in Chicago, and I'm glad you survived! Tell me, how did it feel standing on that ledge when the tremor hit?"

"You really don't want to know! I have always heard your life flashes before your eyes when you come so close to death. Well, I don't know if that happened, but I sure thought it might be my time. I'm glad it wasn't! I can tell you that it felt better than you can imagine for Anders and me when we got our feet on solid ground again. Standing on a glass ledge 1,353 feet in the air is no place to be when an earthquake strikes! I know they said it was *only* a tremor, but it felt like a quake to me standing out there suspended in the air. It's going to take a while to forget that."

"Take a day or two if you need it, Blake. But then we need you back on the ground. Things are changing at warp speed and everybody wants to hear from Blake Thompson. We have to be careful to not let Beth Jennings gain ground on you," he chuckled.

"I appreciate that Ben. We shall see. You know I'm not much for knowing things are happening and being away from the thick of the action. I love my job! I'll be in touch. I'm still researching some things that came out of my time in Chicago anyway. I'm trying to find hard core evidence that the tremor may be leading up to a massive worldwide quake, as the experts are suggesting. If that happens Ben, we are all in trouble. I want to see hardcore evidence for myself instead of taking things I hear and read from others for granted. I know there have been diagrams and endless charts of fault lines, etc., but I want to see something no one else has reported. That is what I do."

Evan and Ally had arrived back at her place with her mom and brothers. There was still no word from her dad. It had been well over three hours since they had awakened and discovered that he was gone. They were beginning to worry now. He had not answered any calls, so they had finally given up trying.

"Let me go out and look for him." It was clear that Evan was concerned about Bruno. That showed in the concern with which he spoke.

"Evan honey, how are you going to find him in Chicago? I know Bruno all too well. He is out thinking. He will be back when he is ready and not until then."

"Maybe Evan and the boys can go, mommy. They can look around the hotel and between there and here. I'm getting really worried about daddy," Ally said.

At that moment, they heard the doorknob turn and the door burst open. Bruno stood in the door. There was no denying the look on his face. He was lit up like a Christmas tree! A big smile went from ear to ear. His cheeks showed streaks where tears had rolled down them. It was as though light was beaming from his entire body. Ally sprinted toward him, her arms open wide.

"Oh daddy, daddy. You believed in Jesus and asked him to come into your life. Evan and I were praying for you. This is the happiest day of my life!"

The hugging party seemed like it would go on all day. It was one big hug fest! Everybody was crying. If someone had walked in and seen it, they would have thought, either something terrible had happened or these people had lost their minds. But this was a celebration! The tears were tears of joy. It was the best day the Fromm family had ever had.

"We need to throw a party," said Ally, even more bubbly than normal.

"No, we are going out for the best American food we can find in this city!" Bruno exclaimed.

"Pizza!" yelled both of Ally's brothers at the same time.

"Not this time, boys. We're eating real food!"

He had not eaten all day. He had left the hotel in such a hurry after the last dream as he slept in the chair that he had no time for breakfast. He had forgotten to turn his cell phone on and rushed out the door, bound for John Baldwin's office. His wife and sons only had a continental breakfast at the hotel. The boys had eaten cereal and she had a bagel and some oatmeal. Ally's fruit loops were gone. So they were all ready for some food!

As they were getting ready to leave, Bruno asked, "Are you going with us, Evan? I know you're hungry. We want you to go!"

Evan had to admit he was hungry. But he had bigger fish to fry, so to speak. It was time to put an action plan together for the Smyrnians. He had to get started. Then it would be time to call the army together.

"Not this time, Mr. Fromm. I'll let the Fromms celebrate together. I have work to do. War is coming, and we have to know the enemy's moves. We need to be prepared for everything that's coming, before it comes. I'm going to have some leftover pizza," he grinned at the boys, "and get to work."

"We can bring you something back."

"Thank you, but I am good. You guys have a great time."

With that he headed for his room, his computer, and most importantly, his Bible.

It was date night and Blake was both nervous and excited. He had dreamed about this day, but never thought it would come. His bed was littered with potential attire for the evening. There was a nice pair of jeans and a polo. The dress slacks and nice button down shirt, or make that shirts, looked appealing too. There were several different shirts lying there that would match the pants nicely. But as he thought about where he was taking her, he realized it called for a suit. He chose a black suit with a royal blue shirt and no tie. Just the right look. He wondered what she would wear, hoping they would not be drastically mismatched. But she knew he was taking her to a nice place, so she would be ready for that. She just did not know it was the Danube. But he had told her nothing but the best for her. So, for him, the suit it was. He was pretty sure she would look stunning. As he was getting dressed, his mind wandered to the future. The Smyrnians would be engaged in constant battle with the forces of evil. As much as he would love to protect Beth from that, he knew it would be impossible. They would be teammates working undercover to gather intel for the team. They would be boots on the ground while Evan and Ally would be hacking every enemy computer they could. All would be well until they were found out. Things would go badly after that. They would be hunted like animals. Many of their comrades would be killed. They would fight to survive for the sake of everyone else in the world. His hope had now changed from hoping Beth would believe in Jesus to praying that she would possibly be his wife. Since he only had seven years or less remaining, he wanted to experience the joy of marriage, but he did not want to experience that with anyone other than Beth. Tonight was really important with that thought in mind. Shew, the pressure was on! He was dressed and had everything as perfect as he could get it. It was go time. So he took a deep breath and was out the door.

True to form, he rang Beth's doorbell promptly at 6:00. His nerves were jumping and his heart was pounding as he heard her footsteps coming toward the door and saw it began to open. It was as though time stood still for a brief period of time until she appeared before him. When he saw her, he was stunned. He had always admired Beth for her style and appearance when she was on the job. But he had never seen her so beautiful as she was at this moment. Her blonde hair lay gently upon a lavender dress. A gorgeous diamond necklace gleamed as it draped around her neck and was accentuated against the dress. The heels she wore made her appear even taller than she already was. The smell of her perfume was intoxicating. He was completely lost in the moment.

"Blake, are you okay?"

He came to his senses. "Beth, you look amazing!" Why in the world would those be the first words to come out of his mouth?

"Well, Mr. Thompson, you look pretty handsome yourself. Don't you think we had better get going? I am hungry, and you promised the lady dinner."

"Oh yes, we had better. I'm sorry. I have to admit that the lady's beauty overwhelmed me for a minute. Let's go. I'm pretty hungry myself."

Conversation flowed naturally once again as they drove to the Danube. As they drove up in front, she said, "Nice choice, Mr. Thompson."

"Blake," he said. "Just Blake."

"Okay, Mr. Thompson," she said with a twinkle in her eye. "From now on, Blake it is."

Blake liked the sound of those words. "From now on" sounded like she planned on them being together, possibly for the next seven years. He could only hope that would be the case. In fact, he was praying under his breath that it would be so.

Ben Abramson was home for the evening and sat alone in his den. His wife knew when he needed some time to think. This was one of those times. Ben sat thinking about the events of the past week. His mind returned to the loud blast and blinding flash that had awakened his wife and him at midnight on Tuesday night. They had rushed outside to find others had done the same. He would never forget the chill that ran through his body that night. After standing for several minutes as he held her close, they had come to a realization and rushed back inside to call their children. Relief came rushing over them when they discovered that all of them were safe, but rattled by the same explosion and flash that had awakened them. His wife had burst into tears. Upon checking the news wires, he began to learn the same thing had happened worldwide. Reports began to surface showing that millions, or billions, of people had vanished without a trace. He had sat in shock, his mind almost unwilling to accept what he saw and heard. The same information came from all over the United States as well. His phone had begun to ring incessantly. He had finally made the call to the ace of the network, Blake Thompson.

Blake was the best newsman, not just in America, but in the world, Ben thought. His promotion to anchor would likely come within the next couple of years. That would distance them from the other networks by a clear margin. Ben was proud of Blake and what he had accomplished. But tonight he could not get his mind off their phone conversation. Blake had sounded different. He could not put his finger on what that difference was, but something was not right. Blake had sounded evasive and almost hesitant to return to work. That was very much unlike him. Typically, he would be champing at the bit to get back out there, working tirelessly to discover and report answers to what the world had experienced on September 11. Had the tremor that had shaken the glass ledge on which he stood at over 1,300 feet in the air also shaken him? Had fear dulled his enthusiasm for being in the thick of the action? Or was there something else? Blake had said he was researching some things that came out of his time in Chicago. Was he failing to be forthcoming with something he knew? No, Blake would never do that. What was it? Ben was anxious to find out. The network could not afford to lose the Blake Thompson the world had come to know and depend on for the news.

Blake and Beth sat at a table in the most romantic section of the Danube.

He had made a reservation and specifically requested that spot. The location had not escaped her attention either. There was no misunderstanding his intentions. She was flattered by his attention to detail. She had the roast chicken with cheese risotto and he the braised beef cheeks in wine sauce. Fruit crepes served as the perfect way to top off the meal. The meal was good, but the conversation was better. A romantic spark had been lit, and it was obvious to both of them.

"Beth, I can't help but wonder if you are feeling anything close to what I feel."

"I don't know Mr. Thompson, uh, I mean Blake. What are you feeling?"

"Well, it certainly isn't anything resulting from the meal we just enjoyed." He smiled, and she chuckled. "Beth, I think I can be honest with you. I have always admired your work as a reporter and have seen you as the female version of myself. But you are also the most beautiful woman I have ever seen. I have always known you are the only woman I could ever see myself with. At the same time, I knew our roles with competing networks would prevent that. But now that we only have at most seven years remaining on Planet Earth, I'm not sure that matters anymore. I'm not afraid to say it: I love you. I really do love you."

She was quiet for a moment causing Blake to feel that he had been too open with his feelings for her and shared too much. But he had newfound courage, and confronted with the small amount of time they had left, felt he had no time to waste. He sat and quietly waited for her to reply.

"Oh Blake, I have been unable to get you off my mind since you consoled me on the street that morning. That was a part of my reason for calling you. I understand that God was probably directing our meeting for several reasons, not the least of which was bringing me to faith in Jesus. But I also think his plan for my life, and yours, may have been even more far reaching than that. I know he wants us to be on the same team as we fight the enemy and try to bring others to Jesus. But I also believe he may want us to be true teammates, with each other. Blake, I love you too."

The joy they felt was something that can only come from true love. Their feelings for each other may have seemed to develop overnight, but in reality, Blake had felt this way about Beth for a long time. Prior to that encounter on September 11, she would have expressed her feelings about him as admiration. But at that moment something had awakened inside her which had been there for years. Each of them was fully aware of what they wanted for the rest of their lives and of the short time they had to enjoy it.

Blake felt his phone vibrating and glanced at it to see who was calling. It said *Ben*. He had never failed to take one of Ben's calls, but this night was different. He let it go to voicemail.

"Do you need to get that?" Beth asked.

"Not this time. They'll leave a message, and I'll get back with them. Right now, nothing is more important than you and our time together."

Ben still sat alone in his den. His call went unanswered, so he waited somewhat impatiently for his opportunity to leave a message. Finally, it came.

"Blake, I assume you have something important on your plate tonight. It is rare for you to miss one of my calls. I want you to be in my office tomorrow morning at 9:00. There is something I need to talk to you about. And Blake, do not be late."

Beth had a concerned look on her face. She could not help but notice Blake's eyes when he saw the name of the person who was calling.

"Who was it Blake? Is everything okay?"

"It was Ben. He normally doesn't bother me in the evenings unless it's an emergency."

"Maybe you had better listen to his message. You don't want to take any chances with your job. Our roles as reporters are going to be vital to the success of the Smyrnians, especially in the early days of our mission."

"You're right. This will only take a moment. But then it is back to *us*. Tonight is about you and me."

He quickly listened to the message. As usual, Ben's message was brief, but to the point. He had never been one for long messages. They were typically just "Call me. It is important."

"Well?"

"He wants to see me in his office tomorrow morning at 9:00. He needs to talk to me about something. And he said don't be late."

"You don't think he knows we are seeing each other, do you? Or maybe he has discovered that you became a Christian. But..."

"But what, Beth? Either of those two things could have me in trouble. I don't think Ben would fire me over either of them. I'm too important to the network. And he knows the others would hire me in an instant. Besides, we are too close for that to happen so fast. But you are thinking something. I can see the wheels spinning in that beautiful head of yours. So tell me, what is the but...?"

"I was just thinking. Maybe this meeting is not by chance. Remember how my meeting with you was arranged by God? Remember how I had been feeling that I was supposed to meet someone who would help me know what my mission was and how I was supposed to spread a positive message to the world? Don't forget that I was the one who called you. You didn't even have to make that call. Now, remember that Ben is one of the people you most want to bring to the faith and the team. Somehow I don't feel like this meeting is a coincidence."

"You may be right. I admit, I wasn't thinking along those lines. But whatever he wants to talk about, I'll try to find an opening to plant a seed about Jesus in there somewhere."

"Well, I suppose we had better get home. Both of us have to get back to work. I'm not sure what our next assignments will be, but whatever they are we have to give them our all, just like we always have. For the time being, I guess we have to keep our relationship quiet."

"I guess we do. But I plan on being with you every chance I get!"

"My plan is the same. I hope the time is not far away when we can be together all the time."

"Now, that is an open door if ever I heard one," Blake thought to himself. He needed to follow up on that very soon. He had already taken care of the bill, so he helped her up from her seat, escorted her to the car and opened the door for her to be seated.

"Be careful Mr. Thompson...I mean Blake. I have to stop doing that, don't I? Let me try that again: Be careful Blake. I could get used to that kind of treatment."

"You had *better* get used to that kind of treatment. I'm going to treat you like a queen!"

As they drove back to her place, love was definitely in the air. Or was it *twitterpation...?*

CHAPTER 20

Evan had been hard at work digesting everything he could from the video of the pastor's sermon and the Bible. He did not understand it all, but one thing he knew was things would be heating up at any time, and he wanted them to be as prepared as possible when they did. He was not sure he was worthy of being the leader of the Smyrnians, and he would never call himself that. But he was the one who had the time to study and do research. His class load was relatively light this semester. And he had Ally helping him. She was invaluable! Besides, she was his very best friend and they enjoyed spending time together. Her family had returned to Germany, a far different group than when they came. He had briefed them on what they would face during the Tribulation and on what roles they could play in Europe. They were ready! Bruno was especially fired up. As difficult as it would be, he had said this would be the big man's time to shine. Evan put together a list and prepared to call a meeting of the team. They were small in number but he was sure their numbers would increase dramatically in the coming days, weeks and months. The meeting needed to happen as soon as possible.

Blake walked into Ben's office ten minutes early. He definitely did not want to be late. The producer was leaned back in his big chair behind a large mahogany desk facing the window. The spacious office and expensive furnishings spoke volumes about the man's success and importance.

"Have a seat, Blake." Ben spoke without turning around. "I'm anxious to hear all about your trip to Chicago, and the last couple of days since you have been home."

"He knows," thought Blake. "He knows about Beth and me. Maybe he knows about what happened in Chicago. Oh well, I am not offering up any information unless I absolutely have to."

"I know all about the tremor and your, what shall I call it, terror at the

Tower. But I would like to hear about the rest of your time there. Who did you talk to? What did you do? What did you learn? I know you said you are still researching some things that came out of your time. Can you enlighten me on a few of those things?"

"Wow, that is a lot of questions, Ben." Blake hoped to lighten the conversation. "As I said, our time was very productive. I met with John Baldwin. You know John. He was studying the tremor closely and how it could have possibly affected the entire earth. He had a theory that it may somehow have been caused by the sudden departure of the alien spaceships. If you think about it, it could be possible that such an explosion of power could trigger seismic activity all around the globe. I think his hypothesis has some validity. He has promised that I will be the first to hear from him if he has further proof of that or other pertinent information."

Blake breathed a sigh of relief at his answer. He did not want to lie to Ben, so he had chosen his words carefully. He had said John *was* studying the tremor and that he *had* a theory. He indeed had a theory (past tense), but now he knew the truth. And his study of the potential worldwide quake continued, not for scientific purposes, but for the benefit of the Smyrnians. As they carried out their mission during the Tribulation, knowing what was coming next and how they and the world would be affected would be imperative.

"Interesting theory. I can see how that could be possible. Personally, I still find the possibility of a worldwide quake very hard to believe. Only a couple of things could cause me to believe it. If John can find absolute proof that it is going to happen, or of course, if it actually *does* happen. But then, I would never have believed an alien invasion was possible either..."

"I believe the quake is coming, Ben. And I think it will be the biggest one the world has ever seen."

"The strongest ever recorded was a magnitude 9.5 in Chile in 1960. Are you telling me you believe it will be stronger than that?"

"I do, Ben. I think we'll be looking at a 10. And instead of the destruction being limited to a specific area, it will be like the *Invasion* and the tremor. It will be worldwide."

"What is going on with you, Blake? Something happened to you while you were in Chicago. I know the tremor happening while you were out there on the ledge had to be a traumatic experience. I am afraid it affected you more than you are willing to admit. I know a great therapist. Why don't you let me hook you up with her, just to help you work through some of that. Look, I'm not saying you are crazy or paranoid. I just think you need to deal with whatever it is that is bothering you so you won't lose your touch and will continue to be who you are, the best reporter in the world."

"I appreciate it, Ben. I really do. But you know me well enough to know that I'm a straight up guy. If something like that was going on, I would have let you know without you needing to have a talk with me. Trust me, the tremor was scary. But I get an adrenaline rush from that kind of thing. You know that. It just made me hunger for more excitement and more adventure. I'm ready to get back into the thick of the action. Put me in, coach. I'm ready!"

"Okay Blake, I'm going to take your word on this. But I'm telling you that something is different about you. I don't know what is going on, but do not let it affect your work. These are the most important and troubling days the world has ever known. I need you to be *you*, the Blake Thompson everyone has come to know, the Blake Thompson that delivers the news first whatever it takes to get it. I need you out there doing what you do. I don't want anything to interfere with that."

"You can count on that, Ben. There is plenty of action available right now; no shortage of adventure, and even danger. The world is going to be a more dangerous place during the next seven years than either you or I can imagine."

"Seven years? Where did you come up with that? Do you know something I don't? Or does that have something to do with what is going on with you?"

Blake had to scramble now. He could not believe he was careless enough to let that slip out. "It came from the things I was discussing with some people as I was trying to track down leads in Chicago. I really think they're on to something, but I need to do some more research before I say anything. Just believe me, if it proves out, it will be news that will shock the world again. There is a lot going on, and I am determined to give the world the answers it needs!"

"I'm not even going to go down that road with you right now. You have gotten me quite excited about hearing this story concerning the next seven years. Do your research, track your leads and get it ready. This could be your most shining moment yet!"

"I have no doubt that it is true, Ben, no doubt at all. This is going to be the biggest story the world has ever heard. And following on the heels of the *Invasion* (he hated calling it that) and the tremor, it will capture the attention of the entire planet. It's something everyone needs to hear. It will literally save lives and give people the knowledge they need to survive. I'm certain we are in for a time like the world has never seen. But I have a lot work to do and need to get on it!"

"Okay, I heard that. Go after it. It sounds like this is a story that won't just grab people's attention. It sounds like a story that is urgent for them to hear!"

"Thanks for calling me in and for your concern. But you have nothing to worry about with me. I am more inspired than I have ever have been. These days were made for Blake Thompson. And Blake Thompson was made for these days. Have a good rest of the day, Ben. I need to get to work."

"Oh, Blake, there is one more thing. I hear you were out with Beth Jennings a couple of nights ago. I know I don't need to remind you who *you* are and who *she* is. You can't go anywhere without being recognized. And you know nothing you do escapes my attention. My sources are just as good as yours! I need to know if something is going on there too. You know she is our competition. If something *is* going on, you need to be very careful."

Now he was on the hot seat. He could not lie to Ben. He had already told him how straight up he always was with him. He took a deep breath and proceeded to explain.

"Okay Ben, you know I have never lied to you about anything related to my work. We have always been very open and honest with each other. I met Beth for coffee night before last."

Ben interrupted. "At that little shop on Broadway, I know."

"You are the consummate newsman yourself, every bit as much a bloodhound as I am. Yes, we were at that coffee shop. You know she lost her mom and dad in the *Invasion*. (That seemed harder to say each time he had to call it that.) She needed someone that morning on the street when she had just gotten the news. I happened to be close by reporting when I saw her sit down on the curb in shock. I went to her to be there for her. She told me about the phone call she had received at that moment and broke down. We went our separate ways after that. I went with Anders to his place, and she left for the airport to fly to Missouri. You know Anders lost his wife and all three kids too, right?"

"I do. My heart goes out to him. If he needs some time, tell him to feel free to take it. And if you know anything the network or I personally can do for him, please tell me. Now back to you and Beth. I'm not finished hearing about that yet."

"She called me the night I got back from Chicago. She needed someone to talk to. I asked her to meet me for coffee so she could get her feelings out. We had a great talk and some incredibly good coffee. We totally clicked. I guess you could say we have a lot in common, huh? And just so you know, if you don't already, I took her out for dinner last night. And we had a great time again."

"Just be careful, Blake. This isn't the first time two competing reporters have been in a relationship with each other. I'm not sure how it would work out if you got the jump on her, as it seems you always do, and beat her to a story. All I ask you to do is think about that."

"Advice taken, Ben. I promise you I will think about it. But I can't promise you I won't go out with Beth again. In fact, I'm pretty sure I will!"

With that, he was out the door leaving Ben to his thoughts. He could not wait to share this information with Beth. At least their relationship was out in the open. He expected to see it on the covers of the tabloids soon. And he expected her to be Mrs. Blake Thompson in the near future! Then something occurred to him. He had gotten so wrapped up in the conversation with Ben and all of his questions that he forgot the most important thing. He had wondered if the moment would be right for it, but with so much out in the open now, he decided this was as good a time as any. Turning around, he walked back to Ben's office. He took another deep breath, tapped on Ben's door, cracked it open and stepped back inside.

"Ben, I want to leave something with you. We talked about my research in Chicago. I hate to leave you completely in the dark. I was contacted by a young man there right after I left my meeting with John. I had a couple of hours before my next appointment, and he sounded like he was serious. He said he knew the truth about the *Invasion* and had proof. You know I will chase down any lead that might yield even the tiniest piece of evidence, so I went. What I saw blew my mind." He pulled a flash drive out of his pocket. "This is a copy of the video he showed me. I ask you to do the same thing I did, watch it with an open mind. Pay close attention to details. They are very important. This is the most significant piece of evidence I have uncovered so far. I made fun of it at first and would have gotten up and walked away if I had not committed to watch the whole thing. But now, I'm all over it. It is the entire focus of my research. Ben, I believe it is true."

"Okay Blake, I will watch it. I was hoping you would let me in on the action anyway." He smiled. "Most people would give anything to know where Blake Thompson is headed before he gets there. But most have to settle for watching your story after you have gotten all the facts. I feel privileged to be on the inside of your investigation. I will be sure to let you know what I think."

"Thanks Ben. I look forward to getting your thoughts on it. All I ask again is, watch it with an open mind. Think about it. A few days ago, you would not have been open to the possibility of an alien invasion, would you? If it had not been verified by world leaders and scientists, none of us would have believed it. But we did. What you are about to watch has far more proof than anything you have heard yet. Make me a promise. Promise me you will not stop watching once you start. Watch it all the way to the end. I won't make you sign anything. All I want is your word."

"Okay, you have my word. I can't promise you how soon I'll get to watch it, but I promise you I will. And yes, Blake, I will watch it all the way to the end." His tone was obviously sarcastic.

Blake was out the door again. He sure was glad to have that out of the way. He started walking...as fast as he could. He was not sure he wanted to be anywhere near Ben when he saw what was on that video. But he prayed that, in spite of his strong Jewish heritage, he might somehow see the truth. If they needed anyone on their team, it was Ben Abramson.

Evan was ready to call the meeting of the Smyrnians. He had a list of things they needed to discuss, getting everyone's input. They needed to get a plan together that would allow them to survive and get the word out to as many people as they could. He would call Blake and have him let Anders and Beth know. He would get the word to Professor Baldwin, and of course, Ally. His plan was to bring Bruno, Mila and the boys into the meeting via Skype. The most pressing question now was where to meet. Chicago was his obvious preference. He hoped the New Yorkers could get there. He needed them present for this one, not just visible and communicating through a computer screen. Hopefully they could fly in for a Friday evening through Sunday noon meeting, possibly even doing their own church service together Sunday morning. That would be different for all of them.

Meeting day had arrived and six Smyrnians gathered in Evan's dorm room. If asked, all of them would have to say it looked like a tiny group in light of the formidable foe they would be facing. But none of them would ever admit that. Their newfound faith made *them* feel like the formidable foe. They were up to the challenge and ready to get the battle started! Evan had created an agenda for the meeting, but he knew the others had much more expertise to offer than did he or Ally. This was a team effort, not a one-man show. The weekend started with each of them getting to know one another. A biology professor, two college students, two reporters and a cameraman. Honestly, they brought a good variety of knowledge and experience to the team. Add to them, Bruno, Mila and the boys on the job in Germany, and their number totaled ten. The Fromms were valuable assets because of their location and fearlessness, especially Bruno. The man was intimidating because of his size and was afraid of absolutely nothing or no one. Now, if they could somehow bring Ben Abramson and Oliver Barton to the faith, the pieces of the puzzle would truly be falling into place. They were well aware of the role the Middle East would play in the next seven years, so Oliver's experience as a Middle Eastern reporter and his knowledge of that area would make a huge difference. And Ben? Well, having a man of such Jewish passion who was now a follower of Jesus would be priceless. A man who could speak to the Jews on their level and who was so well connected in Israel would be a game-changer. Those two men were definitely on the top of their prayer lists for the weekend. Ben had been given a copy of the pastor's message and could respond positively, or he could blow a gasket and become an enemy of the cause. Beth was praying about the best way to share the good news with Oliver. It was anybody's guess as to how he may react. Recruiting the two of them was both a courageous and dangerous move at the same time, because now they would know who the Smyrnians were and what they believed. If they did not come to faith in Jesus, they would clearly see them as enemies of the cause that would consume the people of the world in the very near future. So, they could easily blow their cover before their mission even started. Yes, prayer was certainly a priority for the next three days.

Evan had provided dinner for the evening. He had asked that none of them eat so they could be together and get acquainted over dinner. The meal was a feast of what else...Chicago style pizza. He lightened the mood early on by telling them Chicago pizza beat New York pizza any old day, which brought a fair amount of good hearted debate. Beth, Blake and Anders assured them nothing could be farther from the truth and said they would host the next meeting and give them an opportunity to decide for themselves. Ally and John joined Evan in support of Chicago leaving them tied at three votes to three and no one to break the tie. That is, until Ally spoke up and told them the Fromm boys would say Chicago pizza was the best they had ever eaten! And obviously, Bruno and Mila would agree. This caused Ally, Evan and John to claim and celebrate a decisive seven to three victory. Blake assured them their triumph would be short-lived, almost certainly being overturned after their gathering in New York City.

After thanking God for the food, they all dug in. When they had finished, nothing was left but crumbs. The New Yorkers had clearly shown no lack of enjoyment for the pizza they had devoured. Ally had brought drinks and made a couple of cakes for dessert. They all agreed to save them for later.

Evan told them, since he and Ally had provided this meal, dinner tomorrow evening was on them. They would eat out, and it had better be top of the line! Oh, it would be, they assured him. Dinner was finished now, so it was time to get Ally's family connected and introduced so they could get down to business. Evan pulled up Skype and the connection was made.

"Before we start, I have to settle one issue," Evan said. "Boys, what is the best pizza in the world?"

"Chicago pizza!" they exclaimed without any hesitation. "Right, mom and dad?"

"Without a doubt," said Bruno. "I could eat my weight in the stuff." Mila agreed.

The entire group chuckled as they knew the big man's weight was pretty significant.

"Okay, that settles that," said Evan. "Now let's get to the important stuff."

The first item on the agenda was prayer. It was something they were all still trying to get used to. But they also noticed that it had become something they loved to do. It was as if they were carrying on a conversation with Jesus and he was right there with them. The six in the room sat in a circle, with both Ally's family and them feeling that they were actually all together in the same place. Then they began praying. Words of praise and thanksgiving to God seemed to come pouring out of each of them as they continued in no particular order with each of them speaking multiple times. They were so grateful for having been introduced to faith in Jesus and for their new life in him that the words came freely and from the depths of their hearts. They also praised him for the knowledge that many of their families and friends were with him in heaven at that very moment and they knew they would see them again. They committed the next seven years to him and asked that he would use them to impact the entire world with the good news about Jesus, even in the midst of the chaos that would fill the earth. And they asked him to give them the courage to stand, regardless of what they may face and in any situation in which they might find themselves. Finally, they turned their attention to people they knew who needed Jesus. Four members of the group, as well as four others who were present on the computer screen became silent as they allowed Blake and Beth to pray for the two men whom they most wanted to become part of them.

Blake began. "Dear Jesus, I pray for Ben Abramson. At some point, he will watch the pastor's message. I ask that you will give him that time alone and uninterrupted. Please keep him focused and in tune with the message when he wants to stop watching, and even gets angry or frustrated as many of us did. Let the pastor's words pierce his heart and soul. Help him to surrender his life to you, Jesus. I know it will be hard for him because all of his life he has been taught that you are not who the Bible says you are. Help him to see the truth and put his faith in you. We need him Jesus. The world needs him. You need him. And most of all, he needs you. Please Lord, I beg you for him. Bring him to the faith. I ask in your name, Jesus."

Beth was next. "Jesus, you know how much Ollie Barton has meant to me in my life. He taught me so much and helped me become the newswoman I am today. He has reported so many times from your land in Israel. He has walked there and talked to many people. He has seen for himself the places where you walked and taught and performed miracles. But he doesn't believe in you. I didn't believe either, Jesus, but I do now, with all my heart. Show me what to do. Should I send him the video or call him and talk to him about you? I don't think I can explain it to him as well as the pastor does. I need an answer. I wish I could talk to Ollie face to face. We need him on the ground in Israel and the other nations of the Middle East, places that will surely be in the thick of the action. We also need him to be a member of the Smyrnians. And most importantly, *he* needs *you*. Please give me an opportunity to talk to him and soften his heart. Bring him to faith in you, Jesus. Please bring him to faith in you. I ask this in your name. Amen."

They all responded in unison, "Amen." There was an air of excitement and expectation in the room like none of them had ever felt before. They were definitely ready for action. John whispered, "Bring it on!" Blake motioned to Evan showing him they were ready to get down to business. That was all the prompting he needed. They had to create a strategy, and there was no time to waste.

CHAPTER 21

Evan stood and walked to a large whiteboard that was now attached to his wall, taking up a fair portion of it. John had *borrowed* it from the university assuming no one was going to care once the action hit. Besides, the *Smyrnians* needed it far more. It had just been sitting around unused in a closet for a long time anyway. As Evan approached the board and took several dry erase markers in his hand, he began the meeting.

"Since our time is limited this weekend, I think we need to get right to the most pressing things. None of us really knows what to expect in the coming days and years, but we know it will be bad. We need to come up with a plan now that will allow us to fight the battles we will face and give us the best chance to stay alive for the next seven years. Each of us brings different gifts, skill sets and experience to the table. We need to know how we will use those things to beat the enemy at his own game. We must come up with the most effective ways to communicate with the entire world. And above all, how we can help people come to the faith and become part of the team. This will be our lives. Each of you may continue with your job, but our real jobs will be the cause. The world will ultimately lose this war, but we must win!" He said that last line with all the gusto of a coach preparing his team for a big game and motivating them to go out and give it their all.

"First, let's talk about our team, the Smyrnians." Evan wrote the word TEAM on the board. "I'm a sports fan, so forgive me for using analogies that are familiar to me. Some of you may have some comparisons that work better for you, but I can explain it best using sports. For example, every basketball team has players at each of the five positions, who fit those positions best. Did any of you ever see a six-foot center in Division One Basketball? I don't think so! Why not? Because centers need to be tall. In the same way, you don't see a seven-footer playing point guard and handling the ball. My point is, we are a team. Each of us needs to do what we do best to benefit the team. Now, I have a feeling that all of you have already thought this through and have a good idea of what you bring to the table. So, someone get us started and I'll do the writing on the board."

Ally spoke first. "I can cook and keep us from getting hungry!" She grinned and the others smiled.

"I will start," said John. "I'm a researcher. It's what I do best. I'm all over this worldwide quake right now. I'm mapping fault lines around the globe and trying to determine how it could happen and possibly even when. I don't have answers yet, but I'm seeing clues falling into place that could let us be prepared and help prepare the world as much as possible. I will share some of that with you very soon. But tonight is not the time for that. I'm just saying I can research anything at any time. I feel sure that will be needed in the years to come. It can help us in a lot of ways."

"Good John, uh, I mean Professor Baldwin," said Evan.

"Okay, I know it's not *professional*, but let's forget the student-professor thing. From this point, we are on the same team, warriors in the same army. I would probably get fired for saying this, but you and Ally have more important things to do than study and I have more important things to do than teach. So, go ahead and call me John. After all, we *are* brother and sister in Jesus, aren't we?" John was obviously ready to forget everything else for the sake of the cause.

"Okay, John...I'm sorry, that sounds weird, but I'll get used to it," Evan chuckled. "John is right. That is one huge thing he brings to the table. He has a lot of other gifts too, and I'm pretty sure he is ready to serve on the front lines also." John shook his head 'yes' vigorously! "And trust me, Ally can do a lot more than cook. Am I right, Mr. and Mrs. Fromm?"

"You had better believe it," Bruno said with a loud guffaw. "That girl has always had a mischievous streak. She can be pretty sneaky." Ally acted shocked and shook her head toward the computer screen. "Don't shake your head at me baby girl! I have seen you in action. You're a good spy. You have told on your brothers when they had no idea how you knew what they had been up to. You have always been able to track things down band get information that no one else could get."

"Come on daddy," Ally said, very unconvincingly. "I am not a spy. I was doing things any other normal teenager could do."

"Oh, no you weren't! Remember that time when Sophie stole your tennis racket? You dug around and talked to people until you knew it was her. Then you confronted her and she gave it back. Don't tell me you're not a good spy. That's what you can be for the Smyrnians. You can be a spy!"

"Now, Bruno," Mila whispered loudly enough for all of them to hear. "You can't put Ally's life in danger like that. She would be killed in an instant if they discovered her."

"No disrespect Mrs. Fromm, but all of our lives are going to be in danger every day. And it will get worse as time goes by. We will be laying it all on the line. If Ally can be a spy for us, then she needs to use her talents to gather information about the enemy," Blake jumped in. "I know I'm ready to use everything at my disposal to help. I'm going to be a warrior for Jesus, for the cause and for the sake of everybody in the world who may yield to the antichrist. I want to stop them from doing that, if at all possible!"

"Good, Blake!" exclaimed John. "Tell us what you think you, Beth and Anders can do. I'd say you guys are in a unique position. You're certainly a lot more well-known than the rest of us."

Beth threw her hat into the ring before either of the others could speak.

"God has given us a platform to be able to spread the word! After the *Invasion*...come on, I'm kidding! Just wanted to be sure you are all awake. After the *Rapture*, I was informed about my mom and dad being taken, so I went to their house in Missouri as quickly as I could get there. I admit, it was gut-wrenching as I walked through their house and saw how everything was completely normal, as if they had just disappeared without a trace, without anything being disturbed. But as I stood in their bedroom, something kept telling me that everything was okay and I was going to share good news with everyone in the world and make a difference. I had no idea what that meant until Blake showed me the video and I put my faith in Jesus. Now I know what I'm supposed to do. Now I know where mom and dad are. They aren't on some distant planet being terrorized or tortured by aliens. They're with Jesus! And I have a job to do for seven years!"

"I know what you mean Beth," said Anders quietly. He was not a man of many words and was not very outspoken. "I was crushed when I lost my Angie and our three kids. I didn't see how I could go on without them. Especially knowing they had been taken by aliens. But when I learned the truth, I too came to faith in Jesus and it changed everything. Now I know where my family is. And I know I will see them again in seven years...or less. I'm ready to use my expertise to help people *see* the truth, not just *hear* it. I can do a whole lot of filming, sort of behind the scenes, and get away with it for as long as I can. And even when they discover me, I'll go undercover and provide footage for the world to see. The enemy is not going to like me very well. But I don't care if I become Public Enemy Number One. It will be worth it."

"Well, okay then," said Blake. "It sounds like the news crew is ready to go! We can work at our normal jobs until we're discovered. That should take at least a year or two, maybe more. But when they find us out, it won't stop us. Beth and I are the top dogs at our networks and, not bragging, in the entire news industry. We pretty much have free reign. We can pick the stories we want to cover, while also covering the stories that are assigned to us. We're both bloodhounds when it comes to getting insider information and breaking big stories. And with Ally as our spy, we ought to be on the inside of everything the enemy is doing. So, put us down for news, reporting, getting to the bottom of things, whatever you want to call it. I say we get started right away. I have a feeling things are going to be happening at warp speed!"

Evan was noting all of these things on the board as they talked. "So, we have John doing research, Ally spying (she nodded her head and rolled her eyes as if to say they didn't know what they were talking about) and Blake, Beth and Anders doing their thing as reporters and cameraman. Right?" The others nodded in agreement. The plan was beginning to come together.

"I think we're leaving someone out here," Blake added. "Mr. and Mrs. Fromm, you're going to be the recruiters and organizers of the German, if not the entire European, unit. How do you see your family fitting into this and what do you specifically plan to do? Any ideas yet?"

"Oh yeah, we have talked about it a lot! Isn't that right, Mila?"

She smiled in agreement with her husband.

"Of course, I want to go out there and bust a few heads!"

Mila frowned at that statement and looked a bit perturbed with him.

"I can fight with the best of them," the big man continued. "And I plan to do that! But I have other ideas too. Recruiting is our number one goal. I know we have to be careful, so we'll be selective as we talk to people about Jesus. I'll use the video and explain any parts they can't understand. It makes it a lot easier. This may sound strange, but we're going to try and focus on people with different skill sets; people whose abilities will fit together like the pieces of a puzzle. We need a team, kind of like you have, not just a bunch of flunkies who can't get anything done.

Then whoever we get, we're going to train. We want them to be up to speed on what it's going to be like for the next seven years. We don't need any wimps or people who are going to be chicken and walk away, or worse, turn traitor. And we want to mobilize them, exactly like we're doing in this meeting. We need to know everybody's strengths and weaknesses and what they can and cannot do. We want this unit over here to run like a well-oiled machine! Oh, and Mila? Well, she will probably be the mother hen and nurse for the group. She does that well, you know."

"I admit, I am impressed," John said, his surprise showing far more than he wanted it to. "The German unit is going to be a force to be reckoned with! But we're still leaving someone out. Evan, what do you see yourself doing? How will you fit into the team? You're the one who started this whole thing. Without you, there would be no Smyrnians. You are our fearless leader. Talk to us."

The focus shifted completely to Evan. Every eye was on him, listening for what he would say.

"Well, I really want to be on the front lines, in the thick of the action. There is no way I'm sitting on the sideline. But I do think I can be an organizer and point man for making sure people are where they need to be and getting information out to all of you to keep us organized and up to speed on what each other is doing. Organizing is sort of my cup of tea. I can be like an air traffic controller, making sure all our takeoffs and landings go smoothly and we don't go crashing into each other. I will know where everyone is at any given time and what they are doing. I can also gather information from all of you and help us know what our next steps need to be. And I hope by doing that I can keep us out of danger, at least as much as possible. What do you think?"

"I think that is perfect!" It was Blake again. "We have to have someone hiding out somewhere keeping us all going in the same direction. I think you may be just the man for that job, Evan."

"Hiding out is not exactly what I mean. I suppose I will need to be behind the scenes doing what has to be done. But you're not going to be able to keep me out of the fray, even if you try! I can do both, but I also know what my most important role will be.

Okay, so all of that is decided. I have it all on the board. We can work through the logistics later, but until then we all need to be doing our thing. And keep me posted on everything you do! Now let's talk about something that will be essential: survival. How are we going to survive once we're discovered? We need a plan in advance so we can be working on it. And if I'm going to be hiding out, I'll need a place to hide! We all will. We must survive. All of us won't make it, but we have to make sure we're as protected as possible." He wrote the word *Survival* on the board.

"I have an idea." From the look on John's face, they could tell this was not something that had just popped into his mind. He was serious about it.

"It's something I've been mulling over for a long time. I have done a lot of research about world war, nuclear warfare, any catastrophic event that would make survival difficult. Remember the Y2K scare at the dawn of the new millennium?"

"Ally and I hardly remember that John, since we hadn't been born. And I'm thinking Blake, Beth and Anders are in the same boat since they were all small children at the time. So, no we don't remember it, but I think we've all heard of it. That makes you the old man of the group!"

"Okay, okay, so I'm the old man. But I was alive and in the thick of it. So, for you young whippersnappers, let me bring you up to speed and show you how it fits with what I'm suggesting. In the twentieth century, computer memory was stored using only the last two digits of the dates. So, 1999 would be stored only as 99. It was feared that when the date rolled over to 00, computers wouldn't be able to tell if that was 2000 or 1900. A lot of people bought into the theory that immediately after the clock struck midnight on January 1, computers would crash, power grids would go down and life as we know it would be over. All technology would disappear, electrical power would be nonexistent, there would be no food in stores or fuel at the pumps, and no way to purchase them. Everyone would have to find a way to survive without those things. There was even the thinking that a world power would attack America and be able to wipe us out because we would be effectively crippled. Some people bought property in the middle of nowhere and built houses with their own water systems from springs or wells. They created spaces to grow their own food and bought wood stoves to heat their houses. I researched options for survival. That *is* my gift, remember? And I landed on one that had the most appeal to me. I never followed through because my research ultimately proved that the Y2K scare was nothing more than that...a scare...one that wouldn't happen."

"Well, don't stop there!" It was Bruno via Skype. "Tell us what it was. Is it still available?"

"Absolutely!" John almost shouted. "Underground bunkers. They're made of steel and are virtually indestructible. But they're not cheap. We'll need a big one to house all the technology we need and people who will need to come and go. They make them up to 3,000 square feet and even with hidden rooms, should they be located. Those can cost a million dollars or more. Yep, you heard that right, a million dollars. They have smaller ones for around $50,000, but those won't help us. We have to go big or go home! And by home, I mean home to heaven because we can't survive without full blown protection and space to do everything we need to do."

"A million dollars, John? There's no way we can afford that!"

"Spoken like a true college student, Evan. Here's what I'm thinking. These wheels in my brain never stop spinning. I have a friend who owns a company that builds them. If we can bring him to Jesus, who knows? He would most likely install one for free! If not, you are right. We'll have to come up with a lot of money between us. I sure don't have that much cash lying around. And my Swiss bank accounts are all gone." He grinned. "But there are a bunch of super wealthy people out there who need Jesus. And if they come to the faith...a million dollars is peanuts to them."

"Sounds like exactly what we need, John," said Anders. "You know, somehow I believe God will give us everything we need. I've been reading my Bible constantly. I came across this verse in Philippians 4:19 that says, 'And my God will meet all your needs according to the riches of his glory in Christ Jesus.' I believe that. So, I say we pray about it and trust God to take care of it!"

It was as excited as any of them had seen the man. His eyes betrayed a sense of faith that left no doubt they would have the biggest and best bunker that was made, paid for, installed and ready to use, if they just believed what God said in the Bible.

"Well, we're going to need one of those over here in Germany too!" Bruno wanted to make sure the international unit was not left out. "So, you had better pray for at least two very wealthy people to accept Jesus. We need to survive too. We're going to fight. You know I'm going to fight. But we need a secure location when they come looking for us where they can't find us, no matter how hard they look."

"Okay," said Evan, "that sounds like an item for the top of our prayer lists. *When*, not if, God provides the funds to buy these bunkers, or the bunkers are free of charge, where do we put them?"

"I think I know where ours should go. I know a very obscure place in Missouri that is completely under the radar and the last place anyone would think to look. My mom and dad had a farm that no one knew about. It was willed to them by a friend who had no other living relatives when he died. They took care of him, did his shopping, mowed his yard, things like that for years. The farm is in the middle of nowhere, and seventy-five percent of it is wooded. It seems like the perfect place to me." Beth had a look of determination and excitement on her face.

"Boy, does it ever!" Blake was excited. "What if Anders, you and I stop by there and check it out on our way home? Anders can shoot some footage, and you can describe it as he goes. Then we will send the video to the rest of the group so we will all be in the know."

"We can do that. I know that place like the back of my hand. There are a hundred and fifty acres there. My dad used to deer hunt on it."

The booming voice of Bruno Fromm interrupted. "Don't forget us over here! I know we're thousands of miles away, but we're still part of the team. We need a survival bunker too."

"Now dear, calm down." Mila was ever the peacemaker. She had to be. Her husband could be a loose cannon at times.

"Why don't you scope out possible sites there too, daddy. You're not the only ones who will be looking for a place of survival. There are going to be people from all over the world who will accept Jesus and become part of the Smyrnians. We'll all be out in the thick of battle, but we'll also need a place where we can go and be safe, plan and mobilize. And much of the time it may just be a place to hide."

"Okay. I'll be looking. But we had better pray hard that God will send us the money to buy it."

"There are wealthy people in Germany too, Mr. Fromm."

"Yeah, but we don't know any of them. We're common folks. And all our friends are just like us. We'll have a hard time finding them. We don't run in their circles."

"Faith, Bruno. God will provide. I don't know how, but I know he will. We have to trust him."

"I've never trusted many people. I've always made my own way so I didn't have to depend on anybody else. So, this trusting God thing is new for me. But after what I just experienced when I gave my life to Jesus, I can do that. I'm trusting God to provide us a bunker!"

Evan had filled in all the information about the bunkers under the word *Survival.* They had been hard at work for three hours already. "I think it's time we take a break and have some of Ally's cake," he said. "I've had it before. You are not going to be disappointed! After we finish, we can do a bit more work or turn in for the night. I know everyone has had a long day, especially the New Yorkers."

As Ally began to cut the cakes, Blake's cell phone chirped. He looked to see who was calling and quickly got up. "It's Ben Abramson. I had better answer. He may want to talk about the video." A look of concern was on his face as he stepped into the corner of the room and answered Ben's call.

CHAPTER 22

"Hello, Ben. What's up?"

"Where are you, Blake? I need you in New York and on a story tomorrow morning. If you're in town, that will help. If not, I need you to catch the first flight you can and get here."

"I'm in Chicago, Ben. I'm working on those leads I spoke with you about." He knew if Ben had watched the video, he would understand what those leads were. His urgency about a news story could be nothing more than a ploy to get him home. Was his job in jeopardy? Did Ben know about his newfound faith, something that could put his life in jeopardy? His mind ran amok with thoughts of what could be. He, Beth and Anders would have to leave the Smyrnians meeting and get back to New York. But there was one stop he could not afford to miss.

"Those leads will have to wait. There is something much more important I need you to cover..."

Blake interrupted him in mid-sentence. "I'll get there as fast as I can. Mid-morning should be no problem. I'll work late, all night if I need to, and wrap things up here. Then I'll be on the first available flight to New York."

"Will you let me finish? This is something that could affect the world in a big way and following on the heels of the *Invasion*...I don't know what will happen."

This call sounded eerily like the one not that many days ago when Ben had called at 3:00 in the morning. The same thoughts began to flood his mind again. What in the world was going on that would cause Ben Abramson to be so insistent? Maybe it wasn't him. Could it possibly be something as earthshaking as the Rapture had been? Or maybe...it was the beginning of the Tribulation! This could be it! He heard Ben as he began to explain the reason for his call.

"The Secretary-General of the United Nations has been assassinated. As you know, the UN has begun their meetings at the headquarters here in New York. Earlier today Secretary-General Pieters was killed as he stepped from his limousine to enter the building. No one knows who did it. No group has claimed responsibility. And strangely enough, as many people as are in and around the building, there are no witnesses. And the security cameras clearly show the area during the time Secretary Pieters was killed. But all that can be seen is his limo pulling up, and the next thing you see is him lying on the ground between the limo and the entrance to the building with his entourage surrounding his body. His bodyguards have their guns drawn and are looking for the assailant. It is as if a minute or two of video is missing, but there is no blip or hiccup in the tape. It clearly shows the crowded area with people hurrying about their business, but none of them even stops or looks toward the limo or the building. It is as if a couple minutes of time just evaporated, as if time stood still, then resumed.

But that's not even the weirdest part. He was not shot. There are no bullet wounds. He was strangled. The marks on his neck show two hands that squeezed so hard it nearly popped his head right off his shoulders. But again, there was no sign of an assailant and no real indication of a struggle. Those with him can only remember driving up in the limo, then the Secretary lying there dead. Not stopping, getting out and walking toward the entrance. Nothing. It's the strangest thing I have ever seen. Well, except for the *Invasion*, maybe. NYPD is baffled. They have asked anyone who has any knowledge of the assassination or who saw anything to please come forward. Thus far, no one has."

"Ben, you're not making sense. None of that is even possible."

"Was the *Invasion* possible? I don't think so. That couldn't happen either, could it? But it did happen, just like this happened. Blake, the world is going crazy."

"Crazier than you can imagine, Ben." Again, he wished he had not said that. He did not want to explain so he moved on quickly. "I guess this assassination fits in with the whole picture of a world gone mad, huh? So, what does this mean for the UN?"

"That is why I need you here. The UN Security Council is meeting tonight to come up with a recommendation for someone to fill Secretary Pieters remaining two years. If they can choose a candidate who is acceptable to the General Assembly, he or she should be able to serve the normal five-year term after that, since reappointment is seldom contested. I would think that is very needed during these volatile times. You have to get here to cover the recommendation and appointment. And hopefully, you can get a one-on-one interview with the new Secretary-General. You can be the guy who introduces him or her to the world."

Blake was doing the math in his head. Two remaining years in Secretary Pieters term plus an additional term of five years. Seven years! His skin crawled at the thought and he felt a chill crawl up his spine. He was briefly surprised that his faith in Jesus and excitement for the Smyrnians role during the Tribulation was tempered by fear at what he had just heard. The Tribulation will last seven years. The Secretary-General of the United Nations has the power to control decisions that determine the direction the world will go. Maybe he was wrong. It could be nothing more than a coincidence. But it made that one stop he had to make on his way to New York all the more urgent.

"I'm on it as always, Ben. You know you can count on me. This is one story I do not want to miss. I suspect it may somehow fit into the research I have been doing. Even if it doesn't, it is sure to play a role in the future. I will see you tomorrow and will cover this story in detail. The network can count on me to break the inside information before anyone else. I'll be on the phone and contacting my sources beginning now."

"I never doubt that I can count on you, Blake. I will see you tomorrow."

A thought hit Blake's mind as he was about to end the call. "Ben!" he said louder than he should have. There were only a few seconds of silence on the other end causing him to believe Ben was already gone. Oh well, it can wait for another day, he thought. He felt some relief that the call had ended before he could get out the all-important question.

"Yes, Blake? What is it?"

He had no choice now. So, here goes. His palms were sweaty as he held the phone.

"Have you had a chance to watch the video I left with you?"

"I'm sorry, Blake. I haven't. I intended to watch it shortly after you left my office. But things have been crazy around here and at home. Illness has made its rounds through the kids, so I have had to help Miriam all I can. I do plan to watch it soon. Maybe after this UN story has unfolded. I know we will both be busy, but why don't we try to find a time to sit down and watch it together? I know how excited you are about it. We can have lunch brought in, or maybe some popcorn for the movie. I'm just kidding about that. I really do want to see what you have discovered in your research. I don't often get to do that with the great Blake Thompson."

Wow, talk about fear! Blake shuddered at the thought. But he was not about to turn down his producer. This would be the defining moment of his career. He could either be out of a job and working full time undercover for the Smyrnians, or Ben could become a Christian. He liked the last thought much better!

"I'd love that, Ben. We seldom get to sit down together like we used to do in the early days."

"If you prefer, we can try to find a time to sit down at home and watch it with Miriam. You haven't been to our house in a long time either."

"No, she has enough going on with sick kids. We'll just watch it together. It will give us something to talk about, so let's try to schedule in a little extra time if we can."

"We'll try to make that happen, if time permits. For now, just get back here and cover this story! Time is wasting, and every minute counts. I don't have to tell you that. Of all people, you know."

Blake ended the call, his mind flooded with emotions. The Secretary-General...the strange circumstances surrounding his death...Ben's offer to watch the video with him. He looked at the group. They were talking, laughing and eating cake. None of them, including him, knew what was about to hit them. They knew so little of what the Bible said about the upcoming seven years. Most of them had only heard what the pastor said on the video. They knew the Rapture had occurred and God had taken his people home to be with him. They knew they had missed it because they had not trusted Jesus as their Savior and followed him. They knew the Tribulation was upon them. And they knew it would be worse than any of them could imagine. He walked back over to them.

"Hey, don't leave me out. I want a piece of each one of those cakes! It's past time for dessert."

"What did Ben want, Blake?" asked Beth. "Is everything okay?"

"I'll explain everything after I eat my cake. But I must tell you that I think our meeting is over for this weekend. I have to be back in New York in the morning."

"Blake!" said Evan. "This meeting is important! Do you absolutely have to go?"

"I do, Evan. Now, let me eat my cake so I can explain. The longer it takes me to eat it, the longer all of you have to wait!"

Reluctantly, Ally brought him two big slices of cake. He consumed it. He did not normally eat this late, but the pizza was gone and hunger had set in again.

"Ally, I must say that I like Chicago style cake. It is delicious! I don't know if New York cake can stand up to it or not. The thing I hate most is that we won't get to take you for that awesome dinner tomorrow. I promise I'll make it up to you when you come to New York."

Beth's phone dinged. "It's the network," she said. "I had better take this one too."

She walked to the corner of the room and answered the call. This time the others watched as she talked. Blake could tell that she was hearing the same things he had just heard. Her body language and facial expressions revealed the same shock and disbelief he had felt. He knew she would have to return home too. He wondered if the same thinking had hit her as it had him. The group was silent as they waited and watched. There seemed to be a chill in the air again that they had not felt since the night of and day following the Rapture.

Beth finished the call and walked slowly back over to where they were standing and sitting.

"Blake, did you get the same call I just got?"

"Without a doubt. I could tell by your actions and expressions you were hearing the same things I had just heard. The assassination of the Secretary-General of the United Nations. The strange and inexplicable events surrounding it. The special meeting of the Security Council to decide on a candidate to replace him. They will then recommend that candidate to the General Assembly for appointment. Yes, I heard the same things. There is just one bit of information I wonder if you understand in the same way I did."

"The new Secretary-General will fill the remaining two-year term of Secretary Pieters and likely be elected to the normal five-year term after that. Five plus two. Seven years. The Tribulation."

"Yes. It has begun. I think we will know the identity of the antichrist by tomorrow afternoon."

"I agree," she said. "I'm still trembling. I knew it was coming, but knowing it is here…" Her voice trailed off as she spoke.

"Wait a minute. What are you two talking about?" John clearly did not want to be left out of this conversation. "The UN? Secretary Pieters was assassinated? A new secretary is being appointed by tomorrow? The identity of the antichrist? Let us in on this. You reporters report the news. We are your audience. Fill us in on this breaking story!"

"Okay, back to your seats everybody. This can't be long because Beth, Anders and I have a flight to schedule and a plane to catch. I have a feeling this trip and this story may be even more important than our meeting. Time will tell, but I know Beth and I are both certain that is true."

Beth joined Blake as they both explained their conversations with their bosses and the events which precipitated those calls. When they reached the point of telling how the new Secretary-General would likely fill a total of a seven-year term, their eyes were wide and their faces pale. Each of them felt the all too familiar chill that had been experienced on, and often after, September 11. It was obvious they had come to the same conclusion as the two of them.

"It has begun," whispered Anders.

"It already had," said John. "The seven years began the day after the Rapture."

"Wow," uttered Evan.

Ally seemed to bring them all back to reality in her simple way.

"We have work to do!"

She was right. They had work to do. Their lives were on the line and they knew it. Whoever had killed Secretary Pieters clearly had powers that went beyond human capability. There was no doubt in any of their minds he would be the man appointed as the new Secretary-General of the UN.

"Beth, I'll get to work finding us a flight. But not to New York initially. We need to make a stop on the way. Which means we need to be in the air as soon as possible. We need to be in Missouri well before dawn so we can be at your parents' secluded property by daylight. We need to get the footage and send it to the team. The time is near when we will desperately need a bunker in place."

"I guess I need to get with my friend," said John. "He is our best hope for getting this done. And if it works out as I hope it will, he could be the answer to every bunker we need around the world."

Blake was already on the phone with the airline working on a flight. It did not take long for them to find one for Mr. Blake Thompson and Beth Jennings. But even they could not get an early morning flight from Missouri to New York.

"We are scheduled to fly out of O'Hare in three hours," Blake explained. "That should get us to the Springfield-Branson airport by 4:00 in the morning. How long does it take to drive to the farm from there, Beth?"

"We can be there in less than half an hour. Should be twenty minutes, tops."

"Great! There should be some light not long after we get there. If not, we'll have to make do. Anders is a genius when it comes to filming anyway. But there is only one thing. I can't get a flight to New York until tomorrow evening. I don't know what we are going to do about that. But we *have* to see the property, and we *have* to be in New York by mid-late morning. Can you tell me how that is going to happen?"

"Maybe I can. I have a friend in Ozark who flies a charter service out of Springfield-Branson. I'll call him right now and see what he can do for us. He has come through for me many times in the past when I really needed him. I don't know that I have ever needed him more than we need him right now."

"Call him!" Blake saw a ray of hope in an impossible situation. "You know, God said he will supply all of our needs, right Anders?"

"All of our needs *in Christ Jesus!*" beamed Anders.

"Okay, we're in!" said Beth. Her voice was tingling with excitement. "He said he is clear and will have the plane fueled and ready to go. He'll be waiting for us at the airport. We'll be in the air the minute we can get on the plane!"

"Is this how God is going to meet our needs throughout the Tribulation? If so, it's going to be a great adventure!" yelled John.

"Let's grab our bags and head to the airport. We don't have time to waste. Missouri, here we come!" Everyone else shared Blake's enthusiasm.

Ally looked somewhat sad. "I wish my family could have stayed connected to hear this firsthand. But I'll fill them in as soon as you guys leave."

The New Yorkers grabbed their bags and prepared to leave. Evan halted them before they got out the door.

"I know you have a tight schedule to catch your flight. But we need to pray again before you go. This trip and the next few days are going to be more important than any of us can know right now."

They gathered in a circle once more and joined their hands. Evan led the prayer and the entire group felt the presence of God with them as they had not felt it before. The chill was replaced by a warmth that they felt all over their bodies. He was with them. They knew it. The days to come would not be easy and would get tougher as the years went by. But they were ready. They were a team. They were an army prepared for battle. They were the Smyrnians. The prayer ended and after hugs all around and goodbyes they slowly parted. Each of them was keenly aware that there would be many moments like this in the future when they would part from each other not knowing if they would all be together again, at least on the earth. In ways, it was a somber moment. Blake, Beth and Anders were out the door and in their rental car headed to O'Hare. The next ten hours would be a whirlwind, but they were necessary. They rode silently for much of the drive as they pondered what lay before them. When they talked, it was about the meeting, Ally's cake, the phone calls, the United Nations, the property, the bunkers and the future. But their words were few and far between. Beth rode in the front seat with Blake. He reached over and put his arm around her, then slowly brought it down and held her hand.

"Twitterpation," said Anders. "Just plain Twitterpation." Twitterpation it was indeed.

CHAPTER 23

The plane touched down at Springfield-Branson Airport right on schedule. Blake, Beth and Anders exited and were on the road quickly. They had traveled to Chicago with only a change of clothes in carry-on bags, so there was no need for baggage claim. The 20-minute drive to the farm was anything but silent. It was filled with chatter about the potential of this being the headquarters and safe place of the Smyrnians till the end of the seven years of the Tribulation or until they may be found out, whichever came first. The three of them planned how they would shoot the footage, with audio explanation, as quickly as possible then jump back in the car and head for the airport. If that could all be accomplished in the planned amount of time, they should be able to land in New York by at least eleven o'clock. Close enough to mid-morning. If they could successfully do the filming at the farm in the dark, using any light they could come up with, they would be earlier. It was decided that they would drive the rental car as far onto the farm as they could and use the high beam headlights. Anders always carried a wide-angle flashlight with him that could light up any dark scene. But he said he would come up with a way to get it done so they could stay on schedule and arrive back in New York when they needed to.

Beth was driving since she knew where they were going. "We're almost there. We will turn onto a small road right up there, then onto another road that no one uses in about a quarter mile after that. There is a hidden, unpaved lane that turns from it. Just be ready."

Beth made the first two turns then suddenly turned into what appeared to be a grove of trees. Both Anders and Blake grabbed what they could and braced for impact. They soon realized that they were winding through a stretch of woods on a tiny one-lane dirt road that was surprisingly smooth. The limbs stretching and touching overhead made it appear that they were driving through a tunnel.

"Do you see what I mean by this place being secluded?"

"Secluded isn't the word for it," said Blake. "Neither is hidden. Maybe invisible? From what I can see now, it is perfect. Of course, I can't really see now because it is dark. But I'm guessing this place is almost as invisible in the daylight as it is in the dark. We can drive in and out of here without ever being noticed!"

"You haven't seen anything yet," Beth said with a sense of satisfaction. "I told you this farm is mostly woods. There are a few open areas, small fields scattered about, but more woods than anything. Here is the kicker about this lane coming in. It ends in a circular grove of trees that is as tightly covered as what you are seeing now. Nothing inside it can be detected from the air. It is completely hidden from sight. John mentioned a 3,000-square foot bunker. Even if the span is thirty by one hundred, there is plenty of room inside here." The car rolled into the grove and came to a stop. "As you can see, there is lots of space for parking and as big a bunker as we can install!"

"Wow! My mind is blown," said Blake. "I have never seen anything like this!"

"Of course, you haven't. You're not a farm boy. You're a city guy." She grinned at him. He agreed and grinned back. "Believe it or not, there is an acre of land inside this dome that is entirely hidden from the outside. In case you don't know, an acre is 43,560 square feet. There is room to plant a few 3,000-square feet bunkers in here, don't you think?"

"Absolutely! This is amazing! We'll be as hidden as we could be anywhere. Not to mention that we'll also be underground," Blake laughed.

"Come on, you two." Anders was out of the car with his smaller camera in tow. "We have filming to do and a plane to catch! You may have to put those headlights on low beam, Beth. The high beams are almost too much. They may over-illuminate the place. Let's try the low beams with the car parked just inside the trees. I want to show this spot all around with you narrating. Tell them what you just told us. Make them feel as if they are here seeing it for themselves. We can make sure they get to see it in person soon, but make them feel like they are here instead of watching a video."

He did a trial run and checked it out. It was perfect, almost as if it was daylight, or the grove was lighted electrically. "Okay, let's get to filming," he said. Beth stepped up in her professional way and began to report. She brought Blake in and asked him to share his thoughts on what he had seen. He left no doubt that this was, without a doubt, the place they needed! All three watched a part of the video and approved it as perfectly done. No one would have known they were filming in the dark.

"Anders, you are a genius," Blake raved. "No disrespect to your camera person Beth, but Anders is simply the best in the business. I sure am glad he's on our side." Beth agreed.

"Okay," said Anders, "this is going to be the tricky part. They need to see the drive back here too, and just how secluded it is. I'm going to sit on the hood and film as you drive back out. I think it will come out okay, but it may look a bit spooky...oooohhhh." He laughed at himself. "One thing Beth. You have to drive slow so you don't throw me off the hood!"

"I sure don't want to kill our cameraman before we even get the party started. I will drive slow, and you hang on!"

"Exactly how am I supposed to do that with my hands occupied by the camera? I'm going to be depending on you."

They made the drive back to the first small road then stopped to review the footage once more before exiting the trees and making the turns back to the main highway. It was shortly after 5:00 in Missouri, 6:00 in New York. If things went as planned, they should be back in the air on their charter jet before 7:00 New York time and land by 11:30. This was no time to be messing around. Beth stepped on the gas and they sped toward the airport. Sitting in the back seat, Anders thought they must be flying already. They were, he reasoned, flying low.

Arriving at the airport, the trio met up with Trey, Beth's pilot friend. He escorted them to the plane and they boarded on the tarmac. Once aboard, he talked to them about the flight ahead of them.

"We're in for some rough weather about midway through the flight. Severe thunderstorms are expected throughout the Appalachians. It could get pretty bumpy. I expect a lot of turbulence. If I wasn't doing this as a favor for Beth, I would be very hesitant to fly today. In fact, I probably wouldn't. But I'm well aware of your time schedule and the urgency to get to New York to cover an important story. So, I'm going to throttle back and let her go. Hopefully, the turbulence won't slow us down too much. Just buckle up and hold on. I'll do the best I can." With that, he taxied to the runway and awaited clearance for takeoff. The passengers looked at one another and with a nod, agreed to say a silent prayer for safety during the flight. They were quickly given clearance and were in the air a few minutes ahead of schedule.

Blake and Beth were online researching the UN, Secretary Pieters and potential candidates who might fill his position. News sites were filled with stories, videos and interviews about the assassination. Both of them knew they had missed a chance to be on top of an important world event. But their meeting with the team was more important. At the same time, they also knew they would have to be careful to stay on the job in the future. They could not allow their jobs to interfere with the work of the Smyrnians. But neither could they allow their work with the Smyrnians to interfere with their jobs. It would present quite a conundrum in the future. But for now, they were on the job as bloodhounds who reported the news first. And both wanted to be in that room when the new Secretary-General was announced to the media. They *would* be there.

Ben Abramson was nervously pacing the floor in his office. Where was Blake? He had said he would be there by mid-morning. He had not heard from him since last night. Obviously, he had been on the job in Chicago continuing his research into the disappearances, the worldwide quake and who knows how many other things. He was a bloodhound on the trail of a huge story. No one should ever interfere with a hound that has caught a scent. But he had to call Blake in on this one. It was huge. He did not need to just be a player on the sideline giving input from somewhere else. He knew his top dog well enough to know he also had hold of something else that still had the world reeling and was continuing to unfold every day. He wished his man would call. He needed to hear from him, and he needed him in New York City!

Trey had just alerted his passengers that they were coming into the stormy weather and that turbulence was imminent. All three buckled up and waited. Suddenly it felt as if the plane had slammed into a wall. They grabbed hold of their seats, holding on for dear life. The plane lurched from side to side and began shaking violently. They had been in turbulence before but this felt especially rough. Maybe it was because they were riding in a smaller plane. Then a loud bang and bright flash of light. They had been struck by lightning. Blake began to pray. He knew the others were doing the same. Surely God had not brought them this far and given them a plan for sharing his Word and battling the enemy for the next seven years only to let them die in a plane crash. Then Trey's voice came again.

"Guys, we are going to have to find somewhere to set this plane down. We are not going to make it through this storm. I'm on the radio asking for the nearest airport where we can land."

"No!" thought Blake. "This can't happen!" He grabbed the hands of his partners and yelled, "I'm going to pray. Pray along with me." He began.

"Oh God, I don't know much about the Bible. You know following Jesus is new to all of us. But we have already seen miracles happen in these last two days. You miraculously provided us with this plane to get us back to New York. It's important that we be there on time, Lord. This is the beginning of it all. I know you want us to be there. I have heard Christians talk about Jesus calming a storm for his disciples on the Sea of Galilee. I haven't read it, but I know if you did that for them you can do it for us. We need you right now. Jesus, please calm this storm and let us make it to New York before noon. Please Jesus, show us you are with us. Please, calm our storm!"

Before their eyes had even opened, the plane leveled out. The ride became smooth. No bumps. No lurching. No bouncing. Just a smooth flight. Trey spoke again.

"Sorry folks, I was wrong. We just went from one of the darkest and roughest storms I've ever flown in, to clear blue skies and calm air. I don't understand how that happened, but it did. I'm really shocked. But however it happened, it is behind us now. So, it is throttle up and hang on. We are on our way to New York!"

Applause came from the cabin as Blake, Beth and Anders broke out in celebration. But it was not the usual celebration of relief. It was praise to Jesus for calming their storm.

"I have a feeling these last two days are only the beginning of what we're going to see God do for us during the next seven years," an ecstatic Blake said quietly.

"Yes," said Beth. "Just think about it. He miraculously spoke to us and helped us realize that a bunker is the best option for a safe place as we fight the enemy. I don't know about you two, but I would never have thought about that. And if John hadn't researched it already, starting 30 years ago, he probably wouldn't have either. God is amazing! I sure wish I had realized that years earlier. But if I had, I wouldn't be here with you two today preparing to be God's Army during the Tribulation. It would have been better to have been taken to be with him in the Rapture, but I'm still thankful that I know him now and excited about being a Smyrnian!"

"And," said Blake, "don't forget that God helped you think of the property where our bunker will go. There couldn't be a better place. Now we know why it was given to your mom and dad. It wasn't just a place to hunt deer or a quiet place for your folks and you to get away. God had far bigger plans for it! He planned it all in advance. I can't help but wonder how many things like that he already has planned for us during the next seven years. He knows them, and we get to discover them one at a time as he reveals them to us. Now, that is exciting!

Oh, yes, and the plane! God brought your friend to your mind and cleared his schedule for today. He doesn't even realize that God is using him to make his plans happen. I pray that he'll become a believer in the future. Come to think of it, we sure could use him and his plane. Hmm...it sounds to me like he may be another part of God's plan. We need to start praying for him now! I think he kind of looks like a Smyrnian, don't you? He may not know what is about to hit him."

"And don't forget the calming of the storm," said Anders in his soft spoken voice. "You need to read that story Blake. You too Beth. I read it. I have read the New Testament through twice since I put my faith in Jesus. When you read Matthew, Mark, Luke and John it is hard to see why I didn't trust him before. Who wouldn't have faith in a Savior like him? That story is in Matthew chapter eight. Read it! Then in Matthew chapter fourteen he did it again, except this time he walked on the water, right up to the boat the disciples were in. We have a God who calms storms and walks on water. We are going see things that blow our minds. Seven years full of miracles. And if we don't make it, others who have believed in Jesus will see them. This is going to be quite a ride."

Evan, Ally and John had stayed up all night talking, planning and praying. Now they were anxious to hear from their comrades. They had expected them to call after they had visited the property. Finally, John could wait no longer.

"I'm calling," he said.

"Maybe we should wait until we hear from them," said Evan.

"I can't do it. I have to know." He picked up his phone and called Blake. No answer.

"I'm concerned about them," said Ally. "They should have called before now."

"Let's pray for them," said Evan. And that is what they did. They bowed their heads and started praying immediately. Their prayer was interrupted. Evan's phone buzzed. He said, "It's Blake." They looked at each other in amazement. How many times would this happen? How many times would God answer their prayers instantaneously, even as they were praying? They did not know how many times, but they knew in their minds it would happen again and again. And they knew it was something they would never grow tired of seeing.

"Blake! What took you so long? We've been waiting and waiting. We were afraid something had gone wrong. I'm sorry. I guess I should have said 'hello' and let you talk some too. I'll put the phone on speaker and let Ally and John join our conversation."

"That's okay, Evan. Don't worry about it. Hello everyone. It has been an eventful morning to say the least. I can't talk long. We're about to begin our descent into New York. We just saw a miracle! We encountered some of the worst turbulence either of us has ever seen. The plane was shaking, lurching and bumping. Then we were hit by lightning. The pilot said we weren't going to make it and he would have to set the plane down somewhere. He was on the radio trying to find the nearest airport where we could land. If he didn't find one, I think a crash landing was in order. He saw no way of escaping the storm we were in. He knew it was coming but thought we could make it through it. But it was so bad, there was no way. Anyway, the three of us started praying, asking Jesus to calm the storm. I had heard Christians talk about that happening in the Bible. Right in the middle of our prayer, the storm stopped! The pilot told us we had gone from one of the darkest, roughest storms he had ever flown in, to clear blue skies and calm air. It was amazing! I have a feeling we are going to see a lot of things like that in the days to come."

"Guess what? The same thing just happened here. We were concerned about you guys so we started praying too. And before I had said three sentences, you called. I suppose we had better get used to being amazed, because I think we all know by now that we have an amazing God!"

"Blake, this is John."

"I know it is you, John. I could hardly mistake your voice for Ally's."

"I would hope not. She is much prettier than me too." Blake could almost see John smiling and Ally blushing, even from 800 miles away. "Come on man. We want to hear about the property. What did it look like? Will it work as our safe place and for the bunkers? Is it far enough removed from the populated areas? Describe it for us. We're all anxious to hear about it!"

"Wow. Why don't you just ask me a few questions? Even if I had time, I'm not sure I could answer all of those. I know you are beyond anxious to hear all about it, but we're getting ready to land. I need to turn my phone off. Don't worry. We'll send you the video as soon as possible after we land. Okay, I have to go. Talk to you later."

"Blake!" John yelled. No answer. The call had been disconnected. "Come on now, Blake. Don't do that to us. We need to know. We want to see the property. Evan, I guess this shows us why it's going to be so important for us to stay connected and know each other's every move in the future. Looks like you have your work cut out for you."

Evan nodded in agreement as he shook his head in disappointment at being left hanging by Blake and the others. He tried to remain calm, but he was going as crazy as John on the inside wanting information about the farm.

Blake, Beth and Anders had to admit, they were glad to feel the wheels of the plane touch the runway. Blake looked at the time. It was 11:15 a.m. "Made it!" he thought to himself. He needed to call Ben. As they were moving toward the gate, he grabbed his phone and hit speed dial. Ben answered on the first ring.

"Blake, where are you? Did you make it?"

"We're on the ground and will be getting off the plane any minute. Anders and I will head over to my place, grab showers, get dressed and get to the UN building ASAP. You know how quickly I can make that happen."

"I do indeed. I know it was hard for you to pull this off, but I really appreciate you getting back here. There has been no announcement yet, although one is expected by late afternoon. I will make sure the studio is aware that they can expect you to be on the air soon."

"I'll get there as fast as I can with Anders by my side. I'll try to talk to a few people and get a feel for the process and for everyone's feelings about what has gone on. Then I'll call the studio and let them know when we are ready."

"Thanks, Blake. I know this is a crazy time, but somehow we will find time to watch your video within the next few days. I can hardly wait to see what you have found."

"You got it Ben. I look forward to our *date*." He tried to chuckle at that, but on the inside, he dreaded that meeting and the potential consequences that could come from it. At the same time, he also had hopes of a potential miracle that could happen in Ben's life, as well. But admittedly, his fear of the consequences outweighed his hope of Ben believing in Jesus and becoming possibly the most important member of the Smyrnians. He knew he could not control the outcome of the meeting, so he would make sure the whole group was praying during the entire time they met.

"Let's go Anders. We have to move fast. Beth, I'll see you at the UN. Remember, we need to keep our relationship secret for now. But even as I am reporting, my eyes will be on you. And Beth...I love you." Was it the first time he had said those words? He could not remember.

"Oh Blake, I love you too," said Beth as she embraced him tightly. Neither wanted to let go.

Anders brought the embrace to an end. "Mushy, mushy," he said. "All this twitterpation. I sure will be glad when we can get you two married. By the way, what are you waiting for?"

Blake and Beth looked at each other. "He's right," said Beth. "What *are* we waiting for?"

"Good question," said Blake. "I have never liked to wait." They smiled at each other and walked away. Blake gave Anders a friendly punch on the shoulder.

"Thanks for opening that door for me, buddy. I think it is time I proposed!"

CHAPTER 24

It was not yet daylight in Germany, but Bruno Fromm was up and sitting alone in the kitchen. He had taken some time to read his Bible. He was never a reader, but he was finding that he had a hunger for scripture which intensified every time he opened the book. He was learning but felt like a baby when it came to understanding what he was reading. At times, it was clear and really touched him deeply on the inside. Other times, he did not get it and struggled to see what it had to do with him. But he asked God for guidance every time he read. It was strange to the big, burly gruff German to feel like a baby. But he understood why he did. He prayed briefly. Prayer was still a learning curve for him too. Before Jesus, B.J. as he liked to call it, he would have laughed at people who were "talking to themselves" or simply "talking into the air." But now, when he prayed, he felt like Jesus was sitting right beside him. He had begun to crave that too.

"Jesus, I need to know the names of people you want me to talk to. I know everybody out there needs you, but I also know there are some people that you have ready to listen to the truth about you. And some of them are people you want to be a Smyrnian. And I believe there is someone, or maybe a lot of someones, you know can help us financially if they believe in you. I need to know who they are, Jesus. Please let me know."

With that he picked up a piece of paper and a pen and began to make a list of names. Family members were first. He was sure they would think he had lost his mind. His family had always been staunchly unbelievers when it came to Christianity. But if they could see the video, it would surely make them think about what had happened, an event they still referred to as the *Invasion*. He knew he had struggled with it himself, even after seeing things so clearly pointed out by a preacher who had laid it all out in advance, and it had happened exactly as he had said it would. When all was said and done, he could not deny it. But it had still taken his conversation with Professor Baldwin (John, he had to start calling him John now that they were fellow believers), himself a former hard-core atheist, to bring him to the faith. Now he was sold out, his life and everything about it given to Jesus. Names began to come into his mind. He could even see their faces as they did. A few surprised him but he wrote them down anyway. God was giving him the names. He knew it. He did not hear his audible voice (or did he?) but the names, the faces, kept coming. Before he knew it, he had a list two pages long. His only question now was, where did he begin? "I guess I will just start at the top of the list," he thought. "After all, God probably gave them to me in the order he wanted." He took a moment and prayed for each name, speaking it out loud but softly so as not to wake Mila and the boys. He had also noticed that he saw her through new eyes. He loved that woman like he had never loved her before. He had seven years left to show her and eternity to be with her. This following Jesus thing was pretty amazing!

Ben Abramson sat in his office thinking about the events of recent days. How his life had changed. How the world had changed. It seemed like people had relaxed somewhat and lost the fear that another invasion could happen. Many were still in mourning, but life had returned to normal, if you could call life as it was now, normal. He was glad Blake had returned. He had to help the man get his head on straight and make sure he was not just chasing squirrels as he followed what he saw as leads or research. And then there was the Beth thing. That was dangerous, but he knew he could not stand in the way of their relationship, if it was truly that. Maybe it would play itself out, or maybe it would not. Either way, he had to find a way to keep Blake grounded and focused on his work. He had seen many a good reporter fall by the wayside because of things like this. Not that it would ever happen to Blake Thompson. He had never seen anyone as committed to what he does as Blake. But back to the recent events. It felt like something was not right. He could not put his finger on it. Surely these United Nations happenings were a part of it. Who would the new Secretary-General be? How would his leadership affect the nations of the world? Would he work to bring peace, or would he create division? And how in the world did Secretary Pieters die? How did that happen? No witnesses. Missing video footage. What was the world coming to? His mind ran with so many thoughts that he finally had to shut it off. He heard someone say, "Blake Thompson will be live with us soon. You will not want to miss his report." Oh yes, the TV was on. Now things felt right again. "Come on, Blake. Do your thing, just like you always do. That is why this network's news has been voted the best for 5 years in a row. It is you, Blake. Help us get to the bottom of this. Help *me* get to the bottom of this. The world needs you."

It felt good to Blake to be preparing to report the news again. The trips, the meetings, they were what he needed to be doing right now. But reporting the news, it is what he did. It is what he was born to do. He felt his pulse quicken and an excitement in his mind as he began to conduct interviews and piece a story together. He had spoken with a few people who had been present when Secretary Pieters was assassinated. What they described was humanly impossible. It had to have been produced by supernatural means. No human being could stop time, in spite of people who spoke of moments when time stood still. That was only a metaphor for events that held special meaning to those people. But in this instance, it appeared that time really had stood still. It's like those movie experiences when everyone suddenly freezes as they are while one person keeps moving until they have done something no one is supposed to see. Then the others are released from their spells and continue from where they had been stopped. He had no answers for that. And he certainly could not tell the waiting public what he believed he knew about the man who would be chosen as Pieters' successor. He had left a message for his best source, the one who revealed the information to him about the so-called *Invasion*. His phone rang.

"It's good to talk to you, Blake. We haven't spoken since the big day. This is another big day. I'm not sure I have much for you. No one knows how the assassination happened. It makes no sense. But my source on the inside says Messai is the leading candidate among the council to be Pieters' successor. She is extremely reliable. If she says it, you can definitely take it to the bank."

"Messai? I'm up on world leaders, but I don't recognize that name. Did I hear you right? Spell it for me."

"M-e-s-s-a-i. Just like it sounds. He has just come on the scene. Honestly, I doubt that anyone, including other dignitaries, has heard of him. How he was even mentioned, I have no idea."

"Who is he? Where is he from? What do you know about him?"

"Not much. He is apparently from the Middle East, of Arabic descent and of the Islamic faith, but he has recently relocated to Europe and was appointed as an ambassador to the UN last week. I don't even know what country he is representing. This is all a shocker to everyone. It's unprecedented that someone so new to the world scene, so unknown, could even be considered. But I hear he was nominated by the ambassador from Italy and supported by ambassadors from Saudi Arabia, Iraq, Iran, Egypt,

Afghanistan and others. It appears he's the popular choice because he's a fresh face and a proponent of peace, especially in the Middle East. If he can bring that to pass, he'll be a hero and a leader like the world has never seen."

Blake was certain that last part was true. "Do I have your permission to share that on the air? No one else has even mentioned the name of a possible successor. I never want to violate our agreement or damage our relationship, but I sure would like to break that news first."

"Of course, you can. You know I'll relish hearing that coming from you. But you owe me one, or should I say another?"

"You can be sure that you will be rewarded for this one! You have no idea how much I appreciate you and how much I value our relationship. Thank you for always, and I do mean *always*, coming through for me."

Blake was ready to hit the air with this. But as he prepared to let the studio know he and Anders were ready, something popped into his mind. His source needed to be a part of the Smyrnians! Talk about a spy. Ally would be a good one, he was sure. But this guy was totally under the radar. No one knew who he was, except Blake. His identity was as secret as secret could be. He could get on the inside and gather information like no one else. He was now on Blake's list. The time would come for their conversation, or maybe for the source to watch a video.

Another thought hit Blake's mind. Beth. He felt bad if he *one-upped* her on this one. He did not want to hurt her in anyway. But being the first to break big stories was the name of the game in the news industry. Hopefully, she would not be upset by this. And hopefully the time would come soon when neither of them would have to worry about things like that anymore. There she was. He saw her out of the corner of his eye, looking as professional and beautiful as ever. She was going about her work, as she always did. It was time for him to go on the air. Back to work, Blake.

Word came from the news desk: "Blake Thompson is live outside the United Nations building in Manhattan. Blake, I think you have some breaking news for us."

"Yes, I do. I have just been given the name of the person who is the likely candidate to be nominated by the Security Council."

Ben sat straight up in his chair. How did he do that? No one could know that name until the council came out and made the recommendation to the Assembly. No one, that is, but Blake Thompson. His source on this had to be incredible. He just hoped he was right.

"My sources tell me the potential new Secretary-General of the UN will be a virtually unknown ambassador named Aissa Messai. He is so new to the world scene that no one seems to even know what country he represents. All I can tell you about him is that he is from the Middle East, of Arabic descent and of the Islamic faith. He has recently, as in within the last week or two, relocated to Europe and was quickly appointed as an ambassador for one of the European countries. Again, we don't even know which country. According to my sources, he was nominated by the ambassador from Italy and supported by ambassadors from Saudi Arabia, Iraq, Iran, Egypt, Afghanistan and others. It appears he's the popular choice because he's a fresh face and a proponent of peace, especially in the Middle East." Blake was reading directly from his notes as they had been given to him by his source.

"Blake, let me make sure I have the name right. You said, Aissa Messai? Is that correct?"

"Yes. It is spelled A-i-s-s-a M-e-s-s-a-i. As you know, one of the major roles of the Secretary-General is that of diplomacy. I can only conjecture that his views on peace in the Middle East, and indeed in the world at large, is the greatest reason for his consideration."

"I would guess that you are correct about that, Blake. How else could such a relative unknown be nominated for such an important position that has so great an impact on world affairs?"

"The world has been under such duress for the past couple of weeks. It would seem to me that the council is searching for someone who comes from outside the political establishment. Someone who will bring calm during the storm, if you will." (Blake knew the only real person who could do that was Jesus, even as he said it. But he also knew this man could bring a false sense of peace, if he were indeed who Blake believed him to be.) "As the world remains in shock from the events of September 11 and lives in fear of another such event, people are looking for someone who will bring a positive message. A message of hope and peace. A message that unites rather than divides. Someone who can walk down both sides of the aisle and bring world leaders together. That seems impossible in a world that is so torn by war. It seems impossible in the chaos that currently exists in humanity. But I would think the council is trying to send a clear message that they have the world's best interest at heart. That they care about what people are going through. That they truly desire for the nations of the world to be the *United* Nations, something they have never been."

"Good thinking, Blake. I would agree with you as I hear what you say. Now let's send it over to our panel of experts to see what they have to say about that. Blake, stay tuned and we will be back with you at the top of the hour. We will be anxious to hear what else you may have uncovered. And by the way, should there be word of the council coming out and meeting with the General Assembly to make their nomination, we will certainly interrupt all other coverage and come back to you for coverage of that. As you know, whoever the council nominates has to be approved by a two-thirds majority for the nominee to be confirmed and appointed."

"That is correct. It will be interesting to see how the full General Assembly feels about Messai, if he indeed is the nominee. I will remain on the scene for this all-important decision when the announcement is made. This is Blake Thompson sending it back to you in the studio."

Blake knew that he and Anders had some time before he would be back on the air, unless the council emerged to make their nomination to the General Assembly. They chatted briefly as his eyes scanned the throng of news media and onlookers for the one person he was interested in, Beth Jennings. There she was! It appeared that she was in the middle of a down time too, so he walked over to her and they stepped away from the crowd.

"Blake, how did you know about Messai? I have some good sources, but none of them knew anything about him."

"Just suffice it to say that I have one source that I can count on every time. He has never been wrong and has never let me down. I'm lucky to have found him. Hope you aren't upset with me for revealing that without telling you."

"Of course not. That is the news. It is how it works. You have always seemed to *one up* me, but you have to admit, there have been a few times when I was ahead of you!"

"Yes, there have. That used to drive me crazy, but no more. Besides, this is our job, for now. We both know the day will come when we're found out and will be on the run for our lives. But we'll still be reporting the news, only for a different reason. If it weren't for the fact that our names get us on the inside, I'd be tempted to go ahead and quit so we can get on with it! How about you?"

"So would I. But you're right. We need to be on the inside for now. We can gather information that will not only benefit the team but be vital to the millions of people who need to hear it."

"Let me tell you what came to my mind earlier when I got off the phone with my source. I think Jesus may have put this thought there for me. If my source can come to faith in Jesus, imagine what a spy he can be for us! He and Ally can work together. She can learn from him, if her dad is right about her potential as a spy. He could be dead wrong. We'll find out soon enough.

But this guy, I am telling you, there are no walls he can't penetrate. No secrets he can't discover. No information he can't get. He and I have a good working relationship. It will be dangerous reaching out to him, as it is with most people. He could blow the whistle on us in a heartbeat. But on the other hand, if he will hear me out, or watch a video, he will be a valuable Smyrnian!"

"Great thinking Blake! We need to think in those terms with everyone we know. Some have so much potential that we need to target them for the team. We just have to be careful not to compromise ourselves and the others as we do."

"You're right. You may have to hold me back or temper my boldness at some points. But you and I? We are a team, much more so than the others. While we are talking about that, can you meet me for dinner this evening? Assuming we can both find a few free minutes, that is. I know we'll be working, but maybe we can find time for a quick bite. Meet me down by the waterfront in one of the grassy areas at 5:00. I have something I want to run by you. Is it a date?"

"It is a date, Mr. Thompson." She chuckled, bringing back memories from their first date.

"If either of us gets busy or the announcement is made, let's call. You know my phone will be on, so call me if you need to. But please don't need to." He smiled at her. She grabbed his hand and smiled back. She mouthed the words, "I love you." He mouthed them back to her. Love was definitely in the air, and it was the best thing Blake had ever felt. Right up there with giving his life to Jesus, he thought to himself.

As each of them walked away and back to work, Blake felt his phone vibrating again. It was Ben.

"Blake, how do you do it? How in the world did you get the news about Messai? No one, but no one knew that. Yet, you did. How?"

"Let's just say I have my sources, Ben. And you know as a good newsman, I will never divulge who they are. A reporter's mole is one of the most important people in his or her life. We take care of them and protect their identity at all cost. How do you think I knew about the disappearances being identified as an alien invasion before anyone, including the President of the United States, had announced it? My source. How did I know about Messai? Same source. Invaluable..."

"Well, I just want to tell you that you've cracked some pretty big cases through the years, but these two have been your biggest ever, in my opinion. However you do it, keep it up. I sure am glad to have you back in the saddle.

I am blown away that you could fly in here and by all appearances be behind in the game on a story this big and within two hours be the one to break the biggest story in the world. Are you sure you didn't already have a heads up while you were in Chicago?"

"I'll never tell, Ben. Hmm... But I will say that you know I knew nothing about this until I answered your call in Chicago. Now, I can tell you that I knew nothing until right before I broke the news live on the air. I'm a true bloodhound. Remember?"

"I remember. Now, get back to work. I will be watching!"

"Back to work it is, Ben. Thanks for calling. It is good to know I am appreciated."

With that, he was back on the job. The consummate newsman, that is who he was. The one to break the news, to pull off the surprises, to capture the attention of the people. That was Blake Thompson: newsman, bloodhound, reporter, Smyrnian, follower of Jesus. That last title was his most important. As he walked back toward the UN building, he felt inside the pocket of his suit coat to make sure the item was still there. Yes, there it was. He felt it. It would be revealed soon. And that revelation was sure to be an unforgettable moment!

CHAPTER 25

Ally had returned to her room and tried to lie down and get some sleep. As she did, one word kept coming to her mind: *spy*. Me, a spy? I am not a spy, she thought. She drifted off to sleep. But it was restless sleep. She dreamed. She was a secret agent engaged in espionage. In one dangerous situation after another, she escaped to bring secret information back to her team, allowing them to know the enemy's every move. Then she finally found herself trapped, caught and brought before the evil leader. She was sentenced to die by beheading. With her hands bound and her head secured in the guillotine, she heard the blade released. Just before it hit her neck, she woke up in a cold sweat, shaking with fear. She got out of bed, not wanting to take a chance on the dream recurring.

Was her dad, right? Had she been a spy her whole life? Her mind wandered back to childhood. A friend of the family had called and accused her little brothers of stealing some things from their home as they were there playing with their son. Her dad had brought the boys in and with his face blood red demanded they tell him the truth. They vigorously denied the charges. Bruno had called the accuser and yelled at him for wrongfully blaming his sons. That night Ally had climbed on the roof outside her brothers' window and watched as they sorted through the items they had taken. She saw them place the things in a box hidden in the back of their closet. They were not much, quite invaluable and unimportant. But they had stolen them, nonetheless. She went straight to her father and told him what she had seen and where to look. He stomped to the boys' room, opened the closet door and pulled the box from the back, finding the stolen items inside. He marched her brothers to the friend's house and made them confess, apologize and return the stuff. He then ate crow and apologized for his own actions. When they got home, she had never seen him whip them so hard.

They literally could not sit down for at least two days. That was not the only time she had played the role of spy against her brothers.

Then there was the situation with Sophie stealing her tennis racket when they were in high school. She had walked the halls, hidden around corners and listened to other students talk. She talked with a few privately herself and continued her investigation until the finger was pointed squarely at Sophie. When there remained no doubt, she had confronted her former friend in the hallway when it was filled with students and teachers. Sophie had tried to deny the charges, but when Ally presented the evidence, and brought a witness to testify against her, she confessed, went to her locker and produced the racket. It had ended their friendship, but Ally had prevailed.

Maybe her dad was right. Maybe she was a spy. Come to think of it, she enjoyed it. But was it even biblical? She pulled up a Bible concordance online and searched for the word *spy*. It was there! She got her Bible and read a story from Joshua chapter two. Joshua, the leader of Israel, sent spies into the Land of Canaan to check out the city of Jericho before they crossed the Jordan River and attacked it. The spies went and stayed at the house of a prostitute named Rahab. These were supposed to be men of God and they went to stay with a prostitute? Why would they do that. Ally knew! Only a fellow spy would know that. Rahab was a prostitute. Men went to her house. Everybody knew that. Men who were visitors to Jericho would typically find their way to the prostitute's house. They went there because no one would suspect them of being spies. They were just men who went where so many other men went. Ally understood that. And when they were found out, as almost always happens, Rahab hid them and helped them escape. "Maybe I *am* a spy," Ally thought. There was no question. She was definitely a spy. Espionage! She may have much to learn, but she was ready to start spying for Jesus!

Evan's phone rang. It was Ally. "Evan, I *am* a spy! That is who I am!"

"You are what?" Evan stammered.

"A spy. I'm a spy, just like daddy said."

"You didn't take that seriously, did you? I may have agreed, but it was only for the moment and the sake of not wanting to disagree with your dad. He is pretty intimidating, you know."

"As I thought about it, God reminded me of things from my past. I'm not just a spy. I'm a good spy, Evan. God also led me to a Bible story in the Old Testament about the leader of Israel, Joshua, sending spies to check out the city of Jericho before they attacked it. I read the story and understood why they did what they did. Most people wouldn't get it, but I got it!"

"Got what, Ally? Slow down. You're going too fast."

"The prostitute, Evan."

"The what? Now you are confusing me. What prostitute?"

"Rahab was her name. The spies went to her house and she hid them. Do you know why?"

"No, Ally, I don't know why. They were spying for God. Why would they go to the house of a prostitute? That doesn't sound very godly to me."

"Because no one would suspect them, Evan. No one would suspect them because that is where men went, to Rahab's house."

"Oh, I hadn't thought about that."

"Of course, you hadn't. Do you know why? You don't think like a spy. But I do! I get it. And when the spies were found out, Rahab protected them and helped them escape. Then later they saved her and her family when the Israelites destroyed the city. I'm going to be a spy for Jesus, for the Smyrnians, Evan. I'm ready. I may not be a professional spy, but I know how to spy. I know how to get on the inside and gather information, then bring that info back to the team. I have no question. I am meant to be a Smyrnian spy."

"Okay Ally. You're a spy. You will be a spy. I'm good with that. But I can't bear the thought of you getting hurt. Spies get hurt, you know. They get killed."

"So, we're all going to be in danger every day for the next seven years, if we survive that long. I don't want to sit around and do nothing. I'm like my daddy. I want to be in the thick of the action! I had a dream, Evan, right before God showed me the stories from my past and the story of the spies in the Bible. It was very real. I was a spy and was captured by the enemy. The evil leader sentenced me to death by beheading. They bound my hands and placed my neck in the guillotine. I heard the blade release, but just before it hit me, I woke up. I was cold and clammy and sweaty. Yes, I was afraid. But I believe God showed me through that dream that He will protect me as I do what he has called me to do. There will be some terrifying moments, but in those moments, he will be with me and protect me. I will be like the invisible woman." She laughed.

Evan laughed too. But inside he was crying for the things his closest friend would have to face during the next seven years. One thing he knew: he would be there for her in every way he could.

It was ten minutes before 4:00 and Blake was sitting on one of the grassy areas outside the United Nations Headquarters by the waterfront. A modest, but intentional dinner sat in front of him. Shortly after his arrival, Beth joined him and asked, "May the lady sit down?"

Blake stood and pretended to pull back a chair. "Please sit here. The gentleman would be honored by your presence."

Beth smiled and sat next to him on the grass. "This is so beautiful," she said. "Absolutely perfect. The lady wishes to thank the gentleman for inviting her to dinner."

"Come on now, you know we are past that formal stuff. It's Blake to you."

"I know that. I was just recalling our first date at the little coffee shop."

"So was I. May I serve dinner?"

"You may."

"For you, a white chocolate latte with extra whipped cream."

"Oh Blake, you remembered!"

"How could I forget? The events of that night are forever etched in my memory. Thus, I have my usual *red eye* to drink. After all, I may need it before this night is over."

Beth took a sip of her latte. "It's perfect, Blake. Just right."

"I also brought sandwiches. We need to eat too. I hope they are okay."

She took the first bite and said, "It's perfect too, Blake. You are so thoughtful."

"Nothing is too good for you, Beth. I told you that I have always admired you, not just for your work but also for your beauty. You have always been and still are the most beautiful woman I have ever seen. I've always had trouble keeping my eyes off you. I've never been able to see myself with anyone but you. I am so happy now that we are finally together."

"Me too, Blake. I'm happier than I have ever been. This should not be the time to be happy, should it? We have been left behind after the Rapture and now we face seven years of tribulation before Jesus comes back. But God has given us each other so we can be happy no matter what happens."

They finished their sandwiches and coffee and she moved over to sit right beside him and leaned on him placing her head on his chest. "You know Blake, I really don't care who sees us together now. We may as well get it out in the open."

"Beth, I brought you something else. Call it dessert."

"Blake...the sandwich and coffee were perfect. There was no need for dessert."

"Well...hopefully you will like this. It's pretty special."

"Okay, if you insist. What did you get? I promise you I will like it, whatever it is."

"Okay, close your eyes and wait."

She complied. He reached into his inside suit pocket and retrieved the item.

"Hold out your hand, Beth."

She did so. He took her hand and slowly slid the ring onto her finger.

"Beth, will you marry me? Please say yes."

She opened her eyes and looked at the beautiful diamond that gleamed on her hand. Tears filled her eyes. "Oh, Blake. Yes, yes, a million times, yes. I will. I love you so much."

Blake's heart overflowed with joy. He had dreamed of this moment. Now he had finally been brave enough to propose to Beth. And she said yes. The lady said yes! He was happier than he had ever been in his life. The next seven years with her overshadowed everything else that was going on in this crazy world in which they found themselves.

Then the magical moment came to a perfect end. Beth grabbed him and kissed him with a kiss that he wished would never end. Anders was right. It was definitely twitterpation.

Both were jarred back to reality by the sounds coming from the building behind them. The council had completed their proceedings and would soon be presenting their candidate to the General Assembly for discussion and a vote. Blake and Beth were up in a flash. One more kiss and they were on their way. It was back to work for both, very important work on a very important day. Blake sprinted into the meeting room where the assembly convened. He was warmly greeted.

"Welcome, Mr. Thompson," said the officer in charge of the door, as he pushed other lesser known newsmen and women to the side refusing them admittance. Blake found his place and watched the ambassadors from around the globe arrive and take their seats. He could feel the magnitude of this moment. It was a day and a decision that would determine the direction the world would take for the next seven years. Blake already knew what the decision would be. It had been written about 2,000 years ago in the Bible. He had read it a few days earlier.

Don't let anyone deceive you in any way, for that day will not come until the rebellion occurs and the man of lawlessness is revealed, the man doomed to destruction. He will oppose and will exalt himself over everything that is called God or is worshiped, so that he sets himself up in God's temple, proclaiming himself to be God. 2 Thessalonians 2:3-4

The Day of the Lord began after the Rapture. It was here. It was time for the man of lawlessness to be revealed. The reality hit Blake again. It had begun and he was about to witness it with his own eyes. This man would be their mortal enemy for the next seven years. But not the enemy of the Smyrnians alone, the enemy of the entire world, every person in the world, the enemy of God himself. Blake was anxious to see the face of that man, to look in his eyes and see what was there. It would be a face of peace, but it would have nothing to do with peace. He and the others must keep themselves from being captured under his spell. The world would wonder after him. They must not. "Bring him on," Blake whispered to himself. "I'm ready." He caught a glimpse of Beth sitting nearby. "*We* are ready," he thought. "And the *Smyrnians* are ready. Let's get it on!"

In Chicago, John, Evan and Ally had gathered, this time at John's house, to watch the announcement on his big screen TV. John lived alone, a divorcee whose children now lived in different states. He only saw them once or twice a year. He had snacks and drinks ready, but their interest was focused solely on the man who would soon be revealed. Each of them knew who he was, the antichrist, the man of lawlessness. All eyes were glued to the screen.

In Germany, Ally's family was doing the same thing. Bruno had said he wanted to see the face of the man he would be fighting for the next seven years. He wanted to hear the voice that would deceive the world, but would never deceive him. This was the beginning. Jesus would bring it to an end. Regardless of that, these seven years would be war, and one must know the enemy. After today, they would know him. And so would the world.

Anders was not in the meeting hall, but he was watching too. Sitting outside, waiting for his partner but never leaving him, he watched on his tablet. Like the rest of the Smyrnians, he could hardly wait to see the face of Aissa Messai. This was the man who stood opposed to everything his beloved Angie and his three kids had stood for. Now he stood opposed to Anders and the others. They would fight him with everything in their being, knowing they could not defeat him, but Jesus ultimately would. Nonetheless, they would do everything they could to stop him from wreaking havoc on the unsuspecting people of the world.

Sitting at home in his den with his wife by his side, Ben Abramson was zeroed in on his own network waiting to see who Aissa Messai was. The man no one had heard of. The man without a face, whose face would soon be known worldwide. Where was he from? How had he risen to this position so quickly? Could he help the world recover from the utter devastation of the *Invasion*? There was so much uncertainty. Ben did not know what the future held. But somehow he knew it would be greatly affected by the man who would soon be introduced.

The assembly had reconvened. The president called the meeting to order and began his opening remarks. The entire assembly felt the magnitude of the moment as he spoke.

"Due to the brutal assassination of Secretary-General Pieters, we are gathered for this special and urgent session, and for the business which is being conducted at this time. There are many important items on our agenda, which we have been debating up to this point. But the events of yesterday have made it necessary to table all of them, in light of the all-important decision that now faces us. I want to express the deep grief felt by myself and every representative of our member nations at the horrific murder of the Secretary-General. I also want to send our thoughts and well wishes to his family. A tragedy such as this affects not only the United Nations but the entire world. It is a direct assault on the very peace the UN seeks so desperately to promote and uphold. We do not take it lightly. And yet is necessary for this assembly to now undergo the process of appointing a new Secretary-General to fill the remaining two years of Secretary Pieters term. The Security Council has deliberated throughout the day and night. Now they have reached a decision concerning the person who shall be nominated to this vital position. Without further ado, I would like to introduce the chairman of the Council to formally submit their nomination for the next Secretary-General of the United Nations. I remind you that this will be a defining moment for a world torn by tragedy. It is my desire that we as a group will come together in the spirit of unity that defines the purpose of this body in this election process. And it is my wish that this decision will somehow help to bring hope and peace in troubled times."

The Smyrnians knew it would. But they also knew that hope and peace would be short-lived.

He continued, "I now recognize Mr. Kahn to come and present the council's nomination."

The assembly was as quiet as it had ever been. An eerie silence filled the big, beautiful assembly hall. Blake could feel it, and he could tell by looking at Beth, she did too. He thought to himself, surely the other members of the General Assembly must feel the same. The chill that ran down his spine was unmistakable. It was what the world had felt the night of the Rapture. It was what he had felt during each of his two critical phone conversations with Ben. This time it filled an entire room. Something evil and sinister was about to happen. This was also to be a day like no other. Ambassador Kahn stepped to the podium.

"Good evening ladies and gentlemen of the Assembly. While we rue the reason that has led us to this moment, the members of the Security Council still understand the necessity of fulfilling our purpose of nominating a candidate for the position of Secretary-General of the United Nations. It is our belief that we must seek for a person who can ably fill the shoes of Secretary-General Pieters, who shares his vision and will work as he did to make it a reality. A person who will take up the banner of freedom and carry it proudly, who will work jointly with all nations to bring about peace and allow our children to live in a world without war, who will strive to bridge even the deepest divide that exists between countries and people. We did not take this decision lightly or make it quickly. We deliberated throughout a day and night, without pause. At this time, I would like to express my sincerest appreciation to the members of the Council for their tireless efforts and their commitment to the purpose and work of the United Nations. It goes without saying that each of us is exhausted. However, we come before you today confident that the individual we have selected to fill the role of Secretary-General is the right person for this day and hour, as well as for the future. We feel certain that he will lead in such a way that the world will follow. He is a man of peace, a man of purpose and the leader the world needs for this crucial hour. That man is Aissa Messai. We recognize that many of you have not heard of Ambassador Messai or have knowledge of his previous service. That is one of the reasons we chose him. He is not a member of the long-standing establishment, which includes many of us who have failed to achieve the goals of the United Nations at large, namely the peace and prosperity of the world. However, he shares that common goal with us, and the Council has faith in his ability to finally accomplish it. Simply put, he wants to bring peace to the world. Never in history has there been a time when that is as needed so desperately as it is needed now. Mr. Messai is a native of the Middle East and is a committed Muslim. But he is also a friend of Jews and believes the two can live at peace because of their common heritage and ancestry. In fact, he believes peace can be achieved in the world since the entire human race shares a common bond of humanity. It naturally follows that his primary objectives are the same as ours: peace and security, human rights, economic development and humanitarian assistance. Mr. Messai currently resides in Belgium where he has just been named as an ambassador from that country. The Security Council proudly nominates Ambassador Aissa Messai for the position of Secretary-General of the United Nations."

CHAPTER 26

The room was immediately abuzz following the council's introduction and nomination of Ambassador Aissa Messai. There were shouts of, "We don't even know this man!" and "How do we know we can trust him?" followed by others yelling, "Give him a chance! He's the kind of man we need!" The President pounded a gavel on his desk and called for order. When the room finally quieted, he spoke again.

"Before our deliberations begin, Mr. Kahn has informed me that Ambassador Messai is prepared to stand before us and speak to the things that are dear to him. This way, all of us will have the opportunity to hear him for ourselves. I met him briefly prior to the beginning of our session this evening. He seems to be a delightful gentleman who has a heart of love combined with strong leadership qualities befitting the position for which he is being nominated. I ask that you hear him and grant him the common courtesy of your undivided attention. I present to you Mr. Aissa Messai."

As Messai walked to the podium, he was greeted by a standing ovation from some and icy stares from others who remained in their seats. Blake was taking note of men and women who were a part of each group and listing their names for future reference when he reported on the meeting. He noticed that Beth was doing the same. As Messai came into view and could be clearly seen, Blake also took note of his features. He was a striking man, tall and handsome. His jet black hair was perfectly in place. His sleek and very expensive suit was perfectly fitted and made a bold statement about who he was, almost to the point of being intimidating. His demeanor as he walked was non-threatening but commanding. He felt welcoming and friendly. But Blake took note of his eyes. He had always believed the eyes are a window to a person's soul. He was close enough to see Messai's eyes clearly. Beyond the genuineness of his smile, his commanding walk and striking appearance, his eyes seemed to burn a hole right through Blake. It was as though they could penetrate the mind and invade the soul, gaining access to everything that can be known about a person. Mesmerizing may be the word Blake would use. Possibly captivating. Even hypnotizing. As Messai neared the podium, he looked directly at him. Blake could feel the icy stare, the hypnotic glare, the burning invasion of his mind. He tried to force himself to look away but struggled to do so. The chill. It was there again, but far more intense. It was as if he was saying, "I know who you are." Fear clawed at Blake's mind. His hands shook as he tried unsuccessfully to write. Finally, Messai made it to the podium after a walk of what felt like 30 minutes but was in actuality, probably no more than sixty seconds. As he prepared to speak and looked at the crowd, Blake was freed from the trance. He glanced at Beth and saw her sitting and staring toward the front. He wanted to run over to her and snap her out of it but knew he could not. He did the only thing he knew to do. He began to pray silently and call out the name of Jesus. Aissa Messai began to speak.

"Ladies and gentlemen, it is indeed a privilege to stand before you this evening and an honor to be considered for a position of such magnitude. I have already informed the Security Council that I humbly accept their nomination. I realize many of you do not know me because I am new to the world of government and politics. That is why I want to give you a glimpse into my soul."

"As you are getting a glimpse into the souls of everyone here," Blake thought. "Well, I refuse to give you that right." He prayed, "Jesus, please put a hedge of protection around me and shield me from this evil man."

As Messai continued to speak, one could not help but notice how entrancing his voice was. When he spoke, it seemed that he captured the minds of everyone there and placed them under his spell. The onlookers sat staring blankly ahead. Blake doubted they were hearing a word the man was saying. Even the president sat in an upright position, very stiff, never moving his head or taking his eyes off Messai. The entire room was filled with people who were doing the same thing. If a picture was taken from above the podium, looking down on the crowd, it might appear that seats were occupied by mannequins who were only there to make it appear that people were present. Blake was now an observer who was free to listen and keep an eye on both Messai and the people. What he saw gave him a glimpse into what the future was going to be like for seven years. It was a frightening scene. On a hunch, he looked at Mr. Kahn, then located the ambassadors from Italy, Saudi Arabia, Iraq, Iran, Egypt and Afghanistan. His suspicions were confirmed! Each of them sat smiling and nodding in agreement with everything Messai was saying. They seemed to be fully alert, tuned in and hearing every word. But they were apparently the only ones. Blake looked again toward Beth and found her already looking at him. He breathed a sigh of relief knowing she was not, or at least was no longer, under Messai's spell. She mouthed the words, "God help us." Blake mouthed back, "He will have to."

Beth's notes may as well have been Blake's notes. They both saw, heard and felt the same things. Her mind still felt blurred after Messai had looked directly at her and seemed to look directly into her soul. His eyes betrayed something entirely different from his demeanor and appearance. She too had to pull herself away from his evil glare and pray for God's protection. She had felt the chill running down her spine and goosebumps breaking out all over her body. She knew she was in the presence of pure evil, and the world was never going to be the same again. She found herself praying, "Come quickly, Lord Jesus." But as she did, she knew his coming was seven years away. She was overcome by dread of the Tribulation but was comforted by knowing Blake would be by her side walking with her through it. Everything they faced, they would face together. "Thank you, Jesus, for giving Blake and me each other. I am so thankful that I have him, and that I have You."

The other Smyrnians were tuned in from Chicago and Germany. Their experiences were the same. It was clear to all of them that a meeting and/or conference call was needed as quickly as possible. Even though they had all known this man would be the antichrist, tonight's proceedings had confirmed that a million times over. The problem was, the world would see him not just as a savior, but as *the* Savior. It was obvious that the battle they were preparing to fight would be against a supernatural foe. Had they known that? Yes. But now they knew it in a real way. The odds were stacked against them...big time.

Ally's mind went racing back to the dream she had. She had gotten a glimpse of the enemy when she was brought before him and sentenced to death. Now she was seeing that same face again on the TV screen. The dream had not only been confirmation of God's calling for her to be a spy, it was also a glimpse into the future! She wondered to herself if it would be *her* future. She felt herself shaking. The chill that sent shivers down her spine was unmistakable. She prayed for strength to be a Smyrnian spy without fear of any consequences she may face.

John saw a man who could match his wits and knowledge. In fact, he assumed there was nothing Messai did not know. He felt himself being drawn into the TV screen to do battle with a man against whom he knew he could not prevail. As he fought the pull, he realized his own weakness in the face of one who had been given knowledge beyond the scope of human comprehension. The chill that consumed his body in that moment brought with it fear and trembling like he had never known. What he did know was that this fight would be a battle of the minds for him. But it was a battle that he was determined to somehow win. He prayed for wisdom to outmaneuver the enemy.

Evan found himself wondering how he, a 20-year old college student could defeat a man who was so far superior to him. Messai was likely to be confirmed as a leader who would be looked up to by the entire world as the one who could provide the answers humanity was seeking following a devastating catastrophe. Beyond that, he was also a servant of Satan who received his power from the prince of the power of the air. He was powerless in the face of that, apart from the strength of the all-powerful God! The chill that filled him was something no source of earthly heat could overcome. He needed supernatural strength of his own to win the battle over an otherworldly enemy. He asked Jesus to give it to him.

In Germany, as the Fromms watched, Bruno found himself afraid of another man for the first time in his life. Messai seemed larger than life to him. The big hulk of a man felt like a dwarf cowering before the enemy. He felt fear. He felt a chill that shook him and refused to go away. He prayed for the power of the Lord to be his strength rather than his own. Mila simply sat next to her husband clutching his arm. "I am afraid," she said softly. "So am I," he replied. It was the first time she had heard those words come from his mouth. She silently prayed for him, and for her, the boys, Ally and all the Smyrnians. Their sons were preoccupied with other things and were not watching the broadcast. Bruno and Mila feared for them as they watched them innocently playing games and having fun. They knew the world would be brutal for them as they faced the days to come. They would protect them as best they could and would do their best to turn them into warriors for Jesus, even though they knew it could be a death sentence for them.

And then there was Ben Abramson. Miriam was tending to sick children as he watched alone. She came into the room to find him staring blankly at the television and not moving. She ran to him fearing he had experienced a heart attack and died. Even her screaming at him and shaking him could not break the trance into which he had been lured. It was minutes before she was finally able to get through to him. Standing in front of him and blocking his view of the TV screen was the only thing that worked. Still he sat mesmerized by the sound of the voice coming from the large screen on the wall. The man speaking seemed larger by far than their seventy-inch screen. She found herself sitting down beside her husband and soon caught up in the trance as well. A chill filled the room, but they were unaware of its presence.

Finally, Messai finished speaking. It was time for the Assembly to consider the Council's recommendation and nomination. It became apparent very quickly that his appointment would not happen without a fight. There were 193 member countries, or states as they were called. Thus, approval of Messai as the new Secretary-General would require 129 votes in favor. Blake suddenly realized something. A two-thirds majority was necessary to elect Messai. Two-thirds is a fraction. The decimal of that fraction, he thought to himself, is .666. Six, six, six. The number of the antichrist given in the Book of Revelation! It was no accident that the antichrist was rising to power through the international alliance known as the United Nations with an approval requirement of .666 percent. Some would find humor in attempting to see significance in such trivial details. But Blake knew in his heart at that moment this entire moment had been planned by God. He who had prophesied about the events of the end of days already knew how those events would unfold, even to the most minute details. He took comfort in knowing the all-knowing God was on their side.

It became abundantly clear that two sides were developing in the decision which was about to be made and that it would not happen quickly, and likely not decisively. The pro-Messai side was led by Kahn, European ambassadors from France and Italy, and Middle Eastern ambassadors from Saudi Arabia, Iraq, Iran, Egypt and Afghanistan. They spoke calmly and persuasively, imploring the group to fulfill the duties which had been given them and appoint Aissa Messai to the position of Secretary-General of the United Nations. To fail to do so, they said, would be negligent and a breaking of the trust which had been placed in them by the very countries they represented.

The leaders of the anti-Messai contingent stood vehemently opposed to his appointment. Blake noticed that they were relatively few in number compared to the pro forces. Others were nothing more than a "band wagon" contingent who had been supported by the others in the past. Apart from that, it seemed they had no "dog in the fight." Their input was little more than words in support of the leaders' arguments and were spoken so low they were almost inaudible. The few who were in leadership of the anti-camp, though, were extremely vocal, nearly to the point of being ready to go toe-to-toe with the pro forces and fight. Blake feared if things were not mediated properly, that could happen. The leader of the opposition group was so critical of Messai that he was nearly violent. He had to be held back by the others. But fortunately, at just the right time, an interruption came in the proceedings when the president made a statement calling for adjournment.

"Ladies and gentlemen of the assembly: It is getting late on Saturday evening. It is rare that we would even meet on Saturday. But in light of the special circumstances surrounding this very important time, we have come together to hear the recommendation and nomination of the Security Council for the position of Secretary-General of the UN. We have received that nomination and heard from the nominee. But taking into account the considerable debate we are experiencing between members of this body, as well as the late hour, it seems clear that we will not be able to settle the issue and hold the vote tonight. Due to tomorrow being Sunday and our usual commitment to eschew weekend meetings, I am calling for an adjournment of these proceedings until 8:00 Monday morning. I will entertain a motion to that effect."

The motion was made and seconded. A strong majority was in favor. They seemed to welcome the much needed break, an opportunity to relax and maybe even have a little fun. "The meeting is adjourned," proclaimed the president. "I ask that you please refrain from speaking about this election until we reconvene Monday morning at 8:00."

Blake could easily see that some were not happy with the president's recommendation and the decision to postpone the election until after the weekend. In spite of the admonition against discussing the situation with anyone, ambassadors were already pairing off in groups and talking. The buzz in the room sounded like a swarm of bees leaving the hive. And, Blake thought, it could be just as dangerous. He was convinced that someone was going to get *stung* before this was over. It had already happened to Secretary Pieters. And Blake's fear was that he would not be the last, possibly even before Monday. He did not like having those thoughts, but he could not avoid them. He wished he had a means of warning all the members of the assembly, but he knew that was not possible unless he ran to the microphone and made an announcement. So, he and everyone else would have to let the chips fall where they may between now and Monday. "Well, there may be another option," he thought. He could use his platform as the reporter whom most people would be watching and make a statement that

Pieters' death should serve as a warning to all the members of the General Assembly. He also knew he could not do that. Or could he...

In Chicago, Evan, Ally and John's minds were abuzz. They had so much to talk about. Cameras had been forbidden in the meeting hall following that part of the meeting so as not to show the deliberations that would ensue. "Wise idea," John thought, but he hated not seeing what happened. However, he knew both Blake and Beth were present and would give them all the details. Just as they began to talk about what they had felt, Evan's phone rang. It was Blake.

"Wow, Blake, I'm glad you called! Ally, John and I are talking about the meeting, especially Messai's speech. We can't wait to tell you what each of us saw and felt as he spoke. We wondered if you and Beth felt the same thing sitting in the room."

"I don't have time to talk, Evan. I'm walking out of the hall right now and have to report as soon as I get out. Am I right that next week is Fall Break on campus there?"

"Yep, it started at the end of Friday's classes. We don't go back until a week from this Monday. What are you thinking? Can you get back here to meet with us? I think we have a lot to talk about after what has happened in the last two days."

"There is no way Beth and I can leave here. There is far too much going on for that. But I'm hoping the three of you can come to New York for the week. That will give us an entire week to fill you in on the deliberations after Messai spoke and to talk about all this and how it affects us now and in the future. It was pretty crazy in there. And my guess is, things are about to get a lot crazier."

"I don't know if we can come to New York, Blake. I would love to! If nothing else, I would like to see the city. I've never been there. Neither has Ally. But remember that we are college students. We don't have any extra money laying around for plane tickets."

"Then don't fly; drive. You can get here in eleven to twelve hours, depending on how fast you drive. If you drive like me, you can probably make it in ten! You can stay at my place. I have plenty of room for all of you. And I assure you that you will love the view!"

"I'm ready, if the others will come! I'm not sure what John's plans are, or if he has to work over the break. Profs have to do that sometimes. Let me ask them."

John and Ally had figured out what they were talking about as they overheard Evan's part of the conversation.

"Let's go!" Ally jumped out of her seat. "I'll go and pack a few clothes right now!"

"No problem for me," said John. "I have nothing to do that can't wait until we get back. I think it is urgent that we meet. Besides, who wouldn't want to be in New York for this meeting?"

"Okay Blake, we're all in!" Evan sounded more excited than Blake had ever heard him.

"Can you get on the road tonight and take turns driving? You can be here shortly after daylight in the morning. Beth and I will be extremely busy, but we can all talk anytime we get a break. We will definitely have most of the nights free. Oh, and by the way, you guys may be interested to know that I proposed to Beth earlier today and she said yes! We aren't going to put this off. We will be husband and wife very soon!"

Evan turned to Ally and John and yelled so loudly he almost burst Blake's eardrum. "He proposed to Beth and she said yes! They are getting married and want it to happen soon!"

Blake could hear the celebration. Raucous may be the word he would use to describe what he was hearing, in a positive way, of course.

"Hey, maybe we can have the ceremony while you guys are here. Of course, I haven't asked Beth about that. I hope she will say yes again. She's as excited about getting on with the wedding as I am. The only problem I can think of is, where will we find a pastor?"

"That is a good point. Based on Beth's coverage during the quake, I am guessing that will be hard. But I hope, hope, hope you can do it! Maybe you don't need a preacher at this point after the Rapture. Maybe you can use a judge or other elected official. Or, maybe I shouldn't consider this, but do you think one of the Smyrnians could perform the ceremony? We are the followers of Jesus right now. As far as I know, we are the *only* followers of Jesus."

"First, I'll ask Beth. I'm making *no* decisions without her input. Second, maybe that's something to think about. Let's pray about it. Now again, can you guys get on the road tonight?"

"We will be on the road within the next hour. We can throw some clothes together and hop in the car. Hey, don't forget that fancy New York meal you promised us!"

"If we can find a break that will allow us to do it, the meal is yours! If we can't, I will make a reservation for the three of you, and have them bill it to me. Either way, you are on!"

"We don't want to do it without you and Beth. I really hope you can clear the time."

"Oops. I have to go. Beth is already reporting! I can't have her on the air before me. I'm off here and on the air. I will see all of you tomorrow morning. Call me when you are an hour or so out and we'll be watching for you. I will text you the address to my apartment."

Before Evan could reply, Blake and Anders were gone and back on the job. They did not have time to talk before Blake was called into action.

CHAPTER 27

From the studio: "We have Blake Thompson with us now from the UN building. Blake, you were inside for the meeting of the assembly. We got to see the initial part of the meeting, with the nomination of the Security Council by Ambassador Kahn and Aissa Messai's speech. But we weren't allowed to see the rest of the meeting and discussion of the assembly. We've heard a few things, but can you fill us in? You were in the assembly hall the entire time, weren't you?"

"Yes. First of all, you saw Messai's speech. I'd like to hear your thoughts on what you heard."

"Interestingly, we were all tuned in and listening very closely. But when the speech was over, none of us have a very good recollection of anything we heard. That is very strange."

"That is what I wanted to know. It seems that is the case for most of the people who heard him. As for me, I was listening, but I was also observing the other ambassadors. Their reactions were very interesting. They were not moving; just sitting straight up and still, almost like mannequins. In fact, that is what they looked like, mannequins. If our cameras could have captured that scene from the front, the viewing audience would have sworn the seats were filled with them to make it appear that the ambassadors were there. It was one of the most unique things I have ever seen."

"What do you attribute that to?" Blake knew but did not want to say on the air.

"I'm not sure. If I get the opportunity, I will talk with some of them and get their reactions. With the meeting suspended until Monday, I will try to speak with everyone I can. All I can say at this point is that Messai seemed to have some sort of hold over them. They were spellbound, and I do not take that term loosely. It was as if they were in a trance, mesmerized, hypnotized. I know that sounds strange, but it's how it felt in there. It was a very strange feeling."

"I agree, Blake. It sounds strange. But I have to admit, I felt some of that when the cameras showed Messai walking to the podium. And I was simply watching on television. I can only imagine what it must have felt like being there in person. What do you think that is all about? It seems the man is charismatic and, maybe charming is the word. He appears to be the kind of leader who will command attention and respect, the kind people will follow. Do you get that sense from him?"

"I do indeed. I believe people will follow him, be it for good or bad. I can only hope it is for good."

"It almost sounds like you have an inside track on Messai's record. Do you know something we don't? You always seem to know things before the rest of us."

"I don't know about that. Just let me say something doesn't feel exactly right. I can't put my finger on it. It doesn't even mean that Messai is the problem. It may be the controversy over his nomination and whether or not he can accomplish his goals with that kind of opposition and lack of support. Maybe we will know more after the discussion and vote on Monday."

"Hopefully we will. Thank you, Blake. Stand by. We will be coming back to you periodically as this story unfolds. In the meantime, we're going again to our panel of experts here in the studio."

Blake relaxed and told Anders, "Let's take a break. I will get to interviews, and more, in a little while. But for now, I'm going to catch up with Beth. I can see that she is finished for the moment too. By the way, did I tell you I proposed to her right before the assembly reconvened and we had to hurry inside?"

"No! I can't believe you waited this long to tell me! I know you had to run inside, but couldn't you at least have told me as you were running by?"

"I wanted to, but I had to get in there. It was a big moment. I couldn't afford to miss a second."

"Okay, you are forgiven. But you have to tell me now. Did she say yes? Stop toying with me. I need to know as badly as you needed to get in that room!"

"Yes, Anders. She said yes!"

Raucous celebration happened again. Anders was dancing and jumping up and down.

"I knew it! I knew it! From twitterpation to celebration. I promise you will not hear that word from me again. It has been fun, but I'm retiring it. You will be married now. I can't wait! So, when is the big event?"

"We haven't even talked about it. I think we should go ahead. Maybe this week. Then the others can be here for it too."

"Others? What others? Evan, Ally, John? Is there something else you're not telling me? Why am I suddenly the last one to hear everything?"

"Oh, come on now. You're not the last one to hear things. It's just that all of this happened so quickly. From the proposal to the meeting to rushing back out to report. I had to call them as I was running out here. Next week is Fall Break at college, and we need them here so we can talk about everything that has happened and what it means for all of us and the future. We need to make plans and get as ready as we possibly can. Things are going to be breaking fast. They're leaving now and driving straight through tonight. They should be here around daylight tomorrow morning. Then they will get to experience some of this for themselves and we will get to meet whenever Beth and I aren't working. They will be staying at my place. Why don't you stay there too? Then we can all be together. Especially if we have that wedding within a day or two! Is that wishful thinking?"

"It may be. You'll have to ask Beth and see what she says. By the way, have you thought about where you are going to find a pastor to do the wedding?"

"I wondered the same thing. There aren't any around that I'm aware of. I said that to Evan just before we got off the phone. He suggested that we have a judge or other elected official marry us, or that one of the Smyrnians do it. As he said, we are the only followers of Jesus we know of. And if there is one thing I am sure of, it is that we both want a Christian ceremony."

"I think that's a great idea. We are all new to this Christianity thing, but why not? Wait a minute, don't you have to be married by a licensed or ordained minister, or something like that, for the marriage to be recognized by the state?"

"I don't know and really don't care. I'm not sure I want it to be recognized by the state at this time. The state is going to be an evil regime that is led by an evil ruler. I say forget the state. I'd rather it be recognized by God!"

"Okay, promise me this. The others won't be here until tomorrow morning. Will you ask Beth tonight and let *me* be the first to know when the wedding will be? I *am* your best friend, remember? I would like to be the first to know about at least *one* thing."

"That, I will do. I truly am sorry if I left you out. I didn't mean to. You *are* my best friend. I appreciate you more than you know. So, I will try to get that answer for you tonight. Ah, there's Beth. I will go and see if I can get it right now!"

"I will be waiting right here and watching you two like a hawk. As soon as you get her answer, give me a nod if she says yes, or shake your head if she says you'll have to wait. I sure hope to see you look my way and nod. If you do, I'm coming over there and give both of you a great big hug!"

The Chicago contingent was loaded up and on their way to New York. It took them all of forty-five minutes after the call from Blake to grab some clothes, throw them in John's car and get on the road. Evan and Ally were giddy with excitement because neither had been to New York. It was a dream trip for both, but at the same time it was a vitally important trip for the team. Their only hope was that they would get to do some sightseeing. They wanted to walk in Central Park and stand in Times Square. The Statue of Liberty and 9/11 Memorial were definitely on the agenda. Then there was the Brooklyn Bridge and for Evan, Yankee Stadium. Their list could go on and on. Of course, New York pizza had to be on the list because the gauntlet had been thrown down. It was hard for them to keep their minds on the business at hand, but they knew they must. For now, they had twelve hours to talk, so they decided to make the most of it. They got right into an important topic.

"So, who do you guys think should perform the wedding, if one of us gets to do it?" Evan asked calmly. "None of us has ever done a wedding before."

"I thought you would do it," suggested John.

"Me? I'm too young. You are the one who has the age and wisdom. Not that I am calling you old, or anything. You just know more about things like that than Ally and me."

"It sounds to me like you *are* calling me old, Evan!"

"Now, you know what I meant Professor Baldwin. Oh, that does sound old, doesn't it?!"

"Would you two cut it out?" Ally decided to interrupt their well-intended fun. "I will just do it. Who says a girl can't perform a wedding? I have heard of ladies doing that back home."

"I have a better idea, Ally. Not that I, being the old man of the group, (he glanced at Evan with a wry grin) am any wiser than either of you. Why don't all of us, including Anders, do the wedding together? We can all have a part, and at the end, we can all pronounce them husband and wife!"

"Now, you're thinking. That is a great idea, old man." At that moment, it hit Evan who he was talking to. "I'm sorry Professor Baldwin. I know you told me to call you John. But I sure wasn't showing you any respect. Please forgive me. I was just trying to have some fun. We have a long drive ahead of us. I was trying to break up the monotony."

"You're forgiven, Evan. But I was joining you in the fun. I know how much older I am than Ally and you. That means you will have to listen to my wisdom at times when you don't want to. Wisdom comes with age. I have got that on you. But there is also something good about youth and vigor. There will be times when I will have to give you freedom to decide and act. We're a team. Now, let's do away with this professor and student relationship once again. We're on the same team, soldiers in the same army, followers of the same Lord, Jesus Christ. We have a new relationship in him. The Bible calls us brothers and sister. It's time we act like it. I'm just your older brother."

"Much older! Okay, I will stop. We are glad you're our brother. Right Ally?"

"For sure! Step on it, older brother. I want to be there by daylight!"

John did exactly that. They were headed to New York! No time to waste.

Blake worked his way through the crowd and made it to Beth. "Let's blow this joint baby," he said jokingly.

"I'm ready! Where shall we go?"

"How about back down to the waterfront? There's plenty of light and sure to be plenty of people, but that has suddenly become one of my favorite places."

"Let's go. But we had better not take long. We need to be ready to go when called on, and we need to talk to people and be as prepared as we can be."

"Hey, we can share information while we are together, can't we? That way both of us can be better prepared. And neither of us can one-up the other, unless we hear more after we talk. Then we may just have to see who is better!" He smiled at her with a "You know what I mean" kind of grin.

"Okay, you're on! So, where do we start. Which bit of information do you want to talk about first? Messai? His speech? His entrance? The ambassadors all sitting there like mannequins? How he made us feel when he walked in? The same chill we have felt before when he spoke?"

"All of the above. But it's easy to see that God showed both of us the exact same things. There are two other things I want to talk to you about before we get to all that. First, I invited the others to come and be with us all next week. It is Fall Break at the college, so all of them are free. They have already left and are driving straight through tonight. They should be here by daylight."

"Blake, that is great! With all that is happening, we need to be together. We need to talk about our feelings and Messai and what we now know after seeing and hearing him. I'm sure they were watching the coverage all the way through his speech until they ordered cameras out of the room."

"Yes, they were. I only got to speak to them briefly, but they felt all the same things you and I felt. We can talk about all that when they get here. You and I will be busy but hopefully we can find a lot of time to be with them. We can pick up where we had to leave off in Chicago. But we know a lot more now than we did at that point."

"We sure do. This will be an important time. But as important as it is for the Smyrnians, may I suggest that we also try to find some free time to let Evan and Ally see New York? I may be wrong, but I'm guessing it is the first time here for both of them."

"Absolutely. We may have to rotate shifts to show them around. But we'll do whatever it takes to ensure that they get to see the city! Hopefully, we can all tour together. That will be fun."

"Now, you said two other things. That is only one. What else is on your mind?"

"A wedding, that's what. You have said yourself we don't need to wait. To paraphrase an old saying from the south, "time's a wastin' sweetheart!"

"I said that? Are you sure? What makes you think I want a wedding so soon after I got engaged?"

"I was sure I remembered you saying that. I'm sorry if I jumped the gun. We'll wait as long as you want, even if I would rather not."

"Yes, we will, Mr. Thompson. This is my wedding, and I get to call the shots."

"Yes, ma'am. I'm sorry Beth. Please forgive me."

"Okay, you are forgiven. I say we need to wait at least three or four days."

"Well, you know I will do whatever you want. I apologize again for jumping the gun... Wait, did you say three or four days? That is what I'm hoping I heard!"

"Yes, Blake. I am so ready to be Mrs. Beth Jennings Thompson. I suppose I will need to keep my maiden name for the purpose of reporting the news. What do you think?"

"I think you can use whatever name you want. I will still know that you are my wife! And for seven years, if we survive that long, we are going to both make up for lost time and enjoy being together. I suppose I can wait three or four days, but it won't be easy! Now, to a really good thing about having our wedding this week…"

"So, the others can be here for it, of course."

"You are always one step ahead of me, Beth. Of course! They will get to be a part of our big day. And we can Skype in Bruno, Mila and the boys. It is going to be a wonderful day!"

"But have you thought about where we are going to find a pastor to do the ceremony?"

He chuckled. "Not only have I thought about it, but so has everyone else on the team."

"You mean, they already know before you even asked me?"

"I just told them I proposed and you said yes. I wish you could have heard them celebrating! So, here is our suggestion."

"You have already come up with a suggestion? Wow, you have this all planned out, don't you?"

"Well, we have an idea. I don't think we can find a pastor. There aren't any left. And I don't think we should have our wedding performed by anyone in this godless society, do you?"

"No, I don't! But if there is no pastor, and we won't have it done by a judge, what can we do?"

"I think the Smyrnians should do it. We want a Jesus-centered wedding, don't we? Then why not do it as a group? As far as we know, we may be the only Christ followers on the planet."

"Blake, that may be the best idea you have ever had. I love it!"

"So, maybe John, Anders, Evan and Ally can each have a part in it and then pronounce us husband and wife as a group at the end, right after I get to kiss my bride! I am excited about that part!"

"Stop it, Blake. You will make me blush, even though no one is listening to us. Why not let the Fromms be a part of it too, since they will be joining us online."

"Excellent idea! Hey, this is your wedding. Why don't you decide on everything else from here on out and we will do whatever you say?"

"So, now I get to make the plans, huh? You got it, buddy. This is going to be the wedding of the millennium! Celebrities and royalty will have nothing on us, except a little extravagance and pomp and circumstance. And two billion people around the world won't be watching. But our wedding with the Smyrnians being a part of it will be amazing! I have some planning to do!"

"Oops. I forgot to nod at Anders. He is watching us right over there. See him? Why don't you give him a thumbs-up instead? He wanted a sign that we will have the wedding next week. He can't wait! Sorry. I couldn't keep him from watching. He didn't find out until I had talked to the others. So, he was feeling a little left out."

"So, I'm not the only one, huh?"

"Come on, Beth. I told you I was sorry about that."

"Blake, I am only kidding. I'm just ready for our wedding. I'm glad you let the others know that I said yes and a wedding was coming. And I'm even glad you talked to them about being a part of it and they are on their way. This is going to be the best week of my life! Now, what do you say we stand up and you give Anders a big nod while I give him a big thumbs up? That ought to get him excited!"

"Before you do, I have to warn you. He said if he saw me nod, he was going to run over here and give both of us a big hug."

"I can think of nothing better. He has been hoping for this all along. He is probably almost as excited as we are. Now, let's stand up and let him know!"

They stood together, and Blake did more than nod. He shook his head up and down so hard, it felt like it might fall off. And Beth gave a double-thumbs up, jumping up and down as she did. Anders ran to them in a wild sprint, jumped into them and hugged both as tightly as he could. It felt like the celebration had already begun. All that was left was a wedding. For Beth, it was planning time. For both of them, it was now back to reporting the news. How were they supposed to do that with getting married on their minds? They would. It is what they did. They reported the news, professionals in every way. A wedding...their friends on the way...Aissa Messai...the next seven years... Life was not boring. That was one thing for sure.

CHAPTER 28

Ben was waiting to hear more from Blake. It felt like it had been forever since he was last on. While he liked hearing from the studio, he knew the inside scoop always came from his guy, his future anchor. Come on, Blake. Where are you? It was getting late, and as much as he wanted to keep up with breaking news, he knew he needed sleep. Very little was likely to happen between tonight and Monday. His mind went back to the video Blake had left him. Maybe he should just watch it on his own. After all, Blake was going to be very busy. But he had promised they would watch it together. Blake had called it a date. Maybe he should ask. He gave him a call.

"Hello Ben. What's up?"

"It seems like it has been awhile since I have heard from you on the news. How long has it been since you last reported from the UN building? An hour?"

"It hasn't been that long. I do have other research to do, you know. That is what I do. Research. How else do you think I get the jump on everyone else?"

"Since you mentioned research, that brings me to the real reason for my call. I'm thinking about that video you left with me. I know we made a date to watch it, but I was thinking while there is a break in the action until Monday, I would like to watch it. I want to get caught up with where you are on things. If you would rather I wait, I will. But tonight, while I'm sitting here alone, would be a perfect time for me."

Wow. That was not what Blake expected to hear when he saw it was Ben calling. Everything was going so well. Beth saying yes, a wedding coming up, the Chicago group on their way. The last thing he needed was for Ben to be angry with him, or worse yet, fire him. But the most important thing they needed was for Ben to say yes to Jesus and become part of the team. Maybe this was God's way of ensuring that Ben watched it alone. He sure didn't want to interfere with God's plan.

"That is fine, Ben. I'm going to be incredibly busy anyway. It would be hard to find a time when we could watch it together. Go ahead. But let me tell you before you do, it will be the most important thing you have ever watched. And remember what you promised me. You will watch it with an open mind, and you will watch it all the way to the end. No matter how badly you want to stop watching, you won't. When I first saw it, I was very angry and certainly skeptical, almost rude to the young man who showed it to me. Now I can tell you I know it is right. It has helped me with all the research I have done since seeing it and realizing it is true. Do you promise?"

"I promise, Blake. This must be very important to you. I will watch it with an open mind and hear it out. If it is research that changed your thinking and helped you do the reporting I have seen from you since September 11, it is definitely something I want to see. Can we talk about it after I watch?"

"Absolutely, Ben. Please let me know what you think as soon as you finish. If you need me to come over then, I will get there as fast as I can. I suspect you won't like what you are hearing at first, just like I didn't. But I beg you to hear the man on the video out. Think about what he is saying. It is something he predicted would happen years before it did. And it happened just as he said it would...on September 11, 2029! It is eye-opening, and for me and others, life-changing!"

"Well, if it is that important, I guess I had better get off the phone and get started, right? Keep at it, Blake. But in all sincerity, don't kill yourself. We need you, and we need you well rested and at your best. So, work hard, but be sure you get some sleep and take care of yourself."

"Thank you, Ben. I do need to remember that. These are going to be busy days. They are also going to be critical. We all need to take care of ourselves. You will understand more about what I mean after you see the video. Happy watching. I will be anxious to hear your thoughts. I hope you agree with me. I want us to always be on the same team!"

Blake called Beth. "Ben just called and asked if it is okay for him to watch the pastor's video by himself. We were going to watch it together, but he wants to watch it while he has some down time tonight. He is getting ready to watch it right now. I talked to him about it and tried my best to set him up for what he is going to hear. It's not going to be easy for a man of such deep Jewish faith to watch a video about Jesus. By the way, I called you first this time! Are you thrilled about that? I will tell Anders, then call the group driving from Chicago. We need all of us praying now! Ally can get in touch with her folks. Start praying, Beth. Pray hard. Let's all call out Ben's name in prayer and ask for him to come to the faith after he finishes. Okay, I'm calling the others now. Just pray!"

"I will start praying now, Blake. This is a huge moment in the life of the Smyrnians. If Ben can come to the faith, it will change everything for us as we approach the Middle East, Jerusalem and Jews around the world. Praying! Now, call Evan, Ally and John!"

Anders was standing nearby, still rejoicing about the upcoming wedding. Blake ran to him and shared the news about Ben. "I will pray right now, Blake, and not stop. I want to see Ben come to the faith so bad. We need him. Jesus needs him. The world needs him. He is such a key for us. I'm believing that he will come to faith in Jesus tonight!"

Next, he called Evan. He assumed John was driving and didn't want to distract him. He needed them in New York safe and sound.

"What's up Blake? This must be important for you to call again so soon. Is everything okay with Beth?"

"Everything is great with her. We will have a wedding performed by all of you guys next week while you are here. That is going to be great!"

"Woohoo! I have you on speaker, as you can probably tell. Listen to this."

John and Ally whooped it up too so Blake could hear them loudly and clearly.

"But that's not why I'm calling. Ben Abramson just called and said he is going to watch the video of the pastor right now. We were going to watch it together, but he said while he has some down time for a little while, he wants to watch it by himself. Honestly, I'm glad he is. I need all of us praying that Jesus will be in that room with him and reach out to him in a way that he can't pass up. We need Ben on the team. We need a man who has lived the Jewish faith who can reach the Jews and who has contacts in the Middle East, in Israel in particular. Ben travels there a couple of times a year. He can make such a difference. But more than anything, if he believes, it will mean he is part of the family of God and on his way to heaven!"

"We'll pray the entire trip, Blake, starting now! Please let us know as soon as you hear from Ben."

"I told him to call me after he finishes the video if he needs to talk. I tried my best to let him know how hard it is going to be for him and told him how hard it was for me. Just pray."

"Okay, Blake, let us get off this phone so we can get started!"

"Oh, one more thing. Ally, can you call your folks and have them pray too? Ben doesn't know he will have people praying for him all the way from Germany!"

"I'm on it, Blake. I know they will be happy to pray too."

"Thanks, guys. This can be a great night. I believe. Believe with me, and pray in faith."

"Done," John said. "We hope to hear good news from you within the next hour or two."

Miriam had put the kids to bed and laid down for the night. She knew Ben liked his quiet time alone in the den after they had all gone to bed. She loved her husband very much. But she had noticed that he had not been the same since hearing Aissa Messai speak earlier in the day. Something bothered him about the man. He had not been himself since then. She had heard him talking to Blake on the phone. He was trying to sound like his normal self. He could fool others, but he could never fool her. He had been so interested in a video that Blake left for him to watch. She knew the two of them had planned to watch it together. But she had overheard Ben asking Blake if it was okay for him to watch it by himself. She had seen him get the drive and begin to get ready. He had prepared like he always did. He poured himself a glass of tea and took his medication. It was for his high blood pressure. It wasn't bad, but when he got stressed, it could go much higher than it should. Then he headed into the den. Her thoughts were with him as she drifted off to sleep.

Ben sat his tea down on the table beside his big chair. He had said his prayers and proclaimed his faith in God again. "Hear, O Israel: The LORD our God, the LORD is one. You shall love the LORD your God with all your heart and with all your soul and with all your strength. I do love you Lord," he said. "The world has gone mad. I don't know what is going to happen, but I will maintain my faith in you, no matter what comes. You are my God. You were the God of my parents. You are the God of our fathers, of Abraham, Isaac and Jacob. Show me what I need to do, how to handle the things that are going on. I will not forsake you. Just show me Lord. Show me. Thank you."

He walked over to the TV and popped the drive in. He went back and settled in, then pushed play. He saw the brief introduction, then the pastor came on the screen.

"That is a church and a pastor preaching his sermon!" Ben said out loud to only himself. "I am not watching this!" Then he remembered his promise to Blake. He had always been a man of his word. He had promised Blake he would watch it all the way to the end and listen to the things that were being said. He hit pause for a moment. "I can do this," he said. "God, I will always believe the truth about you. I will not let anything deter me from that. Keep me focused on the truth." He took another sip of tea and hit play again.

Blake was too nervous to work. Besides, he needed to pray. And pray he did. He found Anders and Beth, and the three of them found a place away from the crowd and began to pray together. First Blake, then Beth and Anders. Then Blake again. On and on they prayed without stopping. They called out Ben's name again and again. They asked God to show him the truth. They called out the name of Jesus and asked him to be in the room with Ben and open his eyes and mind to what he was hearing. They prayed and prayed until they noticed they had prayed until after the video should have ended. Blake's phone had not rung, so they prayed some more.

Evan, Ally and John were doing the same. Tears flowed from Ally's eyes when she asked Jesus to touch Ben and give him the faith to believe in him. The guys were not ones to shed tears, but their prayers were from the heart and powerful. They were so focused that more than an hour had passed when Evan spoke softly. "It has been almost an hour and a half. He should be about finished by now, depending on how many times he stopped the video and took a break."

"Please, Lord Jesus," prayed John. "Please open Ben's eyes. Open his heart. Show him the truth. He needs you, Jesus, and the world needs him. The Smyrnians need him. Your people, the Jews, need him. We have heard that your Word says the Jews will turn to you during these seven years. Ben can play a vital role in that. Please, Jesus, please. Be with him right now."

Their prayers continued. They would pray until they heard from Blake. After all, they had a long drive ahead of them. What better thing to do than pray? Especially for Ben.

In Germany, Ally's parents were praying. Bruno had started with "Jesus, you know we're not very good at this praying thing, but I don't think that matters to you. I just ask you to hear us tonight. Ben is watching the video right now, Jesus. Help him to see the truth like I did. It wasn't easy for me. I doubt it will be easy for him. Thank you for giving me John to help me that day. Please help Ben tonight. If he struggles with what he hears like I did, help him to call Blake. He can help Ben. Please Jesus, whatever he thinks, help him to turn to you." Mila was praying along with him, in her own words. Even the boys were praying. Their mom and dad had been teaching them and trying to prepare them for the future. They understood the magnitude of this moment. They did not know Ben Abramson. But they understood how important it was for him to accept Jesus. So they prayed too. "All the way from Germany," Bruno thought. "All the way from Germany we are praying for a man in America to put his faith in Jesus." They prayed and waited to hear back from Ally.

Ben had watched until he got angry. It didn't take long. As soon as he heard the pastor mention Jesus, he paused the video again and stormed around the room. "The LORD our God; the LORD is *one*. The LORD our God; the LORD is *one*," he repeated over and over. He went to the kitchen again and poured another glass of tea. What had happened to Blake? He had surely lost his mind. This was not research. It was heresy! He knew there had been something different about him. He had not been the same man he had always been. Sure, he was still the reporter who could get the scoop and break news before anyone else. He had proven that again today. But, Jesus? Blake had never been a church guy. The news was his life. Whatever had happened to him, Ben knew that he was not interested in what he was hearing. But he had promised. He had sat back down and hit play again.

Blake, Beth and Anders' prayers were suddenly interrupted by the sound of sirens, lots of sirens. They rushed back out to see what was going on. Something had happened at the hotel where the ambassadors were staying. The three of them rushed to the scene. Paramedics were running through the door. Several policemen stormed inside while others stood guard outside. Taking every precaution, most hunkered down behind their cars with guns drawn. No one else could have gotten inside, but Blake Thompson and Beth Jennings did. Blake spoke with a policeman in the lobby who he knew well. He had done a story on the man's daughter who had been extremely ill. By telling her story on the air, Blake had helped the family raise thousands of dollars for treatment and a transplant that saved her life. The transplant happened and all the family's needs were met. They were eternally grateful for Blake's help. Blake knew the man would speak with him.

"Hey, Bob. What is going on? It looks like something really bad."

"You didn't hear this from me, Blake. Okay?"

"You know I would never let that be known, Bob. But it's my job to report the news, and it's obvious that something pretty important is going on here."

"Okay, everybody will know soon enough anyway. The leader of the forces that were so opposed to Aissa Messai's nomination for Secretary-General has been killed. He was in the bar with some of the others who were on his side, and it happened."

"What happened, Bob?"

"The witnesses said he suddenly grabbed his neck as if he couldn't breathe. Some of them tried to get to him to help, but they couldn't. They said, when they got near, they all fell back as if someone had knocked them down. All they could do was watch as the man fought until he turned blue and fell to the floor. When they finally could get to him, he was gone. Just like the Secretary-General yesterday, he had handprints around his neck. But no one saw anyone or anything. Someone strangled him, Blake. The problem is, there was nobody there doing it. This is getting weird."

"Thanks, Bob. I don't know what is going on with all this, but I'm going to try my best to get to the bottom of it."

He did know what was going on, but he was not at liberty to tell it yet. He knew it was Messai, the antichrist, the epitome of evil, Satan's agent in the world for the next seven years. No human entity could defeat him. Only Jesus could. And that would not come until the end of the Tribulation. Things may look bad at this point. But this was only the beginning. If only the world knew how awful it was going to get. But if what he had heard and read about the antichrist in the past couple of weeks was true, things would appear to get a lot better before they got a lot worse. It had begun, and Blake hated knowing the truth and not being able to reveal it at this point. Ben! He had to pray for Ben, even as he interviewed witnesses and first responders and reported the story. He prayed.

Beth was with him. They gleaned the same information together. They appeared to be nothing more than the two primary reporters in America getting all the facts they could get and preparing to break this horrific story. Both had witnesses standing by for interviews and the same facts to report. Both had also contacted their studios with the breaking story. They agreed to go on the air at the same time and begin simultaneously. This time there would be no one-upping from either. Now, it was go time. The studio threw it out to Blake.

"Blake Thompson is on the scene of another tragic situation. Blake, what is going on down there."

"I am live at the ONE UN Hotel in Manhattan near the United Nations Headquarters. Tragedy has struck once again as the leader of the group that was opposed to the nomination of Aissa Messai has been brutally murdered in the same way Secretary Pieters was killed yesterday. I say *murdered*, but again there was no visible killer, just a terrible scene and clear evidence that his death was a homicide. With me, I have one of the witnesses who saw this happen. He was sitting at a table in the bar area when he noticed commotion taking place at the bar. Sir, can you describe for us what you saw?"

"A couple of friends and I were having a nightcap before heading up to our rooms. Suddenly we heard several people shouting the man's name. Then we saw him. He was grabbing for his neck and appeared to be choking. Some people rushed to help him, but when they did, they were thrown back as if someone had shoved them. Every time another tried, it was the same thing. It was obvious that the guy couldn't breathe and was struggling. He was lifted completely off the floor with his feet dangling. It appeared that he was being strangled but there was no assailant. We ran to try and help but couldn't get near him for all the people who were gathered around him trying to help. Finally, he fell to the floor with a thud as if he had been dropped. He was already dead. Everybody knew that. I called 911 as soon as I saw what was happening. Hotel security was called too, but they couldn't help either. They drew their guns, but there was no one to shoot at. It was the strangest and most horrible thing I have ever seen. Just like they said happened to Mr. Pieters."

"This is a frightening scene down here folks," Blake reported. "As you can see, they are carrying out a body bag now that holds the body of the ambassador who was killed. Hotel security weren't the only ones ready to confront an assailant. NYPD officers were hunkered down beside their cars with guns drawn, ready to fire. But no attacker came into view. I don't know what is going on, but all of this comes on the heels of the taking of millions or billions of people. None of this seems to come from human origins. I can't explain it, but there seems to be some supernatural force at work that is far superior to us. I reiterate: every one of us needs to stay on our guard. Who knows what may happen next? Be aware and be prepared."

Then as a few statements were being made by the team in the studio, he realized this was his window of opportunity to warn the other ambassadors of the danger they faced. He interrupted.

"Sorry to interrupt, but if I may, I want to say a word to all members of the UN General Assembly. This makes two of your fellow ambassadors who have been viciously killed within two days. Each of you should be alert and fully aware of your surroundings at all times. I don't want to create a panic, but survival may be the word of the day. A very important decision looms before you. Do not take anything or anyone for granted. You may want to go to your rooms and stay there for the remainder of the night until the assembly reconvenes tomorrow morning. Police protection has been amped up and the National Guard has been deployed to stand ready to fight, if necessary. But folks, I must remind you, it is hard to fight that which you cannot see. Members of the assembly, be careful and be safe."

He felt his phone buzzing in his pocket. Ben! He had to go...now! He abruptly ended his report.

"That is all I have from here. I am sending it back to you in the studio." As soon as he knew the crew in the studio was being shown, he motioned to Anders to turn the camera off and cut the feed.

"Blake, is there anything else you can tell us? Anything we should know? This is a scary situation. Any word on what police or anyone else may be saying at this time?" Silence. "Blake? Blake, are you there...? It seems we have lost our feed from the ONE UN Hotel. My apologies to you, our viewing audience. We will get back out there as soon as we can resolve the issue."

Blake looked at his phone. Ben. Missed call. He told Anders and motioned to Beth. She was off the air too. She had also sent it back to the studio and cut the feed. He did not want to wait. He hit the number. Ben answered. Blake's hand was shaking so much that he could barely hold the phone. "Ben, I've been waiting to hear from you..."

CHAPTER 29

Beth quickly dialed Evan's number and he answered on the first ring.

"Evan, do you have any idea what is going on here?"

"We haven't heard a thing. We've been driving and praying and waiting to hear from Blake. The wait has just about driven us crazy. Has Ben called yet? What did he say about the video? Did he put his faith in Jesus? Please tell us he did."

"Hold on there, impatient one. Just slow down for a minute, okay? Yes, Ben just called. Blake missed his call but called him back as soon as he could. Evan, we are on the scene of another tragedy. This time at the ONE UN Hotel where the United Nations contingent is staying. The leader of the anti-Messai forces who so vehemently opposed his nomination has been killed. It happened the same way as Secretary Pieters assassination. Blake and I interviewed witnesses. It is so bizarre, but I think we all know the answer. It is Messai. His supernatural strength comes from Satan. He is pure evil and is doing away with everyone who stands against him. I hate to think of it, but that is a glimpse into what the next seven years are going to be like. It's what they are going to be like for *us*. We need to be on our toes. I think we must assume he knows who we are. Both Blake and I could feel that when he glared at us as he walked to the podium. It was like he was burning a hole right through us. I don't like it, but I have to admit that I was afraid for a moment. That makes our meeting next week more important than we can imagine. Okay, I have to get to Blake now. He is still on the phone with Ben. One of us will let you know as soon as he gets off. I hope you are still praying for Ben. Blake doesn't seem too upset, so maybe it is going better than we thought. Okay, it looks like he is almost finished. I'll let you guys go. Please drive safely. I look forward to seeing you bright and early."

"Please call us as soon as you can, Beth" said Evan. It sure would be nice to hear that Ben is a brand new member of the Smyrnians!"

"I hope he is!" Beth ended the call and started walking toward Blake and Anders. Her phone rang before she could even take a step. She did not recognize the number, but recognized the England country code immediately. Could it be?

"Hello, this is Beth Jennings."

"Beth! This is your old buddy Oliver Barton in London. I hope you don't mind me getting your number. It took some work, but after all, I am a bloodhound of a reporter, right?"

Ollie! She was ecstatic! She could hardly believe what she was hearing. "It is so good to hear your voice. I have thought about you so often. I wouldn't be where I am today without you."

"Well, I appreciate that, but you didn't need me. You are good, girl! You were always a good reporter, even before you got over here. You had what it takes. That was plain to see. But hey, maybe I did help a little bit. It would be nice to claim responsibility for helping to make the great Beth Jennings the reporter she is today!"

"Stop it, Ollie. But thanks for saying that. It means a lot coming from the best newsman in England. Why are you calling me? I'm sorry, that didn't sound right. How about this: to what do I owe the honor of this call?" she asked in her best British accent.

"Your British still needs a little work," he laughed. "I'm heading your way. You are still in New York City, I see."

"Yes, I am. You are coming to New York? Wow! Now I am really excited! I cannot wait to see you!"

"I am coming on business, to cover the United Nations story. I have seen your reports, and those of Blake Thompson. He is pretty good too, you know."

"He is better than good. He always seems to get one up on me. But once in a while, I get him."

"My flight is leaving London within the hour. I wanted you to know I'll be there. We have to get together. You know, I have never been to New York. I am a Middle East and Europe kind of guy. So, I may need a tour guide, or at least someone to show me where I need to be and how to get there."

"You got it! I just can't believe you are coming. There is so much I want to talk to you about. I know the last few weeks must have affected you as much as they did me...well, so many of us. I lost my mom and dad and so many friends. But I'm okay. That isn't stopping me."

"I'm sorry to hear about your parents, Beth. Maybe you can tell me all about it when I get there, assuming we both can find time to talk."

"We will find time, Ollie. I promise. There is something I want to share with you about the disappearances. During our research, a few of us have found the answer for what really happened. We haven't been told the whole truth. You are my dear friend. I want you to know. It will open your eyes and let you see the whole truth for yourself. It is news to top all news!"

"You know I want to hear that. I hear them calling for boarding on my flight. I don't want to sound presumptuous, but the newsman in me cannot wait to get my hands on information like that! My plane lands at ten in the morning. I look forward to seeing my good friend."

"How about I pick you up at the airport? Are you flying into LaGuardia or JFK?"

"JFK. I would love for you to pick me up. It will save me money on a rental car." He chuckled.

"Great! Give me your flight number, and I will see you there!"

"It is flight 4090. I have to go. Boarding now. See you in the morning."

"Yes sir!"

Beth was amazed at how God was answering her prayer by bringing Ollie to her. "I have believed in Jesus for such a short time, but I have seen God do so many miraculous things," she thought to herself. "Thank you, Lord Jesus. You are awesome!"

Beth got to Blake just as he finished his call with Ben. She heard him say, "I'll get there as fast as I can."

"Well?" she asked in a tone that sounded more impatient than Evan. "What did he say? Did I hear you say you are going to his house tonight?"

"I'm not sure what to think. Ben was different than I have ever heard him. He sounded confused, almost like he was in a stupor of some kind. He said, 'I don't know what to think anymore. The world has gone mad, and I don't know which way to turn or what to do next.'"

"That sounds like he is thinking, then. Don't you think so?"

"I do, but thinking about what? I know Ben. His thoughts can run wild in a lot of different directions. The only way I can know for sure is get there to talk to him. I need to go." He gave her a quick kiss and turned to leave.

"Blake?"

"Yes?"

"I'll be praying for you. And for Ben. And Blake...I love you."

"I love you too, Beth. We both know what is going to happen at the UN meeting Monday. And after that..." His voice trailed off. He had to get to Ben right now.

Ben sat alone in his den, the TV still on, even after the video had ended. His mind wandered back to his childhood. He remembered being taught the stories of the Old Testament by his parents and grandparents. Sabbath worship in the synagogue had been a staple of their lives. His Bar Mitzvah had been a true celebration of his coming of age and being ready to observe the religious precepts of Judaism and take part in public worship. The memories of being paraded through town with instruments playing, the women dancing and men walking proudly alongside were fresh in his mind at this moment. The reception that followed was elaborate and attended by many family members and friends. It was a custom he had witnessed many times as his older brothers and sisters, and many cousins had come of age. But his day was special. Not necessary, but special. He recalled being brought forward to read a text from the Torah and lead the congregation in prayers. He had also gone through confirmation at their local synagogue. Every aspect of both was as vivid as if he was living it again. Why was he reliving those events now? It was not a common occurrence. Why now, after watching the video? Was God reminding him of truth in the face of falsehood? Or was it simply a result of all that had gone on in recent weeks? He was unaware of the time. In fact, it was as if time did not matter. His mind had gone back in time, even as he was keenly aware of what was happening in the present. Back and forth. His wife and kids. His parents. His job. Friends. Family. He jumped...frightened. He saw the image of Messai clearly as if he was standing in the room with him. A chill. Trembling. What was happening to him? What was it about the man that caused him to feel such intense fear? Yes, he was afraid. A chill suddenly crept down his spine. He shivered. Was he ill? Getting sick? Going crazy? An incoming text caused his phone to jingle as it lay on the table next to his chair. He came to his senses. It was Blake.

"Ben, I'm at the door. I didn't want to ring the doorbell and wake your family. May I come in?"

As he made his way to the door and opened it, he had never been more glad to see another human being in his life. He knew why Blake was there. The video. The evidence from the research he had done in Chicago. It had stunned him, not what he was expecting. He had expected something newsworthy, something that would take the world by storm. But this... He had to admit, it was newsworthy. But surely Blake was not crazy enough to break that story. Or was he?

"Ben, are you okay?"

He seemed to come out of a trance.

"Honestly, I don't know Blake. But I'm glad you are here. I don't know what is wrong with me. What has happened to me over the last couple of hours causes me to fear I may be going insane. You know me, Blake. I'm not one to feel like this. Can we sit and talk for a while?"

"Sure Ben. That's why I am here. You are one of the most important people in my life. We can talk as long as you like."

"Can I get you a glass of tea? I know how you like it. Sweet…"

"I could use a glass. It has been a long day and night for me too. Maybe the tea will serve as my red eye coffee for tonight." He smiled, trying to ease the mood and help Ben open up and talk.

Ben returned with the tea. Blake could not help but notice that he did not look like himself. Ben was ever the businessman, confident and in control. But tonight, he looked like a man who had suddenly lost everything, hopeless and helpless. His hand shook as he handed him the tea. He could see it sloshing gently back and forth in the glass. Blake had never ever seen him like this.

"Ben, are you sure you are okay?" he asked as he took a sip of tea.

Ben sat down facing Blake. The television was still on, the video ended. He did not seem to notice.

"No Blake, no. I am not okay. I don't know what is wrong with me. I was fine until earlier today, or I suppose it was yesterday now. I know I should be asleep, and so should you. But there is no way I am sleeping tonight."

"What do you mean you were fine until earlier today? Are you sure you don't need me to drive you to the hospital, or something?"

"No, it's not like that. I don't know how to explain it, but it's not anything physical. Besides, I just had a checkup with my doctor, and everything is fine. Just need to make sure I stay on my medication for high blood pressure. It's something else. I know this doesn't make any sense either, but it started after Messai spoke. I was sitting right here and watching. But I can't remember a thing the man said. It is almost like I experienced a time warp or passed out. When I came to my senses, I didn't feel right. I just don't know what happened during that time. Something happened. I know that. Something happened to *me*. And then, all I could think about was watching your video. I don't have a clue where that came from. It's like it was calling out to me. I had to watch it. That is strange, don't you think?"

"I don't think it is strange, Ben." Blake was trying to speak softly and be as gentle as possible. His boss was a broken man, and he wanted to be here for him. This was the most important moment of Ben Abramson's life, and

Blake knew it.

"The video, Blake. I admit, it made me angry, very angry. If I hadn't promised you, I would have turned it off. I would have destroyed it. But I gave you my word. Blake, how did that man know what was going to happen? How did he explain it so perfectly that far in advance? I didn't tell you, but I had really struggled with the idea of an alien invasion. I didn't fully buy into it. Not only did it not seem possible, the way it happened, but I thought there had to be a reason why some were abducted, while others were not. There was no rhyme or reason to any of it."

"I know, Ben. But I have to admit that I *did* buy into it: hook, line and sinker. I had always believed in the existence of life on other planets. So, it was easy for me to believe it. But then I got that call from Evan Ryles in Chicago. I went to his place because I had some time to kill and because he said he had proof of what really happened in the disappearances. Normally, I wouldn't have given a college student the time of day. But there was something about that call. I felt drawn to him, just like you felt drawn to the video tonight. And I got angry too. I was thinking, 'what a waste of my time.' But as the pastor got to his explanation, and then the date, and saying it would likely be labeled an alien invasion, it was more than I could deny."

"That is exactly how I felt. I don't want to believe him. With all my heart, I don't want to believe him. It goes against everything I have been taught my whole life. It goes against what I have believed and taught to my own kids. A man can't just turn his back on his faith, can he?"

"You know I was never a man of faith. I had no time for such things. But when I heard the pastor's message, I felt something I had never felt before. It was something I couldn't deny. So, Ben, I put my faith in Jesus. And I must tell you, he has changed my life. That is why I wanted you to see the video. I know how strong your Jewish faith is. But I couldn't help it. I had to show you the video. It was too important to keep from you. You're not just my boss; you're my friend. And I care about what happens to you. Ben, Messai is the antichrist the pastor talked about."

"Messai? I don't know that I believe in an antichrist. I don't know what I believe right now."

"You know what you experienced during and after Messai's speech. That is a small glimpse into the future. There are seven years left until Jesus returns. They are going to be the worst years this planet has ever seen. The world is going to be divided into two camps: those who believe in Jesus and those who do not. Those who don't will fall under Messai's spell, just like you did. Like everyone in that room did when he spoke. I was there. Believe me, I know. Those who do believe in Jesus will be on the run for their lives or face certain death at his hands. That may sound bad, but the alternative will be far worse, and eternal. There are ten of us who have believed. Anders and Beth are two of them. Then there are Evan Ryles and Ally Fromm, college students, John Baldwin, you know, the college professor I interviewed in Chicago about the earthquake, and Ally's parents and two brothers in Germany. She is an exchange student. There may be others around the world we haven't discovered yet. If there are, we will find each other. We are determined to fight Messai at every turn. And you need to know that his main targets will be Christians and Jews...and *Israel.* All hell is going to break loose, Ben. I want you to be ready. I want you to believe in Jesus. And I sure would like to have you as a member of our team." His boldness at that moment almost surprised him. But now he was determined to help his friend see the truth.

"I don't know, Blake. I don't know about anything right now."

"Can you deny the things the pastor said?"

"No. I want to deny them. I want to scream 'blasphemy!' But I can't. You have to understand, Blake. For me to believe in Jesus would mean more than turning away from everything I have believed and stood for. It would cost me my family. They will disown me if I do that."

"I can't tell you what to do. But I can tell you what Jesus has done for me in the brief time I have known him. He has changed my life. I'm on his team now and plan to spend the rest of my life, all seven years of it, if I survive that long, living for him. That is all that matters now." Blake wondered if he should have said more. But he did not want to push his boss too far. The *Smyrnians* needed him badly, but he knew Ben's faith ran deep and his family values were strong.

"I'm so confused. This whole thing..." His words trailed off, and his mind seemed to go with them.

"Ben?"

No answer. Just a blank stare. Blake decided to give him a moment. He was afraid to say anything and afraid to not say anything. But for a few moments he sat across from his friend in silence, just watching him...and praying.

John, Evan and Ally were well into their trip. Things were going well, so they decided to stop and eat. It was late, but they found a place that was open all night. They went in and were seated at a table facing a TV showing the news. Blake's earlier report from the hotel was being replayed. Beth had told them about the attack and murder of the ambassador, but hearing the chilling description of the witness as Blake interviewed him painted a picture so vivid they were taken aback. For several seconds after the picture returned to the reporters in the studio, they sat in stunned silence. Ally finally spoke.

"Do you really think he knows who we are? I mean, Beth thinks so. If he does, we are heading right for him. He could be leading us into his trap."

"There is no way to know, Ally." John whispered softly, trying to take her feelings into consideration. "Maybe the three of us and your family are flying under the radar for now."

"Just picturing that man being strangled and lifted off the floor, struggling for air, but not even knowing who was killing him. It was almost as if I could feel his pain and his life slipping away. I could sense his horror. It was as real as if it was...*me*."

"Ally." John put his hand on her shoulder. He felt for his student but knew he could not alleviate her fears, or spare her from what was to come. "We all know what we signed up for. This is not going to be easy for any of us. But we are in it together. And we are not in it to lose! We have seven years. And we are going to fight to win! You are strong. You are a Smyrnian. You can do this!"

"Come on, Ally." Evan was not about to let her lose her courage. "You are our spy, remember? Remember how excited you were when you were shown that? You know what to do. Well, you are going to do it! We are all going to do it. Messai doesn't know what is about to hit him. The Smyrnians are about to be unleashed!"

Just as he said that, the waitress walked up with their food. His outburst startled her. She looked at him strangely and set their food on the table. Then she turned and quickly hustled back toward the kitchen.

"I'm sorry," Evan whispered. "I'm going to have to be a lot quieter than that. In fact, we all are. We can't afford to give away our identity. Lesson learned."

"Lesson learned, all right. You are right. I'm a spy, and a good one at that. I will not be afraid. Thanks, you two, for reminding me who I am. Now, let's eat this food and get back on the road to New York City. I can't wait to get there!"

With that, they finished their meal and were in the car and back on the road. They couldn't wait to see their newly made friends and fellow warriors. And they wanted to personally get a look at the face of the man who would be their mortal enemy for the next seven years, assuming all of them survived that long. Let the war begin!

CHAPTER 30

"Blake?" Ben finally spoke as one awakened from a stupor, yet still somewhat addled. Blake chose to keep silent and let him continue when he was ready.

"The pastor described everything that happened on September 11 perfectly, exactly as it took place. It wasn't an alien invasion, was it?"

"No Ben, it wasn't."

"How could I have missed it all these years? How could my people have missed it? I have read what Josephus wrote about Jesus in his *Antiquities*. He was a great Jewish historian. He tells our story and fills in so many gaps that we would never have known without him. But those few passages, especially one, we have always either denied or just overlooked. I pulled my copy out tonight after I finished the video and read it again. I hadn't read it in years. In fact, I could barely remember it, but I remember my father telling me it wasn't true. He said it must have been added by a later Christian writer to deceive us into believing Jesus was the Messiah. Even though we accept the *Antiquities* as historical fact, we have always taught that passage is fiction. I have it marked here. Will you read it to me, Blake? I want to hear it again just like Josephus wrote it. I want to close my eyes and just listen so I can imagine I am there when he was writing, maybe as if he is telling me the story as he writes. Can you do that for me Blake?"

"Sure, I will Ben. Honestly, I don't know much about Josephus. I have heard of him and listened to brief mentions of him in world history class. It sounds like more research and further proof to me, if it is as you say. And you know I love research! So, I will read it for both of us."

Ben handed him the book called *Antiquities*, written by Josephus and published in AD 93. He read the section Ben had marked.

"Now there was about this time Jesus, a wise man, if it be lawful to call him a man, for he was a doer of wonderful works, a teacher of such men as

receive the truth with pleasure. He drew over to him both many of the Jews, and many of the Gentiles. He was the Christ; and when Pilate, at the suggestion of the principal men amongst us, had condemned him to the cross, those that loved him at the first did not forsake him, for he appeared to them alive again the third day, as the divine prophets had foretold these and ten thousand other wonderful things concerning him; and the tribe of Christians, so named from him, are not extinct to this day." Antiquities 18.3.3.

Blake laid the book on the table next to Ben's chair and waited for him to speak again. He himself was amazed to hear such a clear description of Jesus coming from a Jewish writer.

"He wrote about the crucifixion and the resurrection, and how Christians were still worshiping Jesus up to the time he wrote sixty plus years after it happened. And he said Jesus was the Messiah the prophets had written about. The Jews have been looking for the Messiah to come for over 2,000 years. Is it possible that he did come and we missed him? I can't believe I'm even asking that, Blake. But what I see now is that just as the prophets foretold the coming of Jesus and his death and resurrection, the pastor in the video did the same thing concerning the disappearances. He said it was coming and gave the exact date and manner it would happen. He even said it may be blamed on an alien invasion. He didn't miss one part of it. It all makes sense to me now. As I talk about it, it makes sense. I get it Blake, I get it. The pastor was right. The... what is it you call it... took place on September 11."

"The *Rapture*, Ben. It was the Rapture when Jesus took his followers home to be with him and set the final seven years of this planet into motion."

"Yes, the Rapture. Doesn't that mean something like '*taking up?*'"

"I looked it up. It literally means, '*the act of carrying a person off to another place or sphere of existence.*' Does that ring a bell?"

"That is what happened. Every person who was taken was a believer in Jesus. Churches are empty. Christians are all missing. Babies are gone."

Blake interrupted. "And we are still here, Ben. All of us who never believed in Jesus are still here, left behind. We missed it. But we don't have to miss it when Jesus comes back in seven years. We have been given another chance. I took advantage of that, Ben. Will you?"

"I will Blake, right now. I don't want to miss it again. I can't tell you how I feel. It is like my eyes have been opened allowing me to see what I couldn't see before. I can see Jesus dying on the cross for me. I can see him risen from the grave and alive. I can see some of the people I knew standing with him now. And I can see myself as one of his followers. I am ready."

Out of nowhere, he began to talk to Jesus. It was not like he was praying; more like Jesus was right in front of him and he was talking to him just like he had been talking to Blake. He did not kneel or bow his head or close his eyes. He was not looking at Blake. He was looking at the chair closest to him. Blake felt like he was on the outside looking in, as if he was an invisible guest at an important meeting. It was the most surreal moment he had ever experienced. Why was this so different, so special? Then it dawned on him. Ben was a Jew. One of God's chosen people. Some of his research said they would turn to Jesus during the Tribulation and acknowledge him as the Messiah. Ben was doing that. He may even be the first! That reality hit Blake and overwhelmed him. He just sat and watched as Ben spoke with Jesus. Friend to friend. Like family. This was a special moment and Blake knew how privileged he was to be a part of it.

"I am sorry I missed who you were, Jesus. The prophets foretold that you were the Messiah and that you were coming to the world. How could I have missed it? Micah said you would be born in Bethlehem, and you were. Isaiah described your birth and your death on the cross. It is all so clear now. You are not just *the* Messiah; you are *my* Messiah. As Josephus wrote, I receive you with pleasure! I believe in you. I believe you died on the cross and rose again. I am ready to be a Christian. Here I am Jesus. I am yours."

The smile on his face was…Blake tried to come up with a word. Glorious. Radiant. His entire body seemed to glow. Blake thought he would have to shield his eyes for fear he may go blind just looking at him. The room was flooded with light, a light brighter than he had ever seen before. Something big was happening. That is all he knew. Something BIG! He watched as the light moved through the den and up the steps toward the bedrooms in the large house. Surely anyone who was outside or passing by must see the light. It was beyond brilliant. Maybe that was the word: *brilliant.*

Suddenly Ben's wife and children appeared at the top of the stairs and started down. Were they floating? It was almost as if their feet were not even touching the floor. The same glorious light that shone through Ben and permeated the entire house illuminated them too. The smiles on their faces told of the glory of this moment. They came to Ben and embraced him; first Miriam, then the kids in a big group hug. Then they turned to gaze at the chair on which Ben had been focused. Slowly they knelt in front of it with their faces to the floor. Shortly after, their heads were lifted as if someone had his hand on their chins gently pulling them up. Then their hands reached out and they stretched upward as they were lifted to their feet. Ben stood and joined them. Blake was sure he could hear angels singing. He could not see them but the words came clearly: *"Holy, holy, holy is the Lord of hosts; the whole earth is full of his glory!"* "I don't know about the whole earth," Blake thought to himself. "But this whole house certainly is!"

Now Ben knelt and a hand appeared and covered his head. A voice spoke, *"Whom shall I send? And who will go for us?"* Blake strained to see who was speaking, but he could not see anything because of the brilliance of the light. Then Ben spoke: *"Here am I. Send me!"* And the answer came quickly: *"Go and tell my people..."* That was all Blake heard. The scene seemed to continue for hours, even though he knew it was only a short time. Ben stood. Then the light faded and he found himself sitting in the room again with Ben and his entire family. He stood, reached out his hand and said, "Welcome to the team, Ben."

"You mean the *Smyrnians*, don't you Blake? Jesus told me all about it. We have work to do. *I* have work to do. I have to tell my people. I must let them know that Jesus is the Messiah. This is the greatest night of my life Blake, a special night. This is the beginning. Many of the Jews are going to believe in Jesus! But many others are not. I am a newsman. If anyone knows how to get the news out, it is me. And it is you and Beth and Anders. You...we, weren't chosen by accident. Jesus told me He is the *good* news. We have spent our careers telling people *bad* news. We will have to continue reporting the world's news for now. But we will also find covert ways to share the good news with everyone, especially with my people. Messai is the enemy, Blake. He is from Satan. He is a deceiver. But we have the truth. How soon can we meet with the others? We don't have any time to waste!"

"Funny you should ask, Ben. Obviously, Beth and Anders are here and ready. And just last night I invited Evan, Ally and John to come to New York and meet with us. They are on their way now! This is all God's plan, Ben. I know it. All of us have been praying for you to believe in Jesus and become a member of the team. Your role may be more important than any of ours. You must help us spread the good news in Israel, and indeed throughout the whole earth! Do you mind if I take a moment to call the others right now?"

"Please do! I can't wait to get started!"

Blake called Evan, Ally and John, then added Beth and Anders on a conference call. They were ecstatic, as one might imagine. He put his phone on speaker and allowed the others to talk with Ben and his family. They all celebrated together. A meeting in person would happen at some time during the day. For now, it was 3:00 in the morning. It would help to grab a couple hours of sleep, but Blake doubted any of them could sleep tonight. He suggested they all try, except of course, whoever was driving John's car. Then they needed to meet at 8:00 a.m. sharp at his place. That is where the Chicago contingent would be coming. Blake said goodbye to the Abramsons. As he left, he really could not tell if he was walking on the ground or on air. Tomorrow, well actually today, was going to be an awesome day. He called Beth.

"Blake, I thought you said I should get some sleep. And here you are calling me. Don't you think I need my beauty rest, even if it is only a couple of hours?"

"If that is the case, you had better just stay up. If you get any more beautiful, I don't know if I can take it!"

"Stop it Blake. You are making me blush again."

"I'm just telling it like it is. I love you Beth Jennings. And I am so excited right now that I hardly know what to do with myself! Who knew how awesome a life of faith could be?"

"I love you too Blake Thompson. More than you can imagine. And I am just as excited as you are! Living by faith is real life. But I know you didn't call just to tell me you love me and how beautiful I am, or even how excited you are. What else is on your mind?"

"I thought you may want to come on over to my place. You can lie down and get a little sleep, then already be there when the others arrive."

"That's a good idea. But you have to promise to be a gentleman. We aren't married yet, you know."

"Okay now, that may not be easy..."

"Blake!"

"I'm kidding, Beth. We will both try to sleep, separately, trust me. But that will only be for a few more days!"

"You had better stop that, Mr. Thompson. But I must tell you, I'm as eager for us to be married as you are! So, I'm not going to fuss at you. I should be at your place by the time you get there."

"I can't wait to see you!" He started to end the call, but heard her shout his name just before he did. It startled him. "Beth, are you okay?!"

"Yes. I just remembered in all the excitement about Ben's call and the urgency of you getting over there I forgot to tell you something. Guess who called me and is coming to New York?"

"Well, I know it is not Evan, Ally and John because I already know they are coming. I am stumped. Tell me, who is coming?"

"Oliver Barton!"

"Oliver Barton is coming to New York? How did you find out?"

"He called me! Out of the blue while you were talking to Ben. And told me he is coming here to cover the UN story. Can you believe that?!"

"After everything else we have seen God do, yes I can. You prayed for an opportunity to talk to him about Jesus, and God is bringing him right to you."

"That is exactly what I said. I'm picking him up at JFK at 10:00 this morning. I don't know what that means for our meeting. I'm sure he has a hotel booked, maybe even the One UN. I feel sure they want him nearby to cover the story. I have to find time to talk to him. I told him I have news that explains the disappearances and I want to share it with him. So that door should be wide open. I don't want to wait, but I want the timing to be right too."

"God will answer all of those questions for you. You will know when the time is right. I suppose you plan to show him the video?"

"I think that is probably the best way to do it. I, or we, need to be with him when he sees it. Ollie has always been a secularist, so it won't be easy."

"It wasn't easy for me either, Beth. I suppose secularist would be the best word to describe me before I met Jesus. I was chasing money and fame and never thinking about God. We just need to start praying for him like crazy right now."

"Yes, we do. This is Sunday, and the Assembly reconvenes Monday morning. So, I need to move quickly. I just don't want it to be too quickly. I will let the others know too. Poor Ollie doesn't know what he is walking into!"

"He certainly doesn't! I'm almost home. I will see you in a few."

With that, Blake was off the phone and Beth was on it with the Chicago group. They were blown away to hear about Ollie and amazed at all God was doing in such a short time. They estimated that they were four to five hours away. Soon, they would all be together!

Oliver Barton sat on the plane wondering what information Beth may have come up with. She was so sure it was correct. He knew she was good, but how could she discover not just *an* answer, but *the* answer to the disappearances and worldwide upheaval? She was a true bloodhound and had climbed the ladder of success in the news industry because of it. Maybe she did know. But if she did, why had she not unveiled the story? Questions for which answers would have to wait until he saw her. He lay back and dozed off. He dreamed. Or was it a dream? It seemed so real. Before him stood a man in gleaming white apparel. Ollie was afraid. He wanted to run, but there was nowhere to go. The man carried a large sword which he stretched out toward him. He flinched expecting to feel cold steel piercing his flesh. The man spoke.

"Oliver Barton, you have been chosen by God. I am Gabriel who stands in the presence of God. I have been sent to deliver this message to you. You have spoken with Beth Jennings. She is also my chosen vessel. I have come to tell you the news she has also been given."

"Wh...wh...what news? I have never believed in God. Why would I be chosen?"

"You will believe, and you will be used by God. The disappearances. They did not take place at the hands of alien life forms. On September 11, Jesus, who died and rose again then ascended into heaven took his people to be with him. While he was still on the earth he foretold this would happen. It has happened just as he said it would."

"But how..."

"He said his coming would be with the blast of a trumpet and as lightning flashes across the sky from east to west. Does that sound familiar?"

"That is what happened on September 11."

"Yes. And now has begun the final seven years of the earth. It will be ruled by a man who is anti-Christ. He is the epitome of evil but will come in peace. However, that peace will be short-lived. You already know who he is."

"Aissa Messai..."

"You have said it. Beth will tell you what you need to do and will introduce you to others. Do not delay for you are a chosen servant of the Lord to do his work in the Middle East."

Then as quickly as he had appeared, the man was gone. Ollie was wide awake and had broken out in a cold sweat. His whole body was trembling. Had it only been a dream? He looked at his tray which was now pulled down and out into his lap. It had been put away when he fell asleep! He remembered that clearly. On the tray lay a newspaper. It was plain with no writing, but it was large enough to be a Sunday edition. He picked it up, as he knew he was supposed to do. Every page, plain white paper, no text. He unfolded it until he could pull out the middle section. He opened it and immediately jumped back in his seat. Messai! A full page photo. Nothing else. It was as though he was staring into Ollie's soul. He felt pulled into the page. Fear gnawed at his mind. A chill ran down his spine. He felt fear, pure fear. He could hear Messai's voice. It was loud and directed at him.

"Oliver Barton, you belong to me! Do not believe the lies you have been told. Yes, there are only seven years remaining for this horrible planet. If you will serve me during those seven years, you will be rewarded with everything you have ever desired. You will be the news anchor for the entire earth. You will be by my side as I rule the world. Follow me, Ollie. Follow me."

He crumpled the paper and handed it to a flight attendant. "Garbage," he said as she took it. His mind was in disarray. Beth. He needed to talk to Beth. Gabriel had said she would tell him what he needed to do and introduce him to others. Gabriel. He may not be a Christian or a reader of the Bible, but he knew that name. He was an angel. He remembered hearing him referred to as the messenger angel who brought messages from God. He trusted Beth. He had no choice but to wait for her to tell him more. God. Jesus returning to take his people home. The blast of a trumpet. The deafening sound that accompanied the disappearances. As lightning flashes across the sky from east to west. The blinding flash of light that followed the boom. Messai. Evil. Seven years. He appeared to have a choice: Jesus or him. The need to choose felt urgent. He was shaken to the core of his being. Beth. He had to talk to Beth. He looked at his watch. 4:00 a.m. New York time. Six more hours. How could he wait that long? He had no option. One thing was sure, there would be no more sleep tonight.

CHAPTER 31

Beth sat in the airport, more than an hour early, awaiting Oliver Barton's arrival. She had risen after two hours of sleep, had a cup of red eye with Blake and left so she would be sure to not be late. It was her first ever cup of the strong stuff Blake loved so much, but she was quite certain she was going to need it this morning. Now she sat in a restaurant near Ollie's gate having a breakfast sandwich and more coffee...with a shot of espresso. She wanted to be wide awake when she saw Ollie. Her mind went back to September 11, then began to walk at a brisk pace through the events of the days since then. Her brain had stored those things in its hard drive and now replayed them one at the time as though she was watching a movie in which she had the lead role. How could so much have happened in such a short time? If she had not lived it, she doubted that she would have believed it. The memories came rapid fire: the disappearances, reporting on the scene in Times Square, the news about her mom and dad, Blake...she would never forget him coming to her in that moment of her greatest need. Then there was the trip to her parents' house, walking through it, the sights within, the earthquake, meeting with Blake that first night in the quaint little coffee shop, returning to his place and becoming a follower of Jesus. The memories kept coming: the trip to Chicago, taking Blake and Anders to the place that would soon become the headquarters and safe place for the Smyrnians, the flight back to New York aboard the private jet, the storm, a crash landing about to happen, Jesus intervening and saving their lives. Wow. Falling in love, Blake's marriage proposal, her acceptance, the feeling of euphoria! The United Nations Assembly, the nomination of Aissa Messai to be the next Secretary of the UN, his steely glare, her feeling of sheer terror, the chill down her spine. The news that Evan, Ally and John were coming to New York, the assassination of the anti-Messai group leader, the call from Ollie, news that Ben had become a follower of Jesus, how that happened and what it meant. Her head was spinning with all the little details and acute feelings that had accompanied each individual event. The next seven years. She wished she could see the future as vividly as she could see the past. Or did she? It would be better to take it as it came, not knowing what each day may bring. Even with the trepidation those thoughts raised, her face lit up with a smile as she realized she would soon be Mrs. Blake Thompson...or Beth Jennings Thompson. The choice of name was totally irrelevant.

"Beth? Beth Jennings?" She heard her name.

"Ollie!" she squealed, not caring that she sounded quite unprofessional.

"You sure are lost in another world. What brought that big smile to your face? I'm hoping it may have been the thought of seeing your old pal from the past."

"Oh Ollie, I *am* thrilled to see you! I have been so excited that you were coming. I can hardly believe you are here. Oliver Barton in New York City!"

"Okay, I need to claim my luggage and get out of here. I must talk to you Beth. It is urgent. Let's grab my bags and get to a place where we can do that."

As they hurried to the baggage claim, Beth's mind was a blur again. What did Ollie want to talk about that was so important it could not wait? Was it her? Was it him? Was it the news she had promised to tell him? Her pulse quickened, not from the brisk pace but from anxiety. How would she talk to him about Jesus? She had the video. Should she use it? Would he listen if she tried to explain it herself? Could she do that effectively? "Let's just get the bags and get out of here," she thought.

Blake sat anxiously watching the time as he waited for the Chicago group to arrive. His phone dinged. It was a text from Evan! "We're here!" it read. He leapt to his feet and ran toward the door. A quick reply: "I have cleared you to come on up."

The doorbell rang, and he threw it open. Evan, Ally and John were a sight for sore eyes. He embraced them one at a time, then they grabbed each other in a group hug that none of them wanted to end.

"Breakfast is served," he said. "I'm sure you guys are hungry."

"I know I am," exclaimed Evan. "We didn't want to take time to stop for breakfast. So, I must tell you, those pastries look amazing!"

Coffee, juices and milk were also served, and they all chowed down. The doorbell rang again and Blake jumped up to answer it. It could not be Beth and Ollie. It was too soon. He very slowly opened the door and saw a rather large group of people looking back at him from the outside.

Beth and Ollie had claimed his luggage and were now outside the airport and walking to her car. When they made it, he threw his bags in the back and both climbed inside. As she reached to push the start button, Ollie reached out and stopped her.

"Beth, I need to talk to you now. I can't let this wait another minute."

"What is it, Ollie?"

"Something happened to me during the flight, Beth. Something stranger than anything I have ever experienced. But it was real, very real."

"Tell me Ollie. I'm listening."

"On the plane. We were about halfway into the flight. A man, or an angel or something, I don't know, appeared to me. He was wearing the brightest robe I have ever seen. He gleamed! He said his name was Gabriel, and he stands in the presence of God. He told me the disappearances were not an alien invasion. It was Jesus taking his people home. He described them exactly the way they happened and said that is how Jesus said it would take place. Beth, you know I have never believed in God or Jesus, or any of that stuff."

"Neither did I, Ollie, even though my mom and dad were Christians. That is why they were taken Ollie. Just like every other person who disappeared. They were all Christians, or babies and small children who weren't yet old enough to believe in Jesus for themselves. Blake Thompson showed me a video of a preacher who described it that same way over four years ago. He got every single detail right. That *is* what happened Ollie. Once I knew that, I put my faith in Jesus and received him as my Savior. You would not believe how much he has done for me since!"

"Gabriel told me you would tell me what to do. But then the eeriest thing I have ever seen happened. Right after Gabriel spoke to me, I woke up and my tray came down in my lap. There was a newspaper on it. But it was plain white, no writing. I knew I was supposed to read it. I opened it to the middle and there was a full-page picture of Aissa Messai. I have never felt the evil and fear that I felt in that moment. He talked to me and told me to follow him and I would have everything I have ever wanted. Beth, I knew I had to make a choice: Jesus or Messai. Please help me Beth. What is it that I need to do? Gabriel said you would tell me."

"The same thing I did, Ollie. Just tell Jesus you believe in him and ask him to come into your life. You believe, don't you?"

"I do now!"

"Then ask Jesus right now. Blake, I and a few others have done that. We are a team. There really are only seven years left for this planet. These years are going to be the worst the world has ever seen. And it will all come at the hands of Aissa Messai. He is the antichrist. The Bible says he will come. He will chase down and murder people who believe in Jesus instead of following him. But we are determined to battle him every step of the way and try to survive the seven years!"

"I'm ready Beth. I don't want to wait!"

Before she could say another word, Oliver Barton prayed right there and asked Jesus to be his Savior. What happened even surprised Beth. It was as if an electric shock or bolt of lightning had hit him. He jumped in the seat. The look on his face was one of amazement and wonder.

"He is real, Beth. Jesus is real! You cannot believe how I feel!"

"Oh yes, I have been there, done that, Ollie. Trust me, I know *exactly* how you feel!"

"What am I supposed to do? Gabriel said you would tell me."

"Let me take you to meet the team. That is what we are going to talk about. Welcome to the team!"

"Let's go! Does this team have a name?"

"*Smyrnians*, Ollie. We are the Smyrnians."

"I'm not even going to ask what that is all about. I'm just happy to be on board!"

"Oh, by the way, Blake and I are getting married. I am in love, Ollie. Soon I will be Mrs. Blake Thompson, and I can hardly wait!"

"You are just full of surprises. But I have a feeling the surprises have just begun."

"Right you are, Ollie. Right you are."

In his room at the ONE UN Hotel, Aissa Messai exploded in a fit of rage. "How dare he? How dare he reject me? He will pay. I will make him pay! I will make them *all* pay! They will lose. *Jesus* will lose. I will reign. I will rule the world!" The room shook. Lights flashed off and on. Dark spirit creatures flew around and in and out of the room, screeching and screaming. It had begun. It had definitely begun.

Blake looked into the faces of Ben, Miriam and their seven kids standing at his door. Ben had often said he and his wife had chosen to have seven kids because that was God's perfect number. Blake had joked that forty was also God's number and he was glad they chose seven instead.

"Ben! Miriam! Come in. There are some people here you need to meet. Kids, we have some pastries and juice, assuming Evan hasn't devoured them all."

"Hey, I heard that! I left a few, but they sure are good."

"Ben, Miriam, kids, this is Evan Ryles from Chicago. He is a college student there. He is the one who first showed me the video and told me about Jesus and what really happened on September 11. You might say he started all this."

Ben approached Evan and put out his hand. "Young man, I want to shake your hand and say thank you. Because you didn't hide your belief in Jesus, I am here today as the first Jewish man to believe after the disappearances, uh, *Rapture*. I feel uniquely prepared to get the good news out to my people."

It was the first time that Blake had seen Evan speechless. Tears slipped from his eyes and rolled down his face. "You are welcome, Mr. Abramson. You are so welcome."

No one wanted to spoil the moment, but surprisingly it was Miriam who did. She had always seemed stoic and quite reserved, but it appeared that her newfound faith in Jesus may have changed that!

"Okay, okay. I want to meet everyone too, but these kids are eyeing those pastries. Can we please finish the introductions while we eat?"

Her point was well taken. Everyone was introduced. It was a magical moment. The team was coming together.

"Where is Beth?" asked Ben. "I sure am glad we are on the same team now! I'm anxious to talk to her."

"She is picking up someone at the airport. He is flying in from England. You know his name, Ben. Oliver Barton."

"*The* Oliver Barton? He is coming to New York?"

"He sure is, to cover the General Assembly."

"I thought he was specifically a Middle East reporter?"

"That has always been his beat. But this story is so big that all the big ones will be in this city tomorrow."

"I hope I get to meet him while he is here."

"I hope you do too, Ben. I really hope so." Blake's hope was for the biggest reason of all. He hoped beyond hope that both men would be on the same team before Ollie returned to England.

Beth and Ollie's drive to Blake's place felt like it took five minutes. She was not even sure their tires were touching the road. Before they knew it, they were standing at his door. She opened the door and they stepped inside.

"Hello, everybody. I want you to meet someone. This is Oliver Barton from London. I may be a little biased, but he is the best journalist in England and the Middle East!"

They were all obviously shocked that he was with her. This could be a bit uncomfortable for them with a man who had not believed in Jesus. Ollie broke the ice.

"I know it is early, but why so quiet? I thought you would all be excited to welcome a new member of the Smyrnians. Besides, I am hungry and that food looks delicious!"

"You mean...?"

"Yes, Blake. Ollie believes in Jesus! He has been a Christian for almost an hour now."

That really brought the celebration to a new level. If anyone else could hear, they surely thought Blake Thompson was throwing a party. And indeed, he was! Ollie shared his story from the plane, about Gabriel and Messai and the feelings he experienced. None of them was amazed at anything they heard now. At this point, they felt almost indestructible. They were beginning to think these seven years were going to be the ride of their lives. It would be, but they had no clue what kind of ride it would be. None of them knew the horrors that, not just the world would face, but *they* would face. Would they all survive the seven years? If not, who would and who would not? They needed to enjoy this moment because moments like this would be few and far between in the days to come.

In Germany, Bruno Fromm was dreaming again. He, Mila and the boys were driving somewhere in the Middle East and nearing a military checkpoint. They came to a stop, and he nervously put the window down. As the soldiers walked to their car, he was seized by fear. A large man with his head lowered came and stood directly in front of them. He slowly raised his head and looked into their eyes. Aissa Messai! The chill that had become all too familiar ran down his spine.

"Take the boys!" Messai commanded.

The soldiers held guns on Bruno and Mila as they dragged the boys from the back seat. They were sobbing and crying out for their parents to help them. The men held them several feet away. Then Bruno and Mila were ordered out of the car. The big man instinctively started to charge toward the boys when he felt the butt of an AK 47 slam into his head knocking him to his knees. Dazed he tried to struggle to his feet. The soldiers handcuffed him, lifted him to a standing position and stood him beside Mila. The boys were still crying and begging the men to let them go. Messai came and stood in front of the couple.

"Worship me!" he demanded. "Bow on your knees and worship me!"

"Never!" shouted Bruno. "We will never worship you!" Mila was sobbing softly beside him.

"You!" shouted Messai at her. "You worship me! Do not let this man stop you. I command you to worship me!"

"No," she whispered softly.

"What did you say?" bellowed Messai.

"I said no. I will not worship you, no matter what you do to me."

"Oh, it is not you or your husband that you have to worry about. Worship me or watch your boys die! Bow down now and worship me!"

Bruno and Mila looked into each other's eyes. They knew this moment could come.

"Now!" yelled Messai.

"No." Bruno's voice was no longer the voice of the man Mila had always known. It was soft and shaky.

"Kill them!"

The men backed away from the boys and raised their guns.

"No!" screamed Mila. Bruno tried to pull away but could not.

"Fire!" came the command.

Just as Bruno heard the sound of the guns firing, he woke up. He was shaking all over and covered with sweat. Tears filled his eyes and he was screaming loudly, "No!"

Mila came to him and held him.

"It is okay, Bruno. Everything is okay. You were dreaming."

"The boys... where are the boys?"

"They are in their rooms. They are fine."

He gradually became calm.

"Mila, I am so afraid for them and what they will face during the next seven years. I hope I can be strong. I just hope I can be strong."

"You will be, dear. You will be. I will be with you. Ally and the boys will be too. We will make it."

"I wish I could be as sure as you are about that, Mila. I really do. But I am so afraid."

He had every right to be afraid...very afraid.

Blake lived in a spacious high rise apartment, but there was little extra room as sixteen people crowded inside. They had spent a couple of hours getting to know each other. They felt as if they had known each other forever. But as they were enjoying being together, the day was slipping away. Time was short and they had to make the minutes count. Tomorrow would be a day that would change the world, and they needed to be as prepared as they could be.

"We only have until tomorrow morning," said Blake. "We have to decide what we are going to do. Do we plan, or do we go out on the town?"

Evan was obviously torn by the question. "As much as I want to see the city, we have serious work to do. I say we order up some New York pizza and spend this time planning and strategizing. The rest of us can't get into the assembly tomorrow anyway, so we can see some sites while Blake and Beth, and all you other news people, are there doing your jobs. Hey, someone has to work, right?" He smiled.

"You are right young man," said Ben. He still did not have everyone's names down yet, but he would. "We don't have any time to waste. My people are depending on us. I must get the truth to them! They have been blinded, just like I was. Let's get rolling. You out of towners can see the city tomorrow."

"I agree," chimed in Ollie. "I will be in that assembly tomorrow. That is why I'm here, at least I *thought* that was why I was coming. Turns out there is far more to it than that. I admit, I dread looking Aissa Messai in the face. After what I saw on that plane today, I have a feeling I know what that is going to be like. I'm getting a chill down my spine just thinking about it. But I'm ready to fight him, to fight him every step of the way. What are we waiting for? Let's get to work!"

"The pizza is ordered, but I can't believe you are hungry, Evan." Blake had placed the call as Ben and Ollie spoke. "I have plenty of drinks and snacks. We are set for the night, or however long as we can stay awake. None of us has had any sleep. As important as our meeting is, I still think we need some rest if we're going to be alert enough to make it through tomorrow's meeting. And you Chicagoans can't see the city if you can't stay awake. I say we meet until 10:00, then go to bed. I have room here if you don't mind bunking down wherever you can find."

All were agreed, and Evan took the floor. Blake had the white board in place with plenty of markers in different colors to diagram a plan of action that would guide them as they went to war. Just as Evan started to speak, the pizza arrived.

"Okay, as important as this is, I have been waiting a long time to eat New York pizza. I have a feeling it is not as good as Chicago pizza, but we shall see." He grinned at the New Yorkers.

"You will feel like you have never had pizza before when you taste this!" Anders was finally in on the action.

They dug in, and Evan had to agree it was delicious pizza. Even though the others could see how much he liked it, he would not budge on his opinion. But he did at least put the two different style pizzas on equal status with each other. It was a true pizza feast. Then Evan stood and approached the board again. The room fell silent and every eye was on him. This was the most important time any of them had ever spent. Their very lives depended on these few hours, as did the lives and eternity of everyone else in the world.

Evan went over everything that had been discussed and decided upon thus far. He told the newcomers about the safe place and showed the video Anders had recorded. He asked John to talk about the cost of the underground bunker and how the money would need to be raised to purchase it. The glaring problems were: how they could make such a purchase without giving themselves away, and second, installation. To allow anyone to come and install the bunker would give away their location. They could afford neither. Ben saw no problem with the funding, but the other issues would need a miracle to be resolved. Nonetheless, as the discussions continued, it was evident that plans were coming together. But as good as the plans seemed now, they knew adjustments would need to be made again and again in the future.

"We are a team," said Evan. "But we are like a football team. There is the offense, the defense, special teams, etc."

"Ah, you Americans don't know what futbol is," laughed Ollie. "Let's talk real futbol."

"Oh, I think we have a pretty good grasp on *real* football, Mr. Englishman," said Evan with a twinkle in his eye. "Anyway, as I was saying, we need to work separately in teams also. So, I know we have the news team. What others do we have covered?"

"Well, I am a spy," chimed in Ally. "*And* I am with Ollie on the futbol thing."

Ollie swelled with pride and a sense of satisfaction at that one.

"So, do we have any other potential spies?" Ally asked.

"Okay, newsmen and woman in the living room and spies in the kitchen. John is into research. Anyone with him?"

"Miriam is a good researcher," volunteered Ben. "And I think our kids can join Ally's team. They can get by with a lot without being suspected of anything. Benny, the oldest, is eighteen and Esther, the youngest, is eight. All of them are capable of helping reach my people and fight the enemy."

"I have planned to be the coordinator of the movement, but I am willing to help anywhere I can." Evan was not one to shy away from the action. "I will be walking between teams, giving input and gathering data. But each of you needs to take copious notes as well. Other than that, I will be out there on the balcony praying and looking at that gorgeous view!"

They rolled their eyes at him.

"What?" he asked. "Somebody has to do it."

With that, they were into their teams and hard at work. The planning lasted until nearly 11:00. The meetings were highly productive and they felt ready, at least as ready as they could be after one day of meeting. It was time for bed and rest. Tomorrow would be an important day.

CHAPTER 32

Monday morning had dawned in New York City. Delegates began to gather at the United Nations Headquarters. Blake, Beth and Ollie were set to enter the building wearing their credentials. Anders was there with his camera ready. He would also get to be inside filming and sending a live feed to the world. Blake would be reporting before he went inside. Ben and the others were watching in Blake's apartment. In Germany, the Fromms were tuned in too. They had been fully informed on all the events of the previous day. This was the day. It was go time!

Blake and Anders were set up outside the UN building, as were Beth and Ollie. Each was reporting on the expected election of Aissa Messai as the new Secretary-General. The two murders and uproar at Saturday's meeting were mentioned briefly, but all minds were on what today would bring and what it meant for the future. What role would the new leader of the UN play in leading the world following the devastating events of the recent past. This was clearly the most crucial time in the history of the planet. The Smyrnian news team had a few brief moments to talk before entering the building.

"Okay," Blake said quietly, "we know this is not going to be easy. We must avoid Messai's trance. When he glares at either of us, we will look away, at each other....and pray! Oliver..."

The Brit interrupted. "Wait a minute there, Blake. We need to get this straight. It is Ollie, okay? Oliver to the world, but Ollie to my friends and teammates."

"Got it, Mr. Barton."

Ollie frowned at him and Blake smiled.

"Ollie, it is. I'm thankful to have you on board!"

"No happier than I am to be here, I assure you."

"Enough with the pleasantries. It is almost time to go in. Game faces on, plans in place and minds set on prayer, right?"

Beth was anxious to get inside. "I hope we can sit near each other on press row. But if not, I think we are all ready. I'm not a boxing fan, but Messai's election is the sound of the opening bell. This fight will go seven rounds. We already know who is going to throw the knockout punch in that final round. What we don't know is whether all of us will be here to see it. But I can tell you guys, I am in it to win it! I know you are too. So, let's jump in the ring and let the fight begin!"

It was the most fired up Blake had ever seen his soon to be bride. "Wow, Babe. I am impressed! Boxing, of all things. I would not have guessed that you knew anything about that. But I can tell you that I am ready to put the gloves on! How about you, Ollie? Anders?"

"Ready!" both exclaimed at the same time.

Blake placed a quick call to the others and said, "We are heading in."

"Hey, if it looks like it is going to be a long and boring day there, John, Ally and I may go out and do a little sightseeing," said Evan. "We can watch the coverage on our phones while we are out. If we are needed, let us know and we will be back in a jiffy."

"I think that is a great idea, Evan. You guys enjoy, and the three of us will see you tonight."

With that, the doors were open and a wave of people began to pour through them. The ambassadors walked to their assigned seats while reporters and camera operators jockeyed for position. There was a feeling in the air. It was neither a feeling of anticipation, excitement nor fear. No, it was strange, nothing like any feeling anyone had ever felt. And if one could see it, they would watch it spreading from the UN Headquarters in New York City, like a dark cloud covering the entire world. Ominous indeed. But even more than ominous, it was foreboding.

At 8:00 a.m. sharp the president pounded his gavel and called the meeting to order. Blake could not help but think how much it reminded him of the opening bell of a boxing match. What was that he was feeling? It was different from the familiar chill he had felt. It seemed to permeate the room. On the one hand, it was sinister. On the other hand, it felt serene. Very strange. He, Beth and Ollie were seated together. He whispered to them and both said they felt it too. By looking at the other faces in the room, they felt sure everyone felt it and that the feeling would rule the day.

"Ladies and gentlemen, as all of you know, this is a very important day," the president began. "We are here to consider one item, and one item only: the election of a new Secretary-General of the United Nations. As we continue these proceedings, no outbursts such as we saw Saturday will be tolerated. This meeting will be conducted peacefully and show the true nature of the UN itself. Security has been heightened outside the building, but it is also heavy inside the building. Because this decision is to be made in a democratic manner, we anticipate some disagreement and dissent. But when the decision has been made, it is expected that we will depart as a unified body. Belligerent or threatening behavior will not be allowed. Security has been instructed to remove any member of this group who exhibits either of those. That said, let the meeting begin.

The Security Council has nominated Ambassador Aissa Messai to be the Secretary-General of the United Nations. His election would be to fill the remaining two years of Secretary Pieters term. He would then be eligible for reelection to serve a succeeding five-year term."

"That is *seven* years," Blake whispered to Beth and Ollie. Both nodded. Ollie looked shocked.

As the discussion got underway, it quickly became apparent that a vast majority was in favor of Messai's election. Dissenters came from scattered countries around the globe. A few European ambassadors were joined by others from Southeast Asia, and noticeably Central and South America. These were vocal in their opposition, but not nearly as vocal as before. Seeing what had happened to the previous opposition leader had tempered their willingness to be too outspoken against Aissa Messai. Supporters spoke in glowing terms of the nominee, pointing out his peaceful, yet commanding demeanor and newness to the world scene. Discussion was brief and the time to vote came more quickly than anyone had anticipated. The *feeling* consumed the room and everyone in it. Everyone, that is, except the three reporters sitting in the middle of press row. They felt it strongly, but their minds were shielded by a power that was much greater. They sat and observed.

The vote was taken with each representative stating their *yes* or *no*. The no votes were spoken softly, barely audible. Those who voted in favor did so with boldness and enthusiasm. The final count was Yes: 160 and No: 33. The nomination was approved. Aissa Messai was the new Secretary-General of the United Nations.

Beth reached over and squeezed Blake's hand. He gently stroked the back of her hand with his thumb. Both of their thoughts went to a wedding that would happen soon. He mouthed the word "tomorrow?" She smiled and nodded "yes." There was neither time nor reason to wait.

As Evan, Ally and John visited places they had only dreamed of seeing, they kept abreast of events at the UN Headquarters. Thus far, there were no surprises so they were making the most of the day. They had covered Times Square and walked through Central Park. That was Ally's favorite place. She said it reminded her of home. John and Evan marveled more at such architectural wonders as the Empire State Building and St. Patrick's Cathedral. They knew they were rushing each stop, but who knew what the coming days may bring? They wanted to see as much as they could while they had the chance. High on their priority list were the Statue of Liberty, Brooklyn Bridge, the 9/11 Memorial, and for Evan, eating in Chinatown and Little Italy. They would love to hit the museums, and the Bronx Zoo, Yankee Stadium and Coney Island, if they had the time. Regardless of what would happen tomorrow, they were making the most of today. It could be the last real fun they would have in a long time.

Aissa Messai took the podium to deliver his first address as the Secretary-General of the UN. The *feeling* filled the room.

"Ladies and gentlemen of the General Assembly, I gratefully accept this position and am humbled by your trust in me. I pledge to you my efforts to make the world a better place, with your support. I am a man of peace and will do everything in my power to bring peace through a unified world that includes all nations, united as one. I will begin working immediately with the heads of world government to accomplish this goal. The atrocities of recent weeks will become a distant memory as we move into the greatest time of prosperity the world has ever known. Let us commit ourselves today to coming together to work toward this common goal. To those of you who opposed me, I stretch out the hand of goodwill. To those who supported me, I ask you to do the same. It begins today. It all begins today. Welcome to the *new world order.*"

With that, he stepped away from the podium to thunderous applause. Most were standing for the ovation; a few were not. To watching eyes around the globe, it was a much-needed moment. Who would have thought any person could rise up at this time and bring hope to a hurting world? It was obvious that Aissa Messai was that man. Things were getting ready to change. Yes, things were most definitely getting ready to change.

Among those not standing were Blake Thompson, Beth Jennings and Oliver Barton. Messai seemed to be staring directly at them, even as he smiled and waved to his adoring fans. They could not escape the return of the chill, that came from his icy glare, running down their spines. Ollie had felt it firsthand when Messai confronted him on the plane. He recognized the difference in how he felt this time. And he knew the difference was Jesus.

A huge day behind them, the Smyrnians knew a lot needed to happen in a brief amount of time because the time was short. For one thing, there was a wedding to be had. Ben gave Blake and Anders the next few days off and Beth was able to get the same. Ben agreed to give Ollie the grand tour of the city on Wednesday and Thursday. Newsman to newsman, their stops would be a bit different from those of the others. Anders was more than happy to devote the same days to making sure Evan, Ally and John saw everything they missed and still wanted to see. But tomorrow there would be no touring, no ordering pizza, only one thing: the wedding of Blake Thompson and Beth Jennings. It would be a day of celebration! Fast? Certainly. Too soon? Not at all. They were ready. The wedding would take place at high noon. The Rapture had occurred at midnight under the cover of darkness. The wedding would happen at noon under what was forecast to be a bright sunny sky. And it would be at Blake's place with guests seated in the living room and the bride and groom standing on the balcony. For tonight, everyone would return to their own homes. The Chicago trio would stay with Anders. He was beyond excited about that. They would make plans for their upcoming days of sightseeing. Ally had something up her sleeve and they all knew it. But none of them had any idea what she was thinking. She was giddy about it. But it was her secret. Ollie would stay in the plush hotel room that had been provided for him. They would rest. They would read the Bible. And they would pray. Then tomorrow. They would see each other tomorrow.

At the ONE UN Hotel, a victory celebration was getting ready to begin. That was not just unusual, it was unheard of for an elected Secretary-General of the United Nations. But Aissa Messai was not your typical appointee. His charisma. His charm. There was something about him that clearly elevated him to a position of honor greater than any of his predecessors. And more than a position of honor, his was a role of leadership that transcended his title and purpose. He stood poised to be a true world leader. But far more than that, he was set to become *the* leader of the entire world.

The party was in full swing. The other ambassadors were present, including those who had opposed Messai's election. It was an attempt at portraying a unified front. The bubbly was flowing, and there were hors d'oeuvres aplenty. A band played and people mingled. Messai was in the middle of the action, greeting the people and displaying a calm, yet commanding demeanor. A large screen projected a photograph of him that was larger than life. Napkins were inscribed with his name and the date of his election. The menu had been carefully chosen: braised lamb shanks and mutton curry with vegetables and an assortment of breads. For dessert, there was baklava, tiramisu and lemon and berry cream cheese parfait. An assortment of fine wines, soft drinks, bottled water and Turkish coffee were offered as drinks. It was a black tie gala with a guest list made up only of UN Ambassadors and leaders of a few selected countries. The press was not allowed. This evening had an internal purpose with a specific goal in mind: to rally all 193 member nations of the world around the new Secretary-General and unify them under his leadership. It was working perfectly.

Tuesday morning had arrived. It was the big day! Beth Jennings would become Mrs. Blake Thompson today. Assuming both survived, they would experience seven years of marital bliss, even amid the turmoil which would almost certainly surround them. Blake had the apartment spic and span, with some simple wedding decorations. This event was in stark contrast to the gala of the preceding evening at the ONE UN Hotel. Dress code was casual, except for the bride and groom. He would wear a black tux with lavender tie and she a lavender evening gown which was her favorite. A beautiful wedding cake sat in the middle of the dining room table, directly under the stunning chandelier which hung above it. A fondue fountain sat on the bar that separated the kitchen and dining room, with strawberries in the fridge waiting to be dipped in the smooth chocolate which would flow from it. The freezer contained assorted flavors of ice cream. The punch was already prepared and sitting on the shelf beneath the strawberries. Everything was ready. Blake was now awaiting the arrival of the wedding guests.

The first to arrive were Ben and his family. The excitement of their newfound faith had not dimmed. If anything, it had grown. Ollie came shortly after, and he and Ben engaged quickly in conversation like two old friends, even though they had never met prior to the previous day. Newsmen always have something to talk about. Next came Anders, Evan, Ally and John. Anders had camera in tow and ready to shoot a video which they would have available to watch whenever they wanted. Ally would serve as the photographer. It was her hobby and one she loved. She once had a photograph published in a major magazine. She was very proud of that! Everyone was there. Everyone, that is, except the bride. She would make her entrance at 11:55 sharp and walk out to join her groom on the balcony. They spent this time smiling, laughing and getting to know each other better. They were a team, and everyone in the room could feel the team coming together. It was a special thing, of which were blessed to be a part.

At 11:15, the doorbell rang. "Beth is not supposed to be here until 11:55," Blake thought. It was unlike her to be one minute early or late for an appointment. Evan rose to get the door, but Ally insisted he sit back down. This was Blake's apartment. He should be the one to do that. When Blake opened the door, his surprise caused him to take a step backward. He could hardly believe his eyes. Neither could the others, for that matter. Ollie and Ben were really taken aback.

"Blake!" exclaimed Bruno Fromm with a huge smile covering his face. "You didn't think we would miss your big day, did you?"

"Surprise!" yelled Ally.

"Bruno! Mila! Boys!" Blake was as overwhelmed as Ally had seen him. She was ecstatic! She had pulled off the ultimate surprise. It was what this day needed to be complete.

"Everyone, this is my family from Germany. They are the remaining four members of our team," Ally beamed.

"You had better introduce yourselves quick," said Blake. "Beth will be here in 30 minutes!"

They did just that. Handshakes and hugs all around. Ollie was sure the big man had broken at least one rib with his strong hug. But he was going to like this group. He could tell that. After all, for the time being, they were the only other people on the team who were from *across the pond.*

Everyone was seated by 11:50 and anxiously awaiting Beth's arrival. True to form, she walked in the door at exactly 11:55. As she walked by to say hello to everyone, sitting on the end she saw the Fromms. Her mouth flew open in surprise, and she let out a shriek.

"Bruno and Mila! How, when..." She was overcome with emotion.

"Never mind any of that, dear. We are here. We would not have missed this for the world."

"Come on now, Beth. No tears before the wedding," said Anders.

"I'm sorry everyone. I am just so happy. Having all of you here makes this day very special. Bruno and Mila, thank you so much for coming." They nodded and smiled.

"Come on sweetheart," said Blake. "It is time!"

Standing on the balcony, Blake and Beth faced the team sitting just inside. Blake spoke.

"Dearly beloved, we are gathered here today... Just kidding," he said.

"This ceremony should take about 15 minutes. First, a song. We searched for a Christian song that said exactly what we feel today. Honestly, they are not easy to find now. But we found this one. It says it all. It is 'When I Say I Do.' It was recorded 20 years ago by a Christian artist named Matthew West." None of them had heard of him. They had never been into Christian music until now.

Tears flowed as they listened the words. Smiles accompanied them as they heard "this crazy life." That part made sense as they thought about the days ahead. The song ended, and Blake and Beth turned and faced each other.

"We have each written our vows to the other," Beth said. "We will read them now."

Tears flowed again. Beth could hardly make it through hers. Blake smiled and placed his hands on each of hers as she held the paper. He was next. To his surprise, he could not hold back the tears either. She lovingly placed her hands on his too as he read. It was time for the big moment.

They gently held hands. Blake spoke first, then Beth.

"Beth, I love you. And today I take you as my wife forever. I will love you with all of my heart and always try to love you as God loves you. Today, I say 'I do.'"

She repeated the same words and they simultaneously placed rings on each other's fingers. He then excitedly announced, "Blake, this is the moment you have been waiting for. You may kiss your bride!" The group cheered as he laid her back on his arm and gave her a passionate kiss.

They stood and faced the group, holding hands with big smiles on their faces. "Smyrnians," Beth announced, "I am happy to present to you Mr. and Mrs. Blake and Beth Jennings Thompson!"

They celebrated like followers of Jesus who now knew what true love is. Never in their lives had the couple been happier than they were at this moment. Their happiness was real, but they also knew happiness can be the breeding ground for grief, should tragedy strike. For now, they would hold each other as closely as they could and cling to one another "for better...or for *worse*."

At the ONE UN, as the celebration neared its end on Day 2, Messai had been speaking to the rowdy crowd for about 15 minutes. It amounted to a victory speech, but no one would dare call it that. He recognized a few people and thanked them for their "tireless service and commitment to making the world a better place." Then to the amazement of everyone in attendance, he paused and called one man to join him on the stage: the ambassador from Israel.

"My friend, here in front of this group, I want to pledge to you my support for the Nation of Israel and my efforts to bring peace between your country and the surrounding nations. Being Arab and Muslim from birth, I understand the hostility and division that has existed between our religions, our countries and our people. My goal above all others is to bring peace to the Middle East and between Muslims and Jews worldwide. I wanted all who are present to hear that from my own lips. I hope you will work alongside me in that quest."

Thunderous applause once again greeted his comments. The Israeli shook Messai's hand with an obvious look of uncertainty and doubt on his face. Messai, seizing the moment, raised their clenched hands up and held them there as the applause grew even louder, accompanied by whoops and shouts. As the ambassador left the stage, many wondered, was peace in the Middle East possible? Could it really happen? If it could, worldwide peace was surely achievable too. It was a moment that would define the day, exactly as Messai had planned it.

"Okay, let's eat cake!" Evan shouted, interrupting the congratulatory hugs and laughter. Food was nearly always a priority for him. This time was no different.

"Hold on again, my young friend," Blake replied. "We are not having cake right now."

"Ah, come on. Don't tell me you are going to take an hour for pictures before we get to eat."

"Ally is going to take a few pictures, Evan. We want a few of us and some of us with all of you. They will help all of us remember the joy of this occasion during turbulent days ahead." Beth was not about to let that opportunity pass.

"Fifteen minutes, Evan. No more," promised Blake. "But we still don't get to eat cake then."

"Okay, so you are freezing the whole cake for us to eat a year from now. Is that it?"

"Easy Evan," said Ally. "I have a feeling you will get to eat your cake. Now be quiet for fifteen minutes so I can get these pictures taken. The more you talk, the longer you have to wait for the cake!" He looked at her with consternation.

"So, hurry up and take your pictures. This guy is getting hungry."

Blake spoke up again. "We will hurry with the pictures. If everyone cooperates, they should take no more than ten minutes. Everybody line up.

We want pictures with each group or individual. We can do that fast. Then Beth and I have a surprise for you."

"More surprises, and still no cake." Evan snickered this time showing that he was only having fun. "Tell me, Blake. What is this great surprise that keeps us from having cake?"

"Okay, if I tell you, maybe you will help us get through these pictures faster. Do you remember when we were meeting in Chicago and we promised you a great meal when you came to New York? Well, as soon as the pictures are finished, we are taking all of you out for the best meal you have ever had, New York style! Then we will come back here and celebrate the day away eating all the cake and chocolate covered strawberries you can hold."

"I'm in line!" Evan had leapt up and was standing between Blake and Beth. "Take the pic, Ally. Who is up next? Get over here in line. We have food to eat!" Sure enough, ten minutes later they were on their way to the restaurant. Blake had made reservations, so there would be no waiting this time. The meal was one of the most amazing they had ever eaten. As they ate, talked and laughed, their friendships were growing. They skipped dessert because they knew what awaited them when they returned. After over two hours of chowing down, it was back to the apartment for more celebrating with the newlyweds. The chocolate flowed from the fountain. Strawberries were dipped and devoured until they were all gone. The cake was cut, and everyone had at least one piece. The celebration went on until late in the evening. Then Blake and Beth were finally alone for a one-night honeymoon. Deep inside, each of them believed this would likely be the last day like this they would have. Little did they know just how right they were. The world, the *entire* world, was about to change. But for tonight, the Thompsons may have been the happiest two people who lived in it. Their love would see them through whatever they were about to face.

CONCLUSION

As morning dawned over New York City, the UN meeting had ended, and the ambassadors were returning home. The hustle and bustle of the city was normal once again. The same was true around the world. An unsuspecting populace was feeling good about the future and the man who had risen out of nowhere to bring hope. Memories of the *Invasion* had faded into the past, albeit the recent past. Rays of peace and prosperity seemed to rise with the sun. It was a beautiful day.

The Smyrnians were together again. Here, there was no such optimism. Oh, there was joy. Blake and Beth were filled with happiness and ecstasy. The others put forth their best efforts to continue the celebration of the day before. But their smiles and attempted laughter betrayed the thoughts that filled their minds. Suddenly, without warning, the *feeling* returned. The all too familiar *chill* accompanied it. Each of them felt it and knew the others felt it too. They could see it on their faces. They saw a change occurring outside. The effervescent glow of the brilliant sunshine was fading into an invading darkness. Together, they walked out onto the spacious balcony. A deep, dark haze was settling over Manhattan. As they watched, it began to spread. Instinctively they knew they were the only ones who could see it. It was the emergence of evil, foreboding and fearful.

Blake and Beth held each other tightly, as if to never turn loose. Evan and Ally clasped hands. Bruno gathered Mila and the boys into a strong embrace with his big arms pulling them in. Miriam gathered seven children and spread her arms over them like a mother hen as if to shield them from what was coming. Ben embraced her from behind as she held them close. Anders pulled a picture of his wife and kids from his wallet and clutched it to his chest. John stood silently, his mind filled with thoughts of things that were coming quickly. Ollie's face grew pale as he vividly recalled the face of

Aissa Messai staring at him from a blank newspaper during his flight to New York. They stood for what felt like hours watching the evil fog envelop the earth.

The fog continued to spread. It was clearly spreading eastward, but covering the entire world as it went. The Smyrnians could not only *see* it, they could *feel* it...and *hear* it. A low rumble that sounded like thunder. It seemed to accompany the fog as thunder often accompanies clouds on a rainy day. They knew what it meant. A storm was coming. It would be the storm to top all storms. Not a weather-related storm. Far worse. People were not aware it was coming. How could they be? There was only one way. The Smyrnians had to warn them. And warn them they would, even at the risk of their lives.

Evan softly uttered the words of the verse which had given them both their mission and their name. *"Do not be afraid of what you are about to suffer. I tell you, the devil will put some of you in prison to test you, and you will suffer persecution for ten days. Be faithful, even to the point of death, and I will give you the crown of life."* They *would* be faithful, even to the point of death. Of that, they were sure. War had been declared by the forces of evil. But the Smyrnians knew they were up to the fight. Standing together, with Jesus on their side, they were ready. Whether in life or in death, they could not lose.

They formed a circle, holding hands. They began to pray in unison the prayer they had learned from the Bible. One phrase was foremost in their minds. "Our Father who is in heaven, hallowed be your name. Your kingdom come, your will be done on earth as it is in heaven. Give us this day our daily bread, and forgive us our debts as we forgive our debtors. And lead us not into temptation, but..." Their words trailed off as they held one another's hands even more tightly. *"but deliver us from evil."* Now their voices rose in unison. "For yours is the kingdom, and the power and the glory forever! Amen."

They turned and slowly walked back inside. The inhabitants of the world would be taken by surprise by what was coming. It would impact them all. Surely nothing would surprise this group of twenty people who had put their faith in Jesus. Oh, but it would. They thought they understood, but it would be far worse than they had ever imagined...

INVASION OF DARKNESS

On the heels of the disappearance of nearly a billion people on September 11, 2029, another major worldwide event strikes on December 20 of the same year. An eerie lunar eclipse seems to open the door to the pit of hell from which pours a sinister darkness that engulfs the planet. As evil begins its gradual assault on humanity, chaos and crisis systematically break out around the globe and result in the deaths of another one-fourth of the world's population. Even as it does, Aissa Messai's popularity continues to grow as he seeks to bring peace to the nations of the world, especially in the Middle East. As the Smyrnians work to combat his covert evil intentions, they become enemies of the state. Death and destruction will rule the day, and the earth will be shaken like it has never been shaken before.

NOTE FROM THE AUTHOR

Word-of-mouth is crucial for any author to succeed. If you enjoyed the book, please leave a review online—anywhere you are able. Even if it's just a sentence or two. It would make all the difference and would be very much appreciated.

Thanks!
David O. Bullock

ABOUT THE AUTHOR

David O. Bullock was raised on a farm in rural Kentucky. He left the farm to become a pastor at age 20. He holds Bachelor of Ministry and Master of Divinity degrees. David is married to his high school sweetheart, Glenda. They are still madly in love, have two daughters and six grandchildren, and live in their hometown: Somerset, Kentucky. He's crazy about the Kentucky Wildcats, Cincinnati Reds, Cincinnati Bengals, Diet Rite, and coffee.

Thank you so much for reading one of our **Sci-Fi** novels.

If you enjoyed our book, please check out our recommended title for your next great read!

Culture-Z by Karl Andrew Marszalowicz

In the year 2190, mankind has made great strides forward in the worlds of technology, science, and greed. However, when all three get together one last time, this oblivious generation may not exist much longer.

View other Black Rose Writing titles at www.blackrosewriting.com/books and use promo code **PRINT** to receive a **20% discount** when purchasing.